He walked faster. Having skipped the media circus at the hospital, he'd caught up on his sleep, and his legs felt strong. Past the main quad and nearing the footbridge, he was alone yet had the odd sensation someone was trying to get his attention. He stopped and looked around. Nothing.

He continued. Nearer the footbridge, he felt it again. He didn't stop this time but strode more quickly. He continued through the grove of trees along the iron fence bordering Mt. Seneca Cemetery. Then he was on the footbridge, cars sizzling by on the wet pavement twenty-five feet below.

He was a third of the way across when he heard someone behind him.

The footsteps approached at a jogger's pace, and the back of Gavin's neck tingled. He stopped and turned. The man coming toward him wore a black sweatshirt with the hood drawn tightly around his face.

A potent chill crept up Gavin's back. He turned and hurried toward the hospital end of the narrow bridge, but it was still fifty feet away and the footfalls were closing.

FINAL MERCY

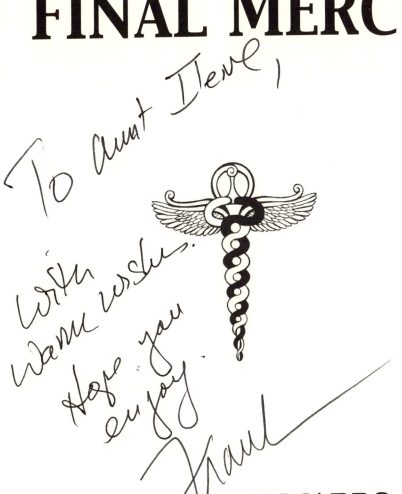

*To aunt Irene,
with warm wishes.
Hope you enjoy.
Frank*

FRANK J. EDWARDS

ZUMAYA ENIGMA   2010   AUSTIN TX

This book is a work of fiction. Names, characters, places and incidents are products of the author's imagination or are used fictitiously. Any resemblance to actual persons or events is purely coincidental.

FINAL MERCY
© 2010 by Frank J. Edwards
ISBN 978-1-936144-20-4
Cover art and design © Kaolin Fire

All rights reserved. Except for use in review, the reproduction or utilization of this work in whole or in part in any form by any electronic, mechanical or other means now known or hereafter invented, is prohibited without the written permission of the author or publisher.

"Zumaya Enigma" and the raven colophon are trademarks of Zumaya Publications LLC, Austin TX. Look for us online at http://www.zumayapublications.com/enigma.php

Library of Congress Cataloging-in-Publication Data

Edwards, Frank John.
  Final mercy / Frank J. Edwards.
       p. cm.
   ISBN 978-1-936144-20-4 (trade paper : alk. paper) -- ISBN 978-1-936144-21-1 (electronic)
   1. Emergency physicians--Fiction. 2. Medical personnel--Fiction. I. Title.
  PS3605.D883F56 2010
  813'.6--dc22
                          2010019485

Dedicated to my wife, Mary Ann

THANKS

I would like to give special thanks Sharon Pyke and Paul Desormeaux for their invaluable help in reviewing the manuscript, and to Liz Burton for her editorial expertise and for believing in this book in the first place.

CHAPTER 1

Jack Forester eased his tall frame into a chair at the nurse's station. For the first time all night, there were no new charts in the rack marked "patients to be seen." Yawning, he closed his eyes and let his mind drift.

For several days, a vivid image had visited him at odd moments, a depressing mental vision he suspected had something to do with being single and lacking much of a social life. It was of a small island with gray waves washing on the beach. The beach was narrow and littered with driftwood and seaweed. Dead jellyfish rolled at the surf line while tattered brown palm fronds clicked in a constant breeze. There were no hills or mountains, no cottages or hotels, not even a shack in the distance. It was just a tiny place crumbling back into the sea, and he was walking alone on the sand.

When he opened his eyes, the disembodied head of an old woman hovered directly in front of him. She had oxygen tubing in her nostrils and was smiling at him.

He rose to his feet. Mrs. Jones, the woman he'd just admitted with pneumonia, sat in a wheelchair on the other side of the counter.

"Sorry to bother you, doctor," she said.

Pushing the wheelchair was a slender man with Rasta braids named Jimmy, dressed in the white scrubs of an orderly.

"Sorry, Doc," he said. "She go upstairs now and want to say goodbye."

"I wanted to thank you again, Dr. Forester. It was so busy when the ambulance brought me in, but you were so kind and patient with me."

Jack stepped around the counter and took her hand.

"Kind of you to say," he said. "We were happy to help you out."

"I hope things stay quiet now. Looks like you could use some rest."

Jimmy began pushing the wheelchair away.

"I tell you a secret, Mrs. Jones," he said. "Never say quiet in dis place."

"Why?"

Their voices receded down the corridor.

"It bring bad t'ings. We get busy."

"Then what should I say—break a leg?"

A door at the back of the ED hissed open, and they were gone. Except for the murmur of two nurses at the far end of the charting station, it was finally quiet. Jack uncapped his pen and looked without enthusiasm at the sprawl of papers in front of him.

One of the nurses came up and handed him a cup of black coffee.

"Bad doctor," she mock-scolded. "Look at all those unfinished charts."

"The flotsam and jetsam of a busy night," he replied, sipping the coffee. "Thanks, Darcy. Must admit I'd like this job more if I didn't have to write down every bloody thing I see, hear, smell, touch, think and suspect just to keep the lawyers happy."

"You're not supposed to complain. You're the director."

"Then I'd better finish up," he said. "It's almost six. Only an hour to go."

They heard it at the same moment—a faint, high-pitched beeping. Darcy groaned. It was an ambulance backing up to the bay.

Since becoming an emergency physician, Jack Forester had seen people impaled by many things—knives, shards of glass, a fork, even a number-two pencil once—but never anything to match this. In the trauma suite, two medics lifted the new patient onto the gurney. Snowflakes melted on their blue jackets.

"Sorry to barge in without calling, Dr. Forester," one said breathlessly over his shoulder. "Our radio's down."

Jack didn't respond. He approached the patient, a man in his early twenties with what looked like a short arrow protruding from his right temple. It was brown and fletched with three yellow vanes. Yet his eyes were wide open. They followed Jack as he approached.

"Self-inflicted with a crossbow, doc," said the medic. "He was awake and oriented times three when we got to the house. His vitals are all normal. Having some relationship problems. We didn't see any seizures or nothing like that, and he's moving all extremities okay."

"I see. Thanks, Vince." Leaning over the bed, Jack said, "Good morning. What's your name?"

"Fuck-up," was the slurred reply rising from patient's mouth on a cloud of garlic-tinged alcohol.

"What's your real name?" Jack insisted, recoiling slightly.

"I fucked up again. That's all I can do."

"His name is Jason Peters," supplied the medic.

"This was really dumb," Peters continued. "I should have gotten a fucking gun."

"No, you shouldn't have," Jack said. "Listen, I have to look you over now. Are you in pain?"

Peters shook his head. It caused the crossbow bolt to tap the side rail, and he winced.

"Hold still."

Jack gently tested the shaft. It felt as solid as Excalibur in the stone.

Returning to the charting station, he ordered an x-ray and stat-paged the neurosurgery resident. A moment later, the phone rang.

"This one will pique your interest," he said, and went on to describe the situation.

"Jesus, you haven't tried to take it out, have you?" The resident's voice was pitched high with excitement.

"Oh, yeah. Sure. I put my foot upside his head and tried to yank on it, but the damn thing wouldn't budge."

"Maybe you wouldn't do something that dumb, Dr. Forester, but half the people who work for you down there make serious fuck-ups every day."

Jack felt his face burning, and he clenched his jaws. The young man on the other end of the line might not have finished his training yet, but he'd mastered the art of disrespecting emergency physicians. Valid or not, his comment was uncalled-for.

Taking a deep breath, he managed to keep voice measured and calm.

"Listen, do you want to come down and take care of this patient, or would you rather discuss hospital politics you know nothing about?"

"That ED is a joke, and everybody knows it. What's hospital politics have to do with it?"

"It's called putting up roadblocks to our ability to recruit good people, Dr. Schwartz, and it's beside the point at this moment. Now, I'm sorry if you've had a bad night. I'd also be sorry to wake up your chairman to talk about your attitude."

When Jack got back to the trauma suite, an attractive young woman with smudged mascara was holding Jason Peters's hand and shaking her head.

"I'm sorry, Jason, but that just looks so weird," he heard her say as he paused in the doorway.

Darcy came up next to him and whispered, "This is one stupid Cupid. And that was good how you handled that resident. You should have bitten the bastard's head off."

Three-quarters of an hour later, as Jack was writing furiously, a portly man wearing a white lab coat and blue scrubs came up to him, his graying hair wet and slicked onto his scalp.

"Howdy, boss," he said. "My turn. You ready to sign out?"

"You bet, Wally. The neurosurg resident just took my last case up to the OR. Top this one—suicide attempt by crossbow. He came in awake and alert with this thing sticking out to here."

Wally Deutch shrugged.

"Not bad, Jack, not bad, but when I was in Baltimore, we had a guy who tried to do himself in with a nail gun. He fired six ten-pennies up to the hilt into his skull, and he didn't even have a headache. Walked up to registration. The triage nurse didn't believe him and made him wait in the lobby for a couple of hours. By the time I saw him, he just looked a little cross-eyed."

"You're full of it, Walter."

"No, God's truth."

"Listen, I have to run over to the faculty meeting now."

"That's right," said Deutch. "Today's the big vote. So, how do you think it'll go? You don't look so confident."

Jack shrugged. "All we can do is keep trying."

"I hate to tell you again, Jack, but if they shoot this project down and we can't get properly staffed, I'm leaving."

"Maybe you and me both."

CHAPTER 2

Taking a shortcut, Jack left the ED and found a world completely transformed. It was mid-October and early for snow, even in this mountainous part of New York State; but the ground was blanketed, and large wet flakes still settled from the overcast sky like tufts of down from a million geese. The air was delicious to breathe, and he felt his mind clearing, the fatigue falling away.

He made his way up the unshoveled sidewalk along Beech Avenue toward the original three-story hospital, a brick building all but engulfed by the new medical school on one side and the clinical towers on the other. He pushed through the tarnished brass doors, stomped off his shoes and entered what had once been the main gateway to New Canterbury Medical Center.

One corner of the old lobby had been turned into a coffee and pastry shop, but the rest had been left to gather dust in its original state—murals, wooden wainscoting, oak receptionist's station, well-worn leather chairs and sofas, three brass-and-crystal chandeliers and a threadbare oriental carpet. Toward the back of the space, a deeply worn marble staircase led up to the mezzanine, where busts of famous physicians studded the granite balustrade. He stood in the dimness and gazed around; the meeting didn't start for another fifteen or twenty minutes.

Someone called his name from the shadows, and a short, slender man with hair as white as the snow falling outside approached. A smile broke out on Jack's face.

"Dr. Gavin," he said. "What a surprise. It's great to see you, sir."

"It's good to see you, too, my young friend. I've missed you."

His old mentor's handshake felt as firm as ever.

"When did you get back?"

"About two this morning. I made it from Rio de Janeiro to New Canterbury in eighteen hours. I should be napping, but I wanted to catch the meeting this morning. I especially wanted to speak with you, so this is fortuitous. "

"What brings you back early?"

"I just found out about Lester Zyman's death."

Jack was embarrassed. "Of course. Please accept my condolences."

"We were very old friends, and he was a great man, indeed," said Gavin. "I'm heartbroken I missed his memorial service. But I was on a research trip up the Rio Purus, and we had no communication."

"We all knew you couldn't get back, sir. Bad luck."

"Bad luck all the way around. When I returned to my office at the university in Rio, there were two unpleasant messages waiting for me. One was the news of Lester's death, and the other was a letter..."

He waited for the older man to continue, but Gavin's face paled, and his eyes lost their focus. Jack took a step closer.

"Dr. Gavin, are you all right?"

When Gavin's gaze rose to meet Jack's, his eyes held a look of anger that in all the years Jack had known the man he'd never seen there before.

"The letter, my young friend, was from Les himself. He wrote it to me the day before he died."

Jack felt his throat tighten.

"Tell me," Gavin continued, narrowing his eyes. "How have things been going around here?"

"How so?"

"Let me rephrase the question. How have things been going since Bryson Witner became the interim dean?"

At the mention of that name Jack stiffened.

"It's been...interesting," he said, after a moment's hesitation.

Gavin nodded. "Go on."

"To be honest, Dr. Gavin, I don't know how much longer I can put up with it," Jack admitted.

"Could you be more precise?"

"It's his arbitrary style of management."

"Arbitrary? That sounds like a euphemism."

"Can I give you an example?"

"Please."

"Okay—I'd been holding open the post of assistant ED director until we could find the right person."

"Of course. That's only sensible."

"Last month, Witner informs me the opening needs to be filled immediately, and he has just the candidate—Humphrey Atwood."

"Hapless Humphrey? Ouch."

"He would have been the last man on earth," Jack agreed. "But it was a done deal."

"That decision should have been your prerogative as director."

"So I thought."

Other voices echoed through the old lobby from up on the mezzanine, where a handful of people in white coats were walking in the direction of the Flexner Room. An orderly pushed the usual cart bearing pastries and coffee.

Jack looked back at Gavin. "Either you're one of Witner's cheerleaders, or he makes your life miserable," he went on. "Frankly, I was shocked when he was elected as the interim dean over Dr. Zyman. How he got enough support, I don't know. There was always something about him I couldn't warm up to. He's obviously brilliant, but he's too…slippery."

"How do you mean, Jack?"

"His personality differs depending on who he's with. He's like a chameleon. You can't pin him down."

Gavin seemed to consider this for a moment then slowly nodded.

"Jack, I should never have gone away on sabbatical. Part of this is my fault."

"Listen, Dr. Gavin, after all you've done for this place, you deserved a sabbatical if anyone did. What worries me is that he may become the permanent dean."

"Trust me, Jack, that's far from a done deal. I still have plenty of influence here, and the search committee is not finished with their work yet. Let's go to the meeting. I could use a cup of coffee."

Halfway up the staircase, Gavin paused, and Jack followed the direction of his gaze to the mural on the west wall.

"I can never look at that without smiling," said the older man.

The old painting depicted a country doctor in a buggy being pulled down a dirt road by a white horse bearing a pair of clumsy-looking wings. The physician's long hair and the tails of his frock coat flew out behind him. Looking down from the upper left corner, a gray-bearded god stood on a cloud holding a caduceus.

"We don't know exactly who the artist was," Gavin went on. "Probably one of the physicians on the original medical staff here around eighteen-seventy, but his ambitions exceeded his technical skills. The poor doctor looks terrified when he should be looking resolute, and Apollo seems like he's about to yell, *Whoa, Pegasus—you're going to kill that boy!*"

"You're right," said Jack, smiling.

"This place is full of ghosts for me. Forty-seven years ago, I came here to train in pathology, right after Korea. Over by that bay window, I proposed to my wife Betty when she was a nurse and I was still a resident." He was quiet for a moment. "Since Colin died, and then Betty, this place is my family."

Jack looked at the old physician and felt a surge of affection.

"I didn't know you were in the Korean War, sir," he said after another moment of silence.

"I never mentioned that?"

"No, sir."

"Yes, and it was quite an experience. I was drafted right after my internship. That's how I got this." He touched a deep scar on the left side of his chin. "A shell landed next to our hospital tent."

More voices were coming from down the corridor now.

"Jack, something very disturbing is happening at this medical center." Gavin's voice lowered to a near-whisper. "The letter Les wrote me the day before he died contained some things about which I can say no more until I've done some research. In the meantime, I want you to promise me you won't quit. Not yet. This is your home, too."

Jack thought back to his first day of medical school at New Canterbury, when Dr. Gavin had given the welcoming lecture. He had talked about the glories and the hardships of a physician's life, the rewards and the toil, and his words—his very example—had made the journey seem utterly worthwhile.

"You've got my promise," he said.

They began climbing again. As they neared the mezzanine, someone recognized Gavin and a hail went up. He was soon surrounded, and Jack let himself be swept along into the old conference room.

For the first time in weeks, he allowed himself a bit of optimism for the future.

Chapter 3

The train headed north out of Pennsylvania Station in darkness, gliding through the stone-and-brick gorges of Manhattan and the Bronx. It crossed the Hudson River as the sun rose, picked up speed and entered a world of hills, forests and occasional small towns.

Zellie Andersen studied the countryside rolling by. For the first time since moving to New York City a decade ago, she was seeing the hinterlands of New York state, and she was struck by how quickly and profoundly the urban world vanished behind her. Though the trees were smaller and the barns and houses constructed for colder weather, she couldn't help but see a resemblance to the Piedmont region of North Carolina, her home state; and she felt nostalgia for people and places she hadn't seen in many years.

They'd already stopped at several stations, and the car was now half-empty, the seat all hers. She stretched, smoothed back her hair and returned to the correspondence she'd been working on.

As she bent over her notepad and began writing, a sudden tingle went down the back of her neck. She looked up. In the seat across the aisle sat a man in his late fifties or early sixties. He was leaning in her direction, and had a look on his face that indicated he'd just asked her a question and was waiting for a reply. She remembered his face from earlier that day when he'd smiled at her as they waited to board the train back in Manhattan.

"Beg pardon?" she said.

The man pulled back as a young girl passed between them, and then he repeated his question.

"Do you know what time we're supposed to get into Buffalo?"

She shook her head.

"Sorry," she said.

"These things never run on time anyway," he said, smiling. "I'm glad I brought a stack of magazines."

It was obvious he was also looking for conversation, but she had never enjoyed small talk with strangers, and the truth was that conversation required a special effort. She went back to the letter she'd been writing.

Zellie had been partially deaf since the age of six, when an epidemic of meningococcal meningitis had swept through Fort Bragg, where her father was a helicopter test pilot. One of the first victims had been Zellie's mother, who worked as a civilian nurse at the base hospital. Zellie had fallen ill just before her mother died.

Much of that time was thankfully a blur now. One of the memories that stayed with her, however, sticking out like a rock in a muddy river, was the day they opened the blinds and she saw her father standing there with his lips moving and no sound coming out. She'd thought he was trying to make her laugh.

The infection had damaged her auditory nerves. She could hear nothing with her left ear, and the right one had about twenty-five percent residual function. A hearing aid could do nothing to help the left ear, but when she wore one in the right ear she had about fifty percent of a normal person's hearing ability. To converse normally, especially if a person spoke softly or rapidly, she needed face-to-face contact, for she had developed an excellent ability to read lips.

Being a good lip reader meant she was also an acute observer of facial expressions. There were times when she could predict what people were going to say before they opened their mouths, and friends joked about her powers of telepathy. Zellie—the BS detector.

She had taken the hearing aid out after boarding the train this morning, liking the way it added to a sense of privacy; and sitting here, she could perceive only a faint clicking of the wheels, though the line between hearing it and feeling the vibrations through the seat would have been hard to pinpoint.

She put the finishing touches on the letter and reread it.

> Dear Amy,
>
> I'm on the train now to a little place upstate called New Canterbury to do another la-di-dah feature story for a magazine. I can't afford to turn anything down these days. Getting my little novel published long ago while I was still in college was too good to be true, and now I'm paying for it, I guess.

Still absolutely no luck getting a second one off the ground. I've made at least twenty starts and have taken a couple all the way to the second and third drafts, but I just can't get them to come alive, if that makes any sense.

So, at the age of thirty-two, I know what it feels like to be a has-been, like the aging fashion model who makes her daily bread posing in underwear for newspapers. But who am I to complain? I've got as much happiness as anybody deserves and plenty of friends and I love living in Brooklyn, even if I don't inhabit the higher literary circles. And I don't have a man in my life since Derek and I split up two years ago to complicate things. Thank God we didn't get married.

And I'm happy writing to my little sister, whom I can't wait to see at Christmas time.

I love the train! Ever since I was sick way back then, I've been uncomfortable in small, closed-in places. So, a train is great—all these windows and the way you can get up and move around. That's how I'll be coming to see you in St. Augustine in December.

I was remembering the time you and Dad and I took the train to Atlanta to see Aunt Rita the year after Mom died. You'd just turned three, and I was seven. You weren't completely potty-trained yet, so Dad brought along some diapers. He stuffed them into that old blue canvas bag of his with the catfish on it, along with our sandwiches, and I recall being grossed out by that. But you didn't need them. I proudly informed Aunt Rita you hadn't stunk up the train.

In any case, I'll see you in a couple of months, kiddo. Write me. In the meantime, please know that it gives me great happiness to think of you and Todd with your two little babies, whom I'd love to kiss and hug right now.

All love,
Your big sis

Zellie

She folded the pages, addressed an envelope, sealed it and placed it inside her big leather satchel next to the several other letters she'd managed to finish since the train had left Manhattan. Zellie was proud to be among the dwindling number of people she knew who still wrote actual letters. She composed dozens every week, the briefest on postcards she bought in bulk from the Metropolitan Museum. It was easier than picking up the phone and gave her far more pleasure than email.

From a computer-obsessed friend named Esmond she'd heard ad nauseam about the internet and how it revolutionized communications. He encouraged her to get hooked up so she could write instantaneous messages to friends anywhere on the planet. The internet was great for research and sending in article drafts, but she wasn't giving up on the postal service yet. In any case, she needed a new computer, and her income had shrunk again this year.

The topic of finances brought her agent to mind, and with a deep sigh, she reached into the satchel and brought out Muriel's latest communication and read it for the fifth time.

> Muriel Gillman Literary Agency
> 19 Park Avenue, Penthouse North
> New York, NY 10019
> October 10, 1992
>
> Dear Zellie,
>
> It pains me to think we became cross with each other, or rather that you became cross with me, because I truly was not upset with you. As I've told you many times, Zel, you are like a daughter, so I have a right to scold you a little. You see, I care about more than just your career, please remember this! You have so much talent, Zellie, so much inside to offer the world.
>
> I know you think this assignment from Coast-to-Coast Magazine is insipid, but you really shouldn't bite the hand that feeds you.
>
> I am as sorry as anyone that your first novel was only a small success and that you can't seem to finish another one. But lots of writers have been in the same boat. It's just a matter of finding out what's really inside you.
>
> Editors tell me that you pull your punches, that you're not writing out of your real self whether its fiction or nonfiction. You get by on sheer skill, but that's only going to take you so far. Readers want the soul. They're like damn cannibals

in that way. That's the difference between a novel selling 3670 copies and one that sells 367,000. But I KNOW you have it in you. I believe in you. The problem is that only you can fix it. And you will. Patience! That synopsis you showed me, the story based on your own life—that's got real potential. I don't know why you won't follow up with it! Please try. Never give up!

Muriel meant well, but these pep talks were starting to sound like eulogies. Here lies an unsuccessful writer who never gave up. She folded the letter and stuffed it back then stared at her hands. She had always felt they were too large, and now they were starting to age. They were ringless, and the nails were cut short and unpolished. On the right middle finger by the last joint was a large callous from holding her pencils and pens. She rubbed it. It was firm and manifest, like a talisman, a testimonial to her ambition...and an eyesore.

She reached into her satchel and took out another piece of paper. It was a handwritten note from the editor of Coast-to-Coast. At the top he had written TALKING POINTS AND IDEAS. She groaned and read.

> Make most of interview with Dr. Bryson Witner, new hotshot dean and star of show. (Photos on file)
>
> New Canterbury Med Center great old place but financial troubles. One of first modern hospitals in East, founded same year as Hopkins, but big endowment almost gone. Once like Mayo Clinic, rural Mecca, but community now is rust belt and dying, sort of off beaten track now.
>
> Emphasize human interest here? What do these suckers do for fun? Night life? Doubtful.
>
> James Gavin, famous dean for 20 years, won Nobel Prize, brought glory but no money. Gavin steps down last year, gives reigns to McCarthy, another star from CA. But McCarthy dies last summer in accident. Good human interest here too. Then Bryson Witner steps up to plate. From Harvard. Genius type. Looks suave. Family? Background? Human interest always good.

Zellie rolled her eyes and continued reading.

> Witner develops plan to put place back on map by televising celebrity procedures. Main reason for this article. You will meet Brenda Waters. Interview is nailed down. This is main thrust. Should be fun. Future bright for this place. Phoenix rising, etc.

The note went on for another page, but Zellie balled it up and tossed it in the satchel. He might as well write the damn piece himself.

Out the window, brightly colored autumn leaves flashed by under a steel-gray sky as the car swayed gently, ticking westwards where, far in the distance, she could see by leaning close to the cool glass what looked like a dusting of snow on the rising hilltops.

CHAPTER 4

Dr. Bryson Witner took a fresh lab coat from the closet in his office and went to the full-length mirror attached to the wall near his door. At six-foot-three, he had to crouch slightly for his image to fit. He smoothed out the coat and rolled up the sleeves, two turns each. Then, he studied his face, tilting his head back slightly, compressing his lips and cocking his right eyebrow. That was his laser-beam look. Very effective on medical students. His black hair, thinning a little on top, was cropped close and needed no further attention. He did up the middle three buttons of the coat.

Length mattered with lab coats, from the blazer-style white jackets that med students were issued to the calf-length ones worn by faculty members—the higher up the pecking order, the longer the working regalia tended to be. Witner had worn the calf-length version until being appointed to the interim deanship several months ago, at which point he'd retired the old ones. His new coat fell an inch or two shy of brushing the floor.

That wasn't the only perk of his new position. Behind him, reflected in the mirror, lay the finest office in the entire university—larger even than the university president's—with hardwood flooring, a Persian carpet, ebony bookshelves, a massive desk, a mahogany conference table with matching credenza and coffee table, a gas-log fireplace, three maroon leather arm chairs, and a wide bay window overlooking the river. All this the university had done for old Gavin after he'd won the Nobel Prize.

Whistling, he gave his necktie a final wiggle, then stopped. His whistle died away. What was this? A tingle of alarm crawled up the back of his neck. He had seen something in the mirror. What was this on the left lapel of his coat?

Looking down and holding his breath, he took out his pen and touched it. The thing was inert. It looked like a piece of brown thread, but you could never tell. He strode into the office's private bathroom, shut the door, opened the medicine cabinet and took out a hemostat, with which he carefully grasped it and lifted it away.

It might well be just a piece of thread, but still. He must not let his guard down.

Setting it on the edge of the sink, he retrieved a butane cigar lighter from a drawer, clicked it on and directed a hissing blue flame toward the object. It made a brief orange flame. With a wad of moistened toilet paper, he wiped away the residue and flushed it down the commode.

As he put the hemostat back in the cabinet, he noted two translucent amber medication bottles, and he paused for a moment. They were like two sentinels standing guard over the dental floss that lay between them. They seemed, in a strange way, to be beckoning him, but they must be ignored. He tore his gaze away and closed the cabinet firmly.

The time for the meeting was drawing close. He peered into the spacious antechamber outside the office and saw Greta Carpenter, his administrative assistant, standing in front of her desk. Her back was turned to him. Greta, who'd been Gavin's assistant for many years, had never warmed to him, which was a pity. She could have been much more useful. Still wearing her overcoat, she was in the process of opening mail, and hadn't heard him. He approached her, stepping softly.

"Greetings, Greta," he said loudly.

With a sharp intake of breath, she spun around, her still-attractive face going pale.

"You look startled."

Her expression hardened.

"No, that's okay. Good morning."

"It is, indeed, a good morning," he said, sniffing. "Is that your perfume? It reminds me of dendrobium orchids."

She was still trying to regain her poise.

"Thank you."

For weeks now, she'd dropped the honorific "sir" when speaking to him, and her manner to him had been growing stiffer every day. Tut-tut.

"Do you have today's calendar for me, Greta, if it's not too much to ask?"

She reached onto the desk, where it lay in plain sight, and passed it over.

"Ah, thank you," he said. "Perfect as always. Perhaps you might be interested in going to the Flexner Room now to greet the faculty council members and give them their handouts before I arrive?"

"That's what I was just about to do."

"Certainly."

Witner went back in and sat at his desk. Eight minutes remained before he had to make his entrance, enough time to conduct a little business.

He dialed Nelson Debussy, whose office was on the undergraduate campus across the highway from the medical center. The president of New Canterbury University a little over a year now, Debussy had been recruited from a college in Ohio, where he'd turned around a crisis similar to New Canterbury's—shrinking enrollment, a neglected portfolio, crumbling local economy and below-the-belt competition from a subsidized state university system.

Debussy answered the call himself.

"Yes?"

"Good morning, Nelson," Witner said. "I see we're two of a kind—we start work before our secretaries."

"Bryson!" Debussy's voice was chipper. "How's my favorite wizard this morning?"

"Splendid, thank you. I'm waiting for this month's General Faculty Council to begin and thought I'd touch base with you."

"How are those meetings going? This is your third, I believe. I've heard good things."

"Have you, indeed? I'm pleased."

He smiled and thought of the various channels he used to insure positive feedback regarding his handling of faculty meetings flowed regularly to the main campus.

"As we've discussed, Nelson," he continued, "the faculty here is ravenous for modern leadership. They're eager for a strong new vision."

"And you seem to be the man to provide it, Bryson."

Witner spiraled his fingertip over the green blotter.

"Listen, Nelson, I wanted you to know that all the arrangements for televising Brenda Waters's sigmoidoscopy tomorrow are complete. She arrives late tonight."

"Dandy," Debussy said. "I must say again, Bryson, the contract you negotiated with Viacom is going to give us a much-needed cash infusion. I'm still not sure how one man could have pulled this together in such a short time. But we're all deeply grateful to you."

"Oh, the *Medical Media* program was a little idea I've been churning around in my spare hours for some years, Nelson. I just couldn't get anyone to share my vision before you. The time is right, and we must not be content with mere survival here."

"That sums it up, Bryson."

"Why shouldn't New Canterbury lead the way?"

"I love it."

"This is just the beginning, Nelson. There'll be celebrities having their pap smears and mammograms here, educating the public and so forth."

"What about vasectomies, Bryson?"

"No reason why not. And all these things performed by New Canterbury physicians under this roof."

"Who needs the Mayo Clinic? That's what we'll tell them."

"I only hope I have enough time during my interim deanship before yielding to the permanent dean when the search committee finishes its work."

"Bryson, don't be coy. I'm your friend, remember? There may be no need to 'yield,' as you put it. Many on the board feel similarly."

"I'm not being coy," said Witner. "I'm a modest man."

"Well, you don't have to be. You're a genius. I promise you, credit will fall where credit's due."

"I would be honored, but in the meantime, I must stay focused. Oh, one last thing, Nelson. I'm sure you're aware that gubernatorial candidate Brad Claxton is making a campaign swing through the Southern Tier tomorrow."

"Right. That crook from downstate."

"A man we'd like to have good relations with. He was thinking of bypassing New Canterbury and going directly to Corning, so I took the liberty of contacting his campaign manager. He'd like to hold a press conference at the hospital tomorrow, shortly before Ms. Waters's procedure. It will give the journalists something to do while they're waiting. I'm hoping you can be there to meet him."

Debussy began laughing.

"Bryson, you're going to own this place someday. Of course, I'll be there."

"Must go, my liege."

"Bye-bye, Bryson. You're the man."

Witner replaced the receiver and leaned back. The opening measures of Mozart's *40th Symphony* came into his mind. Three minutes, thirty seconds till departure time.

It's interesting, he thought, how they see all Mozart's works as special. To me, it's just keeping track of details. But perhaps that is the definition of genius, Mozart turning those notes over and over in his mind, arranging them, thinking them through all the time—child's play for him.

And what I do is simple for me. I've seen the larger plan, and now it begins to unfold. I watch it blossom in slow motion. They see only fits and starts.

But this place is just a tree in a larger forest, and a tree badly in need of pruning. *Clip, clip, clip.*

Closing his eyes, Witner envisioned a big London plane tree like the one he used to climb at the house of his uncle, Bergman Morgan. As a boy, he'd spent two weeks there every summer, because they felt sorry for him. He would climb the tree to hide from his uncle, who liked to drag him into the library and lecture him on whatever came to mind—the Greek city-states, Napoleon, the evils of Marxism. Through the window, he could see the sun, feel the warm breeze, hear the cicadas sizzling.

He'd enjoyed the stories about Napoleon, how he rose from nothing and ended up riding the "best goddamn horse in Europe," leveling cities with his artillery. But old Uncle Craw sipped straight bourbon from a coffee mug, and the more he talked the more history ran together; and he always wound up on the subject of how to accumulate, secure and, if need be, hide large sums of money.

So, Bryson learned to disappear up the plane tree. Playing Napoleon one time, he'd arrested a kitten and condemned it to death, hung it by the neck with a kite string until it stopped writhing, then tied string to its limbs and its tail and turned it into a puppet. The next day it was too stiff to play with anymore, so he made a pyre in the woods.

This medical center was like Uncle Craw's plane tree—never trimmed, never pruned, too many dead limbs blocking light and weakening the whole.

Enough reflection. It was time to work. He gathered up his papers and set out for the Flexner Room.

The hallway was deserted, so he counted out loud to twenty, first in French, then in Spanish, then in German, a habit he'd adopted long ago to limber his voice before giving lectures. His voice was more important than ever now—running the agenda of this faculty committee was like herding goats.

Inside the room, he pulled the doors shut to mark the beginning of the meeting, but something was wrong. Instead of expectant faces staring at him from around the long table, the chairs were almost empty. Most of the council members were congregated at the far end of the room, from which came bursts of laughter. He might have stumbled into a cocktail party. Even Greta was down there. He heard her laugh, and a chill went over him.

At that moment, he caught sight of a snowy head of hair, the center of attention, and he understood.

So, finally, he has left the jungle and returned. The expected has come to pass. So be it.

He vigorously cleared his throat.

"Good morning, everyone. Good morning!"

It didn't work. Something more dramatic, then.

He went to the light switch and turned it off. The voices faltered.

"Good morning," he repeated. "Much business today, I'm afraid. Let's get started. Take your seats, please."

As the attendees dispersed, the old man came fully into view. Gavin was seated in a chair by the windows, his head silhouetted against the gray dawn light. Some gesture of welcome must be made.

Bryson strode around the table toward him, forcing Hal Klinkerman, the chair of psychiatry, to sidestep or be run over.

"Dr. Gavin!" he exclaimed, taking note that Greta still stood next to the old man, her hand on his shoulder. "Good to see you, Jim."

Gavin did not rise to meet him, simply held out his hand to be shaken, which Witner did vigorously.

"Welcome back, sir."

"Hello, Bryson."

"Welcome back, welcome back. By the way, please accept my sympathy for the loss of Dr. Zyman. It was a tragedy for all of us. We'd heard you were out on a field trip when he passed."

"That's correct," said Gavin. "I just learned of it the day before yesterday."

"We understood your absence, as did his family. But the Southern Hemisphere must be compatible with you. You look fit. How long are you staying?"

"I'm not sure, at this point."

"Please, stop by and see me today."

"Yes, I'll be doing that."

"Splendid, then. In the meantime, we'd better get this show on the road."

"By all means," said the old man.

Chapter 5

As Witner called the meeting to order and gave an update on the *Medical Media* program with Brenda Waters's colonoscopy, Jack Forester looked out the window and puzzled again over Dr. Gavin's comments about Lester Zyman's letter. What concerns could he have been talking about?

He glanced at Gavin. The older man's attention was fixated on Witner.

Outside, the snow fell heavier. Huge wet flakes pelted the glass and coated the lindens that separated opposing lanes of traffic on Bracken Avenue, where slush plumed up from the potholes as cars whizzed by. The night was catching up with him. He let his eyes close and could feel his breathing slow. Things were going dark and warm, and he sank into it. He let himself go...

"Good morning, Dr. Forester," said Witner. "Are you still with us?"

Jack looked up and felt his face burn as laughter rippled around the room. He looked at the clock and was startled to see that fifteen minutes had passed.

"Present and accounted for," he said, clearing his throat.

"He was looking for the dog that ate his homework," said Norman Scales, the Chief of Internal Medicine, a slender, silver-haired man.

More laughter. The bastards. When's the last time any of them worked an overnight shift in the emergency department?

"Welcome back," said Witner. "Dr. Bergman had just given his opinion on your emergency department proposal. Horace, would you like to repeat your thoughts for Dr. Forester's benefit?"

Howard Bergman, the chair of Ophthalmology, was a well-fed man with a mane of dark-blond hair.

"Certainly," he said, clearing his throat. "Not to derogate the intent of your proposal, Dr. Forester, but the fact other places have turned their

ERs into showplaces doesn't mean New Canterbury needs to at this time."

"Howard's right," agreed Vincent Marcuso, the division head of Preventive Medicine. "We're talking about a huge expenditure. I don't have to remind people we don't have piles of money buried in the backyard. What do you think, Bryson? I know you've been studying this issue, too."

"It's true I've been trying to perform a reasonable amount of due diligence, out of respect for the excellent work Dr. Forester has put into this proposal," said Witner. "I phoned my counterparts at Cornell, Yale, Boston University and Tufts, and unfortunately, none of them are happy with their new emergency departments, which have floor plans similar to the one proposed."

Several people chimed in.

"May I have the floor?" Jack said, his cheeks burning.

"By all means," said Witner.

"By any standard, our emergency department is outmoded to the point of being dangerous. That's why we've lost three good physicians in the past year, and I've just about given up trying to replace them. It's a vicious cycle. Without modern equipment and a decent physical plant, we will never attract enough trained clinicians with the necessary skill set to fill the schedule, let alone think about starting our own training program for emergency physicians. I can't state it any simpler."

"What's wrong with the care we give in the ER now?" wondered Susan Kingston, Chief of Radiology. "Is it really all that bad? All emergency departments are chaotic from time to time."

"Dr. Forester wants to start his own residency program and become the chair," Scales said. "That's the unspoken agenda."

"Of course, I want to start a training program," Jack retorted, whirling on him. "We're a teaching hospital. I don't care who runs it."

"We don't need reminding what we are," snapped Scales. "The question is, do we need a new program that may have detrimental effects on our existing ones?"

"Would somebody mind telling me what's wrong with the status quo?" persisted Kingston.

"Dr. Kingston has a valid question, Dr. Forester," Witner said. "You've been the ER director for five years now. I was under the impression you had made major improvements down there already."

Shoulders growing more tense by the second, Jack inhaled and looked straight into Witner's eyes.

"We're doing the best we can with what we've got, but we're bursting at the seams and working our staff to death. We need a new ED, we need modern equipment, and we need to fulfill our teaching mission by training emergency doctors."

"If you're short-staffed, why not use more moonlighters?" said Bergman. "There's plenty of residents who'd like to earn a few extra dollars."

"Because emergency medicine is more than just the acute-care side of the other fields. After med school here, I left and did four years of training in it, and I should know. You have to handle urgent medical or traumatic situations with patients of any age in a chaotic environment—days, nights, weekends and holidays. You've got to intubate, put in chest tubes, stabilize fractures, do spinal taps on infants and ninety-year-olds, recognize child abuse, deliver babies, defuse violent patients and much more. Only special training or years of experience can prepare you for it."

"Sounds like a GP on steroids," said Allen Capistro, the head of the Division of Hand Surgery.

This brought a fresh wave of laughter, and Jack's frustration deepened.

"Allen, if a member of your family comes to the ED, who do you want taking care of them—a trained emergency doctor or a moonlighting resident?"

Norman Scales leaned forward and smiled.

"I wouldn't be so hard on moonlighters, Dr. Forester. For one thing, the moonlighting resident doesn't think he or she knows it all. They are more likely to call for help when they need it."

"Dr. Scales," Jack said, "you make my case. A training program teaches the emergency physician what his or her limitations are."

"Jack." Scale's tone was patronizing. "There are only so many patients. If we add more trainees down there, what happens to our existing internal medicine and surgery residents? I'll tell you what'll happen. The quality of their educational experience will be diluted."

He turned then to Jacob Hansen, the salt-and-pepper-bearded Chairman of Surgery. "Jacob, you're a major stakeholder in this, and we haven't heard from you yet. What are your thoughts? Do you not see this as diminishing the training of your residents in the emergency room?"

Hansen appeared to study the backs of his hands for a moment, his face solemn. The room quieted, and he looked up and down the table.

"For one thing, the major issue here is building a new ED. The training program would come later. But, in general, when faced with the prospect of change, we should consider foremost how it would affect patient care. So, the question is this. If we vote to fund a new emergency department, and we then create an emergency medicine residency program, would the result be better care for our patients?" He paused. "I think the answer is yes."

"Definitely," Jack assured him, feeling hope rise in his breast.

"Your surgery residents would be pushed aside, Jacob," Scales said. "What about *their* future patients?"

Hansen turned to him. "I grant you they would probably see fewer patients—not that they'd complain about that." A few chuckles greeted this. "But I suspect they'd be better taught and supervised in the context of a program like Dr. Forester envisions, and they'd certainly benefit from working in a modern environment with state-of-the-art equipment. The net tradeoff should be positive."

Scales frowned. "There's no guarantee it wouldn't be the reverse—and I, for one, don't want to tamper with the hard-earned reputation we have for training internists."

Several other people began speaking simultaneously, and in a few seconds, the entire table was in a hubbub.

"Ladies and gentlemen," Witner shouted. "Please! We must move on if we're going to finish the agenda this morning. I'm going to call for a motion. Are we ready to take this step, or not?"

"I move we drop it," said Bergman.

"I second that motion," Scales said.

The hubbub rose again.

"Silence, please," Witner ordered. "There's a motion on the floor to drop the proposal for a new emergency department. Any more discussion?"

"Yes." Gavin rose to his feet. "Colleagues, would you mind if I weighed in with a few words, ex officio?"

Witner stared at him and cleared his throat. "Certainly, absolutely, we were hoping you would," he said, his voice neutral. "The chair recognizes Dr. Gavin, *ex officio*."

Gavin approached the table.

"I'll get right to the point. Before stepping down last May and passing the deanship to poor Bob McCarthy, I was a firm supporter of Dr. Forester's vision. I remain so. I'm personally convinced we need a new emergency department, along modern designs, and I believe we can find a way to fund it."

"Thank you, Dr. Gavin," Witner said, his voice rising. "Your input is appreciated. Now—"

"I'm not finished, Dr. Witner. Furthermore, I believe emergency medicine would be a good addition to the list of our fine training programs. There are not enough good emergency doctors—able clinicians like Dr. Forester here—to go around. There's no reason I can see why we shouldn't train our own, and it will be a blessing to the entire region.

"This isn't revolution, as the adage goes, it's just evolution. In light of the additional revenue this *Medical Media* program will generate, I think it makes sense to proceed. If we want to continue attracting the best students, this is an investment we need to make, and the sooner the better. That's all I have to say, thank you."

A murmur spread around the table as Gavin sat back down.

"With all due respect," Scales said, "this may be putting the cart before the horse."

"Thank you again, Dr. Gavin," said Witner. "To view this proposal as evolutionary seems reasonable, and New Canterbury has always stood for progress. The problem here is one of finances. I agree with Dr. Gavin that funding this project is an essential step, but one which will, unfortunately, take a great deal of study. Is there any further discussion?"

The second hand swept around the clock. Chairs shuffled and throats were cleared, but no one else spoke.

Witner nodded. "Then, we have a motion to table this proposal pending further study, and it has already been seconded. All in favor—a show of hands, please."

Gradually, the hands rose—some hesitantly, some boldly. But more and more rose until all Jack could see was a clear majority against him.

Chapter 6

His anger rising with each step, Jack trudged down a seldom-used stairwell near the Flexner Room. Though not the most direct route to the emergency department, it was the least used, and he did not want to run into anyone.

Yanking open the door at the bottom, he found the basement corridor empty. A growl escaped his throat, and he flung his briefcase at the old cinderblock wall, which was smooth from countless layers of paint applied over the past century.

The case bounced and slapped onto the floor, the sound echoing down the corridor. Not only would he like to have it out with Witner, he'd also love to have a personal discussion with Norman Scales, who was obviously power-hungry.

Until Witner entered the picture as interim dean, Scales had gotten used to the idea that change in the emergency department was inevitable. But Witner had rekindled his opposition—nurtured it and fed it. What Witner stood to gain, Jack had no idea. Maybe he was just doing Scales a favor so Scales would support him for the permanent deanship. These political games were making him sick at heart. He was sure finances weren't at the core of the matter.

Aiming a kick at the old briefcase, he watched it flip and bang against the wall again. Panting, pinpoints of light flashing before his eyes, he heard the sound of rapid footfalls approaching. He didn't come this way often and had forgotten that the main security office wasn't far away.

The footsteps grew louder, and a tall, portly man wearing the green pants and white shirt of a security guard appeared around the corner. He halted ten feet away and looked at Jack in surprise. Then he glared at the briefcase, which miraculously was still closed.

Tim Bonadonna, assistant chief of security for the medical center, had been a close friend of Jack's since they met in the fourth grade at

New Canterbury Elementary School, where Jack had been the taller of the two. At six-foot-four, Tim now loomed over him.

"It sounded like someone was being murdered down here. You okay there, partner?"

They approached and shook hands.

"Howdy, Tim. Me and the case just had a little tiff."

"Well, I'm glad to see you're the one still standing. Those little buggers are tough." He pointed at the case. "You want me to arrest the son of a bitch?"

"No, we've already made up."

"What the hell's going on?"

Jack released a breath and looked away.

"Things didn't go so hot at the meeting this morning, Tim. I can't believe it. They shot it down."

"You're proposal? I don't believe it, either."

"The whole damn thing. Tabled."

Tim shook his head.

"That really sucks, buddy. I know how long you've been working on this."

"I can sum up the problem in two words—Bryson Witner."

"I never liked that bastard, Jack. He floats around this place like King Tut on a golden barge."

"Only two people spoke up in favor of the proposal—Jacob Hansen and Dr. Gavin. He'd gotten to everybody else."

"Dr. Gavin? He's back from Brazil?"

"You bet. Got in last night."

"Well, there you go." Tim thrust out his jaw. "Maybe he'll throw that arrogant dude out on his arse."

"We can hope."

"And we'll throw a party when it happens," Tim added. "Speaking of entertainment, when are you going to come catch a performance?"

Tim Bonadonna was an actor, and a very good one. He was currently playing Falstaff in a University Players production of *Henry IV, Part 2*.

"Soon, man, soon."

"You keep saying that."

"I mean it."

"You'd better. Hey, watch this."

The large man drew himself up, arched an eyebrow and pointed at the briefcase.

"Be this some novel sport, Doctor—abuse of the attaché? Or did the undoing of your scheme at the morning's assemblage of swineherds also undo your wits? But, yes, a plague upon me—your visage bespeaks it all! By the nonce, I shall help to scourge thine enemies. I will lift Witner on a pike!

"But what is this change I see in your eyes? Can it be that if I continue these silken words you might grow vexed and strike me? Ah, but now I recall me how once you did bloody the nose of Harry Lee, bully foul, when I was but a runt and he did push me into a nettle bush, and because of this, I will this cajolement cease, and—"

"Please, you've cheered me up. Jesus Christ, I'll come. I promise."

"How'd you like it?"

"Not bad. In fact, that's pretty good."

"Excellent. Let me buy you a coffee."

"Raincheck, Tim, I've got to work. But glad I ran into you."

"Likewise. How's your brother doing with this change in weather?"

Tim Bonadonna was one of the few people who seemed to enjoy the one-sided nature of conversations with Jack's reclusive brother Tony.

"Fine. He moved into the barn last night."

"Good. Listen, don't forget dinner at our place next Friday. Sonia asked me to remind you, being familiar with the way you neglect your friends."

"Thanks, and give her my love."

Jack watched the bulky figure disappear around a corner, then examined the briefcase for damage—nothing major—and headed down the corridor toward the emergency department, which was on the far side of the complex. He strode rapidly, despite his fatigue, past the tunnel that led to the old nurses' residence, by a row of teaching labs that were only storerooms now, by the pathology department offices and the morgue. Finally, he arrived at one of several back entrances to the ED, his heart pounding as if he'd just run a mile. He set his jaw and stepped in.

The noise, action and brightness hit him like a refreshing wave. He had never liked the term "emergency room." It was true this had once been a single room, but that was long before his time, back when that single room was staffed by just a nurse and maybe an intern, and there'd been a portico outside for horse-drawn ambulances. That had long since given way to a bustling warren of corridors and thirty-five separate rooms, though most of them were just tiny cubicles separated by curtains. Some were set aside for special purposes, like the eye-nose-and-throat room, and the two gyn rooms with stirrup stretchers for pelvic exams; and there was the large suite that contained all the necessary equipment to deal with several major trauma cases. There was a cardiac arrest room and three psychiatric rooms with padded walls, and a room near the lobby with wallpaper, soft lighting and a couch where loved ones could grieve. When all the rooms where full and people kept arriving, as happened almost every day, patients were simply put on stretchers up and down the hallways.

Though the New Canterbury emergency department was a cobbled-together, noisy, bustling, congested warren, it was still his. Jack gazed around almost fondly.

Just to his right, here in the very back of the department, was an area that had once belonged to the pathology department. Walls were moved, and it was now called Suite X, an observation area that predated Jack's tenure here; it could hold three stretchers, separated by curtains. It was space the ED needed, but it was less than ideal for two reasons.

For one thing, it was remote. For another, it was right next to the main autopsy room, separated only by a sheet of drywall, meaning patients lying in there could hear the sound of necropsies being performed—the plop of organs tossed into the weighing bucket, the whine of a bone saw removing the top of a skull.

Not long before Jack arrived five years before, an elderly woman had died in Suite X, unattended and forgotten by the staff, discovered dead by a family member the next morning. So, one of his first actions as the medical director had been to install a video camera connected to a monitor in the central station.

However, the only real solution to this ED's problems—of which this was just one of dozens—was new construction, period.

He stepped around a stretcher in the hallway, dodged a sprinting RN and entered Suite X. Over by the back wall, near a door that, for some reason, still gave access to the autopsy room, lay an elderly man reading a magazine. He had a bandage on his head. Next to his stretcher sat an old woman, knitting. The autopsy room was quiet.

"Everything okay, folks?"

"Yes, thank you, Doctor," said the woman. "They told us he could have something to eat, but they haven't brought anything in yet."

"I'll check," he said, going back into the corridor.

At the California hospital where he'd taken his emergency medicine residency training, Jack had worked in an ultramodern ED. It was designed in six semicircular "pods"—one for acute medical cases, one for minor cases, one for pediatrics, one for trauma, a psych pod and, lastly, a dedicated and well-monitored observation area. Each region had a raised central station around which the rooms were arrayed, so that every patient was visible. No one got stuck in a corner and left alone. That's what the proposal had been all about, a variation on this paradigm.

He stopped a technician and asked her to check on a meal for the patient in Suite X then went by the central station toward his office.

The central station sat roughly in the middle of the department and measured about twenty-by-fifty feet. It was bordered by a waist-high counter, and it served as a work area for nurses, medical students, residents and physicians. Two secretaries occupied alcoves on either wing to answer phones, take care of pages and operate the pneumatic tube system that sent specimens of body fluids to the laboratory. His office lay at the front end of the central station next to Gail Scippino's; she was the new ED nursing supervisor.

Several nurses and residents and the secretaries greeted him as he passed. He nodded and smiled, careful to hide his disappointment. It was the people who mattered—the staff and the students and the patients—not the politics. He knew most of them believed he was going to make things better; he had never been shy about sharing his vision and hopes. Now what could he tell them?

Wally Deutch was bent over a chart at the far counter and hadn't seen him. Jack slipped by. The time to tell him would arrive soon enough. God willing, Wally wouldn't really just quit. At some point soon, he'd have to break the news to all the others, too—all the colleagues who'd looked to him for leadership and believed in his vision. But not now.

Chapter 7

The Amtrak swayed, and Zellie Andersen felt the clicking become fainter and less frequent. Leaning close to the cool glass, she watched the superstructure of a bridge flash by. Down below, she made out the dark band of a river. Having studied the map, she knew it was the Seneca River. They would reach New Canterbury in a matter of minutes, and sure enough, buildings began to flash past.

Out on the platform, a gust of frigid air took her breath away—it had to be twenty degrees colder here than in Manhattan. She strode into the little station, taking note of the junk food wrappers and ticket stubs littering the floor. The windows were thick with grime, and the air was stale. A rolled-up disposable diaper lay on one of the orange plastic chairs. Hopefully, the rest of the town wasn't like this. If it were, she wasn't going to linger. *Do the article and go home. No, just take notes and bolt.*

Zellie retrieved her suitcase from the porter and went to the ticket counter. She waited for a girl to look up from a magazine.

"Could you tell me if the Seneca Hotel is within walking distance?"

The girl turned away and seemed to be speaking to someone in the office behind her. She turned back to Zellie and said, "Just go out the front and head left at the next intersection. It's not too far."

Zellie felt a tap on the shoulder. It was an elderly man wearing an Irish tweed cap. Thankfully, he didn't have a mustache or a beard so his lips were easy to read.

"I beg your pardon, Miss, but I overheard you asking directions. You must be a stranger to town. My wife and I are getting a taxi home, and we'll be going right by the Seneca Hotel. You don't want to walk it. It's half a mile, and you'd have to stroll through a rather rough neighborhood."

The taxi driver loaded their suitcases in the trunk, and Zellie sat between the man and his wife. The cab lurched out onto the street and sped away from the station.

"So, you're going to stay at the Seneca?" the woman said. "A very good choice. John took me there on our first date to see the Duke Ellington Orchestra. We're just getting back from a cruise. We had a wonderful time, didn't we, John?"

"Yes, indeedy."

Zellie had to keep her head a-swivel to follow the conversation.

"So, what brings you to town, my dear?" asked the woman. "Is this your first visit?"

"It is, yes."

"Work or pleasure?"

"I'm writing a magazine piece about the medical center."

"How interesting! I'm so glad people are writing about our hospital. It's such a fine place. My sister-in-law used to write children's books under the pen name Emma Goldenrod."

"So, you folks are natives?"

"I am, but John is a transplant from Schenectady. Now that we're retired, though, we like to wander, but how good it feels to be back home."

"Where was your cruise?"

"Iceland, and it was fabulous. I'm not a traveler by nature, but give my husband a boat and he'd paddle around the world."

"Primarily upstream," John said.

Zellie grabbed the front seat for support as the taxi veered around a corner.

"Speaking of articles," said the woman. "There was a wonderful piece about this region recently in *Yankee* magazine. You should look it up. It was called 'New Canterbury: A Town for All Seasons,' and how true. We have Lake Stanwick for summer fun and a ski slope not far away, and in the autumn people come from all over to see our leaves. Unfortunately, we're two weeks past the peak. And then there's the university and the medical center. And there it is! Driver, please slow down so we can see. That's the main campus of the university on our left. That big thing with the dome is the library. That's where I used to work."

But Zellie's attention was drawn to the other side of the highway, where an even larger complex of buildings lay.

"So, that's the medical center over there?" she asked.

"You bet," John said. "That's where Brenda Waters is going to let the nation look up her rear end tomorrow."

"John, that's disgusting."

"Tell that to all the people who'll be tuned in. That's why we came back, Zellie."

"No, it was not," his wife protested.

The medical center was much larger than she had expected—multiple interconnected buildings on a scale that would have done justice to a much larger community. As they drew closer, she could see a big archway of brick and glass that looked like the main entrance. In front of this was a fountain with a a stainless steel caduceus in the middle, which in warmer weather, she suspected, would be bathed by a ring of water jets.

Then they were past, and the driver accelerated, pushing Zellie back into her seat.

Chapter 8

All the senior faculty members at New Canterbury—deans, interim deans and department chairs included—rotated through the clinical teaching schedule. This was Bryson Witner's week to serve as the Blue Team teaching attending.

Directly after the faculty meeting, he strode to the East Clinical Tower, obsessed with the image of walking into the Flexner Room and seeing Gavin sitting there surrounded by people. He found the team, a group of eight residents and students clustered near a coffee shop on the ground floor, waiting for him to begin morning rounds. He motioned for them to follow and continued marching down the green-carpeted corridor toward the elevators. They quickly fell in behind like a flock of white-coated ducklings.

To his side drew young Dr. Randolph Delancy. Blond-haired and little-boy-faced, Delancy carried a large notebook, for it was his job to make sure the team stayed on target.

"How did the meeting go, sir?" he asked. "Anything interesting?"

Witner looked at him. There was no trace of guile in the young man's face. The news of Gavin's return was still not widespread.

"Nothing unexpected, Randy, and nothing that won't be appropriately dealt with in due time."

"That's good, sir."

"Yes, that is good, Randy."

Witner was pleased with his choice of Delancy as chief resident for the Blue Team. He had separated the man from the ranks of senior residents back in August and elevated him to the newly created position. None of the other three internal medicine teams—Gold, Green and White—had permanently assigned chief residents, but neither did the other teams have the interim dean taking them on as special projects.

The Gold Team was a non-teaching service devoted mainly to rich locals who wanted VIP treatment, along with a sprinkling of Canadians wealthy enough to opt out of the assembly line up north. There was also a small but steady trickle of Saudis and Kuwaitis who, thanks to Nelson Debussy's representatives in Riyadh and Kuwait City, arrived in large white cars and paid in cash from briefcases carried by assistants with British accents and Brooks Brothers suits. They received special meals, deluxe nursing care, private rooms with a southern view, and no exposure to medical students. The Gold Team was fine as it stood.

"Tell me, Randy, how did things go last night with admissions?" Witner asked. "You're not letting any good cases slip on to White and Green, are you?"

"No way, sir. A potential pheochromocytoma almost got admitted to White, but I got wind of it in time."

"Good lad."

"They were not happy about it."

"Their happiness isn't the issue," Witner said. "You're only doing your job—and doing it well."

Green, White and Blue Teams, unlike Gold, were training-focused, but the Blue Team had a special niche—it took only the most interesting patients. Its history dated back to the 1940s when the dean at that time, George Blankenship, decided to put the brightest house staff in contact with the most rewarding clinical material by creating a special team for that purpose. Let dullards deal with the routine pathology—the strokes, pneumonias, drunks with pickled pancreases, and so forth.

Blankenship's successor, James Gavin, had allowed the Blue Team's special mission to degenerate until it became indistinguishable from Green and White. That had been a shame, and when Witner took the helm in July, he encouraged a more-than-willing Norman Scales to resurrect the Blankenship paradigm.

They created the post of Blue Team chief resident, empowering him with the right of first refusal for all non-Gold Team admissions; and Witner had selected Delancy, who was bright, ambitious, circumspect—and whose father was chairman of the university's board of trustees. Among the benefits of giving Randy this appointment was that Witner was now a frequent dinner guest at the Delancy home.

He smiled as he ushered the team into an elevator, watching them press shoulder-to-shoulder. He entered last, pushed the button and stood by the door, inhaling the familiar odor of medical people in training. Someday, he should mention this in an article—the sour pheromonic smell of young humans spending the prime of their lives caged inside hospitals and libraries, poring over books into the wee hours, or who'd been up all night with patients. It was a miasma of stale clothing and body odor, fading deodorant and perfume, and mixed with it the carroty, yeasty smell given off by a vegetarian. For it never failed—there was always a vegetarian or two among the residents and students.

The door slid open, and he stepped with some relief into the hospital smell of isopropyl alcohol and urine. He resumed marching.

"Where do we start this morning, Randy?"

"Room sixty-four-thirteen, sir. The patient's name is Gladys Vanderwulf, and she was admitted last evening with fever and weight loss."

He liked the enthusiasm in Delancy's voice; it was proof the young man remained grateful for his position. And well he should be. Every resident on the Blue Team had cause for gratitude. Not only did they get the most exciting patients—the carcinoid tumors, the histiocytosis X cases and the hairy cell leukemias, the pituitary dwarfisms and the Marfan syndromes, and all the exotic parasites that came to these shores so rarely—but their call schedule was only one night a week, even for interns, allowing them maximum time for reading and knowledge absorption.

The other medical teams were on call every third night.

To sweeten a Blue Team rotation even more, the residents were handed free meal passes to the faculty club, where filet and prime rib were served at lunch, along with unlimited gym access and a dedicated Blue Team conference room with couches, a well-stocked fridge and a TV.

"Dr. Witner," Delancy said, lowering his voice, "I just wanted to mention what a pleasure it's been having you as the teaching attending this week. We all wish you'd do it more often."

"I would enjoy that, Randy." Witner lowered his voice as well. "But I must spread the wealth around."

Which was true enough. Internal medicine faculty members were clamoring to teach the Blue Team. That was one of the reasons Norman Scales had been delighted when Witner revived the team—it was a perfect political lever for rewarding those who deserved it, and he and Witner doled out those favors behind closed doors.

Delancy looked at his notebook. "Here we are. Room sixty-four-thirteen."

Witner stopped, and the team gathered.

"Who's the first-year resident, the intern who worked up this case?" he said.

"Me," replied an anorexically slender young woman.

"And you would be?"

"That's Dr. Chen, sir," said Delancy. "Mary Chen."

"Present the case, please, Dr. Chen."

Mary Chen had black hair pulled into a tight bun and a face marred by dark circles under her eyes and a general look of fatigue. Her lab coat had a large coffee stain on the lapel. She'd obviously been up most of night researching in preparation for this presentation, her moment of glory. She stole a look at her notes and began to describe the case.

The patient was a forty-nine-year-old woman who'd developed a recurrent fever five weeks ago. Blood smears for malaria were negative, and all the other serologic testing had so far been inconclusive. As she grew weaker, her family doctor finally referred her to New Canterbury. Chen had reviewed the symptoms, discussed her past medical history, and then noted the woman and her husband, a Baptist minister, had returned four months previously from a mission to Central America.

The husband had not gotten sick.

Chen droned on, and Witner began tapping a fingertip with increasing rapidity against his chin. It was an excellent presentation for an intern, better than most second-year residents. Chen had obviously spent a great deal of time reading the case presentations in the *New England Journal of Medicine* and was attempting to equal that level of precision and detail. Her presentation was so good, for an intern, it reeked of arrogance.

He abruptly raised his hand.

"I believe you've gone into these details far enough, Dr. Chen, if you don't mind," he said. "We are awaiting your differential diagnosis, please."

"I was just about to go there," she said, shooting him a glance.

Petulance? Was that *petulance* he heard?

"I see," he said, thoughtfully. "Then perhaps, Dr. Chen, you could answer a little question for me before you proceed. Tell the group exactly why you believed it was important to mention that your patient's spouse was a Baptist minister? Does this expose her to certain diseases that a Catholic might escape? Or a Mormon?"

The laughter that erupted was hearty enough to draw attention from the nursing station at the end of the hallway. Mary Chen frowned. She tried to hide her embarrassment with a smile, but it wasn't convincing.

"Or a follower of the Buddha, Dr. Chen?" Witner continued.

He had timed it well, and the laughter redoubled. Mary Chen's eyes now betrayed a flash of anger and pain.

Witner raised his hand. "Continue, Dr. Chen, and please, try to be relevant," he said. "We have three more patients to see. Unless, of course, there really is something about being married to a Baptist that anticipates an illness."

Another wave of mirth ended with a clearing of throats and a final retrospective chuckle. Clearly, the others had found her a little too competent and were enjoying her comeuppance.

Like a fatigued horse thrown off its stride by a bolting fox, Chen began again but immediately tripped over the word *interstitial*. Three times her tongue twisted it unsuccessfully. She finally took a deep breath. Moisture welled in her eyes, and her chin trembled. On the fourth try, she got it right, however, and began to trot again.

Oh, yes, she was strong and smart, no doubt about it. In a moment, she would start discussing the differential diagnosis, the part of her presentation she'd probably done the most research on. She might even find a clever way to get back at him. That would never do. He must decapitate her without delay.

"That will be enough for now, thank you, Dr. Chen," he said crisply. "Who's the second-year resident on this case?"

Mary Chen's mouth made a gasping motion, and she turned her head to the left and right. Delancy consulted his list.

"Sullivan, sir."

"Dr. Sullivan," Witner ordered, "kindly take over and discuss the differential for this patient, and please demonstrate to Dr. Chen the value of brevity."

Edwin Sullivan stepped forward, his expression displaying no guilt that he was about to capitalize on the work done by his intern while he'd slept. Why should it? Similar things had happened to him during his internship. It was the nature of roundsmanship, and Mary Chen would have plenty of time to repay someone else in kind over the next couple of years as she rose up the pecking order.

With six hours of solid sleep under his belt, Sullivan summed up the case then discussed the various possible diagnoses and focused ultimately on protozoan parasites vs. liver flukes vs. possible tickborne rickettsial syndromes. Pending confirmation by laboratory testing, his first choice was dengue fever.

"Thank you, Dr. Sullivan," said Witner. "Very fine. By the way, does this disease have a predilection for those of a Baptist persuasion?"

The team then entered the room and gathered around Mrs. Vanderwulf's bedside. She was a wiry woman, sallow and emaciated. Witner introduced himself and asked how she'd rested.

"Gracious," she said, smiling weakly. "I've never been so poked and prodded. I feel like a pincushion."

Witner called the medical students forward and made each of them demonstrate an aspect of the exam. That done, the team departed, Mary Chen now fallen to the rear of the crowd, a look of dejection on her face.

After visiting eight other patients, the team came to the last patient, a twenty-five-year-old man comatose after being resuscitated from a cardiac arrest precipitated by a viral inflammation of the heart. Witner performed the initial chest auscultation himself, wanting a chance to use the new Krackendorf Professor model stethoscope with its solid silver head he'd just taken delivery on from the factory in Vienna. As he skipped it across the bony arch of the young man's wasted ribcage, listening, the sounds were clear and loud—it was like taking a Ferrari for a spin.

He straightened and removed from his ears the earpieces (custom shaped from a mold of his ear canal).

"Medical students, come forward and observe." He lifted both of the young man's eyelids with his thumbs, placed his fingers on either side of the man's head and slowly moved it side-to-side. "Miss Singh, tell me what am I doing."

She was a shy-looking third-year student with dark skin and deep red lipstick.

"You are checking for the occulocephalic reflex, Dr. Witner," she said in a lilting Indian accent.

"Good, yes."

Winter located Samuels, a senior medical student with acne-cratered cheeks and oversized ears. Samuels wanted to be nothing more than a family doctor. He stood in the far back, trying to be invisible.

"Mr. Samuels, come here."

"Sir?" Samuels's his face turned crimson.

"Come, step forward and tell us about the occulocephalic reflex."

"The occulocephalic reflex." Samuels repeated, hesitating. He blinked. "If I recall, it checks for cerebellar dysfunction."

Chuckles spread through the group, and Delancy rolled his eyes.

"Really?" said Witner. "Tell us more about this theory of yours."

"Well, maybe it's the pons nucleus and not the cerebellum."

"The pons nucleus? Mr. Samuels, while you're trying to remember some basic neuroanatomy, why don't you step closer—come, come—and demonstrate your auscultation technique."

Samuels froze.

"He won't bite. Come forth, Mr. Samuels."

The other medical students parted, the majority of them looking relieved that today it would be Samuels burned at the stake. It was shaping up to be quite a conflagration, too.

Witner folded his arms.

"Before you start," he said, "tell us what you see when you look at this patient."

"Well," said Samuels, "this is a young man who is unresponsive."

Witner turned to Delancy and indicated with a nod that the latter could take over the line of questioning. Delancy beamed like an apprentice butcher given a prime carcass.

"How do you know he's unresponsive?" he demanded.

"How?" Samuels said, slightly defiant. "Well, because he's not responding to anything."

Delancy shook his head.

"Maybe he's just asleep." His tone was derisive. "How do you know?"

"Dr. Delancy raises a very important point, doesn't he?" interjected Witner. "Is there anyone who can tell Mr. Samuels a more definitive way of determining a patient's state of responsiveness?"

Several hands shot up.

"Prick him with a pin," said one.

"Put an ammonium capsule under his nose," said another.

"Do a sternal rub," offered a third. "Or press something hard into his eyebrow."

Witner nodded. "Yes, all of those things could be done, but isn't there something simpler?"

"A rectal exam?" suggested an intern.

"Dr. Delancy," Witner said, "enlighten us."

"Yes, sir. The first step in determining a patient's level of consciousness is to try verbal stimuation. You *talk* to the patient."

"Thank you. Simple things first. Now, Mr. Samuels, assess his level of responsiveness."

Samuels shuffled his feet. "You mean try and talk to him?"

Witner looked toward the window and tapped his toe on the floor. Samuels sighed and bent toward the patient.

"Hello, there," he said. "Hi, how are you feeling today?" He then straightened and stepped away from the bed. "Okay, well, I guess he's not responding to that."

"Now, auscultate, Mr. Samuels," Witner ordered.

Samuels again leaned over the comatose patient and began listening to his chest. There was a problem, however—he had forgotten to put the earpieces of his stethoscope in his ears. They were still clamped around his neck.

Witner held up his hand to silence the chuckles that began erupting. The pyre had been lit, and the flames were now licking up Samuels's legs. He continued for another ten seconds, and then his ears suddenly turned the color of ripe tomatoes. He straightened and slipped the earpieces into their proper place, and would have continued if Witner hadn't broken in.

"That's quite enough, Mr. Samuels. Quite enough. Tell me something. You've gone through four years of college and are now in your fourth year of medical school, is that not correct?"

"Yes, sir."

"That makes eight years of post-high school education focused on a career in medicine."

"Yes, sir."

"Such effort usually means an individual truly wants to become a physician."

Samuels nodded, his temples and forehead glistening.

"However, I have to wonder, as I suspect your colleagues are also wondering, if that's the case with you. Do you really possess that desire?"

"I was a little nervous."

"People standing on thin ice usually are. And you are on very thin ice." *Not to mention that you're ugly, unambitious and probably one of the Infected already.*

Samuels's lips parted, but no words came out.

"Let me put it this way," Witner continued. "Until the moment you graduate in May—that is, *if* you graduate—please consider yourself under the lens of a very high-power microscope. I will be watching you, Dr. Delancy will be watching you, all the house staff will be watching you, the nurses will be watching you, the entire faculty of this medical center will be watching you.

"But most of all, your classmates will be watching you, because as a reward for all their hard work and dedication, it would be unfair to make them share the honor of achieving a medical degree in the company of someone unworthy of it, don't you agree?"

Samuels stood like a statue.

"Tomorrow morning, you will give us an exhaustively referenced twenty-minute lecture on the nature of the occulocephalic reflex. Goodbye to you all for now."

Back out in the hallway, the team scattered, leaving Witner and Delancy to continue to the elevators. Witner felt as fresh as if he'd just stepped from the shower. There was something so invigorating about teaching.

Delancy looked up at him.

"Dr. Witner, I just wanted to tell you I agree with the way you handled Samuels."

"You don't think I was too harsh, Randy?"

"Definitely not. You were more generous than he deserved. Samuels started slacking off when he came back from emergency leave last week."

"Oh? What was he on leave for? To have his teeth fixed? No, it couldn't have been that."

"His father died suddenly."

"What did his father do?"

"A shoe salesman or something like that."

"Keep the thumbscrews on him—I don't like his demeanor. There's something sullen and crafty about his face. If he quits, excellent."

"All of us appreciate the way you're trying to raise the bar here. And personally, for what it's worth, sir, I truly hope you'll accept the permanent deanship."

"Thank you, Randy, but I'm like George Washington. I'm happy to serve when the country's need is great, but when the crisis is over, I'll return to the farm—in my case, the laboratory and clinic."

"George Washington became president."

"But he didn't campaign, Randy. He didn't campaign. I'll leave that decision to the board of trustees."

"They'd be crazy not to keep you on. Look at all you've done. The media program is so exciting. And the Blue Team."

Witner put his hand on Delancy's shoulder.

"By way of returning a compliment, my young friend, if ever I were to assume that office, I would want people like you on the faculty—bright and trustworthy young clinicians who share my vision of renewed greatness."

Delancy blushed furiously.

"There's nothing I'd like more than to join the faculty here."

"Then consider it a promise, doctor. If I become permanent dean, you will be offered an assistant professorship."

"Sir...did you say assistant professorship?"

"Given your abilities and your contributions this year to the Blue Team, I'm sure we can arrange for you to skip the clinical instructor phase. Especially if you were to write a couple of good papers before, say, June?" Witner gave his shoulder a pat. "Onwards," he said. "New challenges wait. As an aside, Randy, if the deanship is offered to me, I'd like to rename the Blue Team the Dean's Team. What do you think?"

The young man was most appropriately enthusiastic.

Chapter 9

Jack called upstairs and learned that surgery to remove the arrow from the attempted suicide's skull had gone smoothly, and the man was now stable in the surgical intensive care unit awaiting a psychiatric evaluation. As he sat in his office, exhaustion hit him. He shuffled listlessly through a stack of letters and reports. He should go home and sleep, but there was paperwork to catch up on.

In any case, he had too much to think about. It was hard to concentrate on anything except the meeting this morning, and Dr. Gavin's return, and most of all perhaps, the letter Gavin had mentioned.

He laced his fingers behind his head and leaned back, his gaze coming to rest on a poster of Mount Everest above the filing cabinet. A woman he'd dated a couple of years ago had given it to him. In red letters across an azure sky was the phrase *Because it's there.*

He looked away, eyes burning. Maybe it had been an impossible idea all along, to bring a modern emergency department to New Canterbury. He'd been warned by plenty of people in California that coming back here was a mistake. The East Coast wasn't ready yet for real emergency medicine.

That might have been true back in the 1990s, but this was a new millennium. Nor was it a problem with the entire East Coast. It was New Canterbury, Bryson Witner and Norman Scales.

The woman who'd given him the poster had been an attorney Sonia Bonadonna introduced him to. She'd wandered into his life and wandered out again. It had been the same with the other women he'd gotten close to since returning to New Canterbury half a decade ago. They'd been frustrated by his work schedule, his frequent breaking of dates, and they'd all been less than thrilled when they found out he had a younger brother living with him, an atavistic hermit with an untrimmed beard who seldom spoke and who prowled the woods hunting.

That was a facet of his life he had neither the power nor the desire to change.

He stared down at the carpet, listening to the sounds of voices and activity swirling in the department just beyond the thin wall. What had he accomplished in the past five years? No much, really—a teaching award and a few articles published. The ED was still a work in progress, with four- and five-hour waiting times on busy days, never enough staff, an inefficient layout; and now any chance of moving things forward was on hold for who knew how long?

The phone rang. It was Kathy, ward secretary for the ED's acute side.

"There's someone here to see you, Jack," she said. "Were you expecting a Mr. Fleusterman?"

"Who's Mr. Fleusterman?"

"I think he's a patient with a complaint."

"Great." Jack looked at his watch. "As long as I'm here, I'll see him."

Out by Kathy's post in the eastern alcove of the central station stood a stoop-shouldered old man with rather long but well-combed gray hair. He had on a black cashmere overcoat and held an ivory-handled cane in one hand and a black beret in the other. A green scarf hung around his neck. He did not look happy.

After escorting the man to his office, Jack arranged two chairs while Mr. Fleusterman scrutinized the walls.

"So," the old man said in a gruff voice. "What have we here? Bachelor of Arts and Sciences, University of New Mexico. Phi Beta Kappa. Doctor of Medicine, New Canterbury University. Alpha Omega Alpha, whatever that might be. And 'Be it known that the below named physician has fulfilled the requirements set forth by the California Board of Regents for completion of the Residency Program in Emergency Medicine at the University of California, Los Angeles.' And here's an award. 'The City of New Canterbury presents this with gratitude in honor of Dr. Jack Forester's contributions to the training of volunteer ambulance services, 2010.'"

"Please have a seat."

The old man turned to face him. "All of you love to flaunt your education, you medical men, don't you? You put hardwood frames around your degrees then hang them up where people must look at them."

"I thought patients wanted to see a doctor's credentials."

"That's because half of what you do is show business. At any rate, I came here to lodge a complaint, and I will not be brushed aside. I want to be heard and I want satisfaction, or I will go to every newspaper and attorney who will listen to me. I've lived in this community for seventy-five years. Am I making myself clear? No, I don't need to sit to talk."

"Why don't you tell me what happened?"

Fleusterman drew himself up. "Three weeks ago, my daughter brought my ten-year-old grandson here because the boy had been acting clumsy, dropping things, fumbling with words. That particular day, he stumbled in gym class, and his ankle swelled up."

"I see."

"They put Rory in a cubicle, and after about two hours of waiting he went to sleep despite the fact they'd put a loud and obnoxious drunkard in the next cubicle."

"That was a bad choice of rooms," Jack agreed.

"Hah, that's nothing! One of your doctors—a genuine moron—comes in and grabs Rory's ankle and makes him cry. He tells Susan it's probably a sprain, but he's going to get an x-ray. Fine, but then Susan starts describing Rory's recent behavior, the clumsiness and all. She's worried, you see."

"Do you remember who the doctor was?"

"His name was Heartwood, or something like that. Susan said he had red hair and a mustache."

"That would be Dr. Atwood."

"Yes, that's the one. So, Susan starts telling him about Rory's recent problems, and he just cuts her off and then—" The old man stopped and gathered himself. "Do you have any idea what he asked her?"

"No, I don't."

"He asked my daughter if she has an alcohol problem."

"What?"

"Yes. He asked her if she or anyone else in the family drinks to excess."

"He must have smelled the patient in the next room."

"There!" said Fleusterman. "You, sitting here three weeks later, can figure it out. Susan says no, she doesn't have an alcohol problem, thank you, and what does that have to do with the price of beans? But he keeps going. Well, has she considered the possibility Rory's been getting into the liquor cabinet, and that might explain his behavior?"

Jack closed his eyes.

"Susan reacts as any concerned mother would act and tells the dinglebrain off. So, what does he do but huff out and call the Department of Social Services to investigate my daughter! When Rory gets back from having the x-ray taken there's a social worker waiting to interview him."

"Mr. Fleusterman," Jack said. "I am deeply sorry."

Fleusterman's eyes were all but glowing with rage.

"Story not finished, Dr. Forester. The ankle was sprained, and they wrapped it and sent him home. Next day, the Department of Social Services comes to their *house*. Once a doctor makes a referral, you see, they've got to carry through. They not only visited Susan, they called the school and they spoke with the neighbors—oh, yes, the neighbors, too.

"Meanwhile, Rory's clumsiness was getting worse. So, Susan took him to see their pediatrician, who actually..." Fleusterman jabbed his finger toward Jack. "...listened to her. He listened to her, and he examined Rory, and then he sent him right away for one of those scans of his head."

"A CT scan," Jack supplied.

"What have you," said Fleusterman, whose voice broke slightly."

He paused, and Jack stepped closer. He knew what the answer would be before he asked.

"What did they find, Mr. Fleusterman?"

"My grandson has a brain tumor, Dr. Forester. If that quack, Atwood, had listened and not jumped to ridiculous conclusions, the diagnosis might have been made a week sooner, and my family spared public humiliation."

The old man's voice was drained of anger and outrage, and he looked like a drifting ship. He sank as though exhausted into the chair.

Forester went to his desk. He reached for the phone and dialed the Department of Internal Medicine's secretary.

"Hi, this is Dr. Forester. Could you get a message to Humphrey Atwood for me? I need to talk with him ASAP."

"Don't do that for my benefit, Dr. Forester," Fleusterman protested. "I do not want to see the man—not unless it's to watch him get tied to a rail and covered with tar and feathers."

"*I* need to talk to him," Jack told him. "How's your grandson doing now?"

"He's scheduled for surgery tomorrow in Boston. We could have had it done here, but no, thank you. Not after this."

After getting a security guard to help Mr. Fleusterman out to his car, Jack returned to his office. He got on his computer and reviewed the chart for Mr. Fleusterman's grandson—it was exactly as the man had described—then called to have Atwood paged again. Ten minutes later, his phone finally rang.

"You wanted me?" said an impatient voice.

"Yes, Humphrey. Can you come speak with me?"

"If you want to tell me about the failure of your proposal, I've already been apprised. So sorry to hear it."

I'm sure you are. "No, it's something else."

"About my new study, then?"

"There's been a patient complaint filed against you," Jack said.

"Anything to be concerned about?"

Jack thought of several responses to that, all of which he knew he would regret. He bit his tongue.

"Yes, Humphrey, it *is* something to be concerned about. Can you stop in my office?"

"This is a busy day for me, Forester. I have to work an ER shift this afternoon, and in the meantime, I've got administrative chores."

"Humphrey, I consider it a mandatory part of your job as the assistant ED director to respond to my request for an urgent meeting, unless you're dealing with a life-or-death situation. I'll be waiting here for you."

He didn't give Atwood a chance to respond, re-cradling the phone vigorously. Almost every shift Atwood worked in the ED there were problems of one sort or another. He had a cold and supercilious bedside manner—if it could be called a bedside manner at all. He had no tact in dealing with the nurses, treating them like servants. He'd been trained as an internist and had precious little interest in pediatrics and a near-total paucity of skills for dealing with trauma. When he was on duty, he let the residents and medical students do nearly all the real work.

About the only thing the man could do decently was give a lecture.

Until Witner had shoved Atwood down his throat, Jack had never really thought much about why some physicians chose academic medicine instead of private practice. Now the truth of the old saying was clear—if you can't do it, teach it.

Someone rapped on the door.

"Come in."

Humphrey Atwood was in his mid-thirties, a red-haired man of medium height with blue eyes and a neatly trimmed mustache. Today he wore a dark maroon shirt and a paisley tie. His right hand held a cup of coffee, his left a glazed doughnut.

"Shut the door and have a seat, please," Jack said.

Atwood bit into the doughnut then moved the chair farther from Jack's desk with his foot and slowly occupied it.

"Can we make this quick?" he said, dabbing icing from his mustache with a napkin he took from his shirt pocket.

"Sure, Humphrey, we can make this quick. Let me tell you the story I just heard." He described the events as the old man had reported to him.

Atwood shrugged and screwed up his eyebrows dubiously as he swallowed the last of his pastry.

"He's sure it was me?" he said.

"Unequivocally."

"Ah, yes. Now I remember. Yes, interesting. Well, it goes to show that even the best of us can be fooled. I'm an internist, after all. I mean, a kid comes in with a sprained ankle and ends up having a brain tumor. Osler himself couldn't have figured that one out.

"This clearly indicates why we should move in the direction of having three separate physician staffs in this ED, as it used to be—adult medicine, pediatrics and surgery. That's been my idea all along. We should return to the standard model."

"Sure, let's step backwards, Humphrey, so we can have three physicians on at any given time instead of one real emergency doctor."

Atwood chuckled. "We'll never see eye-to-eye on that one, will we?"

Jack felt his jaw muscles tighten.

"In any case, this situation has nothing to do with how to run an emergency department, Humphrey. It's about practicing medicine—it's about jumping to unfounded conclusions. You mentioned Osler. Do you think he would have generated this kind of complaint?"

"What gives you the right to talk to me about practicing medicine? Is that what you're implying? That I'm some kind of quack? Forester, I cannot win with you. Never."

"For the sake of argument, let's assume this child had, indeed, been getting into his parents' hooch and I'd failed to notify Social Services? Where would I be then? I'll tell you where I'd be—I'd be standing right here on this same carpet."

"I doubt that, Humphrey. You failed to empathize with that mother. You didn't listen to her. You made a cockeyed snap judgment."

"Open your eyes, Forester. This is an emergency department. I erred on the side of caution. I should be patted on the back, not vilified. It was busier than usual that night, and I did what I thought was right, and I'd darn well do it again. Complaints are part of the rough-and-tumble."

"Not necessarily."

"They've been a part of every ER I've ever worked in."

"Maybe it's you, then," Jack snapped, regretting the words the instant they left his lips.

"All right, be insulting," Atwood cried, his eyes bulging. "Meanwhile, I've got a major bone to pick with *you*." He jerked to his feet and glared. "When are you going to install my special pager system?"

A wave of heat suffused Jack's cheeks. Atwood's special paging system was a major bone, alright—a major bone sticking in his craw.

When he'd first taken on the directorship, New Canterbury's emergency department often lacked a supervising attending physician on duty. Even when there was one, he or she often wandered the hospital doing other things, leaving the interns and residents unsupervised for hours on end. One of Jack's first actions had been to ensure that at least one attending doctor was on duty 24 hrs a day, and he'd mandated they stay in the department. It had taken two years to get to that point, and even now half the shifts were filled by not-well-qualified moonlighters—or worse, boobs like Atwood.

Atwood folded his arms and continued staring.

"Well, when is it going to be in place?"

Atwood wanted to be able to leave the department whenever he chose, as in the old days, and intensely disliked Jack's policy. If they needed him, they could page him. But because the standard paging system still didn't reach all corners of the hospital, he wanted a special system just for him, "to free me up for more important duties than babysitting residents," as he put it. "They need to learn how to swim in the deep end."

The new system would require the installation of a few hundred dollars-worth of new antennas. Witner, to no surprise, had authorized the expenditure. It was Witner who had foisted Atwood on him as the assistant director and given him privileges beyond his value, for reasons that continued to mystify Jack.

So, he had been dragging his feet on submitting the paperwork, and he intended to continue to drag his feet. Atwood, of all people, should not be allowed to break the rules.

"Humphrey. The bottom line is that, when you're on clinical duty, I want you to stay in the department with the trainees. I'm not going to compromise on this."

"We'll see about that," said Atwood, his mustache twitching. "Is this all, or do you want to waste some more of my time?"

"As a matter of fact, it's *not* all." Jack leaned forward and rested his arms on the desk. "I want you to write a letter of apology to that little boy's mother."

"You *what*?"

"You heard me, Humphrey. Draft an apology letter. Let me see it first."

Atwood snorted.

"Fine, a letter, wonderful! And maybe I could also attach a list of malpractice attorneys so she can sue me. I'll write it as a confession of negligence so she can use it in court." He shook his head and snorted again. "Forester, you are out of your mind. You've gone too far. I'll see you later." He turned to leave.

"Humphrey, I want it by this afternoon."

"Forget it." Atwood gripped the door handle. "I believe it's even against hospital policy."

"No, it is not against hospital policy. You simply apologize for the fact she had a bad experience. You tell her you would be happy to speak personally with her. You don't admit to negligence. These things *can* head off lawsuits."

"Ridiculous."

Jack rose and leaned over his desk.

"Listen, I don't care what you think. You're going to do it."

"I refuse."

"I beg your pardon?"

"It's against my better judgment and general principles, and I refuse to lower myself."

"Fine, then immediately resign as my assistant director."

"I am not *your* assistant director. I am *the* assistant director. I am not your lackey. We'll see what Dr. Witner and Dr. Scales have to say about this."

"Humphrey, that family deserves an apology from you personally, and I suspect the board of directors of this hospital, who are very sensitive to public opinion, would agree."

"So, you're threatening to take this to the board?"

"You bet, my friend. I will take this to the board in a heartbeat. Have you ever thought, Humphrey, about what will happen to you if your special pal Bryson Witner doesn't get the permanent deanship? Were you also aware Dr. Gavin is back in town? Remember him, the man who was dean here for a quarter-century, my friend and mentor? He was at the general faculty council meeting this morning. I don't think he's very happy with Dr. Witner and his changes."

Atwood's mustache twitched violently.

"We'll continue this later, Forester," he said, his tone less arrogant. "I've got projects to attend to."

"The letter, Humphrey," Jack repeated, tapping the middle of his desktop. "It needs to be sitting right here by tomorrow morning. Or else it'll be time for a shitquake—with you at the epicenter."

Atwood slammed the door.

Jack let out a breath. His shoulders were aching.

Chapter 10

Zellie strode into the lobby of the Seneca Hotel and looked around in surprise. It was quite large, and its decor was straight out of the 1890s, with gilded wall sconces and polished pink marble columns. Clawfoot sofas and chairs had been artfully arranged among large potted ficus trees. On her way to the registration desk, she passed a violinist playing in an alcove—a girl dressed in a black T-shirt and pants, her bow arching up and down, making notes Zellie could not hear.

After checking in and settling her things in the room, she decided to take a walk, both for the exercise and to get a better feel for the place. A sharp wind was blowing down the sidewalk under a low sky of broken clouds that contained more shades of gray than she thought she'd ever noticed before. Turning her back to the gusts, she headed out, passing other strollers walking into the wind with heads lowered and collars pinched closed.

The hotel was on a street called West Avenue, where the storefronts were old and elegant. A few minutes later, she came to the intersection of West Avenue and Main Street and realized she was probably in the center of town. There were department stores and office buildings, the tallest of which rose five or six stories above the street. Beyond the buildings, she could see tall snow-dusted hills—small mountains, really—rising close by the town on three sides and giving the impression it sat alone in a deep valley like one of those villages in a liquid-filled glass ball you shake to create a snowstorm.

She found a post office, mailed the letters she'd written on the train, then went into a little bookstore across the street. It appeared deserted at first.

As always when entering a bookstore, Zellie ambled to the fiction section and looked under A to see if, by some outlandish possibility, her novel might still be on the shelf. Only once in the last five years had she found a copy.

It wasn't there, of course, and despite her having armed herself against disappointment, her heart sank a little. It was not that her book had failed to find a permanent place on the shelves—for such was the natural fate of most novels, no matter how good or bad—but that she still couldn't bring into being another one.

Vibration in the old floorboards told her someone was approaching. She stepped away almost guiltily and turned to see a bespectacled man of about sixty with a potbelly and a gray beard. He had a kindly smile, and a twinkle in his eyes.

"Something in particular you're looking for?"

"Just browsing. I was looking for some local history."

"Ah, indeed," he said, beaming. "Well, that will be over in Regional Interest. Here, let me show you." He led her to a row of books near the front of the store and began pulling titles out. "Now, these three are a series about the frontier days in this part of the Southern Tier, written by a local newspaper reporter back during the fifties. But they're verbose and apocryphal—a lot of Injun Joe stories, if you know what I mean—so I couldn't recommend them if you're really interested in local history. I take it you're not from around here?"

Zellie shook her head

"Visiting relatives, are you?"

"Nope. Here on business. I'm writing a piece on the medical center."

"Ah, why didn't you say so?"

He was obviously eager for company. He introduced himself, and they shook hands, and a few moments later he was brewing a fresh pot of coffee. He pulled up a chair for her behind the counter.

Jonah Peters was head of the New Canterbury Historical Society, had, in fact, written one of the books on the "Regional Interest" shelf—a copiously illustrated history of barn construction in the Seneca River Valley titled *From Post and Beam to Laminated Trusses*.

After describing how the book combined his love of history and photography, he went on to give her the highlights of the region's settlement from precolonial days to the present—the original Iroquois tribes that had hunted and fished here, how the land grants brought the first white settlers, how the Iroquois had unfortunately sided with the British during the Revolution and lost their lands as a result, how the canal and railroad spurred an explosion of development in the 19th century, how New Canterbury produced more ball bearings than any other city in North America just before World War I.

"But sadly, as you can see by looking at the empty factories on the other side of the river, we're a region in decline," he said. "The ball-bearing works finally closed five years ago. We're just too far off what's now the beaten path, and—oh, the winters. They're something."

"But the university and its medical center seem to be thriving. Aren't they?" Zellie said.

"They're under threat, too, I'm afraid," he replied. "Their glory days may be over."

"Why's that?"

"Part of it is due to population shrinkage, Ms. Anderson, and part of it is financial. I'm not a pessimist by nature, so I'll keep my fingers crossed, but New Canterbury is a private university, you see, not state supported, and they face a lot of competition from the public system nowadays. Their endowment isn't what it used to be. They lost buckets on their investment portfolio they'll probably never recover."

"I can imagine."

"And the medical school has been through a lot of turmoil lately, ever since Dr. Gavin stepped down as the dean. James Gavin had an international reputation, and he really put the place on the map. Did you heard what happened to the man who replaced him?"

"Not really, no." Her curiosity was now officially piqued.

"Terrible tragedy. He was scuba diving in Lake Stanwick, exploring caves—though for the life of me I can't understand why that particular sport would appeal to anyone in their right mind. In any case, he apparently got lost in a cave and ran out of oxygen. Never made it out."

"How horrible." A shudder passed through her. "What an awful way to die."

"Indeed. Now, this new fellow who's taken over, a man from Harvard by the name of Dr. Bryson Witner, is really shaking things up, they tell me."

"He's the one who started the *Medical Media* program I'm going to write about."

"Exactly. He's a real mover and shaker, apparently. I hear some folks like it and some don't. Some say he'll put us back on the map."

"I'm scheduled to interview him tomorrow," she said.

"That should be interesting. I hear he's quite the charmer. You'll get a good story, I'm sure."

"Maybe," she said.

"Why maybe?"

"Oh, I'm just being negative," she admitted. "I'm under relatively strict guidelines about what to write. I must be upbeat and positive. As my editor said, 'Fry the egg any way you want as long as you make it sunny-side up.'"

He laughed, and his belly shook, his glasses sliding halfway down his nose.

"Well," he said, after a moment's pause to recover his breath, "I guess we must do what we must do to survive. If I had my way, I'd be roaming around shooting pictures of dilapidated old country stores right now for a second book, to the dismay of my long-suffering better half. I'll probably never get around to it, though. I guess I only had one book in me. I'm old, and the fire is almost out."

"I hope you do," said Zellie, wondering if she'd make a similar comment when her own hair was gray.

"But, editorial restrictions or not, you should use this opportunity to tell a grand story. Youth is full of adventures."

They talked for another half-an-hour before Zellie finally thanked him and went back out into the cold, her satchel now weighed down with a complimentary copy of *From Post and Beam to Laminated Trusses* he'd presented her with a bow when they said goodbye. She wondered what tomorrow would bring, and found herself for the first time since boarding the train that morning intrigued by this assignment, and even by the thought of meeting Bryson Witner.

Chapter 11

Bryson Witner slowed as he approached the dean's suite, partly to admire the elaborate arched molding of fluted cherry wood that distinguished his new office from all others in the medical center, and partly to eavesdrop on Greta, whose desk sat near the entrance. He was glad he did. It was not Greta's voice he heard but that of James Gavin.

He listened intently. Gavin was using the telephone on Greta's desk, having a one-sided conversation of which Witner couldn't make out the words except for the final goodbye. Then, Gavin murmured something to Greta.

Witner rounded the corner and cleared his throat. Greta blushed, her eyes widening. Gavin turned to face him, his expression neutral.

"This is a pleasant surprise, Jim. I was hoping you'd stop by sooner rather than later, but this is excellent timing. I just finished rounding with the Blue Team."

"Greta says you have the rest of the morning free," Gavin said.

"Greta never lies. Hope you haven't had to wait long."

"No, we've just been catching up."

"She often lets us know how much she misses you. Greta, would you bring us some coffee or tea?"

"That won't be necessary," Gavin said. "I ran into Norm Scales, and he told me what you've done with the Blue Team. You certainly move fast."

"When the sun shines, as they say. Shall we?"

Witner unlocked the door and ushered the older man inside. They sat on red leather-upholstered chairs in front of the fireplace, the coffee table between them.

"So, Jim," Witner continued, lacing his fingers together, "how's your jungle research coming along. Is semiretirement being kind to you?"

"You're really getting used to this, aren't you, Witner?"

"What? Your old office?"

"Everything. The trappings and levers of power."

"Not really. I'm just temporary help, Jim. I'm an individual lost in shoes ten times too large. I'm a little man drowning in a sea of past—"

"Spare me the rhetoric," Gavin interrupted.

"Jim, have I done something to offend you?"

He watched the old man's eyes spark with anger. Good. Let him lay his cards on the table.

"Witner, you know as well as I that the role of an interim leader is to keep the ship on course and running smoothly—period. It is not to change directions. It is not to derail long-standing projects."

"Are you referring to that business about the emergency department?"

"That's just one of many. Like what you've done to the Blue Team."

Witner smiled. "As far as the emergency department goes, there was general opposition to Dr. Forester's proposal. I said relatively little."

"You expect me to believe that? When I left here almost everyone except Norm Scales was enthusiastic about it."

"Dr. Forester misunderstands me."

"Oh, does he? The role of an interim dean does not include alienating good faculty members. Nor is it to create from whole cloth entirely new projects like this *Medical Media* thing. Neither is it to increase the size of the medical school class, as I hear you're trying to do, by lowering admission requirements, or what you've done to the Blue Team—shortchanging the experience of many to benefit a few.

"You're not acting like an interim leader, Witner, so drop the pretense. You're pandering to the board. You're campaigning. I see hidden agendas, and I see power abuse. And I will tell you right now, I suspect there are other things going on of far graver concern."

He had never seen Gavin's face like this—rigid and red, with a faint sheen of perspiration on his forehead.

"What might those things be, Jim?"

"You'll know when the time is right, Witner. I still can't believe this. When I hired you, I thought I was bringing on board a reserved, promising, sincere individual who'd just recovered from an unfortunate problem and who deserved a chance to grow in the sun."

"And I grew. So, what's the issue?"

"This isn't growth. This is some kind of metamorphosis. Or maybe this is what you were all along. Whatever—I've come to believe you're an artist at manipulating people."

Witner smiled and shook his head.

"You overestimate me. You make it sound as if I'm a threat."

"To be perfectly honest, I believe that having you selected as the permanent dean would be an unmitigated disaster."

"Jim, your negative feelings toward me are very distressing."

"Odd—you don't look distressed. I think that somewhere inside you're enjoying this. You think this is a game, and you think you're the master."

"I don't know how to respond to that."

"I know what *my* response is going to be. I'm going to have myself placed on the search committee."

"That's your prerogative, of course."

"I suggest you wipe that smile off your face. My opinion will be heard."

"As well it should." Witner looked down at his watch. "Listen, I don't want you to think I'm brushing you off, Jim, but I've got work to do, I'm afraid."

"You amaze me, Bryson. There's no crack in your facade. You sit there like we're at a garden party."

Witner unlaced his long fingers and studied them for a moment, then looked up at Gavin and let his face turn grave.

"Power is a strange thing, Jim. Some people compare it to the wind. But I think power is more like the sail a person raises to the wind. The wind is, for lack of a better term, fate. When a person—such as yourself, for example—gives up a powerful position, as you did, he lets his sails down. When the wind is blowing strong, it may be very difficult to raise them again."

Gavin's eyes bulged with fury, and the old man rose. He said nothing for a long moment as his face grew calmer.

"Witner, just who the hell are you?" He didn't wait for a response. He strode to the door and let himself out, closing it quietly.

Witner went to his desk, and sighed. The battle was engaged, and that in itself was a relief.

With a key from his pocket, he opened the bottom left drawer of the desk and removed a small digital recording device he'd installed two months before that allowed him to monitor all telephone activity on Greta's extension. Because a number of people considered Greta a reliable confidant, he had learned many things of greater and lesser value, and that was the major reason he tolerated her insolence.

This recording device was, in fact, how he'd discovered the threat the recently deceased Lester Zyman had posed. Zyman had made the mistake of leaving a message on Greta's answering machine one day—a message, fortunately for her, she never received—and had paid the price.

Witner fast-forwarded through several routine calls, then came to the one Gavin had made. Leaning back, he listened.

"Hello, is Chief Bedford in?"

"No, he's not. May I ask who's calling?"

"This is an old friend, Jim Gavin. Dr. Jim Gavin."

"Oh, hello, Dr. Gavin. This is Agnes. How can I help you today?"

"Thank you, Agnes. Listen, I'm calling from the hospital. I've just got back in town and was hoping I could see him this afternoon."

"The chief will be sorry he missed you, but he's at a law enforcement conference in Albany today. He'll be back the day after tomorrow. That's Saturday, but I know he's going to spend the morning in his office catching up. Would you like to see him then?"

"I guess that will have to do."

"Certainly, sir. Just stop over. I'll leave him a message. How's eight o'clock?"

"Fine. I'll be there at eight o'clock Saturday morning."

"Can I tell him what it's about, sir?"

"It's a private matter, Agnes, but you could mention I want to talk about the deaths of Robert McCarthy and Lester Zyman. Maybe he could pull the files."

"I will certainly let him know, Dr. Gavin. Nice to speak with you."

"The same here, Agnes. Goodbye, now, and thank you."

Witner nodded. *So, the old man thinks he's on to something.* Resetting the recorder, he placed it back in the drawer and carefully relocked it. Then he unlocked the drawer below it and removed a large fireproof metal box secured with both a combination lock and a padlocked chain that ran through the handle and over the top. He spun the combination dial, then fished a key out of his pocket and unlocked the chain.

Inside lay a leather-bound book the size and thickness of a volume of the *Encyclopedia Britannica*. The words *Society Carnivalis* were inscribed on the cover and, below that, his initials *BMW*.

With his left thumb and index finger, Witner lifted the front cover to a forty-five degree angle and looked at the clock. He watched the second hand complete a sweep, and then he opened the cover fully.

Not long ago, he had been called away from the office for some urgent clinical matter—a Blue Team patient taking an unexpected turn for the worse. He had locked the office door, of course, but he had not put the book away, had left it lying on the desk. It was a shocking lapse into complacency that could not be tolerated again. No harm came of it, fortunately, but he lost sleep castigating himself.

How gratifying, the way life had fallen into place since that day he'd felt compelled to enter a little bookstore in Cambridge. Almost against his will, he'd gone to a dusty shelf in the back where his eyes came to rest on this book. To anyone else it would have been a relic from the days before personal computers, the kind of elegant ledger that would have been at home on his grandfather's desk; but for some reason it drew him like a magnet, and when he opened its cover, the voices began talking to him.

They were not the strident voices he'd used to hear. They were calm, measured, professional and comforting. *You are the one. Take this Book and fulfill your mission. We will teach you all you need to know. We will reveal to you the truth.* Not only was this Book the medium though which he had been recruited to the Society, it would make visible, through what he wrote, the plan of action that must be carried out.

After all these years, he still didn't know who the others were, or how many souls like him existed. It was enough to know that, in due time, all would be revealed. That is, if he succeeded. Perhaps there were thousands like him, indistinguishable from the Infected ones.

When he took it to the counter and paid for it, the Book had been blank. For many weeks back then, he'd written and written, articulating the steps and the reasons for each one. After he moved to New Canterbury, he began making entries on every individual of significance, from the head of housekeeping to the chairman of the board of trustees, with coded notes regarding their potential to harm or further the mission.

Jack Forester. Let's see. He turned to Forester's entry, took up his pen and briefly noted the outcome of today's meeting. Forester was a 12B3—meaning he had no potential to assist and was potentially disruptive. His resignation should be encouraged.

As for Dr. Gavin...

Witner flipped the page. Gavin was 1T2B—a dangerous impediment to progress. He picked up the pen and added the code tag XR. *Expedite removal.*

Setting down the pen, he thought for a moment then dialed Nelson Debussy. Debussy's secretary picked up the line and informed him the president was out.

"Give me his cell number, please."

"He left his mobile here, I'm afraid, Dr. Witner."

"Kindly tell him to return my call when he gets in. Let him know it's urgent."

Turning back to the Book, he leafed forward to the chronology map and studied it. With a fingertip, he traced his rise from associate professor of medicine to interim dean to permanent dean. The timeline didn't stop there, of course. Once he had gained a national reputation, it would be on to the directorship of the World Health Organization, which would occur in approximately fifteen years at this rate.

Only then would the real battle against the Infection commence.

The intercom crackled.

"Dr. Atwood is here," Greta said.

He pressed the button.

"I already have a brief meeting scheduled with him this afternoon. What's the problem?"

"You'll have to ask him. He just wondered if you had some time, and I said yes."

"All right. Send him in, in exactly four minutes."

He returned to the Book. Closing the cover halfway, he watched the second hand sweep from twelve to twelve before ending the session.

When Greta showed Atwood in, it was obvious the man was agitated.

"Sit and state your business," Witner said, pointing at the chair recently vacated by Gavin. "Then I've something to discuss with you."

"Thank you for seeing me early, Bryson. This is about Forester."

"What about him?"

"He's trying to crucify me over some silly little patient complaint. Believe it or not, he's ordered me to write an apology letter. It's insane."

"Ordered you to write an apology letter? What was the complaint about?"

"Oh, this child came into the ER with a sprained ankle and a few weeks later was diagnosed with a brain tumor. I missed the brain tumor, ergo, I'm a bad physician."

"That was all?"

"The crux of it was that I made a Social Service referral because I was concerned about parental neglect, and the family felt insulted. Forester wants me to write the boy's mother and admit my mistake. He's threatening to take it to the board of trustees."

Witner tapped his fingertips together and sighed. Atwood's ability to empathize with patients was painfully limited, and he could easily imagine him unintentionally insulting a family. People don't easily forget that sort of thing.

"Humphrey, I assume you know what happened to Forester's proposal this morning?"

"Indeed, sir," said Atwood, flashing a smile. "A victory for common sense."

Witner shrugged. Forester's plan actually made considerable sense.

"Humphrey, you have to realize that Forester's upset," he said. "He's lashing out because his plan was crushed. It might be wise to humor him."

It was Jack Forester himself who made the plan unacceptable. If Forester had shown the appropriate amount of deference, like Atwood and Delancy—not that he'd have needed to be as obsequious as that pair—Witner would have helped him. But ever since Forester voted against him becoming the interim dean in favor of Dr. Zyman, the man's true nature was clear. Forester had chosen the rocky road.

"I see what you're saying, Bryson, but it's the principle of it."

"Principles, schminciples, Humphrey. By refusing to write this letter you give Forester power over you. Imagine standing before the board of trustees trying to explain why you won't say you're sorry. You'll get little pity, believe me. You'll come across as callous and petty, and because I have supported you, it may tint my reputation as well."

"Do you really think he'd take it to the board?"

"Our friend Forester is a frustrated fellow right now. I wouldn't rule it out."

Atwood looked at the floor and fiddled with his mustache for a moment.

"I would never want to tarnish your image, Bryson," he said finally. "You've been very good to me."

"Console yourself, then, with the thought that I believe Dr. Forester will resign within a month or two. When he's gone, I will see that you get the directorship. It's just a question of time. Meanwhile, don't pick a fight you can't win."

"I see your point."

"Go ahead and draft the letter and let me see it first."

"It shall be done. On a brighter note, Bryson, I've got a great idea for a new study. Can I run it by you?"

"Make it quick—I've got something else to cover with you."

Atwood leaned forward, excited, his eyes gleaming.

"Sir, I believe I've hit on a revolutionary way to reduce overcrowding in the emergency room that's far cheaper than building new rooms. Let me give it to you point by point.

"Point one, most ER patients are not true emergencies—the sore throats, the headaches, the chronic back pains, little rashes, insomnia—and many of them are uninsured to boot. They're bad debts that clog up the system. It's a loss any way you cut it."

"Short and sweet, Humphrey."

"Okay, point two, people with trivial problems will sit in the waiting room for hours until they see the physician, when they don't need to see one to begin with. But there they sit, hour after hour, tying up resources. Why?"

"To the point."

"The reason is so obvious we overlook it, Bryson. It's due to some extent simply because the waiting room is a comfortable place to lounge. We provide them with a TV, magazines, vending machines, carpeting, even upholstered chairs. It's warm in the winter and it's cool in the summer. There's even a volunteer to answer questions and hand out tissues. In essence, we reward them for sitting there and waiting. We've created a paradise for hypochondriacs and malingerers where they can relax and socialize with each other."

"And therefore...?"

"Therefore, I propose that for three months we remove all amenities and install simple wooden benches—like church pews. I even kicked around the idea of restricting use of the restrooms, but the State Public Health Code mandates them. We could, however, reduce the frequency they're cleaned and stocked, and we could remove the air fresheners."

"I think we'll leave the bathrooms alone," said Witner, glancing at his watch.

"Even so, Bryson, I hypothesize that a significant number of people who don't need the ER will get frustrated by the Spartan conditions and walk out. Fewer of them clogging up the system means faster turn-around times for the sicker cases. We'll do a simple before-and-after comparison. I believe this has got *New England Journal of Medicine* potential." Atwood leaned forward, his face brimming with excitement. "So, what do you think?"

Witner looked at him for a moment.

"You're proposing we encourage people to leave by making the waiting environment inhospitable?"

"Not inhospitable—just barren."

"I see. Had you thought about irritating music at loud volume, too?"

The touch of sarcasm was lost on the younger man, who smiled enthusiastically.

"Yes! Just loud enough to discourage conversation, like a short Bach fugue played in an endless loop."

"Or maybe something by the Monkeys, Humphrey?"

"The Monkeys? Hmmmm. Interesting. You know, we could have separate study arms using different music."

"All right," Witner sighed. "Enough of this. Have you run your idea by Dr. Forester yet?"

"Are you kidding? He treats every little boo-boo with the same intensity he devotes to myocardial infarctions. His approach to overcrowding is to hire more staff and whip them into working faster. I'm interested in getting rid of the little boo-boos entirely."

Witner smiled.

Good, then, this may be the straw that breaks the camel's back.

"Humphrey, your plan may require some modifications, but I want you to draw up a formal proposal. Run it by me, and we'll submit it to the IRB, and I'll make sure Forester gets a copy. I'm sure Norm Scales would be happy to make this an Internal Medicine-supported study. You, I and Dr. Scales can be the major authors, and Dr. Forester will just have to accept it."

"Or leave, right? Thank you for the support, Bryson. Forester's never been receptive to any of my ideas. I'm still struggling to have my paging system installed."

Witner frowned.

"Are you telling me the paging system I personally approved for you has not been installed yet? I sent him authorization over six weeks ago."

"No. He's stalling."

Witner's frown deepened.

"So, Bryson, you really like my idea?"

"Humphrey, sometimes you remind me of a dog that can't get enough petting."

Atwood laughed.

"Nancy's accused me of the same thing sometimes. Oh, I wanted to show you something."

"Can it wait?"

"Won't take a minute," Atwood said, removing a photo from his lab coat pocket. "This will be our Christmas card this year. That's nine-year-old Jeremy standing by me, and Nancy's holding Brianna, who'll be twenty-two months."

"Yes, very nice." Witner gave it a glance.

"No, take it, please—this copy is for you."

Witner took it and dropped it on the coffee table.

"Humphrey, tomorrow is going to be an extremely big day here. Not only will we have our first televised medical procedure, but Brad Claxton, the gubernatorial candidate, is passing through the region and wants to give a press conference here."

"So, he wants to tag on to Brenda Waters's publicity," said Atwood. "I'm rooting for the Republican candidate, Bob Simpson. How about you?"

"Humphrey, who gets elected has no more significance than who wins the Super Bowl. Individuals do not drive history. If there hadn't been Napoleon, there would have been someone else. Just so long as the winner keeps us in mind, and that's why we're going out of our way to accommodate him. Now pay attention. *Coast-to-Coast* magazine has assigned a journalist to write a feature on the *Medical Media* program. She's arriving tomorrow morning."

"Great."

"Whatever else *Coast-to-Coast*'s redeeming qualities may be, it has a large national circulation, and a glowing story will improve our name recognition. Therefore, we want a completely positive report. We do not want this journalist exposed to any of the naysayers around here, and there are a few left. I want to take no chances. To that end, Humphrey, you being one of the most optimistic people here, I'd like you to be her constant escort tomorrow. You stay glued to her elbow, do you understand?"

"Bryson, it'll be an honor."

"Honor or not, stay with her and keep her entertained and properly informed."

A dreamy look came over Atwood's face.

"Bryson, I just have to say this. All of us are amazed at what you've accomplished over the past few months. The *Medical Media* program alone would have taken a team of people half a year to organize, and yet you just set to work and—bang—it exists. You did it. Astonishing. You must have great connections."

Witner narrowed his eyes, paused and studied Atwood's face.

"What do you mean by connections?" he growled.

Atwood's smile faded.

"It's just an expression, Bryson."

Witner leaned towards him, slowly.

"Do you have any reason to think that I might not work alone?"

A puzzled look came to Atwood's face.

"I asked you a question. Answer me."

"No, I don't think that, Bryson. I was only—"

"I work alone. Do you comprehend that?"

Atwood cleared his throat and shifted on the chair.

"Yes, absolutely, Bryson. I didn't mean—"

"You will tell me immediately—and I mean *immediately*—if you become aware of any rumors regarding connections I may or may not have. Is that perfectly clear, Dr. Atwood?"

Atwood blinked rapidly. After a moment, Witner leaned back in his chair, his expression softening.

"I only mean to say that reputation is very important in my situation, Humphrey."

"Yes, certainly, sir. And I only wanted to say that I'm proud to be standing in your shadow."

Just so long as you stay there.

CHAPTER 12

The western sky held only a pale scarlet glow when Bryson Witner rose from his desk and went to the window. He had worked out a plan for dealing with Gavin, and there must be no further delay. He leaned on the broad sill and regarded the black shape of the Seneca River, curving by the undergraduate campus in the twilight like a sickle blade before it straightened and ran through the center of New Canterbury.

He lingered for a moment, gathering his thoughts, then dialed Fred Hinkle's home number. He listened impatiently as Hinkle's wife said Fred wasn't home. Hinkle shouted something in the background and, a moment later, came on the line.

"Domestic bliss, Fred?"

"What do you want, Witner?"

"Fred, I have another electrical problem at my house. I need you to come check things out this evening." Witner heard him breathing. "It's that same old circuit breaker panel again," he added when Hinkle didn't respond.

"Does it have to be tonight? I promised Martine a movie."

"I'm very concerned about fire."

"How about the morning?"

"There's a real danger of fire, Fred."

"Jesus Christ."

"I'll see you at seven-thirty. Come around the back way."

Witner got his overcoat from the closet, donned a blue baseball cap with *NCMC* embroidered on the front, then made his way down the dim hallway. He felt a little foolish wearing a baseball cap—with a logo, no less—but it enhanced the regular-guy image he cultivated in the minds of younger faculty members. He'd never worn one at Harvard, but maybe he should have. Things might have turned out differently.

He let his white Volvo warm up then eased down the ramp of the parking garage. A freezing drizzle had fallen late that afternoon, and when he turned out from under the overhang at the bottom of the ramp, the station wagon slid and the right front fender scraped concrete with a sickening crunch. He released a long breath through his teeth.

The garage attendant, Lloyd, a man who suffered from chronic open sores on his forehead, sprinted from his booth.

"You all right, Dr. Witner?"

Witner rolled down the window.

"I was doing less than five miles an hour—of course, I'm alright. I'm more concerned about my headlight. Take a look up there—and throw down some salt."

"Doc, the glass looks okay," Lloyd said when he returned, "but the molding frame is bent, and the headlight wiper is dangling."

"Blast it!"

"A car with wipers for the headlamps. Boy, that's something."

"Yes, exciting, isn't it?" Witner snapped, jerking the shift lever into drive. "Now, move away, or I might fishtail into you."

He hated damage to his vehicle, but repairs would have to wait. Ordinarily, he would have gone straight to the Volvo dealer, which stayed open till nine. However, the meeting with Hinkle took precedence over everything, even this evening's business meeting of the Pet Partners Club; he had already called to inform them he couldn't make it.

His membership in Pet Partners was a matter of no small political expediency. At the first dinner party at the Delancys', right after Randy became the Blue Team chief resident, Witner discovered Mrs. Delancy presided over a pet therapy group. The organization was dedicated to the proposition that demented senior citizens living in nursing homes benefited from mingling with domesticated animals. When he'd mentioned his ferrets, Hex and Rex, Belinda had recruited him.

"Oh, Dr. Witner, that would be wonderful! Cats and dogs we've got aplenty. We need more exotics, like my Nguyen. Hex and Rex, how charming."

Nguyen was Belinda's potbellied pig.

So, for the past eight Sunday mornings, Witner had driven over to the Delancy house, where Abe Delancy, the board chairman, dressed for golf, would give him a warm handshake.

"By God, Bryson, it's an honorable thing, this pet business, but better you than me. I wouldn't have guessed you for a ferret man."

Off Witner would drive with Belinda in the passenger seat, his ferrets in a cage, and the pig reclining on a plastic tarp in the cargo area.

"You know, Bryson, the first time you brought Rex and Hex, I had my doubts—the way the brown one scuttled up that poor old woman's arm. But she loved it."

How surprised Belinda would have been if she knew the real reason he kept Hex and Rex—their presence kept his house free of Infection.

The flow of traffic stopped just before the Seneca River Bridge. He checked his watch and ticked his fingernails on the steering wheel. It would not do to miss Hinkle. He probably should have left the hospital earlier. Even though home was only forty minutes away, at times like this he wished he lived closer to the university. That, however, would have meant a loss of privacy. His house on the lake was surrounded by woods, and the nearest neighbor lived a quarter-mile away.

That degree of isolation was good for now, but when the deanship was his, he must get a second place in town. There would be entertaining to do.

The traffic crawled forward, and he saw flashing red lights up near the bridge. A car was on the side of the road, its front end buckled. Three police cars, magnesium flares, a fire truck and an ambulances—idiots. As usual, the paramedics were strutting around.

He detested emergency medics. Many of them were obese physician-wannabes in love with uniforms. They loitered in the ER, scattering cigarette butts over the ambulance ramp and flirting with the nurses. Their champion, of course, was Jack Forester, who trained them and encouraged them.

But that would soon end. Atwood's idiotic study would certainly drive Forester out.

He was almost at the accident site now, and realized he couldn't just drive by like the average citizen. He might be recognized.

He rolled down the window.

"Hello, there, sir!" he yelled to one of the medics. "This is Dr. Witner. Can I be of help?"

"No, sir, everything's under control. But thanks for asking."

"You're sure? I'm Dr. Witner, from the medical center. I'd be glad to help."

"Thanks much, Dr. Witner, but it's under control."

Witner smiled and waved.

Often, when Witner worked in his basement during the cold months, he would don his academic robe from Harvard. It was warmer than a sweater, and put him in a reflective mood. He was wearing it when Hinkle came to his cellar door at the rear of the house, which was at ground level due to the slope of the land toward the lake.

"Sorry I'm late," Hinkle said, stepping out of the cold and shutting the door. "Martine was really pissed. You owe me."

Witner marveled how men of a brutish nature like Hinkle let themselves be dominated by a woman. Sex was the cause, the need to slake their lust.

"Well, Fred, I feel sure you'll discover a way to make it up to her."

Hinkle peered around, eyes wide below his thick Neanderthal brow, a bit of supper stuck to the corner of his mouth.

"Why are you wearing that get-up?" he demanded.

Witner smiled and took a few slow, challenging steps toward him. Although Hinkle was burly, with the shoulders of an ox, Witner towered over him by more than a foot and was wide in the shoulders himself.

"Does it bother you, Fred?" he said, folding his arms and staring down.

Hinkle glowered for a moment then dropped his eyes.

"I don't give a damn what you wear, Witner."

"Good. Now, come with me."

He led the way down a path between old furniture, metal filing cabinets and stacked boxes to his sanctum sanctorum, the workshop where he worked on his marionettes. Crafting puppets out of wood and fiberglass and animating them electronically was a hobby he'd picked up as an undergraduate. Seven lifesized figures sat in a semicircle of chairs, each in accurate period clothing.

Hinkle gave a cynical laugh.

"I still can't get over these things," he said, shaking his head. "So, these are supposed to be old doctors?"

"That's correct, Fred," Witner replied after a moment. "Hippocrates, Galen, Paracelsus, Harvey, Rush, Cushing and, last but not least, Sir William Osler."

"Oh, yeah, let's not forget Osler." Hinkle chuckled, giving him a challenging, stupid look. "You just make them and leave them sitting around down here to mildew?"

"No, Fred. Sometimes they come upstairs."

"And that's all you're going to do with them? It's nuts. Why bother?"

Witner approached him.

"What's you're favorite hobby, Fred? Rolling cigarettes? Or maybe it's knocking your new wife around?"

Hinkle glared back, his eyes narrowing.

Witner stepped closer, smiled down on him.

"You think you're stronger than I am, don't you, Fred?"

"Don't press your luck, Witner."

"You're thinking right now that you could kill me if you wanted. I can see it in your eyes. You like the thought. It energizes you. All those things you told me about being an Army brat over in Germany when you were a boy, having to fight those skinheads just to get to school, and then becoming a SEAL, and about your time in the Persian Gulf, killing prisoners. Death is in your blood."

"You're off your freaking rocker."

"If anything were to happen to me, Fred, I've arranged for the right people to know about what you did to your first wife, and to Dr. Robert McCarthy and Dr. Zyman. Now, shall we proceed?"

"You're in this just as deep."

"I think not. You must have misinterpreted some idle comment I made, and given the well-documented degree to which you hated and abused your late wife, I doubt you'd get much sympathy from a jury. Nor is there any possible way I can be tied to Dr. McCarthy's terrible accident."

"You were the one who suggested I kill Madeline in the first goddamn place!"

"What possible motive would I have to do something like that? When you shared with me that she was addicted to prescription narcotics and alcohol, and was making your life a living hell, and the way she was forcing you to raise your stepdaughter singlehandedly, I sympathized with you, Fred, of course. But Madeline was a patient of mine—it was only natural I should try to comfort her husband. When you queried me about the lethal doses of certain medications, I had no idea you wanted to put her out of her misery and collect her life insurance.

"But sitting in a safe in my lawyer's office, Fred, is all the evidence the police would ever need to hang you, just waiting for something to happen to me. Now, sit."

"Fuck you, Witner," Hinkle snarled. "Screw you to hell." Still, he pulled out a chair and sat.

Witner went to his workbench. He opened a drawer and drew out three white candles. Placing them in a triangular pattern on a table next to Hinkle, he lit them with a kitchen match.

"I don't understand you at all, Witner."

"Of course, you don't. That's the way it must be."

He switched off the fluorescent light above his workbench so the only illumination came from the candles and a row of tiny bulbs on the ceiling above the mannequins. He sat across from Hinkle and watched the candlelight ripple over the man's face as his jaws clenched and unclenched.

"So, Fred, let's stay on the same team, shall we? You'll get what you want, and my needs will be met as well."

"When will this be over?"

"When I am the permanent dean and all challenges to that situation are eliminated," Witner said. "It shouldn't be long, assuming I can call upon your assistance again tonight."

"What's the deal?"

"I now believe that, just before he died, Dr. Zyman contacted a certain party who, therefore, must be removed."

"Is this the last one?"

"I don't know. There may be more."

"Will there be bonuses?"

"My silence should be bonus enough."

Hinkle leaned forward, his eyes narrowing. Witner held up his hand and smiled.

"Of course, there will be bonuses, Fred. You won't be disappointed. When my goal is reached, there'll be double the total."

"And then I'm selling the marina and clearing out of here. That's it. No more."

"That's your business. Unless, of course, you come to wish your new wife were also sleeping six feet under."

"You're an asshole, Witner. I love her. We've only been married two years."

"You should have taken my advice and not married a woman half your age who doesn't like your stepdaughter. How is she doing, by the way? She's, what, twelve years old now?"

"Katrina's thirteen, and you're right. They hate each other."

"You should have listened."

"Martine sits at the supper table and blows smoke at her. Katrina's sick half the time."

"This is what I like, Fred. You and I sitting here chewing the fat like a couple of old friends. That's the way it should be."

"Give me a break."

"Would you care for some sherry?"

"Fuck you and your sherry. I promised Martine I'd be back in an hour."

"So you will."

"Who's the party?"

"Dr. James Gavin."

"Christ."

"Not hardly."

CHAPTER 13

Jack took his coffee out onto his deck; Arbus followed and sat at his feet. He gazed out at the sloping field below his house. There were still patches of snow, but they were rapidly melting. The dog looked up at him, panting steam, an expectant look on his face. He reached down and scratched his head.

"No time for a walk today, buddy."

Tossing the dregs of his coffee over the rail, he went back through the sliding glass doors into his living room with its open-beamed ceiling. After collecting his briefcase, he slipped on a trench coat and a pair of duck boots and headed outside through the side door carrying his good shoes in a shopping bag. Arbus bounded down from the deck and caught up with him as he crossed the yard.

"Don't give me that look, Arbus. Tonight we'll hike to the bluff. Then I'll build us a fire in the woodstove, and we can commiserate."

The dog's mouth dropped open into a smile, and Jack had to laugh.

"Wait a minute, boy. We'd better check on Tony."

He set the briefcase in the garage then trudged to the old gambrel-roofed barn sitting fifty yards uphill behind the house. The barn had been the only building of his great-grandfather's farm still standing when he'd inherited the land and built his home on the fieldstone foundation of the original farmhouse, which had burned to the ground a generation ago.

Sliding open the doors, he saw a small green tent pitched near the tractor. Arbus shot past and disappeared inside it.

Jack's younger brother Tony, his only sibling, had lived with him for the past three years. The arrangement was an odd one. From early spring until the streams froze over, Tony camped outside. Though Jack kept an aluminum chest by the side door stocked with canned food, vitamins and batteries for his MP3 player, Tony lived otherwise off the land. Sometimes, he set up his tent on the ridge behind the house, sometimes down below near the bluff.

When the weather turned foul, he would camp inside the barn, and only in mid-December would he move inside, staying in a room Jack had made for him in the basement.

Jack approached the tent.

"Tony? You awake?"

A wooden long bow leaned against a hand-hewn wooden column, and a leather quiver bristling with hunting arrows hung from a nearby peg. The bow was a thing of beauty Tony had made from a kit, and he kept it polished. He used it to harvest rabbits and turkeys and the occasional deer. He never used a gun, and didn't need one.

At Tony's boarding school, archery had been a major activity, and he had developed remarkable skill in it. He could shoot two-inch patterns at forty yards by the age of twelve, and had been urged to try out for the Olympic team. But Tony wasn't interested in becoming famous. It was difficult to say exactly what his true interests were, except that he liked being alone and out-of-doors, with his bow and arrow and a penny whistle.

He was eight years younger than Jack, and when they were growing up, the doctors speculated Tony had a high-functioning form of Asperberg's disorder, which corresponded with what Jack had learned as he trained to become a physician. It was partly concern for his brother's condition that had drawn Jack into medicine.

The only noise coming from the tent was Arbus, panting. Jack pulled aside the flap and, in the green half-light, saw the dog attempting to lick his brother's bearded face.

"Looks like winter's coming early," Jack said.

Tony nodded and yawned.

"Keep warm. And let me know if you need anything."

Two contrasting vehicles occupied the garage—a weatherbeaten 2001 Ford half-ton pickup and a gleaming black 1972 Jaguar Series 3 E-Type roadster, a restoration project Jack had found in a barn near Syracuse. Tossing his briefcase and shoes into the Jag, he squeezed behind the polished wood steering wheel and turned the key. The V-12 was finicky on colder days; this morning it caught quickly but idled rough then died. Never a good omen. One shot was usually all he got.

So, a few minutes later, he pulled out of the driveway in the truck, its tires sloshing though snow as he wound down the narrow road toward New Canterbury. He slowed as he neared the Carters' place, his closest neighbors. Wilfred Carter, dressed in a bright orange vest and Carhartt overalls, was crossing the road, heading from the barn back to his house. He waved, and Jack slowed.

"How about this white stuff, Wilfred? You gotta love it."

"You can have it, doc," the old man replied. "Where's the British go-cart this morning?"

"It took a vacation."

"Wouldn't mind heading south myself. Can't drag Beth away from here, though."

Speeding back up, Jack turned his thoughts to the hospital. The memory of yesterday's meeting welled up, along with that conversation with Dr. Gavin. He pondered again the letter Dr. Gavin had mentioned, the one Lester Zyman had written the day before he died. Why didn't Gavin want to talk about it? What did he have to research?

The temperature had dropped below freezing during the night; he crunched on frozen slush up the steps into the old lobby. He'd intended to buy a cup of coffee at the vendor before going to the emergency department, but an unusual sight greeted him. Someone was occupying the reception desk, just like the old days, and the place was buzzing with activity.

The receptionist was a lovely elderly woman by the name of Eleanor Lane, who headed the hospital's volunteer auxiliary. She had on the auxiliary's trademark pink jacket, her cheeks heavily rouged and her hair freshly blue-tinted.

"Good morning, Dr. Forester," she called out cheerfully. "My goodness, how about all this fanfare? Isn't this exciting?"

"Looks like the circus is coming to town. What's the occasion, Eleanor?"

"Don't tell me you've forgotten. Shame on you."

"Ah, yes," he said, taking off his gloves. "It's Public Colonoscopy Day."

"And Brad Claxton's press conference, too," she said. "He's going to do it right here in the lobby. Look."

She pointed toward a group of technicians in jeans and T-shirts who were assembling a platform and unpacking lights. Electric cords snaked across the old carpet.

"Brenda Waters is already upstairs. I saw her come in about an hour ago. She's very well-preserved and taller than I imagined."

"So, they've got you working early today."

"That's the nice thing about being a volunteer—it doesn't feel like work. I'm seventy-nine, and the reason I stay healthy is because I come here every day. Do you know I began doing this in nineteen-fifty-nine?"

"You're definitely part of the family. I couldn't imagine this place without you."

"Thank you, and I still remember when you were just a medical student. And now look at you, doing such great things in the emergency department. Are you working there this morning?"

"Just desk work today. I'll be back tonight at eleven for another clinical shift."

"I don't remember this much excitement since Richard Nixon came here with a kidney stone," Eleanor said.

"Richard Nixon was here with a kidney stone?" Jack grinned.

"Oh, yes. I was volunteering in the emergency room that day, and I almost bumped into him. He was on a tour of some kind just before he threw in the towel. Probably needed to take a break from Washington. He was holding his stomach with one hand and Pat's arm with the other, the sweat dripping off that nose of his, and he was cursing like a sailor. Dr. Gavin came in to take care of him. And isn't it wonderful that Dr. Gavin is back? He's my next-door neighbor, you know."

"Have you seen him yet today, by the way?"

"Not this morning," she said. "So, are you coming to the press conference?"

"If I don't, you can tell me the important parts, Eleanor. You're a good Democrat, aren't you?"

"There are some things you should never ask a lady," she said, wagging her finger.

As he joined the line in front of the coffee vendor, he noticed a strikingly attractive young woman standing near the staircase. His eyes lingered on her, déjà vu coming over him—she looked familiar. He studied her again, and the sense of familiarity deepened. He had definitely seen her somewhere. No—it was more than just having seen her before; there had been an interaction of some kind.

He racked his memory but couldn't get the image to crystallize.

She had an oval face and above-average height. Her figure was willowy, and she had dark-blond hair that was almost brown. He had an excellent memory for names and faces, but for some reason hers—and how he knew her—was eluding him. The harder he thought, the more certain he was, but the more it evaded him.

She was looking around, as if searching for someone. Her attention briefly lit on him, but she gave no sign of recognition.

The man behind Jack cleared his throat, and Jack realized he was holding up the line. He moved forward. There were still three people between him and the counter. When he looked again she was gone.

Then he spotted her over by the reception desk, where she was studying the mural of Pegasus giving the country doctor the ride of his life. Was she smiling? One thing for certain—she was lovely. Transcendently lovely.

California—that's where it must have been, during his training. Had he dated her? Utterly impossible. He would never have let someone like her slip out of mind. He sighed with frustration. The memory would bubble up in his memory, he was certain—probably after she'd gone.

Then something did surface, but it was fragile. A forest. The sound of surf breaking in the distance. He probed, but the thread dissolved.

The man behind him again cleared his throat, this time quite aggressively. She was crossing the lobby toward the staircase.

"Sorry." He broke away and marched toward her. His throat tightened as he watched the swirl of her dress as she moved. She stopped again near the base of the steps and read from a piece of paper in her hand.

"Excuse me," Jack said.

She didn't look up.

"Excuse me," he repeated.

Again, no response. She probably thought he was a stalker, given the way he'd been staring at her. He was about to back away when she looked up and noticed him standing there.

"Forgive me," she said, not unkindly. "Were you saying something to me?"

Jack's head felt little light.

"I hate to bother you, but I think I know you from somewhere."

Her face was even more striking up close. She had a dimpled chin, and a beauty mark on her left cheek.

"That sounds very convincing," she said, one eyebrow rising and her smile turning wry. "But I don't think so."

"No bells?"

"Nope."

"Have you ever been in Los Angeles?" he said. "I did my residency at UCLA."

"Never been west of the Mississippi."

"Maybe I saw you in a movie or something," he said. "Are you an actress?"

"Ah, there you go. You must have caught me as the Tin Man in the tenth grade."

Smiling, Jack shook his head.

"This is driving me crazy. I know I've seen you somewhere before."

"Maybe *you're* the actor."

"No, I couldn't act my way out of the proverbial wet paper sack. Listen, my name is Jack Forester. Does that trigger anything?"

"Nada."

"And you might be?"

"I might be Zellie Andersen," she said, shaking the hand he extended. "A pleasure to meet you, Jack Forester."

"Seriously, either you have a double, or I'm losing my mind. I take it you're not a local."

"No."

"Are you a medical person?"

"A writer," she said. "I'm here for the story."

"I see. Listen, while my memory is trying to sort itself out, would you care for a cup of coffee?"

"Thank you, but I don't have time." She looked up the staircase. "In fact, the person who fits the description of the man I'm supposed to be meeting is coming right now. Red hair and a white coat."

Jack followed her gaze, and his heart lost a beat. Skipping down the broad marble staircase toward them was Humphrey Atwood.

Atwood propelled Zellie away so quickly, bounding up the staircase with her in tow, that she didn't have a proper chance to thank the man named Jack Forester for his coffee invitation, nor to wish him luck with his memory crisis, if that's what it was. If he'd simply wanted to meet her, all he'd had to do was say hello. In any case, he had a very nice smile. A very nice face.

Halfway up the stairs, she turned and saw him watching her. She winked at him and had to laugh—the look on his face was so genuinely puzzled. But she was sure she'd never run into him before.

At the top of the stairway, Dr. Atwood ushered her left down the mezzanine and into a corridor and finally stopped in front of an elevator. He seemed flustered for some reason, his face pink. As they waited for the elevator, he bowed and handed her a presentation folder stamped with the university seal.

"Inside this, Ms. Andersen, you'll find your full day's itinerary along with a comprehensive fact sheet about the medical center and, of course, about the procedure being performed on Brenda Waters. It's all copied out and has also been loaded on a complimentary thumb drive for you. It's all in there."

"Thank you," she said. "You're doing all my work for me."

The elevator door opened, and they stepped inside.

"Dr. Atwood, I must tell you that I have a hearing impairment. I'll understand you best if I can see your face."

"I will speak plainly, then," he said, still seeming distracted. "Listen, I noticed you talking to Dr. Forester." He pressed a button for the fifth floor. "Do you know him?"

"No."

"Good," Atwood said. "I mean, it's good I wasn't interrupting a conversation or anything."

Zellie had begun forming the impression Dr. Atwood was a strange bird.

"He'd just come up and introduced himself," she explained. "What do you know about him?"

"Not much to tell. He works here. Well, again, I'm happy to welcome you to New Canterbury, Ms. Andersen. You have a big day ahead of you.

You'll start by meeting with Dr. Witner, the interim dean. That will be quite a treat for you, and I know he's thrilled you're here."

The elevator door slid open.

"Your medical center is bigger than I expected," she said, gazing up and down the long corridor.

"Forgive me if I brag, but this place is one the best-kept secrets in the nation. We are the regional referral center, and we have almost every specialty you can imagine. We also boast a prestigious medical school and many NIH research grants. You'll find all this and more in your fact sheet. Consider yourself free to use any of it verbatim in your article."

"How kind."

"You also need to know, between you and I, Ms. Anderson, that Dr. Witner is the reason all this is happening today. The *Medical Media* program was his baby. He's the prime mover. By the way, my wife Nancy is a great fan of your magazine. I promised to get her your autograph. I told her you probably wouldn't object too strenuously." He chuckled. "Was I correct?"

Zellie smiled at him.

A few minutes later, he led her beneath an arched entry off the corridor into an anteroom where a pleasant-looking woman was sitting behind a desk. She rose to her feet and came toward them.

"You must be Zellie Andersen. I'm delighted to meet you. I'm Greta Carpenter."

"You'e the one who arranged my accommodations," Zellie said, shaking her hand. "Thank you very much. The hotel is great."

"Isn't it a lovely old place?"

Dr. Atwood cleared his throat.

"Mrs. Carpenter, would you kindly let Dr. Witner know we're here? His schedule is tight today."

Greta glanced at him.

"Certainly." She turned back to Zellie. "Please let me know if you need anything else."

"Well," said Zellie, "if you wouldn't mind, I'd love to interview you to get a non-doctor perspective."

"I'd be delighted," Greta said, giving Dr. Atwood a smile as she pressed the intercom button.

A moment later, the oak inner door opened to reveal a well-dressed man who looked to be in his mid- to late forties. Zellie was struck by how straight he stood, how formal his bearing, and how white his lab coat was. It almost hurt her eyes.

"Bryson Witner, at your service, Ms. Andersen. Welcome, and do come in. You may join us if you like, Humphrey."

"I'd like nothing better, sir."

Except maybe bending down and kissing his buttocks, Zellie couldn't help thinking as she crossed the threshold into Witner's office.

Atwood took her coat and hung it in a closet while Witner showed her to a chair by the fireplace.

"What a lovely office," she said. "It must be a wonderful place to work."

"Yes, indeed, it is, and thank you. I trust Dr. Atwood's been giving you what you need?"

"I'd love to know more about the history of your hospital."

"I have just the thing for you. Humphrey, would you bring me that copy of *A Century of Greatness*. It's next to the dictionary. And switch on the fireplace while you're up."

Atwood returned with volume and handed it Zellie, making another little bow as he'd done when he'd given her the itinerary.

"Thank you."

"With our compliments, Ms. Andersen," Witner said. "The university published it to mark the hospital's first century—from the turning of the initial shovel to the building of our new clinical towers and research wing. Lots of old photos and alumni essays, many of which are redundant and overly nostalgic, but it will give you a glimpse of our past."

"That's kind, thank you again."

"Now, can we get you a cup or coffee or tea, or maybe a soft drink?"

Declining, she took a notepad out of her satchel.

"So, tell me about what's going to happen this morning, Dr. Witner."

"This morning, Brenda Waters will become the first personality to grace our *Medical Media* program. When I welcomed her this morning, by the way, I arranged for you to speak with her. I hope you don't mind. We can do that right after the Claxton press conference."

"Claxton, the candidate for governor? He's involved in your program?"

"No. Coincidentally, he happens to be giving a press conference here this morning. It won't take long, and I assumed you might like to meet him, also."

"Sure, why not?"

"Settled, then."

"So, tell me more about your *Medical Media* program? How did it begin? What's its reason for being?"

"Let me begin by saying that modern medicine has made great strides in the prevention and early detection of conditions that cause early mortality..."

As she took notes, Zellie couldn't escape the impression he was speaking by rote—that much of Witner's mind was elsewhere. There was something unsynchronized between his words and his expression. It was subtle, something perhaps only someone who depended upon reading lips to one extent or another might notice, but it was real. The impression it gave her was that, as he spoke, he was trying to appease her while, at the same time, he was actively analyzing her, categorizing her. It was strange, and a little unsettling.

"But early detection procedures are for naught," he was saying, "if, out of ignorance or fear, people don't take advantage."

"Or from simply not knowing such things are available," added Atwood, who stood by the fireplace, his hands behind his back.

The glance Witner shot him contained a spark of irritation.

"As I was saying, Ms. Andersen, this is the impetus behind New Canterbury's *Medical Media* program—showing the public they have nothing to fear from such procedures. We estimate that fifty-five million Americans will be watching next week when Brenda's procedure is aired on the Learning Channel."

"That's very interesting," she said. "What other procedures are you planning?"

"Your fact sheet will tell you that we have commitments from William Camden for a transurethral prostatectomy, Roger James Kilburn for a polypectomy, Sharon Ropeling for a lumpectomy, and Bernice McLain's going to have her hysterectomy with us."

"And we've got a tentative agreement with Robert Beddington, don't we, Bryson, for his vasectomy?" Atwood piped up.

"Dr. Witner, what benefits do you see your medical center reaping from this?"

Witner smiled.

"Ms. Andersen, some might call this an elaborate publicity campaign, but I assure you, it's not. Our top priority is to spread information about the miracles of modern preventive and palliative medicine. It's already well known that New Canterbury is a national resource."

"Dr. Atwood says this was your idea," said Zellie, putting down her pen.

Witner laughed and shook his head. "Well..."

"Don't be modest, sir," said Atwood. "Dr. Witner has done the work of ten people pulling this together. When the university chooses a permanent dean, we hope that Dr. Witner will not have to move from this office."

"I can imagine," said Zellie, stifling a yawn.

"Dr. Atwood overstates the case," said Witner, glancing at his watch. "Well, this has been a very pleasant interlude, but I'm afraid we must go meet the candidate. You can leave your coat here."

"Thank you," Zellie said, rising to her feet. "By the way, I'd like to have a brief interview with your assistant, Greta."

"Might I ask why?"

"The more perspectives I get, the better."

"Of course," he said. "Would three-thirty or four o'clock this afternoon be acceptable?"

A short while later they were back on the mezzanine above the old lobby. The dais below was fully assembled. She looked in vain to see if, by some chance, Jack Forester was still there, and was startled by Dr. Witner's sudden grip on her elbow as he guided her toward a set of doors labeled "The Flexner Room."

A half-a-dozen people were clustered inside, talking to a swarthy, good-looking man she recognized as Brad Claxton. The atmosphere was festive.

A portly man broke away from the group and strode toward them.

"Hello, Bryson."

"Good morning, Nelson. Please allow me to introduce Ms. Zellie Andersen, the writer from *Coast to Coast* magazine I mentioned. Ms. Andersen, this is the Nelson Debussy, the marvelous president of New Canterbury University."

"A pleasure, Ms. Andersen," Debussy said. "Delighted you're here."

"Nelson," continued Witner, "have you seen Dr. Gavin? I'm surprised he's not here."

"No, I haven't, Bryson. He's probably catching up on rest after his long voyage. He is scheduled, however, to come see me this afternoon."

"I would like to speak with you before then."

"Fine, we shall do that," Debussy agreed. He turned back to Zellie. "Please come and let me introduce you to the candidate. He's quite a fellow, even if he does belong to the wrong party."

As they approached him, Claxton's eyes latched onto her, and such was the man's charisma the smile he beamed at her was among the warmest and most exciting she had ever received. He didn't give Debussy a chance to make introductions.

"So, this must be Dr. Bryson Witner, the top gun around here. It's truly a great pleasure to finally meet you, Doctor. I've heard nothing but inspiring things about you and this extraordinary hospital. It's one of the jewels in our state's crown."

"Thank you, sir," said Witner. "We welcome you to our institution and to the wonderful community we live in."

"Call me Brad. Someone like you, a healer and a scientist, a great New Yorker, I automatically consider a friend, and I hope you will give me the honor of a first-name relationship."

"I would suggest the honor is mine," purred Witner. "May I introduce you to Zellie Andersen, a journalist who's writing about us for *Coast to Coast* magazine?"

"Ah, Ms. Andersen," he said, beaming at her. "Your publication brings a good deal of pleasure to people."

"And this one of our junior faculty members, Dr. Humphrey Atwood."

Claxton pumped Atwood's hand like he was trying to raise water.

"Nice to meet you, Hump. I'd guess you took some ribbing in your younger days about that nickname."

Face crimson, Atwood mumbled something unintelligible as laughter filled the room.

Ten minutes later, the group descended en masse down the grand old staircase. Atwood offered Zellie a seat between him and Nelson Debussy behind the dais.

"Thanks for the honor," she said. "But I need to see faces, remember?"

She stood out front as Debussy introduced Witner, who uttered a few pleasantries and then introduced Claxton, who leapt onto the platform and started off with a joke about a Long Island farmer and a tax collector. Then, after praising the *Medical Media* program, he launched into a discussion of New York's broken political system and how he would go about fixing it.

Growing bored, Zellie looked around and noticed with a wave of pleasure that Jack Forester stood on the mezzanine, leaning over the balustrade. A moment later, his gaze met hers, and he smiled. Straightening, he waved.

There was something decidedly interesting about him. Why not interview him? Get his perspective on things. Yes, she would approach him once Claxton's press conference was finished. Maybe he'd figured out where he knew her from. Likely story.

But by the time Claxton's speech was over, Jack Forester had disappeared.

Chapter 14

Dr. Forester, please report to the emergency department.

Jack missed hearing it the first time as he stood on the mezzanine watching Zellie Andersen, more than ever convinced he knew her, and wondering if he should wait until after the speech to join her.

Dr. Forester, please report to the emergency department, stat.

He heard it this time. They wouldn't have called him unless it was something important. He tore his gaze away and strode off, but when he reached the ED everything appeared calm, the hustle and bustle if anything less than usual.

He marched up to the unit secretary's station.

"What's up, Kathy? I was stat-paged."

"It's Gail. One of the nurses is having a breakdown or something."

"Since when am I a psychiatrist?"

"She tells me, I page."

At that moment, Gail Scippino, the ED nursing director, scurried around the corner. She had taken the position only two months before, and now wore the flustered expression of someone who'd crash-landed on the wrong planet.

"Thank you so much for coming, Jack," she said. "I hate to bother you, but I need some assistance."

She explained on the way to her office. Darcy, one of her best nurses, was about to walk out.

"I'll let her tell you the situation. You've known her a lot longer than I have."

Gail flung open her door. Darcy McFeely, elbows on Gail's desk, sat with her face buried in her hands and her shoulders shaking, wads of tissue scattered over the desk like the aftermath of a snowball fight.

"Hi, there," Jack said as Gail closed the door behind him.

"It's no good, Jack," Darcy informed him. "I've got to get the hell out of here before I completely lose my mind. I've had it."

Gail opened the door and handed him two foam cups of coffee then shut the door again. He set a cup in front of Darcy. She looked up. A pretty woman in her early forties, her eyelids were swollen, and mascara had run down her cheeks.

"You want to talk?" he said, pulling up a chair.

Mechanically, she lifted the cup of coffee, blew on it and sipped.

"Tell me what happened, Darcy," he persisted.

"You name it, Jack. My ex-husband is being a bastard about custody again. I covered somebody's shift last week and left the twins with a sitter he doesn't like. He'll use any excuse. I covered the shift, you see, because Joan was sick, and guess what? Today I'm feeling like crap myself, and do you think I can find anybody to relieve me? Fuck, no! Nobody gives a shit. And then there's this little son-of-a-bitch schizophrenic I triaged this morning who calls me a stinking old whore and spits on me. I can take that crap, but what pushed me over the edge was when I heard you're leaving."

"What? Who told you that?"

"I heard it when I took a patient to radiology. People are saying you're upset because they voted down your plan. They said Dr. Witner is trying to get you to stay, but you've decided to go, and that Humphrey Atwood is going to take your place."

Jack felt his forehead grow hot. He shook his head vigorously.

"It's true I was upset, but I have no intention of quitting, Darcy. They're wrong. Dr. Gavin is back, and things are going to get better."

She looked up at him with bloodshot eyes and an unconvinced expression.

"I couldn't blame you if you did," she said, sniffling. "I've come to believe this place is run by a bunch of assholes."

He laughed.

"My leaving is a false rumor, I promise you, and I'm sorry you're not feeling well."

"Thank you."

"Did you ask Gail to help find someone to cover the rest of your shift?"

"Can I tell you something else?" she said.

"Sure."

"I don't want you to tell a soul."

"I promise. What is it?"

"Jack, I've started having fantasies about killing patients. Has that ever happened to you?"

He paused.

"I'm not sure I follow you."

"I can see myself marching some of them outside and shooting them. Like that drunk yesterday who caused the fatal accident. And the schizophrenic who spit on me today."

He reached over and put his hand on her arm.

"I'm glad you shared that, Darcy, and I know it's not you. It's stress. You know that."

"But just the thought I can have ideas like this, Jack—I can't stand it."

"Do you have any vacation time left?"

"I used it up when the twins had summer break."

"Let me talk to Gail about maybe getting you a week of R-and-R."

She swirled the coffee in her cup and sipped again. Then she looked him in the eyes.

"Okay," she said. "But I want you to promise me something."

"Name it?"

"If you do leave, give me some warning. If that jerk Atwood gets your job, I'm out of here. I have to work with him this afternoon, Jack, and it makes me want to vomit. He's lazy, he's arrogant, and he's mean to patients. He likes to work the three-to-eleven shift because you're not here most of that time. He lets the residents do all the work and disappears. We can't find him when we need him. Somebody's going to get hurt, Jack, and I don't want to be around when it happens."

Before the applause died away, Brad Claxton jumped off the platform and began shaking hands and patting shoulders. Zellie was still looking around for Jack Forester when Atwood found her in the crowd. He escorted her down a long corridor, through the chrome-glass-and-tile new lobby, then down another corridor and up in an elevator to the endoscopy floor to the VIP. Room. A few minutes later, Zellie was sitting across a small table from Brenda Waters, and wondering aloud how Waters could make an ordinary pale-blue hospital gown look exotic and glamorous.

Waters laughed. She was unpretentious and likable.

"That's the nicest thing anyone's told me all day," she said. "No, I take that back. A litter of medical students came by this morning. I say litter because they were like little puppies. You want to scratch their ears. God, to be that young again."

A woman peered around the doorway.

"Brenda, they'll be coming to give you an IV in about half an hour."

"Well, bully for them. Tell them to bring it on."

"Yes, ma'am."

"There," she said. "Zellie—what a lovely name."

"Thank you, Ms. Waters—"

"Brenda, please."

The same woman reappeared in the doorway.

"George wants to know if you'll need makeup?"

"Makeup? They're not going to see my face, for God's sake. Tell George if he can figure out how to beautify the inside of my large intestine, he can be my guest. Tell him I want a colonic makeover. Now, leave me alone for a while. Wait a minute. Zellie, would you like something to drink?"

"I'm fine, thank you."

"Beryl, there's some Perrier in the little fridge."

"You're not supposed to have anything by mouth, Brenda."

"Thank you very much. I know that. I'm not asking for myself, though Lord knows I'm thirsty. I shat myself crazy yesterday. I must have lost ten pounds. Have you ever had this done, Zellie?"

"No."

"Anything else, ma'am?"

"Peace and quiet."

"After they start the IV, Brenda, they're going to give you a sedative."

"Well, there's something to look forward to."

"I'll let you know when the nurse is here."

"I have no doubt."

The woman disappeared again.

"Zellie, I suppose you want to know why I agreed to do this in the first place?"

"Bingo."

"Because it would be the worst thing in the world to die of an illness that could be easily cured. I watched my father die of colon cancer, and he was in such misery you wouldn't believe. I was eighteen, and he'd been the rock of my life. I'm doing this for him. I'm not making a cent on it. You can write that down."

"I will."

Brenda Waters leaned across the table towards her.

"Zellie, is that some kind of new bluetooth in your ear?" She reached over and lifted Zellie's hair. Zellie felt herself blush.

"No, it's a hearing aid," Zellie acknowledged, leaning back.

"Are you deaf without it?"

"Not quite."

"I'm so sorry."

"Nothing to be sorry about."

"What happened? Were you born that way?"

"No."

"What's it like? I mean when you're not wearing it?"

"What do you mean, what's it like?"

"To not be able to hear. I ask you that as an actor, sweetheart. I liked you immediately."

"No, you didn't."

Brenda Waters smiled and looked at the tabletop.

"I do now," she said.

Beryl reemerged.

"Nurse is here, Brenda."

"Thank you, Beryl. Another couple of minutes." Brenda took Zellie's hand in both of hers. "That was true about my father," she said. "I'm not a vicious person. But, please, tell me what it's like. Take me inside your mind for a moment. Just one sentence."

Zellie smiled.

"I can perceive smells better than you."

Zellie found Humphrey Atwood just outside leaning against the wall, his arms folded, looking bored.

"How'd it go?" he said.

"She's...interesting."

He took her to a small café located on the ground floor of the medical school. They sat by a window and ate sandwiches. The courtyard outside was scattered with wet leaves, and beneath a maple tree lay patches of snow. Dr. Atwood chatted away about his work and his background.

"So, as you can imagine, me having grown up in San Francisco, I find this a cultural wasteland. Still, I suppose there's an up side. The lack of distractions allows me to focus more on my career."

"What exactly is the focus of your career, Dr. Atwood?"

"Good question. You see, I'm a general internist by training, but my academic interests range from endocrinology to health care resource utilization."

"Ah."

"Yes, indeed. My latest study involves finding a simple way to reduce inappropriate usage of the emergency department, and I think I've hit upon a great idea. Are you interested in that sort of thing?"

"What other things are you studying?"

"Oh, I'm also trying to come up with a cost-effective way to screen hospital employees for breast cancer."

"I see. That sounds like a worthy thing to study."

"Very much so. I must admit, I don't know where I got my scientific bent from. My mother was an accountant and my father just a dentist, though he had a very upscale practice. My great-grandfather was a mining engineer, though, and he did a lot of inventing. Maybe that's where it comes from."

"Maybe so."

"Well, Ms. Andersen, do you think you've seen enough of our hospital for the day?"

"I'd love to wander around some more. I'd like to visit, oh, let's see, a lecture hall, and the place where you keep cadavers, and the library. I've always wanted to see what a medical school's library looks like."

Atwood pushed his glasses back up the bridge of his nose and sniffed.

"I was hoping to do a little paperwork this afternoon. Then I have to work a clinical shift in the emergency room from three to eleven."

"I didn't mean you had to tag along. I don't mind going by myself, really."

He stiffened.

"I'll be delighted to keep touring with you. It's easy to get lost in this place."

For the next two hours, they explored the complex, and finally arrived at the library.

"Humphrey, you look pooped. Why don't you cool your heels while I look around in here?"

Atwood readily agreed.

She passed the checkout desk and entered a room full of students crowded around computer terminals. She found the rare book room and browsed the shelves, stopping to study a glass display case that contained medical artifacts, including a Roman scalpel, corroded but easily recognizable, from the fourth century AD. She sketched it in her notebook, then found a metal stairway that spiraled down into the stacks, which were several dimly lit floors containing bound journal collections.

They obviously never threw anything out around here. The first volume she peered at was called *Acta Anaesthesiologica Scandinavia*, Vol 245, 1896, with subsequent years running down the shelf and around a corner. The stacks were deserted except for a young woman scanning old journals page-by-page into a computer.

Zellie pulled out a huge green-bound book. Written on its spine in white ink was *Journal of the American Medical Association*, 1938, January-May. Leafing through it, she came upon a full-page advertisement. A young physician stood next to an examination table, a mirror on his forehead. He wore a short-sleeved white smock and was holding up a pack of Lucky Strikes. The caption read: "Luckies, the brand recommended most often by physicians for its purity."

Except for the curly black hair, the doctor was a close facsimile of Jack Forester.

Smiling, Zellie showed it to the girl.

"How can I get a copy of this?"

"Just tear it out and keep it," she said. "We don't scan ads, and once this issue is in the computer, it'll be thrown out. Can you believe they used to do that?"

Zellie thanked her, carefully removed the page and slipped it into her notebook. Climbing the stairs, she passed a fluttering moth.

Humphrey Atwood had gone to the gift shop while she was gone. He handed her a copy of the current issue of *Coast-to-Coast* and his pen. Though she had no work in that issue, Zellie wrote across the face of Angelina Jolie on the cover *For Nancy Atwood, with Warm Wishes, Zelinda Andersen.*

A few minutes later, he dropped her off at the dean's suite, in plenty of time for the meeting with Greta Carpenter Witner had told her he'd arrange. But Greta was gone, her desk tidy. Maybe she'd stepped away for a moment.

A hand on her shoulder startled her. She whirled around.

"So, you're done," Witner said.

Her breathing returned to normal. She took a step away from him.

"Where's Dr. Atwood?" Witner continued.

"He had to work. I came to see Greta. I thought we had a meeting."

"I'm afraid she's already gone for the day. A family situation or something. I couldn't catch her in time."

She watched his face. *He doesn't mean that. I'm being played.*

"You'll be happy to know the procedure went perfectly, and Brenda is doing fine. I just called over. Not a hitch."

"Glad to hear it."

"When are you heading back to New York?"

"Tomorrow afternoon."

"Very good. Well, we can't thank you enough, Ms. Andersen, and I look forward to reading your article. If you have any more questions, I'll be working in my office tomorrow. Saturday is my catch-up day. Just give me a ring."

"Thank you, Dr. Witner. It was a pleasure. My coat?"

Witner helped her into it and extended his hand. It felt as cold as stone.

Walking back toward the main entrance, where she could catch a cab, Zellie decided the only person she'd met that day she'd care to meet again had been Jack Forester. Might his claim of knowing her have been more than just a pickup line? She was starting to think he was telling the truth. Maybe she did have a double.

Her route took her through the old lobby, which was quiet, dim and empty. Motes of dust hung in a shaft of late-afternoon sunlight.

Jack climbed out of the truck, closed the garage door and strolled to the barn, swinging his briefcase. Tony had headed back to the woods, and

Arbus lay where the tent had been pitched. The dog trotted over, looking up with expectation.

"That's right, I promised a walk. Let me change. Why am I talking to a dog? Because there's nobody else around."

By the time they returned, it was dark. Jack went down to the basement. Lying on the exercise bench, he lifted weights and let his mind drift back to Zellie Andersen. He knew the only way to recover the memory, if ever he could, would be to take his mind off her and stop trying. Easier said than done.

"Frustration, Arbus," he said to the dog. "I'm probably having temporal lobe seizures."

Arbus stopped gnawing on his nylon bone and looked at him. Jack slowly set the weights down.

"Wait a minute."

Moments later, he was upstairs pawing through a bookcase that occupied a full wall in the spare bedroom that served as his study, and a few moments after that he let out a whoop.

He stared at the photo on the back of the dust jacket, then opened to the cover blurb.

> It's always remarkable when a debut novel is so wise and well-written, so strong and poignant. That such a book flowed from the pen of a 21-year-old simply astonishes. *Burning Down the Boardwalk* tells the story of Craig Timberlane, who grew up an orphan in Morganton, North Carolina, and became a marine in the first Gulf War. When Timberlane tries to settle into his old life, he discovers his family is unraveling, and Timberlane must decide where his true loyalties lie. Bubbling with insight and humor, *Burning down the Boardwalk* is an unforgettable journey.

He turned back to her photo and shook his head in amazement.

She was standing on a beach, either in the early morning or at dusk. Half-turned toward the camera, her face and figure were unforgettable. There must have been a breeze, because the gauzy white dress was hugging her legs and a strand of hair had wafted across her forehead. Her face was every bit as striking still as in real life.

He'd read it eight years ago, during a break from internship when he'd spent a week on the Monterey Peninsula, having found it in a little bookshop in Salinas. He clearly remembered liking the first page, then turning to the back photo and buying it. Hiking the next day along the ocean, he'd read more than half of it in a single afternoon, sitting with his back against an oak. That's where the memory of trees and surf came from. His high opinion of the book was confirmed by the fact he'd never given it away or traded it in.

Arbus nuzzled Jack's knee. He lowered the photo for the dog to view.

"Is that loveliness or what, boy?"

A string of saliva dripped from Arbus's jowls.

Jack laughed.

"You're a swine, but that's alright. I forgot to feed either of us. So, I shall. Then it's a nap for me because I work the night shift. Tomorrow, I will write a letter to her in care of the publisher, which will probably be a waste of time because they never forward them. Unless, of course, she might still be in town. I could try calling the hotels. It's probably hopeless."

Arbus barked.

"Okay, you be the optimist."

Chapter 15

James Gavin buttoned his overcoat and stepped out into the cold night, which felt good after the stuffiness of Nelson Debussy's office. He never understood why some people kept their thermostats turned up so high.

It had been, all-in-all, a very discouraging meeting. He'd expected more objectivity from Debussy, but Witner obviously had the man in his pocket. In retrospect, it wasn't surprising. Debussy was focused on the university's shaky financial state, and Witner's *Medical Media* program could become a windfall, increasing their referral base and stimulating alumni donations. Debussy wasn't going to bite the hand that fed the coffers. It was clear in the way his eyes glazed over when Gavin had tried to talk about Witner.

As for Gavin's request to join the search committee, Debussy had smiled politely and changed the subject.

He looked up at the lights marking the windows of Debussy's office. He and Witner were probably on the phone right now. Good, let them talk. It might make Witner nervous. Tomorrow was Saturday, and he was going to meet with Chief Bedford. Things would start rolling then.

His route back to the hospital took him down a tree-lined path that led through the undergraduate campus to the footbridge over Beech Avenue and the medical center. The air was cold and damp. Streetlamps silhouetted the bare branches and cast a maze of shadows. The pathways were full of students, most of them bareheaded and dressed in clothing more appropriate to spring. He and Betty had come this way hundreds of times from the hospital to meet friends for lunch or dinner at the faculty club on the undergrad campus.

Chief Bedford was a solid, smart man who would take this matter seriously and knew how to conduct a proper investigation. Gavin felt inside his jacket. Lester Zyman's letter was in his breast pocket. It would be the key.

He walked faster. Having skipped the media circus at the hospital, he'd caught up on his sleep, and his legs felt strong. Past the main quad and nearing the footbridge, he was alone yet had the odd sensation someone was trying to get his attention. He stopped and looked around. Nothing.

He continued. Nearer the footbridge, he felt it again. He didn't stop this time but strode more quickly. He continued through the grove of trees along the iron fence bordering Mt. Seneca Cemetery. Then he was on the footbridge, cars sizzling by on the wet pavement twenty-five feet below.

He was a third of the way across when he heard someone behind him.

The footsteps approached at a jogger's pace, and the back of Gavin's neck tingled. He stopped and turned. The man coming toward him wore a black sweatshirt with the hood drawn tightly around his face.

A potent chill crept up Gavin's back. He turned and hurried toward the hospital end of the narrow bridge, but it was still fifty feet away and the footfalls were closing.

The ringing of the phone interrupted Witner as he was making notes in the Society journal. He glanced up at the clock and smiled. After the third ring, he lifted the receiver.

Nelson Debussy's voice was somber.

"Jim just left my office, Bryson, and I'm afraid you're right. He is not the same man."

Witner sighed loudly.

"It breaks my heart to see him suffer, Nelson."

"I understand, my friend, and I'm grateful you discussed it with me."

"As much as anything, I wanted your opinion. I need to make sure I'm not overreacting."

"No, I don't think you are."

"This certainly puts a damper on today's success."

"So goes life, Bryson. But today was wonderful, and you should be very proud. I don't think things could have gone any better."

"The production crew was very pleased with the footage they shot. They're already on the way back to California for editing, and Brenda is spending the night here for a good rest."

"Splendid."

"So, how did it go with Jim?"

"It was just like you said it would be. He told me he has reasons not to trust you, which he couldn't discuss, and he believes you should not be the permanent dean. He wants to be on the search committee. I told him it was probably too late, but he wasn't satisfied. As for the *Medical Media* program, according to him, we might as well sell ourselves to MGM."

"Yet, the emails he sent me from Brazil—as recently as two weeks ago—were completely positive. He praised me, and everything I've tried to do here. I welcomed him into my office yesterday expecting the same friend and mentor as always, but it was the difference between day and night."

"You mentioned possible Alzheimer's when we talked earlier."

"I'm not a psychiatrist, Nelson, but everything points toward it. Early on, patients often develop intense paranoid delusions."

"Do the symptoms come on this suddenly?"

"They can, but, you know, I'm remembering an email he sent me a couple of months ago where he mentioned something about the CIA planting a listening device in his car."

"Oh, boy."

"And he made a remark about Norman Scales and the Mafia. Again, I brushed it off as a joke. So, here we have an elderly man, no more family left, by himself in a foreign country. His entire life revolved around this medical center, Nelson, and now he's no longer in charge—which may explain why I've become the focus of a delusion."

"Because the baton was passed to you."

"Exactly. Then comes the death of Lester Zyman. I think this may have accelerated the disease process."

"What can we do, Bryson?"

"He needs a psychiatric evaluation, even if it means an involuntary commitment. Without treatment, suicide is a risk—especially in people who've been functioning at such a high level as Jim. They realize what's happening and want to end the slide before they loose control."

"You think he may be suicidal?"

"When we were talking yesterday, he mentioned being tired of seeing things change, that he felt the world might be better off without him."

"This is not good."

"Damn it, Nelson, I should have done something earlier. I've been in denial."

"Bryson, you're only human."

"I'll never forgive myself if anything happens before he gets help. Was he headed home after he left you?"

"I don't know. I assume so."

"Then I'm going to his house immediately."

Gavin reached the end of the footbridge and was about to start down the steps when a hand grabbed the collar of his overcoat. He reached out and caught hold of the railing.

"You're coming with me."

"The devil I am," Gavin braced his feet and gripped the railing now with both hands.

"Suit yourself."

"If you want my wallet, I'll give it to you. Let me go."

The man tore his grip from the railing. A hand clamped over his mouth. He was dragged toward the middle of the bridge.

A car whizzed along the pavement two stories below. His assailant stopped and crouched. When the noise of tires had faded away, Gavin was lifted. He flailed with his arms and kicked out, but the man was powerful, and he felt a sickening sense of weightlessness that seemed to have no end.

He became aware of a strange white crackling noise.

Korea. He was lying outside the hospital tent, his face in the grass, the explosion of the shell ringing in his ears. The tent was gone, and so was the young soldier he'd been sewing up. He felt something warm run into his left eye.

Or had he simply tripped and twisted his ankle? He would get up, brush himself off and apologize to Betty for being clumsy and embarrassing her in public.

A terrible pain shot through the left side of his chest when he tried to move. He touched his left eye, and there was moisture, and then he smelled blood, or was it tar?

What was he doing in a tar pit?

Would the North Koreans drop another shell in the same place? Or were they up against the Chinese this time. So much for the big red cross on the tent. The world was going insane, and where was that young soldier? He had almost finished taking care of his wound, and there were other cases waiting. He shouldn't be lying here like a fetus. They'd think he was drunk. Up and at 'em. You're in the Army now and not behind a plow.

He tried to work his elbow underneath him, but that stunning pain in the left side of his chest struck again, and he sagged back.

Nelson Debussy, a pompous ass if ever there was one, had been sitting in front of him only a moment ago, but now it was dark.

No, it was mud he smelled, not tar.

The pain was making it hard to breathe, so he lay still and he thought of his wife and his son.

He sat next to Betty on the bleachers watching Colin play football. The boy was a fine little quarterback, aggressive and fearless. But he wouldn't listen to anybody. A wave of fear for his son's life passed through him.

Now there were voices nearby. Stop mumbling and come to the point, Colin. Have I ever been unfair to you? When are you going to wake up and smell the coffee?

He blinked. Something up there was glowing. Yes, it was the top of the New Canterbury caduceus, all lit up. So be it. He was at work, and that was all right.

"He must have fallen from the footbridge," said one of the bystanders, pointing up.

The medic knelt and began assessing the old man while his partner carried over a green blanket and an orange tackle box. Another medic came jogging with a wooden backboard shaped like a coffin lid.

"I don't know how long he's been lying out here," said a man. "I was driving by and noticed some movement."

"Can you hear me, old fella?" said the medic.

"Yes. Help me up, would you?"

"No, you lie still. Can you remember what happened?"

"I stumbled, and I'll be fine."

"What day is it?" said the medic.

The old man thought for a moment.

"How about the year?" said the medic.

The old man thought about this, too.

"What happened?" he asked.

"Looks like you fell off the footbridge, sir," said the medic. "You're lucky you hit the median and not the pavement."

"There's the median, the mean and the mode," the injured man muttered, his voice slurring. "Which one do you really want?"

"Who are you, sir?"

The response was indistinct.

"Did you say Dean? No, sir, please don't try to move. We're going to slip this collar on to protect your neck, okay, old buddy? Listen, where all do you hurt?"

"What happened?"

"You fell."

"Where's Colin? Did the others make it? Damn those Chinese."

"Please hold still, sir."

They carefully slipped the backboard under him and lifted him onto a gurney, covering him with a blanket and placing an oxygen mask over his mouth and nose. The gauze bandage taped over the gash on his forehead was already soaked with blood.

"Hey," said the medic, "we're close enough to the ED we could just hike the stretcher up the rise and wheel him there."

"The sidewalk's rough. It'll be easier to drive around."

Two minutes later, siren screaming, they pulled up to the ambulance bay doors, having had time to give only the briefest of radio reports to the ED staff.

"They'll be pissed we didn't call earlier."

"They're always pissed. You can't win. I hope Dr. Forester's working."

CHAPTER 16

The EMS radio crackled to life in the ED.

"This is Canterbury Seven with an elderly man, fall from a height, positive loss of consciousness, hemorrhage from a head laceration, tenderness of the left chest. Possible rib fractures. Unknown other injuries. BP 105 over 55, pulse 118, respirations 25 and erratic, Glasgow 12, over."

The medic sounded anxious. Darcy didn't like it when they sounded anxious. She'd be going on vacation in a couple of weeks, thanks to Jack Forester and Gail. An extra week of paid vacation! Though the thought had been enough to rejuvenate her, she didn't want to see any more blood today.

Fat chance.

"Copy that," she responded. "What's your ETA?"

Nothing—they'd cut off the radio. They were at the damn doors already. Jesus Christ. A gurney flew through the ambulance entrance on a wave of cold air. Darcy jogged out from behind the counter.

"Take him to the trauma bay—and give us a little warning next time."

The medic winked as he passed.

"Darcy, you're looking good tonight."

"Eat your heart out."

The surgical intern, Dr. Steve Brasio, had just sewn up the thumb of a woman who'd cut herself slicing tomatoes. Peeling off his gloves, he headed for the charting station to write up the case but stopped when he saw two blue-jacketed medics wheel in a stretcher with a patient on a backboard wearing a neck collar. There were bloody bandages on his head.

Brasio's mind and body tensed. Trauma. The Chairman of Surgery, Dr. Hansen, said he wanted surgical interns to get involved in every major trauma case that rolled through the doors when they were doing their

ER rotations. Brasio grabbed a fresh pair of gloves from a dispenser on the counter and dashed after the stretcher.

This was only the second day of a six-week emergency medicine rotation for Brasio, a twenty-seven-year-old former college hockey player who'd graduated from Tufts Medical School just five months before. Until now, things had been routine. He'd sewn up lacerations, evaluated belly pains and treated a few burns, but nothing major. He had been well aware, however, that one day something awful was going to roll in the door and test his mettle. It might be somebody with an arm cut off, or a throat slashed, or a bullet wound to the chest. Fortunately, there was always an ER attending on duty to back him up.

With that in mind, he took a deep cleansing breath—he and his pregnant wife were going through Lamaze classes—and strode into the trauma suite. Two nurses had beaten him in and were preparing to move the new patient onto the trauma gurney.

"What happened?" he asked.

Nobody seemed to hear. He repeated the question, louder, and one of the medics looked over at him.

"Doc, this guy apparently fell off the footbridge, about twenty-five feet," he said. "Nobody saw it, but that's what we think happened."

Brasio was still hovering about ten feet away.

"I see," he said.

"I bet he jumped," said one of the nurses. "The railing's too high to just fall over."

Brasio edged closer. It was obvious the man had a head injury—tufts of bloodstained white hair peeked over the top of the thick orange neck brace. On the count of three, the medics and nurses lifted the backboard and transferred the man onto the trauma gurney. As they did, a blood clot slid out from under the man's head and plopped onto the linoleum.

It might be a good idea to get the attending in here—Brasio wasn't quite sure where to start.

He strode back out into the hallway, but there was no sign of Dr. Atwood at the charting station. He checked the cross corridor, and still no sign of him. A nurse passed by, but when he asked her if she knew Dr. Atwood's whereabouts, she rolled her eyes and laughed. Should he go look for Atwood himself? No, that would waste precious time, and he hadn't even examined the patient yet.

He bolted into the trauma room.

"Hey, intern," one of the nurses yelled. "Help us get him undressed."

"Sure, right, okay," said Brasio, trying to recall all he'd learned in the Advanced Trauma Life Support course he'd taken back in July with the other interns.

Patients with major trauma need to be exposed so you won't overlook serious injuries.

"Right, we need to expose him. Let's get him exposed."

Heart pounding, he took out his bandage scissors and began helping the nurse cut away the man's clothing.

Begin your evaluation with the ABCs.

A: Assess the integrity of the airway. Is there massive facial trauma? Is there blood or foreign material in the mouth?

No, not from what he would see.

B: Note how the patient is breathing—look for rise of the chest wall, listen for noises.

Yes, the chest was rising regularly, and the breathing wasn't noisy.

C: Check for circulation. What's the blood pressure, and does he have a good pulse?

Brasio reached for the old man's wrist. He felt a strong, fast pulse.

"What's his blood pressure?" he asked the nurse.

"One-ten over fifty-eight."

Okay, so that was the ABCs. Now what?

Then perform a quick secondary survey from head to toe, looking for things that need immediate attention like hemorrhages. Examine the chest, abdomen and pelvis for signs of internal bleeding. And—Jesus Christ, the neck—don't forget the patient's neck. Head trauma always carries the possibility of a neck injury—so obtain a lateral c-spine film early on.

Brasio had heard stories about people with broken necks having their cords severed by careless interns who moved their heads before getting an x-ray.

"Let's get a neck x-ray stat!" he ordered.

"Already called for it, Dr. Sherlock," said the nurse, a tiny brunette whose name was Bridgett.

The medics found this humorous.

"Okay, then, I need to check his chest and belly," said Brasio, blushing.

"Be my guest," said Bridgett, who had wrapped a rubber tourniquet around Gavin's arm and was stabbing a vein with a huge IV needle.

The other nurse was hooking him up to the cardiac monitor.

"Don't you want chest and pelvis x-rays, too?" she suggested.

It's always wise in patients with significant trauma to obtain routine chest and pelvis films so as not to miss potentially life-threatening injuries.

"Definitely—let's order them."

"Already done," said Bridgett. "How fast do you want the IVs going?"

Brasio hesitated.

"How about wide open," she said. "His pressure's a little low."

"Yes, wide open," he agreed. "Good idea. Wide-open lactated Ringers." Brasio leaned over the man's face. "Sir, can you hear me?" he yelled.

The man's eyelids fluttered.

"How are you feeling?"

"What happened to me?"

"You fell, sir," Brasio told him. "Listen, you're going to be okay, we're going to take care of you. What's your name?"

The man didn't respond.

"We don't know either," said the medic. "He called himself Dean."

"Is your name Dean?" Brasio asked.

"Jim."

"Jim? Jim who?"

"Jim Gavin. What happened?"

At that moment, Brasio heard Bridgett gasp. He looked at her, afraid he'd stepped on her foot.

"Oh, my God, I recognize him now," she said. "This is Dr. Gavin, our old dean."

"Holy Mother of God, you're right, Bridge," Darcy cried. "It's Dr. Gavin."

Every muscle in Brasio's back seemed to tense. He looked toward the door.

"Somebody, please go find Dr. Atwood," he commanded.

"Good idea," Darcy said as she punched the intercom button that connected the trauma suite to the charting station. "Kathy," she yelled. "Find Dr. Atwood and send him into trauma, STAT."

"You're going to be okay, Dr. Gavin," Bridgett assured him. "You had a little fall."

"Ah," Gavin murmured. "Thank you."

"Dr. Gavin," said Brasio, "could you squeeze my fingers, please? Good. Now wiggle your toes. Good. Where all do you hurt?"

"What happened?" Gavin asked again.

"You fell."

"Okay, thank you."

"What do you remember?"

"I'm not sure," he said. "Did Captain Peters make it?"

He obviously had a concussion, so there was no point in trying to get any more history. Brasio continued with his examination. Gavin had a big laceration on the left parietal scalp, and Brasio could see the glistening membrane over the cranial bone.

"Let's order a head CT as soon as possible," he said. "How are the vitals doing now?"

"I've got him on the automatic cuff," the second nurse said. "You can see up there yourself."

Brasio looked at the monitor screen mounted on the wall above the patient's head. It showed a blood pressure of 105 over 50 and a heart rate of 124. The pressure wasn't all that bad, but his heart rate was higher than it should be. That might mean impending hemorrhagic shock.

Or he was in shock already?"

Brasio felt sweat rolling down his neck. There was obvious bruising to the left side of Gavin's chest, but his arms, shoulders, legs and hips seemed okay, and his abdomen was soft and didn't seemed tender. Where might he be hemorrhaging from? Maybe he'd lost enough from the scalp laceration to make him shocky.

"Have we located Dr. Atwood yet?"

Bridgett snorted.

"No, and don't hold your breath," she snapped. "We'll page him again."

"Sir, tell me where you have pain," Brasio continued. "Does your neck hurt?"

"Tell Nelson to go to hell."

Reassess, always assess and reassess. Brasio quickly reviewed the situation. Definite head injury. The x-rays of neck, chest and pelvis would be done shortly, and the labs would soon be back. The guy seemed reasonably stable. Then the head CT. The vital signs—he'd keep a close eye on them. Atwood would show up any minute.

Brasio began to relax. Perhaps he would manage to negotiate this minefield, and what a story he'd have to tell on rounds tomorrow—treating the former dean of the medical center by himself because they couldn't find the attending!

"Bridgett, could you help me get ready to suture the scalp laceration?" he said. "I don't want the bleeding to kick up again."

"Wait," Bridgett cautioned him. "Take a look at his heart rate."

Brasio's eyes shot to the monitor screen. The series of green squiggles representing the heart rate were coming even closer together now; the digital read-out said 140 beats a minute. An alarm went off inside his head.

"His BP is bottoming out," Bridgett yelled.

Brasio looked. It was now 82 over 39.

"He's going into shock," Bridgett said.

"He's probably bleeding inside," Darcy added. "We'd better hang some blood."

"Yes, right, definitely," Brasio said. "Let's get two units. And call for help—call the chief resident if they can't find Dr. Atwood."

Bridgett punched the intercom button.

"Kathy, page the surgical chief super-STAT."

Gavin's skin had gone pale and clammy, and he was breathing in rapid gasps. A wave of pure horror washed over Brasio.

"Pressure's down to seventy," said Bridgett.

"Open the IVs wide," he ordered

The worst thing he could do was panic. Think. What was going on? Why was this guy going down the tubes? Where the hell was the attending? If he were sitting in a classroom right now analyzing this situation, the solution would probably be obvious.

Gavin was losing blood, but his abdomen was soft, so it wasn't likely a ruptured spleen. But it could be. Or he might he be bleeding into his pelvis? But he wasn't tender there, either. He could be bleeding inside his skull, but if that were the case he should be unconscious, or so the book said. But the book also said that any internal hemorrhage can give misleading symptoms, or no symptoms at all until it was nearly too late to correct the problem.

Or could it be from something else? What the hell was going on?

"Are you still with us, Dr. Gavin?" he asked.

No response.

"I can't get any pressure now," Darcy said. "Oh, shit, look—he's gone into V tach."

Gavin's cardiac tracing looked like a picket fence. Bridgett hit the button again.

"Kathy, call a code in the trauma suite."

Racing back to the bedside, she elbowed past Brasio and started pumping Gavin's chest with her palms. Darcy took out the defibrillator pads and began squirting electrode paste on them.

New Canterbury's General Surgery residency program was of the pyramid type. Fifteen interns started out each June, and each year their number declined. By the fifth and final year there were only three left—a trio of chief residents who had been tempered in the flames of unrelenting responsibility, continuous evaluation and hundred-and-twenty-hour work weeks. By that fifth year, they were proud and tough—some would have said arrogant as well.

Thirty-year-old Sarah Hopper, the on-duty surgical chief, was in the ICU checking on a subclavian line she'd placed that afternoon when the ER paged. Her first impulse was to run down and take command. Experience had taught her, however, that if she didn't put up at least a token resistance, she would soon be busy beyond any human's capacity. So, she strolled to the phone and called the ER desk.

"Hopper here. What's up?"

"They need you in trauma," Kathy said.

"I assumed that much. For what?"

"Because there's a patient dying down here."

"That doesn't tell me anything."

"Listen, all I know is that a very good nurse told me to page you STAT, okay?"

This didn't sound like the usual bullshit. She felt her heart quicken. The landing craft was grinding against the beach, the ramp swinging down and bullets thwacking metal.

"Okay, but the next time, some more information would be helpful."

She slammed the phone down and took off at a dead run. You never knew what might be going on down there. Some of the ED docs, like Jack Forester, knew acute trauma management, but others couldn't manage their way out of a paper bag. They'd call you down to evaluate a fucking hangnail. Nurses, though, tended to know their stuff. Bad sign when a nurse calls uncle.

Down six flights of stairs she dashed, and she wasn't even out of breath when she hit the ground floor. She bashed through the back door of the ED, hit the trauma room and slammed on the brakes.

There stood one of the new interns with a deer-in-the-headlights look in his eyes and a sheen of sweat on his brow. Nurses and techs of all varieties were milling around, and in the middle of the crowd a tiny nurse stood on a stool doing CPR.

"Out of the way," she commanded. "Stop the CPR for a minute."

Though not much larger than Bridgett, she picked up the nurse by her elbows and set her aside.

"You," she said, pointing at Brasio. "Tell me what the hell's going on."

The room fell silent as the intern described the situation.

"Jesus, this is great," Hopper said when he'd finished. "You've got the Nobel Prize-winning former dean of the medical center falling off a fucking bridge, and you didn't call me sooner? Where's the ER attending?"

"Good question," Bridgett growled.

Hopper knew exactly what the problem was within several seconds, and she started barking orders. Then her eyes bored into the intern.

"Brasio, this patient's got an obvious tension pneumothorax. Look at how his trachea's deviated, and he's got crepitus up and down his left chest. That's why he's hypotensive, goddamnit. You should have done a needle decompression of his chest ten minutes ago. CPR is just making it worse. Somebody give me a fourteen-gauge angiocath needle and bring me the chest tube tray and a seven-point-five ET tube so I can intubate him. Quickly, people. Watch close, Brasio."

In one deft movement, Hopper stabbed the needle high in the front of Gavin's left chest. As trapped air under pressure escaped through the needle, a hissing sound was audible across the room.

"Step one."

"I can palpate a pulse now," Bridgett announced.

"Of course," Hopper said. "He had no venous return due to buildup of pressure in his chest. He's probably bleeding inside the chest, too. Have you ordered blood, Brasio?"

"Yes."

"Good." Hopper bent over and slipped a tube through Gavin's mouth into his trachea. "Have you looked at the chest x-ray yet?"

Steve Brasio said nothing. His vision was blurry from the sweat running into his eyes. The chest x-ray. He'd ordered one, hadn't he? Had it been done? He wasn't sure. All he knew was that his career was over. He would be drummed from the program. His family would be disgraced. His wife would leave him out of shame. His child would never know a father.

Hopper swore but didn't skip a beat. She tore open the chest tube tray and began placing one into Gavin's chest to keep the lung inflated.

"How's the pressure doing now?" she asked.

"Much better," Bridgett told her. "One hundred over fifty, and his pulse is down to a hundred and five. His color's getting better, but he's not waking up yet."

"He may not go dancing tonight, then. Please call for another chest x-ray to check the tube and make sure the lung's re-expanding. And let's get him over to CT. We'll do his head and neck, and his chest, belly and pelvis while we're at it. And call for a bed in surgical intensive care."

She turned again to the stunned intern.

"Come with me," she said, crooking her finger. "We need to talk."

They ran into Humphrey Atwood at the door of the trauma suite.

"Hello, there, Sarah," he chirped. "What brings you down here?"

Chapter 17

Lights were burning in Wilmer and Joyce Carter's living room window when Jack drove by at a quarter to eleven. He tooted the horn three times, letting them know he'd be at the hospital all night. The Carters were in their early eighties, both still active around the farm, and Wilmer had been a friend of Jack's grandfather. He reminded them often to call if they needed help for any reason. In the rearview mirror, he saw the porch light flicker in acknowledgement.

Ten minutes later, he pulled into a parking spot near the ED and saw that something beyond the ordinary was transpiring. The Channel 11 TV van sat near the portico, and vapor rose from the exhausts of three police cars idling at the curb. Police cruisers in front of the ED were not all that unusual, but the news van certainly was, at least at this hour.

He strode inside and found a half-dozen people milling near the entrance. One of them was Susee Baker, an anchorwoman who often came to interview him for stories.

She intercepted him, her cameraman jogging to catch up.

"Dr. Forester, can you give me a minute?"

"Sorry, I just got here," he said. "I don't know any more than you do."

Curiosity skyrocketing, he cut through registration directly into the clinical area and saw Bryson Witner and Nelson Debussy standing by the charting station. He stopped. Witner was dressed in a baseball cap and navy blue overcoat, and Debussy in a maroon New Canterbury University sweater and duck boots. Witner saw him, alerted Debussy, then motioned Jack over.

"Dr. Forester," he said. "I take it you are not aware of what happened?"

"No. What's going on?"

"They're waiting for us in your office. Come."

"Who's waiting? Would you mind telling me what's happened."

Neither Debussy nor Witner answered.

He entered his office and was astonished to discover Humphrey Atwood and the Chairman of Surgery, Jacob Hanson. Dr. Hansen was in jeans and docksiders, obviously roused from home. Hansen nodded a greeting, his expression grim. Atwood's skin was an alarming yellow-gray, and his attention was fixed on the wall near the Everest poster, as if he were contemplating an ascent.

Debussy spoke first.

"Alright, Dr. Hansen, you know the details better than anyone. Would you bring us up to speed? Especially Dr. Forester here."

The gray-haired senior surgeon began.

"A little after six this evening, Jim Gavin had an accident and suffered serious injuries."

Jack felt the blood drain from his face.

"He's alive," Hansen continued, "but he's in a coma."

Jack looked around in disbelief, unable to speak for a moment, grief mounting in his chest.

"What kind of accident?"

"There were no witnesses," said Hansen, "so we don't know, exactly. A passing driver found him on the median strip below the footbridge over Beech Avenue."

The grief mingled with horror.

"You mean it was a hit-and-run?"

Hansen looked over at Debussy. The university president drew a deep breath.

"Jim and I met in my office just before this happened. He was going back to the hospital, and he would have taken the footbridge."

"But how could he fall off the footbridge?" Jack said. "The railing's chest-high."

"We have reason to believe he tried to take his own life, Dr. Forester," Debussy said, looking at the floor.

"What reason?" Jack cried. "I don't believe it."

"Nevertheless, it's very possible, and the only reason he didn't succeed is because he landed in shrubbery on the median and not on the pavement. That's a two-story drop."

Despite his shock, Jack thought of the letter Gavin had mentioned, and Gavin's words echoed in his head.

"I still don't believe it," he insisted. "You're wrong."

Witner cleared his throat pointedly.

"Regardless of your opinion," Debussy continued, his voice rising in anger, "what happened to him outside is only one issue. We need to talk about what happened after he got to this emergency room."

Jack didn't like the sound of this at all.

"What do you mean?"

"Keep going, Jacob," said Debussy, his voice still simmering.

"Jack, I find the idea of Jim Gavin trying to commit suicide hard to swallow myself," said the surgeon. "But, in any case, when he got to the ED, he was coming around. Steve Brasio, one of my interns, was working on him. Unfortunately, being just an intern, he failed to appreciate the presence of a developing tension pneumothorax, and Jim went into cardiac arrest."

"Explain what that is again, for my sake," said Debussy.

"When Jim fell, he suffered, along with a concussion and a scalp laceration, three broken ribs. One of the broken ribs punctured his lung, which caused air to escape and build up pressure inside his chest cavity to the point his heart couldn't pump blood. The condition is easily reversed by relieving the pressure with a needle. Sarah Hopper, the chief resident, immediately did the right thing, and Jim's blood pressure normalized. If someone had done it five minutes sooner, Jim would probably be talking to us right now."

Jack felt as if his own chest had just been punched.

"Humphrey," he said, after a few seconds, trying hard to contain his voice, "you were the attending on duty. What happened?"

"Dr. Atwood had left the department," said Hansen. "He couldn't hear his page."

"Mother of Christ," Jack hissed.

"Which brings us to the issue concerning you, Dr. Forester," said Debussy. "I understand you had been charged by Dr. Witner with installing a special paging system for Dr. Atwood. Would you mind telling us what happened to that?"

Jack looked around, his face prickling.

"I'm waiting for an answer, Dr. Forester," said Debussy.

"It was against departmental policy."

"What the hell is that supposed to mean? How does your policy trump what the dean tells you to do? What kind of place is this? Unsupervised interns running around killing people? Jesus H. Christ." Debussy turned to Witner. "Bryson, would you untangle this for me?"

"I do not like pointing fingers of blame," Witner replied calmly, "but Dr. Atwood told me some time ago there are too many internal dead spots for his standard pager, and we all know the overhead speaker system can't be heard everywhere. So, in light of the fact Dr. Atwood's administrative duties sometimes necessitated his leaving the ER, I authorized Dr. Forester to install a special paging system for Dr. Atwood. I sent a memo authorizing it and gave him an account number to utilize.

"Unfortunately, this evening I learned that no steps had been taken in this direction and, in fact, that Dr. Forester had decided of his own volition to leave it undone."

"Is this true, Forester?" said Debussy.

"Mr. Debussy, when I took the job as director, long before Dr. Witner became the interim dean, I set a policy mandating the on-duty emergency medicine attending stay in the ED with the trainees, whether it was busy or not. Nobody else has problems with it. The overhead speaker is sufficient when the attending remains in the ED."

"So, you disagreed with Dr. Witner's decision?"

"Very definitely. The attending needs to be in the ED supervising."

"Did you personally discuss this disagreement with Dr. Witner?"

Jack paused, his mouth dry.

"No, sir, I did not. It is part of my job description to set policies like this, and I saw no reason for making an exception."

"You saw no reason to follow a directive from the interim dean of the medical center, and you saw no reason for discussing it with him—is that what you're saying?"

Jack swallowed.

"That's correct."

Debussy now turned on Atwood, pointing at him.

"Dr. Atwood," he growled. "Yes, you. Despite the fact you knew you might be unreachable given the lack of this new paging system, you decided to leave the department anyway?"

Atwood's mouth opened, and his eyes darted to Witner.

"Tell him where were you, Humphrey," Witner advised him.

"I wear many hats, Mr. Debussy," Atwood said, then paused.

"One of them being to supervise the interns, I assume?" Debussy persisted. "Where, exactly, were you?"

"I was working on a study in a room no more than a hundred feet from the ED," Atwood said.

"Calm down and answer accurately, Humphrey," Witner ordered. "You told the unit secretary where you'd be, didn't you?"

Atwood looked at him and swallowed. He nodded.

"Yes, sir. I told the unit secretary where I'd be."

"That's a load of crap," Jack blurted.

Debussy glared at him.

"Keep a civil tongue in your mouth, Dr. Forester, damnit," he spat.

"The nurses could easily have located me," Atwood continued, his words coming out in a rush now. "Easily! But I don't think they really tried. Mr. Debussy, you can ask anybody about the negativity of the nurses here."

"Negativity!" Jack shouted. "How would you know? You never talk to them except to give commands."

"This ER has nothing but problems," Atwood pronounced. "It's a hellhole, and I've been unable to improve things."

"Shut up, both of you," Debussy cried. "I've heard enough. You stand here blaming each other while the great man who gave his soul to make this hospital what it is lies mortally injured upstairs—and I think both of you are at fault."

"I agree," said Hansen. "I feel sorry for my intern, too. He deserves no blame for this."

Debussy rubbed his face and shook his head.

"We have failed Jim Gavin at his time of greatest need. What are we going to tell those news people out there? What are we going to tell the rest of the world? Bryson, for God's sake, give me some reasonable thoughts."

Face grave, but calm, Witner nodded.

"The issue of responsibility will be easier to settle in the cool light of day," he said. "I agree with Jacob that his intern should not bear any blame."

"Give us your honest prognosis, Dr. Hansen," said Debussy. "What are the chances he'll come out of this?"

"There's no way to tell at this point. It's a matter of how long his brain was deprived of oxygen during the resuscitation. He could make a complete recovery, or he could stay in a vegetative state. We'll have a better idea in a day or two. It is to be hoped he'll wake up and be able to tell us exactly what occurred."

"Yes," Witner concurred. "That is what we'll pray for. And when he recovers from the physical trauma, we'll make sure he gets the help he needs from a psychiatric standpoint."

"I talked to him yesterday, and I know you're way off-base," Jack protested, staring at him. "Dr. Gavin did not try to commit suicide. He was in the process of checking out something that was going to change things around here. People with suicidal intent don't talk like that."

"What makes you an authority on the subject, Dr. Forester?" Debussy wanted to know. "Maybe this was what he was talking about. I'm personally grief-stricken about this," he added, looking at Witner. "His behavior was strange, and I never should have let him leave my office."

"Nelson, don't second-guess yourself," Witner assured him. "As you know, he was acting disturbed when I met with him, too, so I'd be equally responsible. The fact is that you and I were talking on the phone and coming to the same conclusion about the time he did it."

"No," Jack insisted. "I can't believe you're jumping to this crazy idea."

Debussy glanced at him with unmistakable dislike.

"You, Dr. Forester, can believe whatever you want," he said. "In the meantime, we need to speak with a single voice to the media. We keep comments about what happened out there—and what happened in here— to an absolute minimum. Dr. Gavin suffered a complication following a fall. Nothing more. Both the complication and the fall are under investigation."

Jack looked at the wall clock.

"If there's nothing more for me to say, I need to get to work," he said gruffly.

"You'll stay until we're finished," Debussy commanded. He reached over and put a hand on Witner's shoulder. "Bryson, you and I will go and make a statement along those lines to the press. Has anyone contacted Jim's family yet? Did he have any relatives in the area?"

"No," said Hansen. "Jim had some distant cousins in Canada, but his closest kin would be Daphne, his son Colin's wife, and I believe she's living in California now."

"Yes. I remember hearing about her. Wasn't there a scandal of some sort?"

"She supposedly had an affair while Colin was dying of ALS," Hansen explained.

"Colin Gavin had Lou Gerhig's disease?" Debussy asked.

"That's correct," said Witner. "It was four years ago, Nelson, long before you arrived."

"Good Lord, was it true?"

"To the best of my knowledge, it was all circumstantial," Hansen said. "But the rumors took on a life of their own. You know how it goes. Jim felt it was true."

"I really need to get out there to see patients," Jack said.

"Believe it or not, Dr. Forester," Debussy said, "life will go on without you."

"Jacob's right." Witner was still focused on the alleged scandal. "It was all circumstantial. Colin was a brilliant surgeon, but he lacked his father's conservative morals, and his wife Daphne was a little unstable and flamboyant. Jim never liked her."

"We'll still have to get in touch with her, of course," Debussy insisted.

"Leave that to me," Witner said. "It should be easy to track her down. I'll personally make sure she's informed, and I will also contact any other relatives we can locate. She can probably help with that."

"Thank you, Bryson. I can't thank you enough." Debussy then spun to confront Jack. "What time are you done working in the morning?"

"Seven-thirty."

"Please come straight to my office. And, Dr. Atwood, *you* are not off the hook. Not by any stretch."

After the others left, Jack closed the door and sat on the edge of his desk. A few minutes later, the door swung slowly open.

"Can I come in?" Darcy asked.

Jack looked up, still numb, and nodded.

"I saw the muckety-mucks leave. Does this mean you can fire Humphrey Atwood now? We couldn't find him, Jack. He came prancing in after it was all over."

"How busy is it out there now?"

"We're backed up about twenty patients, and they're getting hostile."

"I'd like to go up and see Dr. Gavin."

"Maybe you could wait until there's a lull?"

Jack rubbed his eyes and sighed to the bottom of his chest. His first duty was to the patients in the department now.

"You're right. I'll go up later."

"Hey, I bet he'll do fine, Jack. They give great care up there. You should have seen Sarah in action."

Jack looked up at her, a thought crossing his mind.

"Darcy, do you know if anyone took away Dr. Gavin's garments yet?"

"I'm pretty sure. Why?"

"He was carrying a letter with him yesterday. I remember him reaching into his pocket and touching it."

"Something important?"

"I don't know, but I wouldn't want it to get mislaid. It meant a lot to him."

After speaking with the press, Witner and Debussy left the ED.

"I'm parked by the old entrance," Debussy said.

"I'll walk you there, Nelson. I'm parked beyond it in the west ramp."

"As long as it's not out of your way."

"No, no, no," Witner insisted.

"Lord, what a way to end a day that started out so beautifully."

"Nelson, as tragic as this is, I don't see it holding us back. I'm sure the excellent publicity we enjoyed today will help outweigh this situation, and in a month or so, it will be a distant memory. We'll move beyond this, I'm sure. We just need to keep encouraging people to focus on our bright future."

"It'll be an uphill battle for a few days."

"As they say, the wheel of fortune keeps turning," Witner said. "We'll survive."

"Bryson, I've never seen a man take things in stride the way you do. You're a born leader. I want you to get that ER straightened out. Do whatever the hell it takes. Both of them need to be out of there."

"Understood."

"Tomorrow morning, I'm going to order that footbridge be fully enclosed."

"Excellent. Visible evidence of our commitment to safety."

When they reached the old lobby, Debussy stopped and looked intently at the interim dean.

"You're convinced it was a suicide attempt, Bryson? I need to hear you say that."

"As painful as the idea is, yes."

"You don't think he might have run into some lunatic out there?"

Witner smiled sympathetically and shook his head.

"Though I could almost wish that were the case."

Debussy shook Witner's hand with both of his, then pushed through the doors into the night.

As Witner turned away, he felt a buzzing at his waist. It wasn't his pager, but his cell phone. He opened it and studied the number. Hinkle. He frowned, and looked carefully around before putting the phone to his ear.

"In the future, you page me, and I'll return the call from a secure phone. Is that understood? We've talked about that."

"I know we talked about that," mocked Hinkle. "It's done, but I needed to discuss my little change of plans."

"You call the difference between a campus footbridge and the Seneca River bridge a little change of plans?"

"Whatever, Witner. You left the details up to me. I saw an opportunity, and I took it. Getting him into a car and driving out there would have been a major hassle and dangerous. Anyway, it's done. Nobody his age was going to survive a fall from that footbridge."

"That's probably true, Fred, if somebody his age had hit the highway instead of the median."

There was a pause.

"What do you mean?"

"I mean that he landed in some bushes that broke his fall."

"He's alive?"

"And in a coma."

"Motherfucking hell, Witner. It was dark as sin. I couldn't see anything down there."

"Obviously."

"But I don't see the big deal. He's right there under your nose. I'm sure you can finish the job yourself, Dr. Death."

Witner thought for a moment.

"I'm disappointed in you, Fred, but perhaps there's a reason why it turned out like this."

"How so?"

"We have many resources, my friend, and I see ways we can benefit from this complication."

"Who? You and me? I don't see how."

Witner's eyes widened at the slip. With his left index finger, he sketched a circle in the air three times clockwise, then three times counterclockwise.

"Of course, I mean you and I, Fred," he said. "Don't be obtuse."

"You know, Witner, I wonder about your sanity. No, I don't wonder. I know. Maybe you should see somebody."

The Surgical Intensive Care Unit was like the bridge of a starship—a discrete world with no external windows, only screens and gadgetry. Its lighting was bright and never varied, day or night, and neither did the ebb and flow of staff members. At any given time, there were nine nurses, a respiratory tech, two ward clerks, a second-year surgical resident and, usually, two pulmonary fellows assigned to the unit. Above the head of each bed sat a bank of monitors, each set to sound an alarm at the least variance.

Many of the staff knew James Gavin personally, and knots of people from all over the hospital came and went, standing at a respectful distance while his primary nurse and her assistants hovered over him. A plastic endotracheal tube attached to a hissing ventilator protruded from his mouth, and a large IV catheter ran into his internal jugular vein, dripping saline and an antibiotic. He also had a catheter inserted into the radial artery of his left wrist, giving a continuous reading of his blood pressure and oxygen saturation. A Foley catheter had been inserted into his bladder, and a thermal probe placed in his rectum.

Shortly after midnight, a young man in surgical scrubs with deep circles under his eyes came into the SICU and stood looking at Gavin from the doorway. His attention moved from the man on the bed to the monitors and back again.

"Yes?" the nurse said.

"Just wanted to see how he's doing."

"Are you one of the new SICU residents?"

"No, I'm nobody," Steve Brasio said.

Sarah Hopper had been quite kind to him, as had Dr. Hansen. Sarah told him a war story of her own, about having missed a case of appendicitis when she was an intern, and how hard it had been on her emotionally, but that she'd learned a great deal from the experience. Dr. Forester had shaken his hand and told him it wasn't his fault, that he hadn't had the backup he'd needed.

Brasio knew all this was true, but it barely eased his shame and guilt. He could have saved a life. Instead, he may have destroyed a great one.

Chapter 18

Jack leaned close to the old man's ear.

"Dr. Gavin, if you can hear me, it's Jack. This is my hand. Can you squeeze it?"

The fingers lying on the blanket didn't move. They felt unnaturally cool and smooth. Only Gavin's chest moved, rising and falling as the ventilator fed him oxygen through the endotracheal tube.

It was Saturday morning, and Jack's shift was over. Unable to break away during the night, he'd called upstairs a number of times, hoping to hear that Dr. Gavin was waking up. There was no such news.

A nurse came to the bedside and stood next to him. She must have assumed he was one of the caregivers. She smiled at him, then looked up at the monitor and began writing on a clipboard.

Jack read her name badge.

"Hi, Becky," he said. "I'm Dr. Forester from the ED."

"Yes?" she said, glancing over.

"Listen, I think Dr. Gavin had a letter on him when he fell, and I know he'd want me to have it for safekeeping. I'm a close friend. You've haven't seen it, by any chance?"

"No, sorry."

"Could you tell me where they put his clothes?"

"They're in the little closet next to the bathroom, right over there."

During the night, on the off-chance the letter might have fallen out of Gavin's pocket while he was in the trauma suite, Jack had checked the room carefully but found nothing. The medics who'd brought Gavin in had transported another patient to the ED later that night, and Jack had questioned them. Had they seen anything that looked like a letter? They hadn't. It had to still be either in Gavin's pocket, or back there on the median, thrown out during the fall.

He opened the closet. Gavin's overcoat and suit jacket hung inside, the former still wet and covered with mud and darker stains. Jack searched all the pockets but nothing. A red plastic bag lay on the floor of the closet. He fished inside and discovered Gavin's pants, which had been cut off him, and a bloodstained white shirt and blue tie. All the pockets were empty.

After adjusting an IV line, the nurse came up to him.

"Any luck?"

"Zero," he said.

"Then it's probably with his wallet and personal effects."

"Which are where?"

"They'd be with security. Valuables get locked up somewhere downstairs."

At the SICU nursing station, he dialed the security office number, but Tim Bonadonna wasn't in.

"Ask him to call Jack Forester as soon as he arrives, please. Tell him it's very important." Then he checked his watch. Nelson Debussy could wait a while longer.

After asking the SICU unit clerk to call him if there were any changes in Gavin's condition, Jack headed down to the old lobby to grab a cup of coffee.

The lobby was nearly empty. He trotted down the steps from the mezzanine, his briefcase swinging, still dressed in last night's scrubs, and he saw a single person standing at the coffee vendor's counter. His eyes and senses may have been heavy and numb, but his heart suddenly leaped.

Zellie Andersen had just paid for her coffee and was arranging her big leather satchel over her shoulder. She saw him coming, and to his great pleasure, she smiled at him.

"I was afraid you'd left town," he said.

"I was going to, but I postponed it after what happened last night. I read about it in the paper this morning at the hotel. What a tragedy. It's a far more interesting story than yesterday's. I'm going to write a second piece about it."

The memory of walking into the ED and seeing Witner and Debussy and hearing the news, and of seeing Gavin a few moments ago in the SICU, all came crashing back in on Jack, and his spirits plummeted.

"Yes, I can understand why," he said.

She was studying his face.

"You knew him well, didn't you?"

"I did."

"I'm sorry. I hope he recovers. Were you involved in the case?"

Jack's heart clenched again.

"No, but I wish to heaven I had been."

She gave him another smile, kind and understanding, and nodded.

"Well, listen," he said, trying to shake off the sadness. "I've solved the mystery of who you are."

"Mistaken identity, right?"

"Far from it. Have you got a minute."

"Dozens of them."

He ushered her over to one of the old leather sofas. Opening his briefcase, he took out the book, thanking his lucky stars he'd brought it with him last night. He always carried something with him to read in case the department got slow in the wee hours—a rare event in the past few years.

Handing it to her with the back cover photo up, he relished her look of astonishment.

"I've been waiting a long time for an autograph," he said.

"Wait a minute." She shot him a skeptical look. "You're telling me you remembered me from this awful picture. If this is a joke, I don't find it funny. Where did you get this?"

"I bought it when I was an intern. Eight or nine years ago. And I think it's a wonderful picture."

"No."

"Yep."

"I don't know what to say."

"You believe me, don't you?"

She looked at him again with those intense eyes.

"Yes, I suppose I do."

Jack took a pen out of his scrub shirt pocket and handed it to her.

"Would you?"

"How could I refuse?" She opened to the title page. "Is Forester with one R or two?"

"I'm flattered you remembered my name. One."

She thought for a moment then wrote, and when finished, she read it aloud.

"'For Dr. Jack Forester—of elephantine memory—one good line deserves another. Warm wishes, your friend, Zellie Andersen.'"

Jack noticed the lack of rings on her left hand.

"I was afraid I wouldn't run into you again."

"Why did you bring the book, then?"

"I was rereading it."

"So, you really liked it?"

"I did. What have you done since then?"

She hesitated.

"I've got one in the works. We'll see."

"I'll look forward to it."

"Have you heard of second-novel syndrome?"

He shook his head.

"Some writers never get past their first book."

"Ah, but I'm sure that doesn't apply to someone who writes as well as you. I'll tell you, the scene where the little brother falls off the breakwater and gets stranded with the tide coming in—I can *see* it."

"Okay, now I believe you. Well, thanks. That's kind of you to say."

"You wrote so well from a male point of view, if you ever did a book from the female perspective, it would have to be fantastic."

He was surprised to see her eyes suddenly cool.

"But what do I know about writing?" he added quickly. "Listen, I'm running very late for a meeting, but you know, if you're going to be in town and didn't have any plans, could we talk some more over dinner tonight?"

A moment passed, and then she nodded.

"How could I turn down my only remaining fan?"

Late or not, Jack wanted to check something out. He went to the steps leading up to the footbridge but turned into the trees and worked his way down the embankment until he reached the highway. The Saturday morning traffic was light as he crossed the eastbound lanes to the median strip.

The temperature was in the high thirties, and there were many footprints on the muddy ground. He saw a dark-brown stain near a bush, which had to be blood. There were no skid marks on the pavement nearby. He looked up. Had Gavin fallen from the bridge or been hit by a car? It could have been either, but it had to have been the latter. Suicide was out of the question. How could those idiots even think it?

After searching for several moments, he found something rectangular and mud-soaked that looked about the size of an envelope. Peeling it away from the muck, he looked at a pizza shop bulletin offering free delivery to the dorms.

He heard the distant scrape of footsteps on the bridge above. A man in a dark overcoat was striding over it, coming from the medical center toward the main campus. He was silhouetted against the overcast sky, and there was no doubt—it was Witner. Jack froze as the man glanced in his direction, but Witner made no sign of having seen him.

When he arrived in Debussy's office, Witner was there.

"Sorry I'm late," Jack said.

"Just as well. It's given Dr. Witner and I a chance to talk some more." Debussy motioned him toward a chair and waited a full minute before speaking, his hands folded on the desk, his face unsmiling. "Dr. Forester, first-off, you are no longer the ER director."

This was not unexpected, but Jack still felt heat suffuse his cheeks as the words hit him. He glanced at Witner, who was, as usual, a portrait of serenity.

"You understand why, don't you?" added Debussy.

"Sure," Jack said, keeping his voice contained. "One of the emergency physicians under my supervision leaves the ED, despite departmental policy, so I'm being fired for having set the policy."

Debussy leaned forward, his belly folding around the edge of his desk.

"You can spare me the sarcasm. Do not think for a moment Dr. Atwood is forgotten. He will own his share of responsibility, but at this point that not your concern. I'm talking about the fact you decided to ignore Dr. Witner's decision about that paging system."

"Look, Mr. Debussy, as I said last night, setting policy fell within the job description I was given. There was no reason to make an exception."

"Except when the dean *tells* you to make an exception. What's so hard to understand about that? You have a direct line of responsibility to Dr. Witner, and you brushed it aside."

"It went against the good of the department. And I'll tell you another thing, sir—Dr. Gavin did not try to kill himself."

Debussy's face was going from pink toward crimson. He raised his hands, looked at Witner and shook his head.

Jack continued.

"I'm here for you to fire me, so let's get it over with."

Witner cleared his throat.

"If I might interject. First of all, Dr. Forester, your opinions are always valued, and Mr. Debussy is not firing you. It would be prudent to remain respectful."

"Very prudent," said Debussy. "Forester, you've done many good things here—I've heard that from many sources. We need good doctors, and we're not going to toss you out in disgrace. I have relieved you of your directorship, that's all. We would like you to continue in your clinical and teaching roles in the emergency department. But, as far as administrative activities, no. I've got a leadership team to maintain, and it's obvious you don't want to participate in the command structure."

"Not with the way things stand."

Debussy leaned back in his chair, paused a moment, and went on.

"On the other hand, I'm also offering you the chance to resign with no black marks against your otherwise excellent record. If you choose to leave, there will be no mention of this conflict over the paging system in your letters of reference. You can depart New Canterbury with a clean slate and a separation package of three months' salary. Many faculty members and students will be sorry to see you go, but if you have to move on, we'll do it with a handshake, in recognition of your service."

Jack looked down at the oriental carpet and felt something he hadn't in a long time. Hot tears were forming in his eyes. He blinked hard.

"I know you worked last night, Jack," said Debussy. "Call me Monday and let me know what you'd like to do. As for Dr. Gavin, I guarantee you there were signs I personally witnessed suggesting he was far more ill than might have been apparent to you. I know you were close to him, and I'm sorry. We all are."

Jack glared up at the ceiling. He knew of a job in Denver. All he had to do was call. Three months would give him plenty of time to prepare Tony for the dislocation. There were bigger mountains and plenty of rivers in Colorado; very likely, his brother wouldn't complain.

Maybe the promise he'd made to Dr. Gavin didn't matter now, anyway. The one about not leaving.

As he crossed back over the footbridge, Jack's legs felt heavy. A stiff wind was blowing from the east now, and the air temperature had dropped. The mud below would soon be frozen solid. In his jacket pocket, he felt a piece of folded paper. It was just some notes he'd made a few days ago for the next ED staff meeting, the meeting he would not be leading. He tossed it over the railing.

Halfway across, his cellphone rang. It was Tim Bonadonna.

A few minutes later, in his office in the basement of the medical center, Tim pulled out a chair for him and shut the door.

"Pardon my French, Jack, but you look like *merde*," said the big man, laughing. "Get it?"

Jack sat staring at his shoes.

"Man, are you all right?"

"I've been better."

"That was awful about Dr. Gavin last night. He was such a great guy. He'd say hello every time I passed him in the hallway. Even remembered my name. How's he doing?"

"He's still in a coma."

"Why in hell would he try to commit suicide?"

"That's the official story, Tim, but I'm having a real hard time believing it."

"Hang on a second." Tim returned a moment later with a cup of very dark coffee. "You look like you could use some of this."

Jack took a sip and winced.

"Tim, this is fucking vile. It must have been sitting on a hotplate all night. Are you trying to poison me?"

"Oh, come on. Don't be such a wuss." Bonadonna took a sip and grunted. "Sorry, mate. Let me brew a fresh pot."

"Never mind. Listen, I've got to tell you something."

"Yes?"

"I may be leaving New Canterbury."

"Come again?"

"I have been fired from the ED directorship and invited to resign from the medical staff."

"What the fuck? Why?"

"Dr. Gavin coded in the ED because the intern didn't recognize a tension pneumothorax and the emergency physician on duty—that son-of-a-bitch Humphrey Atwood—had left him unsupervised."

"I heard about the intern, but not the business about Atwood. Why does that put *your* neck on the chopping block? I don't understand."

"It's a little more complicated."

Jack explained how he'd blocked the special paging system Witner had authorized for Atwood.

"But you did right, Jack," Tim protested. "Even I can figure that out."

Jack looked up at his friend.

"I'm not so sure anymore. The fact is, if I'd installed the paging system, Dr. Gavin would not be upstairs maybe dying right now."

Tim groaned and shook his head.

"Well, there's a fine piece of creative self-flagellation, Forester. It's bullshit. Two wrongs don't make a right."

"It's true, though, Tim."

"So, you're just going to let Witner and company toss your poor little cadaver out the window?"

"You should have seen how tight Witner and Debussy are. I don't stand a chance here anymore."

Tim shook his head and sighed.

"Ah, Christ, what a mess. Not to change the subject, but if Dr. Gavin didn't try to kill himself, what the hell did happen to him?"

"You want to know my honest opinion?"

"I'd prefer that to your lying opinion, yes."

"Either he was the victim of a hit-and-run, or someone pushed him over the railing."

"You mean like a mugger?"

"It's possible someone tried to mug him, and he fought back."

"The police would have thought of that. There was no mention of his wallet being gone or anything."

"I don't know, but one of the reasons I called you this morning was to see if you could help me take a look at his personal belongings. The SICU nurse told me security would have them."

"Sure, we can do that. Are you looking for anything in particular."

"I think he was carrying a letter with him. I ran into him before the faculty meeting, and he mentioned a letter he'd gotten from Dr. Zyman written just before Zyman died."

"Zyman was the anatomy professor who had the heart attack a couple of weeks ago?"

"Right. An old friend, best man at his wedding, that sort of thing."

"So, what's the big deal about the letter?"

"I don't know. Gavin said it contained some disturbing news, and that the letter was why he decided to rush back."

"Strange. He didn't tell you anything else?"

"He wouldn't go into details. He said he had to do some research. But it was obviously upsetting him. I don't know if it has any relevance to what happened, but I want to see it, and I'm pretty sure he would have still had it on him. I've looked everywhere else, so hopefully it got secured with his things. I even looked around the area where he fell."

"Wow, you really do think this is important." Tim looked up at the ceiling for a moment, then back at Jack. "Amigo, I smell a plot."

"Oh, do you?" Jack said ironically.

"Gavin comes back from the Amazon with a letter and gets thrown off a bridge. Ten-to-one, he discovered a new medication down there. He'd been sharing information with Zyman, and Zyman got whacked."

"Zyman had a heart attack."

"Where's your imagination? This is a no-brainer, man."

"Think of Occam's Razor, Tim. The simplest thing is usually the truth. If Gavin were pushed off the bridge, it's simpler to imagine that a mugger did it than what you're concocting."

"You think you're so smart, Dr. Forester? Catch this: *Pluralitas non est ponenda sine necessitates*. William of Occam, thirteenth century."

Jack laughed and shook his head.

"How in the hell did you know that?"

"I occasionally read more than Robert Ludlum."

"Why in the hell didn't you finish college, Tim? You could have been running this place instead of Nelson Debussy. Or you could have been in Hollywood."

"We've had this discussion before. There's more than one way to lead a happy life, and I am a happy man. In any case, think of it, Jack. Brazil, rain forest, orchid extract, cancer cure. Gavin returns to test the formula, but he knows he's being followed. He feels safe on the campus, though. He's lulled. There he is on the bridge, it's night, and he's alone. Along comes one of their henchmen. Gavin goes over the edge...bang!

"My first guess would be makers of chemotherapy agents. Within six months, we'll see some amazing new cancer drug hit the market. That'll be the smoking gun. Can't you see it?"

"No, but I've seen the movie *Medicine Man*. The plot's a tad similar."

"So, maybe that gave them the idea."

Jack chuckled and rubbed his eyes.

"Tim, I've got to get some sleep. But I want to find that letter."

"Tell you what, my friend. I will personally track down his belongings and give you a call. You go home and get some rest."

"Thank you, Tim. I'll have to tell you about an interesting woman I met the other day, but not this morning."

"It's about time." He paused a moment. "You're not really thinking of leaving, Jack, are you?"

"I'm supposed to decide by Monday. They told me I could stay and be just a staff ED doctor."

"What's wrong with that? Why do you always have to be the boss? You were like that as a kid, too."

"Naw, you just needed someone to crack the whip, or you'd have sat in front of the tube all day channeling Harrison Ford."

CHAPTER 19

Witner barely had time to settle in and start entering his daily notes before someone knocked on his door. Being Saturday, there was no Greta to screen visitors. Who could it be? He put the journal away and locked the drawer.

"Come in, the door is open."

A familiar face peered in.

"Do you have a moment, sir?"

"I always have a moment for you, Randy. Come in."

Delancy approached with a strained expression and hesitant steps, as if expecting a trap door to open underneath him. Witner studied him.

"Why the mournful expression, Randy?"

"Sir, there's something you need to know."

"Is there, now?"

"It's about the disaster last night."

"I'm well aware of it."

"Have you talked to Dr. Atwood about it yet?"

"Of course. I came in last night, and I'm due to see him in a short while. What's the issue?"

"You know he was out of the emergency room when Dr. Gavin came in."

"That fact is well-established."

"And he told you what he was doing?"

"I'm not sure I see your point. He was working on one of his projects. I don't know which one, not that it matters. Randy, why won't you look me in the eyes?"

The young man opened his mouth to speak, then closed it again, his face coloring.

"Listen, Randy. Let's not waste time here. If you've got something to tell me, out with it, please."

"I know you and Dr. Atwood are quite close."

Witner grunted and began tapping his pen on the desktop.

"If you fancied we were friends, I'll disabuse you of that idea. He's one of my junior faculty members who performs some useful roles, nothing more. Please, either share your thoughts or let me get back to work."

Delancy's Adam's apple slid up and down.

"This isn't easy, sir."

"Obviously."

"Dr. Atwood wasn't working on a project last night."

"What do you mean?"

Delancy took a deep breath.

"An orderly saw him go into the old fluoroscopy room last night with one of the radiology techs and lock the door. The tech was a woman."

"For Satan's sake, Randy, tell me she's not young and attractive."

"I wish I could, Dr. Witner."

"That's where he was when Dr. Gavin was brought in?"

Delancy nodded.

"I don't know if it's an affair, sir, or what. I just know word is starting to spread, and that you needed to be aware."

Five minutes after his appointed time, Atwood appeared at the door. He was less tidy than usual, his hair uncombed and circles under his eyes.

"How are you this morning, Bryson?" he said

"Perfectly wonderful."

"Sorry I'm a little late. I was polishing the draft of a new paper and lost track of time. It's a literature review of Addison's disease presentations in the elderly."

"Is it, now?"

No matter how much Atwood wanted to make a name for himself, his ambition would never outweigh his native stupidity.

"Yes. I'll be sending it out Monday." Atwood continued. "It's so satisfying to get one's thoughts down. I love it. Just love it. Don't you, Bryson?"

He was, at best, third rate. No—fifth.

Witner tilted back his head and stared at him. The younger man's smile slowly evaporated, and he swallowed, tugging at the neck of his shirt with a finger.

"I hope you slept better than I did, Bryson. I understand Dr. Gavin is status quo this morning."

"That's correct. Unchanged."

"If only I had pushed harder for the paging system and not put up with Forester's BS."

"You should have let me know he wasn't complying."

"And that, yes. I should have let you know. But I wanted to take care of it on my own, and spare you the trouble."

"Take a seat over there, Humphrey."

"Over there? By the coffee table?"

"Yes, Humphrey. Over there by the coffee table."

Witner followed and sat opposite him.

"Shall I light the fire, sir?"

"No, I think not."

He kept his eyes fixed on Atwood's forehead.

"Humphrey, you are relieved of your duties as assistant ER director. Nelson Debussy's suggestion."

"I hope it will only be temporary, sir."

"I imagine you do."

Atwood was looking increasingly worried.

"Bryson, if you're angry with me, I can understand."

Witner brought his fingertips together and made a little tent.

"Humphrey, I'm going to ask you a question."

"Certainly, anything."

"What were you really doing last night?"

"We already talked about that."

"Humphrey..."

Atwood took a deep breath and did not seem inclined to release it as Witner leaned toward him.

"You lied to me, Humphrey. You weren't working on a research project."

"I absolutely was, sir. You see, I've always been interested in using the emergency room as a site for hospital employees to receive routine health care services in order to reduce expenditures and so forth. Let me explain. You'll remember me telling you about this, I believe last December—yes, about the middle of last December. I remember you were very interested."

"Poppycock," Witner growled.

Atwood rushed on.

"I wanted to determine the cost-effectiveness of screening hospital employees for cancer in the emergency room. That's what I was working on."

Witner leaned over and picked up Atwood's family snapshot that was still lying face-down on the coffee table from two days before. He looked at it, then stared up at Atwood.

"Humphrey, talking to you is like peeling the bracts off a rotten artichoke."

"Nice metaphor, Bryson."

Witner voice suddenly soared.

"Don't nice metaphor me. I'm waiting to hear you tell me the truth."

Atwood cleared his throat and began with a stammer.

"The truth, ah, is that undetected breast cancer in young women is a serious problem. Our hospital employees include a large population of younger women, most of whom do not undergo routine screening. My hypothesis is that routine breast exams done in the ER on this captive population will lower the rate of morbidity and mortality. I happened to stumble on the perfect subject, my index case."

"She is a radiology technician—correct?"

Atwood cocked his head in surprise.

"Well?" Witner spat.

"Well, what, sir?"

"I want the truth, and I want it now."

"She told me she had a lump in her breast. Her mother had died young of breast cancer, and she didn't have a family doctor. I've been examining her regularly."

"How regularly?"

"Well, whenever she thinks the lump in changing."

"Which is how often?"

"Sometimes once a week. But that's the nature of fibrocystic disease, as you well know, which is what I think it is."

"You examine her weekly, all by yourself, in the old fluoroscopy room?"

"It makes an ideal setting. Once the study gets rolling, I was hoping to get some funding to set it up as a formal consultation room."

"How old is she?"

"Ah, I believe she is twenty-two. This is going to be a wonderful study for New Canterbury, and I was hoping you'd be a co-author. Anyway, if Forester had ordered my pager, this wouldn't have happened. Nothing changes that."

Witner gazed at the ceiling.

"I am humbled to be in the presence of such a genius—able to justify why he was fondling the breasts of a twenty-two-year-old woman behind locked doors while his intern was flubbing the case of the century."

"I wasn't fondling—"

"Shut up," ordered Witner, rising to his feet. "Stay there."

He checked the antechamber—it was empty—then firmly closed the door and threw the lock. Returning, he stood beside Atwood's chair.

"I can see it now, Humphrey. Can't you? Front pages from *The New York Times* to the *National Enquirer*. 'New Canterbury Doctor With Nymphomaniac While Intern Butchers Former Dean!'" He leaned close and let his voice rise unchecked. "You are a first-caliber moron! Why didn't you tell me yesterday? I'll tell you why. Because somewhere in the porridge of your brain, you know exactly what a bumbling ass you are."

Atwood leaned away from his rage.

"You blithering numbskull! This is going to finish your career and could drag me down as well! I flay myself for any modicum of trust I ever extended you...you bleeding varlet!"

Atwood's head tilted like a traffic light in a gale. Witner brought his face even closer.

"You are a contaminant! Utterly Infectious! If I didn't know the depths of your worthlessness, I'd suspect you were an agent sent to destroy me."

"What are you talking about?" Atwood murmured, his voice trembling.

"That's none of your business."

Witner held the photograph in front of the man's face, tore it into pieces and stuffed them into Atwood's shirt pocket.

"A study of the value of screening breast exams on hospital employees—rubbish! You are fit to study nothing but the twisted little worms that pass for neurons inside your skull. Have you even submitted this study idea to the institutional review board?"

"Not completely, no, sir. It's high on the to-do list."

"Not completely. How dare you breathe the same air? Do you know what I would like to do right now?"

"Ask me to resign?"

Witner lowered his voice.

"I would like to pop you open like a bug."

"Bryson, I'm sorry. Please—"

"Shut up!"

The last words showered Atwood's face with spittle. Witner straightened, inhaled deeply, then paced around Atwood's chair, twice clockwise, twice counterclockwise. When he sat back down a few moments later, the storm was ebbing, his expression beginning to relax as he considered all the options. Finally, he took another deep breath, and when he spoke again, his voice had resumed a nearly normal tone.

"You'll understand, Humphrey, I had to get that out of my system."

Tears streaming down his cheeks, Atwood gaped at him, speechless.

"However, if you think anyone will believe that cock-and-bull about a study, you're stupider than I thought. If a dozen people know about this today, two hundred will by tomorrow, and it's just a matter of time until the media gets wind. Within a week, I think it's fair to say the entire world will be reading about it. And your friend, Dr. Forester? Just imagine the joy he'll feel watching you roast."

Atwood's mustache worked up and down.

"Nancy," he said. "I don't want her to know about this."

"Well, she'd have to be even less astute than her brilliant husband to miss it. This will be like a big chocolate cake for the press."

Atwood fumbled for his handkerchief, wiped his face and blew his nose.

Witner looked at his at his watch.

"And to think you were on the threshold of a brilliant career."

"I'll resign."

"How generous of you. You'll be unemployable, anyway, at least as a physician. The state health department will pull your license, you can be sure of it. I wouldn't be shocked if they initiate criminal charges against you for patient abandonment. Do you expect your index case to stand up for you? Even McDonald's will probably turn you away."

Atwood groaned into his handkerchief.

"As for me, Humphrey, who's going to want me for the permanent dean after I trusted the likes of you? My only hope for survival lies in aggressively putting as much distance between us as possible. I have no choice but to join the incipient chorus of condemnation, and even that might not remove the stain."

Shoulders shuddering, Atwood mumbled something unintelligible.

"Beg your pardon?"

"I'm sorry. You're right, it was incredibly stupid."

"You know, Humphrey, in the little scum pond of your mind, I believe you really thought you were doing some form of science."

"I was, Bryson. I even have a data log."

"Pointless." Clearing his throat, Witner fished out a pocketknife and began cleaning his fingernails. "But, Humphrey, it occurs to me there may be a way to salvage the situation."

Atwood looked at him with swollen eyes.

"What do you mean, Bryson?"

"When faced with terrible odds, my friend, most people resign themselves to defeat too quickly. But, as the old Confucian proverb goes, every crisis contains the seeds of opportunity. All that's required to sow and harvest them is clear, ruthless thinking, creativity, and courage."

Atwood blew his nose again.

"What's your idea, Bryson?"

"It's drastic. I don't know if you'll be up to the challenge."

"I'll do anything to make this right. What is it?"

"I mean very drastic, and painful—physically as well as psychologically."

"I don't care about myself. It's my family I don't want to hurt. And you." Though his mustache was still soggy, Atwood's tears were starting to dry. He sniffed.

Witner slid to the edge of his chair. He leaned over and put a hand on Atwood's knee and spoke in a voice barely above a whisper. As the words sank in, Atwood's eyes grew shocked, and he shook his head, pulling away.

"Bryson—you can't be serious."

"There's nothing else that will divert attention from your indiscretion while generating sympathy for you. If you can think of an alternative, please let me know."

For several moments, Atwood stared out the window. Then, finally, he turned back to Witner.

"But it will be like an admission of guilt."

"Not at all. Not at all. It will simply indicate genuine remorse, which is not the same thing. The key factor, Humphrey, is that I will be there to publicly moderate the response people will have, and to see that the proper interpretation is made by all parties concerned. If you haven't noticed by now, I've a talent for shedding the right light on things. I will help people see you as a good person suffering severe remorse and trying to make amends."

"What if something goes wrong?"

"How could it? I'll be there to make sure it doesn't, every step."

Atwood ran his hands through his hair and gazed down at the floor, blinking, as if trying to imagine the scenario Witner had just described.

"Think of your family, Humphrey. They'll be stunned, but they'll still have you—and you'll still have your license, if all goes well, and perhaps even your old job. The sympathy factor in your favor will be huge. And you'll have my continued support. I'll tell how you were victimized by Dr. Forester's failure to install a paging system. Furthermore, I will explain I was aware of your study and had personally authorized it, believing the paging system I'd authorized was already in place."

"You mean you'd lie for me?"

"It would go against my grain, but to save a loyal friend from destruction, of course, I would. Anyone would. In the overall scheme of things, it's not a great untruth, and I will be helping myself as well. What's good for me, I believe, is good for this institution."

And for the world.

This was confirmed by a chorus of voices only he could hear.

For the next several minutes, they detailed their plan, and when Atwood left the office there was purpose in his stride. Witner had barely sat back down at his desk, however, when Atwood peered in the doorway again.

Witner cocked his eyebrow.

"Don't tell me you're having second thoughts already."

"No, sir, not at all. Ms. Andersen is here. She wants to know if you can talk to her."

Witner stiffened. He motioned Atwood to his side and spoke in a whisper.

"Where did you find her?"

"Out in the hallway."

"Are you sure she hadn't been in the anteroom?"

"No, she was just coming down the corridor."

Witner paused.

"All right, tell her to come in, but do not speak with her. Mention you wish you could stay but are coming down with something."

"No, I insist, Ms. Andersen. You couldn't have come at a better moment. Please, have a seat."

Witner seemed more tense than yesterday. She watched him go to the fireplace, switch it on and adjust the flame.

"I apologize for barging in, Dr. Witner, but you mentioned you'd be in this morning."

A wave of blue fire licked over the artificial logs.

"No apology needed. I gave you an open invitation and am happy to see you." He circled around behind her for some reason before taking a chair across the coffee table. "Excuse my curiosity, Ms. Andersen, but is that a hearing aid you're wearing, or some kind of communication device?"

He was frowning.

"It's a hearing aid."

The frown lightened.

"Seriously, now, it's not a Bluetooth?"

"No, this little guy gives me about fifty percent hearing in my good ear. The other one's too far gone."

"I see. I hadn't noticed yesterday. Were you wearing it then?"

"I always wear it, except when I'm sleeping."

"Your hair conceals it well. How can you converse so well with only fifty percent hearing in one ear?"

"I've become a good lip reader."

"Yes, of course. That explains something I'd noticed about you yesterday."

"What's that?"

He smiled disarmingly.

"The way you stared at me. I thought it was because you thought I was handsome."

Zellie felt herself blushing. She returned a noncommittal smile.

Witner continued.

"I'm a reader of people's faces, too, Ms. Andersen, so we have something in common. How can I help you today? Wait, I believe I can guess. It's about what happened last night."

"Yes."

"There, you see. I'm reading your face."

Something intense and excessively personal in his gaze increased her discomfort. Like yesterday, it was as if someone else peered out of his eyes, observing her as if she were some kind of lab specimen.

"Ms. Andersen, I hope last night's tragedy won't cast a negative light on the article you're preparing for *Coast-to-Coast*."

"Actually, I finished that article already and emailed it out. It was done before I saw the news last night."

"I know Dr. Gavin would not want his personal tragedy to cast a shadow over the good things happening here."

"As I said, the *Coast-to-Coast* article is already with the editor in New York. But I spoke with my agent this morning, and she's arranged for me to write a piece about Dr. Gavin for *U.S. and World Current Affairs*."

A change inched over Witner's face, as if he first had to look for and select a suitable expression. It happened to be a smile tinged with sadness.

"Congratulations, Ms. Andersen. We stand ready to help you in any way possible, despite the grief we all feel. But I've forgotten my manners. Would you like some tea or coffee, or maybe a glass of sherry?"

"That's kind of you, but no thanks. I'd just like a few minutes, if this is a good time for you."

"Dr. Gavin was such a beloved figure at New Canterbury, I can't tell you. I'm sure you noticed a change in Dr. Atwood when you met him outside the office."

"He said something about his diverticulitis."

"Always the one to put on a brave face. You see, Dr. Atwood was working in the ER when Dr. Gavin arrived, so you can imagine the burden he feels."

"Do you mind if I take notes?"

"Please do."

"Why do you think Dr. Gavin had become suicidal, Dr. Witner? Did he have a history of depression?"

She noticed the slightest wrinkling of his brow and tightening of his jaw muscles. Here was a man who never uttered a word without weighing it first.

"A good question. Why would a man like James Gavin try to end his own life? First, let us hope against hope that he may recover and be able to tell us himself."

"What are his chances, sir?"

"Not good, I'm afraid. As to your question about why, it's clear he was suffering from the acute onset of a clinical depression. Nelson Debussy and I—you met Nelson the other day, our president—he and I had both noticed signs of it. Neither of us realized how serious the situation was. Even seasoned psychiatrists have difficulty predicting when people will try to end their lives.

"His condition was no doubt exacerbated by the losses he's suffered recently, including the death of a good friend and the fact his career was coming to a close. His career became his entire life after the death of his wife and only son."

"I see."

"Stepping down from the deanship after twenty-five years was difficult. We believe it all caught up with him."

"What is your specialty, Dr. Witner?"

"Why do you ask?"

"Just out of curiosity."

"Geriatric endocrinology."

"Do you still see patients?"

"Of course. In a supervisory capacity."

She looked up from her notepad and noticed the residue of a frown on his face.

"Dr. Witner, I heard that the intern taking care of Dr. Gavin made a serious mistake. What can you tell me about that?"

"That we're still investigating the situation."

"I understand."

"But..."

"Yes?"

"But that's not true. I'd be lying if I told you I didn't know exactly what happened in the emergency room last night. You're not the sort of person I'd want to lie to. I sense that empathy is one of your talents, along with your obvious literary skills. I researched your name on the internet, by the way, and read about your book. It was very well reviewed."

The look on his face seemed sincere. She felt herself blushing again.

"I don't mean to flatter you," he continued. "I'm just saying that I'm tempted to give you the real story here and now. The details won't be officially released for at least another day. This would give you a leg up."

"Listen, Dr. Witner, I don't want you to say anything you aren't comfortable with."

"I wouldn't do that, of course. But it would actually feel good to unburden myself."

"I can say it came from a highly placed administrator, if you'd like."

"That would be best. Okay, given that cloak of anonymity, I will tell you what occurred.

"A simple collapsed lung, caused by a broken rib, was overlooked by an intern in our emergency room, which led to Dr. Gavin's going into cardiac arrest. It was overlooked because the intern's supervisor, who was none other than Dr. Atwood, had briefly left the ER for administrative work. He was not called back in time because a communication system that was supposed to have been implemented had not yet been placed in operation."

Zellie wrote furiously.

"Do you need a moment to catch up?" he asked.

"No, go ahead, please."

"Very well. As I said, a communication system for Dr. Atwood had not been installed as it should have been."

"Got it."

"The reason it had not yet been installed is that the ER director had neglected his duties. He did not set the ball in motion, as he was supposed to have done. That, Ms. Andersen, is the story in a nutshell, and you're one of the few people in the world to know about it at this point."

"So, what happened in the emergency department was completely preventable?"

"Correct."

Zellie felt stunned.

"That's awful."

Witner lowered his head, shook it and sighed deeply.

"Dr. Gavin is dying, and Dr. Atwood is in a state of emotional turmoil, and all due to a matter of administrative negligence."

"Can you tell me the name of the ER director?"

"I assure you, he's no longer the ER director. That was Dr. Jack Forester. "

Zellie felt as if she had just been body-slammed. She looked up at Witner, who was gazing to one side, a misty, sad look on his face.

She clipped her pen to the cover of her notebook. Witner appeared to collect himself and turned to lock his gaze with hers. She felt another chill.

"What's wrong, Ms. Andersen?"

"It's just that the whole thing is so unfortunate."

"Even in an institution like ours, unstable people are sometimes placed in positions of responsibility, and that was the case with Dr. Forester. He was apparently unhappy with his job and was thinking of leaving. Unfortunately, he didn't leave soon enough. I have to tell you, I'm worried about what this is going to do to Dr. Atwood." Witner looked at his watch. "I wish I could give you more time today, but allow me to do this. I can arrange for you to spend some time tomorrow with Dr. Randy Delancy. He can affirm the details I've just given you."

"Tomorrow's Sunday. I wouldn't want to disturb him on a Sunday."

"Not a problem. I will speak with him, and I know he'll be happy to help you. After all, you need to hear this from different angles to maintain your objectivity."

Chapter 20

Faint sounds of jazz filtered through the brick wall separating a nightclub from the restaurant where Jack and Zellie sat at a small table. They had been there ten or fifteen minutes, and during that time they had not spoken more than twenty words.

Ever since he'd picked her up at the Seneca Hotel, Jack's best efforts to start a conversation had gone nowhere. Not only was she subdued, she avoided eye contact—was sitting now staring at something on the other side of the room, rotating her wine glass in her fingers and blinking occasionally, as if lost in thought.

He cleared his throat.

"Well," he said, "I have a confession to make."

She glanced at him with no great show of interest.

"Beg your pardon?"

"I said, I've got a confession to make."

"What's that?"

"I've never been to dinner with a writer before."

He'd meant it to be whimsical, but the comment dropped like a bird that had just slammed into a window. He cleared his throat again and took a long sip of wine.

"We're even, then," she said, not sounding the least bit interested. "I've never had dinner with a doctor before."

Jack forced a laugh.

"So, did you get some good research done today?"

She appeared to consider the question a moment.

"A fair amount."

"That's good. How much longer will you be in town?"

"It's hard to say at this point."

"I wanted to tell you they make an excellent grilled salmon here."

"I'm not that hungry."

"You like seafood?"

"Sometimes."

"So, you're originally from North Carolina?"

"That's right."

"I like your accent."

"I've lost most of it."

"Whereabouts in North Carolina are you from?"

"Several places. We moved around."

Jack waited a moment for something to follow. When it didn't, he sighed and raised his hands.

"Listen, have I said something wrong?"

"No." She glanced at her watch.

"Okay, then. You know, if you're not hungry and not interested in talking and not enjoying yourself, I can take you back to the hotel, if you'd like."

"That might be a good idea."

He felt like he'd been slapped.

"Fine," he replied, trying not to let his feelings show. "But I have to say, we seemed to be almost friends this morning. I can't tell you how much I've been looking forward to spending a little time with you tonight."

"I'm sorry," she said, finally looking into his eyes, if only briefly. "I'd been looking forward to it, too. Things changed."

"What things?"

"I almost wish I hadn't stayed here to do this new story."

"Why's that?"

"Because I'm going to have to write about you," she said, now glaring at him. "Haven't you figured that out? Don't you think I'm disappointed, too? I shouldn't have come out with you tonight. It isn't fair to you."

Jack felt his face flush. It was the most she'd spoken to him all evening, but he was now only more confused.

"Why isn't it fair to me?"

"Do I really have to spell it out? I'm talking about what happened in the emergency department. The medical error. The reason it happened. Dr. Witner gave me an exclusive interview this morning. I know all the details."

Jack drew in a breath, and understanding crystallized in his mind. He leaned back in his chair and nodded.

"So, you talked to Dr. Witner after I saw you this morning?"

"Right. Not long after."

"And in Dr. Witner's version, I'm responsible for everything that went wrong."

"He described things quite clearly. I'm sorry."

"He told you about the paging system?"

"Yes."

"That I didn't install it?"

"That's what he said."

"You've been Witnerized."

"Excuse me?" Her voice rose in anger as she stiffened. "I make my own, objective decisions."

"Then you need to hear things from a different angle."

"So I can be Foresterized?"

"I'm sorry for that. Listen, I'm glad you told me. You could have led me down the garden path and gotten a candid interview without me knowing it."

"Well, I'm glad to know you think I might have done that to you. I don't operate that way."

Jack felt the situation spiraling out of control. She was gathering up her satchel.

"No, I know you wouldn't have done something like that. That's not what I meant, honestly."

"You talk as if you know me. Reading a book doesn't mean you know the writer."

"Speaking of that, it really was a great book."

"Please cut the flattery," she snapped, beginning to rise.

Jack held out his hand.

"Wait. Would you like to hear my side of the story?"

She froze.

"You don't owe anything to me," he said. "You owe it to yourself."

She sat back down, shaking out her hair. The waitress came.

"Sorry I couldn't get back sooner," she said. "Are you ready to order yet?"

"Not quite," Jack told her.

"Can I get you another glass of wine?"

"I'd like a double Gibson, if you don't mind," Zellie said, "on the rocks."

"Certainly. Sir?"

"A Talisker. Make mine a double, too, and a couple of ice cubes."

"You got it."

"So," Jack went on after the waitress left, "may I say something straightforward?"

Zellie was drumming the red-checkered tablecloth with her fingertips. She stopped.

"It's a free country," she said.

"I don't care if you want to pick my brains. Well, I do care, but I'm going to enjoy this evening one way or the other. I'm happy to be here with you, and I hope you have a pleasant time. You needed to talk to Witner—that's your job. I'm just sorry his version seems to have interfered with our having a pleasant night. So, maybe we should clear the air."

"I agree."

Her eyes met his again, and this time a smile curved her lips.

"Frankly," she said, "I *would* like to hear a perspective other than Dr. Witner's. You're right. I owe it to myself. And to my last fan in North America."

The waitress set down their drinks and took orders for dinner.

"Okay, are you ready for my side?" he said.

"To be honest, no. Not yet. Tell me something about yourself first. All I know is that you're a doctor with a precocious memory for cheesy book jacket photos. Where are you from?"

"Africa."

"I'm not interested in having my leg pulled."

"Seriously. My dad was a civil engineer, and he took long stints abroad. Mom would sometimes go with him. So, I was born in Mozambique. I never saw home in New Canterbury till I was three years old."

"So, you grew up here?"

"Pretty much, until I was sixteen. Then we went to Bolivia."

"You went to high school in Bolivia?"

"I did. And college in New Mexico."

"What was high school like in Bolivia?"

"Well, it would have been handy to know a little more Spanish before I got thrown into the deep end. My brother was younger, and he stayed here in boarding school. But it was okay. Still, I would never do the same sort of thing to my own kids."

"You've got children?"

"I mean hypothetical kids. I'm unattached."

"How did you end up back here?"

"I came back for medical school, then went to California for residency, and after that I returned to take a job here. All the family is from New Canterbury. My great-grandfather settled here before the Civil War. I now live on what's left of the old homestead."

"Where are your parents now?"

Jack paused.

"They died, in a plane crash in Bolivia."

A look of sympathy appeared on her face.

"I'm sorry to hear that. I lost my mom when I was young, and it's never easy. I can't imagine losing both at once."

"In any case, that's pretty much it. I've been here at the medical center for the last five years."

"Just one brother?"

"Just one. His name's Tony, and he lives with me now."

"I hate to make this Twenty Questions, but what made you want to be a doctor?"

"When I was a kid, it was a toss-up between baseball and archeology. But the summer before my folks died, I went fishing with some friends out on Lake Titicaca."

"Fishing in Lake Titicaca?"

"You bet. It's full of catfish. In any case, we ran into a couple of thieves, and my friend Enrique ended up getting stabbed in the chest. We had to drive him forty-five minutes to the closest city to find a doctor."

"Did he make it?"

"No, he didn't make it. He died. My friends wanted to get guns and find those guys, but I just wanted to know why this tiny wound had killed Enrique. It wasn't much bigger than your fingertip, didn't even bleed much. The damage was all internal. I kept wondering what I could have done to save him. Something told me he didn't have to die."

"And that got you interested in medicine?"

"I think it woke something up in me. That, and the fact my brother has a developmental handicap. I believe that kind of experience makes a person interested in fixing broken people."

A hand clamped down on Jack's shoulder, and he looked up into the face of Tim Bonadonna. Standing next to Tim was a petite brunette—his wife Sonia.

"I beg your pardon, miss," Tim said to Zellie, "but don't believe a syllable that passes this man's teeth—especially if he says he wants to leave town."

Jack made introductions. Sonia Bonadonna stared at Zellie with congenial curiosity. Jack invited them to share the table. Sonia was reaching for a chair when Tim put his arm about her.

"Most incredibly kind of you, Jack, but we're running late for the movies."

"How long will you be in town, Zellie?" asked Sonia.

"I'm not sure yet."

"We'd love to have you out to our place."

"Yes!" Tim agreed. "But, anon—we must leave you. Miss Andersen, the good doctor is not only my best friend but a reasonably trustworthy person. A prince, indeed, and he can even hold his liquor. You are in good and relatively non-debauched hands. I hope we see you again."

In the Bonadonnas' wake, the waitress returned and took their dinner orders. When they were finally alone again, Zellie's former reserve had transformed into amusement.

"So, how about you?" he said.

"What about me?"

"All I know is that you write and come from North Carolina."

"Where do I start?" she said. "Well, my father was a helicopter pilot in the army, a Vietnam vet, and my mother was a nurse. I went to college in Chapel Hill and got lucky with publishing a little book, and now I live in Brooklyn and wish I could write another and be rich and not have to write stories about Brenda Waters's colonoscopy. I'd buy a house on Okracoke Island, and keep a tan, and write, and take walks whenever I feel like it. That's me. Oh, and I've got a married younger sister living in Florida. My parents are both gone, too."

Jack took a sip of his scotch.

"Not married, then?"

"Contentedly single," she said. "I can see myself either alone and happy fifty years from now, sipping brandy and reading a book all by my lonesome or, on the other hand, surrounded by grandbabies and baking cookies. Who knows? I think the less you worry about those things, the better."

"I'll drink to that," Jack said. *How can such a lovely woman be unattached?* "So, what are we doing now? Is this still an interview?"

"What do you want it to be?"

Jack grinned at her.

"I suppose writers and doctors never leave their jobs behind."

She raised her glass in a mock toast.

"Well said. Let's just talk."

"No hidden tape recorders," he agreed, clinking his glass against hers. "Conversation sounds good. My closest confidant now is a dog."

"I see. Why's that?"

"I work too much."

"Listen, as long as we're opening closet doors, there's something I want to show you. Maybe you'd already noticed." She turned her head and pulled back her hair to expose a beige plastic hearing aid in her right ear. "It'll spare us both embarrassment later on, in case it seems like I'm ignoring you."

"I hadn't noticed."

"With this in, my hearing is about fifty percent, better with low frequencies," she explained, letting her hair fall along her cheek. "Without it, I can just barely hear the sound of your voice. Lip-reading helps either way."

"You lip-read?"

"I do."

"That's got to be extremely difficult."

"Not if you have some training. Here, you try it. Press your ears closed and watch me talk."

He obeyed.

"I can still hear you," he confessed after a moment.

"I'll make it hard for you to cheat by whispering."

He concentrated, but it was more the lips themselves, and the face, that drew his attention than whatever she said.

"You're reciting the Gettysburg address," he guessed.

The waitress came up and gave him a puzzled smile.

"Is everything okay?"

"I'm trying read her lips," he explained.

"Okay."

He saw Zellie chuckle.

"So, what were you really saying?" he asked.

"I'm not going to tell."

"How long has it been like this for you?"

"I got sick when I was in the first grade."

"Meningitis?"

"Yes, doctor. My mother and I both had it." She looked down for a moment. "She didn't survive."

"My turn to say I'm sorry."

"Lord, that was so long ago," she said.

Jack watched sadness sweep across her eyes before she continued.

"I was completely out of it for almost two weeks and didn't know she'd gone. My father told me by writing on a little chalkboard. He sat down on my bed, and I knew something was wrong by the way he kept wiping it off with his hand and starting again, and when I saw he was crying I knew."

Jack nodded.

"Funny thing," she mused. "I can remember that chalkboard better than I can recall her face. What I mean is that, for some strange reason, I can't put together in my mind a complete picture of her. I know what she looked like from pictures, but in my mind's eye, I only see individual parts—her eyes, her hands, her hair, her neck. And forgive me for babbling on like this."

"No, please, go on."

"I remember the way her neck smelled. Isn't that strange? The perfume she used. They say I've got her neck and her little feet, but my father's big bony hands."

She held them up and turned them over. Jack didn't think he'd ever seen a more graceful or lovely pair of hands in his life.

"I'm sure your mother was very nice," he said.

The meal came, and they ate for a while in silence.

"You're right, the salmon is wonderful," she said.

"Glad you like it. You know, I'm not a person who gets angry easily, but knowing Dr. Witner wants to hang the blame on me makes my blood boil."

She looked at him. "You'll have to repeat that. I wasn't watching you."

"Sorry," he said. "I was just saying that being blamed for what happened to Dr. Gavin makes me angry."

She nodded.

"It's not only unfair to me personally, but I loved—love—Dr. Gavin. He's been a mentor to me, and a friend."

She set down her fork and folded her hands.

"Please tell me about it."

"No, finish your dinner. I'm sorry."

"No, please," she insisted. "Tell me. I can eat and watch you at the same time. You just have to pause a little when you see my eyes move away from your face. It's all the ambient noise in this place that makes it harder for me to hear, I think."

Jack nodded. Having to watch her closely didn't bother him in the slightest.

"Well, let me give you some background. After med school, I decided to specialize in emergency medicine."

"The kind of doctor who could have saved Enrique?"

"Right. It just felt like a good fit for me. I like the mix of cases, the breadth of things you see, and I like knowing that I can deal with the really bad things that roll in the door. So, I did a four-year residency, got board certified, and found out New Canterbury was looking for a new ED director. Ordinarily, they wouldn't touch a person fresh out of training for a job like this, but they were having trouble recruiting. Dr. Gavin was the dean then, and he was willing to give me a try."

"And that was five years ago?"

Jack nodded.

"My friends thought I was biting off more than I could chew, but I was inspired by the challenge. Might as well leave a mark on my alma mater, you know?"

"Why were they having trouble recruiting?"

"There were too many turf battles. Emergency medicine is still a relatively new specialty, and New Canterbury is still a very conservative place. Emergency medicine encroaches on other fields."

"How so?"

"Lord, when I first got here, some of the old pediatricians didn't trust me to take care of sick infants, and there were surgeons who didn't want me putting in chest tubes. The anesthesiologists were resisting the ED use of paralytic drugs for intubations, despite my training."

"Intubations?"

"That's when you place a tube directly into the patient's trachea so you can breathe for them and protect their airway."

"Is it hard?" she asked.

"Sometimes—but it's the most important thing an emergency doctor can do in a life-or-death situation. If you can't control the airway, the game is over immediately."

"But the anesthesiologists consider that their turf?"

"They used to, at any rate, and they're excellent intubators, of course. They do it all day long in the operating room. The problem is they're not here at two a.m. when the combative drunk arrives with a bad head injury who needs to be paralyzed and intubated before he gets his CT."

"You can't wait."

"Not if you really want to help these people. Throw in heart attacks, strokes, seizures, infections, trauma and a lot of minor things all demanding attention at the same time, and you've got emergency medicine in a nutshell."

"Sounds like you enjoy it," she observed.

"I do."

"I liked *ER* on TV. Was it accurate?"

"So I hear."

"You didn't watch it?"

"I caught it once. For me, it was like getting hit on the head with a bunch of cliches."

"I see what you mean. So, you won some turf battles when you first got here?"

"A few. There was a lot of low-hanging fruit when I arrived. The nurses needed a better triage system, the physician staff needed upgrading, we were missing all sorts of equipment. We've made a good deal of progress, but believe me, we're not halfway where we need to be."

"Like what sort of things?"

"Mainly, building a new ED and starting our own residency program—things that take a tremendous amount of time to get off the ground. When Dr. Gavin was dean, he was very supportive, and so was his successor, Bob McCarthy. But everything was put on hold when Dr. Witner stepped up."

"When did Dr. Witner take the job?"

"They named him interim dean after Bob McCarthy died back in July. Now, it looks like he's going to get the permanent slot. And as far as my plans for the emergency department go, he's been nothing but negative. He helped make sure they got blown out of the water—actually, just a few days ago."

"Why?"

"If I tell you, Zellie, you'll think I'm being childish."

"Try me."

"Well, I believe it's because he knows I don't like him."

"That's why? Just because you don't like him? What is this, elementary school?"

"I didn't join his fan club. Many of the other people who don't support him are planning to leave. Meanwhile, his friends are being elevated."

"Would that include Dr. Atwood?"

Jack grimaced and took a sip of wine.

"That's right, you've spent some time with Humphrey. What do you think?"

"I think the whole situation here is bizarre. But keep going."

He explained the purpose behind his long-standing attending-stays-in-ED policy, and how Atwood had resisted.

"That's why you stonewalled the paging system?" she said.

"Witner was telling the truth—I ignored his instructions. I thought I was doing the right thing, but..." He let his voice trail off and stared at nothing for a long moment.

"But what?" she encouraged him.

"I told Tim Bonadonna this morning that when you do what you think is right, and it ends up hurting someone, maybe it really is time to move on."

"So, that's why he mentioned something about you leaving town."

"I can't follow my instincts here anymore."

She set down her fork, still maintaining eye contact.

"What other conclusion can I come to?" he added.

"I see the conundrum."

"And they've made me a great financial offer if I resign."

Her eyebrows rose.

"Who has?"

"Witner and his pal Nelson Debussy, the university president."

"So, they're accusing you of having made a terrible mistake, and yet they're offering you a golden parachute if you leave?"

"They'll even scrub my letters of recommendation of anything negative."

She looked thoughtful.

"That just seems very strange."

"Witner's cleaning house. I don't mean to puff myself up, Zellie, but I really haven't done such a bad job here. The med students voted me clinical teacher of the year twice in the past five years. For the volume of patients we see and the antiquated physical plant, our frequency of patient complaints isn't that bad, compared to other places. I've managed to help get a couple of research projects off the ground. Staff morale is reasonable. This could have been a great emergency department in five years."

"I was just thinking about my meetings with Dr. Witner. I know this is going to violate every tenet of journalism, me saying this to you, Jack, but there's something very odd about that man."

"Like how?"

"I'm not really sure. It's as if his outside and his inside don't come together. I sensed a disconnect between the inner and outer man, if that makes any sense. I don't know why I'm sharing this with you."

He held her gaze.

"I appreciate your trust."

She smiled.

"I'm very glad I heard your side. Things are beginning to make more sense, but I still feel like I'm wandering in a maze."

He nodded.

"I'm wondering what it's going to feel like walking into the ED tomorrow morning and not be the director anymore—I'm working the day shift. At least, they're not afraid to let me practice medicine."

"How is the staff likely to take it?"

"They've seen directors come and go before. They'll be fine. I hope."

"So," she said, changing the subject, "you say your closest confidant is a dog, Dr. Forester?"

"Indeed, right after Tim Bonadonna. Or maybe before. His name is Arbus."

"Someone who never talks back. Sounds great."

"Actually, he's more critical than you might imagine."

"Really? What does he find to criticize?"

"My housekeeping. Well, okay, he doesn't really mind that as much as the laziness. I don't go for walks enough, and I talk to myself."

"You say that with a straight face."

"You don't know my house and habits."

Watching her as she teased him, he could only smile. That lovely face, those intelligent hazel eyes—the image he had carried around in memory all these years. Could there be the remotest possibility she might like him?

"You know something," she said, turning serious again for a moment. "I agree with your friend. I think you should stay. I don't believe you should take their offer."

"Are you taking sides?"

"Don't press your luck."

CHAPTER 21

Three nurses were talking animatedly by the door of his former office when Jack arrived in the emergency department the following morning. He'd spent a while in the SICU checking on Dr. Gavin, whose condition remained unchanged—still on life-support and unresponsive.

"Good morning," he said to them. "What's up?"

"Dr. Forester, we can't believe they did this," said Bridget. "I think we should all just walk out."

She pointed to a sheet of paper taped to his door. They parted so he could see. The memo was on Bryson Witner's letterhead and simply stated that, effective immediately, Dr. R. Delancy would be serving as acting medical director of the emergency room. Jack's nameplate had been unscrewed from the door, leaving a rectangle of bare wood slightly paler than the rest.

Jack hadn't slept well. While showering that morning, and all during the drive, he had mentally prepared himself for the change, but even so, this struck him with a wave of almost nauseating anger and disbelief.

He tried the door. It was unlocked. Sometime during the night they had cleaned out his belongings, and a half-dozen boxes now sat stacked by the desk. Everything—the contents of his desk, the books and journals, his files—all was packed away. His diplomas were gone, even the Everest poster. The only thing they'd missed was a little trinket sitting on top of the bookshelf, a porcelain figurine of a golden retriever that resembled Arbus.

The three nurses had followed him.

"You don't deserve this," Sheila said. "We should picket the dean's office. And we don't deserve Randy Delancy."

"He's just a resident!" said Bridget. "This is such an insult to all of us. Jack, are you okay?"

He was leaning against the desk, staring at the boxes. At least Zellie Andersen had agreed to have dinner with him again that evening. That would be his link to sanity for the remainder of the day.

Several hours later, Jack was at the charting station writing up a case when Randy Delancy came up. Jack saw him out of the corner of his eye but kept working on the chart.

"Good morning, Dr. Forester."

"Hello, Randy."

Randy thrust his hands in his pockets, then took them out and folded his arms. Jack looked up at him. His face was unsmiling, embarrassed.

"I've heard the news, Randy," Jack said. "Listen, I'm not angry with you. It is what it is."

"I'm sorry, Dr. Forester. They asked me to help out, and what could I say? I don't have any qualifications to do this."

"All Dr. Witner wants is obedience, Randy."

Jack returned to his chart.

"Dr. Forester, I was wondering if I might be able to use you as a resource?"

"Sure. My best advice, first of all, is to listen to the nurses. Second, don't come to work drunk, and third, always take notes at meetings so you can remember what the hell you promised people. But the major thing is making sure you get the physician schedule out on time."

"The physician schedule?"

"Oh, they neglected to mention that? As medical director, you make sure all the shifts are covered. We're chronically short-staffed, however, so it's a little like putting out brush fires with your bare feet. You'll have to ask people to do things like work seven nights in a row."

"Don't you have a secretary do the schedule?"

"They don't have enough clout. Gail Scippino and I share Bonnie Grimes. She'll make some calls for you, but she'll be out the door in ten minutes if you ask her to do the whole thing. Besides, if you've got an open shift, a secretary can't work it, right?"

"What happens when there's an unfilled shift?"

"As director, you are the ultimate backup."

"Does that happen often...I mean, the director having to fill open shifts?"

"It varies. Around the major holidays and in summer, once or twice a month, maybe."

Delancy cleared his throat again.

"I've only worked in the ER as a resident before."

"Well, the schedule may get a little tougher. If they have their way, there's a good chance I'll be packing my bags, and that'll leave open ten clinical shifts a month. Wally Deutch's almost gone, too, and Susan Redwater has been talking about taking a job in Pittsburgh. Of course, you can always return to using every moonlighter you can dig up who wants to make a few extra bucks, but then you'll be dealing with more complaints and more errors. Maybe you can get Dr. Witner to pull a few shifts. Or Dr. Scales."

"Are you serious?"

Jack looked up and laughed, then handed Delancey one of his business cards.

"If you get overwhelmed, Randy, as long as I'm still around you can give me a call. That's my cell number."

Delancy took it, a numb expression on his face.

"Randy, this ain't bad at all," Jack lied. "All I'm doing now is taking care of patients."

It was a typical hectic Sunday. Immersed in dealing with the problems of others, he gave no more thought to Bryson Witner until the man's name came up in a completely unexpected context.

He went in to see a thirteen-year-old girl with abdominal pain. She was accompanied by a woman who sat in a chair reading *Cosmopolitan* and didn't seem terribly concerned. He read her name on the chart.

"Hi," he greeted the patient. "I'm Dr. Forester. You must be Katrina?"

The girl nodded. She was small for thirteen, underdeveloped and very thin, her face pale and her hair in need of washing. An image came to his mind of a doll forgotten in the corner of an attic. He turned to the woman.

"You're Mrs. Hinkle?"

"I am, but I'm her stepmother."

He took note of the heavy makeup, the leather pants and stiletto-heeled boots, the mass of jewelry on fingers and ears, and the bull's-eye tattooed on the back of her right hand. Martine Hinkle smelled of too much perfume and too many cigarettes.

He turned back to the girl.

"Katrina, tell me where you hurt."

"All around," she said.

"Point to where it's the worst."

Her index finger circled the middle of her belly.

"How long have you been hurting?"

The girl looked at the woman and shrugged.

"Do you have the pain now?"

"Sort of."

"Katrina," the stepmother snarled, "I brought you all the way in here, now you tell him about it. It's all she talks about at home."

The girl flinched.

"Does it hurt more after you eat, Katrina?"

She didn't reply, but her lips quivered slightly.

The stepmother dropped the magazine on the floor and stood.

"She's been complaining about it for months, especially when she doesn't want to go to school. She started crying this morning, and her father wanted her checked out. He had to go to the marina as usual, so here we are." She turned to the girl. "I hope this isn't going to be another waste of time."

Jack cocked his head. The name Hinkle suddenly connected. A man named Fred Hinkle ran the largest marina on Lake Stanwick.

"Would that be Deepwater Marina?" he asked.

"Yeah," the stepmother said. "You got a boat there?"

"Not since the place changed hands. I keep my little sailboat at a friend's house now."

"Listen, she'll probably talk more if I leave, and I need a cigarette anyway. Katrina, talk to the man, or we'll just go."

With the stepmother gone, the girl indeed began opening up. The pains had been going on more than a year, almost every day. Her appetite was poor. The more Jack heard, the more he suspected the problem was functional, something non-organic. Her vital signs were normal, and her abdominal exam completely unremarkable.

"Katrina, we're going to run a few tests on you, but tell me how things are going. Is there much stress at school, or maybe at home?"

Her eyes met his for a second, but then she looked away, shrugging again.

"No, I guess not."

"Hey, listen," he assured her. "It's safe here. You can say anything you'd like."

She kept her eyes averted.

Jack walked out to the central station with a heavy feeling in his chest. He ordered a blood count, electrolytes, a urinalysis, and decided to include a pregnancy test, too. He'd been surprised too many times in the past, remembering a fourteen-year-old who'd come in with abdominal pain and delivered a full-term infant an hour later, to the shock of her mother as well as to Jack.

He went on to new cases; and about an hour later, when the tests were back, he returned to Katrina's room. They were all negative.

"Where's your stepmother, Katrina?"

"She went out to smoke again. Have you found out what's wrong?"

"I think you might have what we call irritable bowel syndrome, Katrina. It's where the intestines cramp up and cause pain. But there could be other things going on." Like depression. "Do you have a family doctor?"

"My dad took me to see Dr. Witner last summer when I had a headache."

That statement shocked him.

"Do you mean Dr. Bryson Witner?"

Katrina nodded.

Witner was an internist, not a pediatrician or a family doctor, and this was the first he'd heard of the man seeing private patients outside the hospital.

"How did you get to see him?"

"My father and Dr. Witner are friends, but I don't like him. His hands are like ice."

This was extremely odd.

"Katrina, where's your real mother? Does she live around here?"

The teenager looked down and swung her legs.

"No. My mom's dead."

Forester found Martine Hinkle in the waiting room. He took her into the family consultation room to discuss his impressions with her.

"So, you're saying she's just faking?"

"No, no, not at all. The pain is real. She's not pretending anything."

"So what the heck do we do now?"

"First off, she needs a full workup by a good pediatrician."

"What about Dr. Witner? Fred does some work for him, and he doesn't charge us anything. He lives right down the lake."

"I don't think so, Mrs. Hinkle. This is way out of his field. I'm going to refer you to Virginia Sortelli. She's got an office on the west side of town. Her name and number will be on the discharge instructions."

He didn't mention that Virginia was a former med school classmate of his, and she was especially good with teenage girls from broken homes, having been one herself.

As for Bryson Witner taking care of a troubled kid, the idea chilled him to the marrow.

CHAPTER 22

Jack found Zellie sitting in a booth with a notepad in front of her, her pen sailing over it; a candle burned in a small red globe on the table. She looked up and smiled.

He slid in across from her.

"Working on the long-awaited second novel?"

She closed the notebook.

"Maybe."

He took a small package from his jacket pocket and slid it across the table. It was a white cardboard box tied with black silk suture material, the only thing he'd had on hand.

"What's this?"

"Open it."

She hesitated.

"Listen, this is kind of you, but I shouldn't be accepting gifts."

"Believe me, it's not worth much. I'd have brought cash if I wanted to bribe you."

She picked it up and turned it over.

"So, what is it?"

He smiled at her.

"That's why God made fingers. Open it."

She slid off the string and lifted the lid. Nestled in gauze pads was his china dog.

She held it up and examined it.

"It's a golden retriever."

"Yes."

She wrinkled her nose at him and grinned.

"Your dog wouldn't happen to be a golden retriever, would he?"

"This is Arbus the Second."

"Why are you giving it to me?"

"When they came to my office and cleaned it out, this was the only thing they didn't toss into a box."

"You're kidding. They've cleared out your office already?"

"Sometime last night. So, this little guy needs a new home. Do you like it?"

"I do," she said. "But I really shouldn't take it."

"Listen, if I wanted to influence your opinion I'd find something a little more dramatic."

"Alright, then, he'll be our chaperone." She set it near the candle holder, adjusting it. "There. He's our journalistic watchdog. Thank you."

"You're welcome."

"That must have been lousy, finding your office invaded like that. How cold."

"It was like a spin-kick below the belt, if you really want to know."

"I can imagine. How did the day go otherwise?"

"Not bad. No one handed me a single administrative problem. All I had to do was be a doctor."

"And that was okay?"

"Yeah...I think. It was different. I don't know."

"Ambivalence, Dr. Forester? Sounds like the kind of thing you need to discuss with your canine advisor."

"But he hates it when I waffle. Actually, I did have one administrative task today."

"What was that?"

"I had a brief meeting, in between patients in the afternoon, with our nurse manager, Gail. She's new to the job, and she believes this is going to make her job harder. I'm afraid she's right, but there's not much I can do to help at this point."

"Here comes the waitress," Zellie said. "Listen, this is Dutch treat. I'm on an expense account."

After they'd given their orders, he asked her how the research for the Gavin article was coming.

"Not bad, for a Sunday," she said. "I went over to the hospital and had a little interview, which was fairly pointless but short. After that, I went to the medical center library and looked up some old articles Dr. Gavin had written, not that I could understand much of it. Then I had a lucky meeting with one of the volunteer ladies, who was very eager to chat, and she told me a bunch of Dr. Gavin stories. Did you know he treated Richard Nixon for a kidney stone?"

Jack laughed.

"That must have been Eleanor Lane."

"Yes, what a sweetheart. After listening to her, I can understand why you admire the man so much. Your name came up, too, by the way. She's quite a fan."

"Likewise. This place would fall apart without people like her."

Zellie nodded, her face turning serious.

"Jack, I want to ask you a favor."

Jack turned to the statuette.

"Are you monitoring this, Arbus Two?"

"Seriously," she said.

"Ask away."

"Would you take me to visit Dr. Gavin?"

Jack looked at her. She wasn't joking.

"You know he's still comatose, right? I went by after work."

"Yes, I understand that."

"Well, we could drop by the hospital after dinner, then, if you'd like."

"I would, very much. While we're there, maybe you can show me your ER."

"You're on. But call it an ED, not an ER."

"What's the difference?"

"A pet peeve," he said.

"I don't understand."

"The term *ER* goes back to when there were no trained emergency physicians, and I find the term belittling. You know, they don't call surgeons 'OR docs.'"

"I can see you're sensitive about it."

"And now you can forget about it. So, who did you get to interview today?"

"Oh, I wanted to tell you about that. It was Dr. Delancy."

"Delancy?"

"He told me he's just been assigned to your old job as the ER—excuse me—ED director. He's so young, though."

"Good Lord, how did you get hooked up with Randy Delancy?"

She held his eyes and pursed her lips.

"Take a guess."

"Witner?"

She nodded.

"Dr. Delancy said some very respectful things about you, but regarding the paging system, you're guilty as charged."

"Of course. What did he have to say about Dr. Witner?"

"My God, if I hadn't met Dr. Witner myself, I'd have come away believing the man was an amalgamation of Christ, Einstein and Edison."

Jack couldn't help but laugh.

"I feel bad for Randy. He's in way over his head."

"He also told me Dr. Witner and Dr. Gavin were close friends. Is that true?"

Jack's smile died abruptly.

"Absolutely not, Zellie."

"I didn't think so. On the other hand, I don't think he was lying to me. He believed it."

"Zellie, trust me—"

"I do trust you. I'm just saying *he* believed it."

"Then he'd been coached, and I can imagine Witner loading the dice like that."

"Why?"

"He's got a fetish about polishing his image."

"Or is he trying to hide something?"

"How do you mean?"

"Something very strange is going on around this place. I thought medical centers were supposed to focus on medicine."

"You should be writing detective stories."

"Are you poking fun?"

"Not at all."

"Well, you're right, I am a good people reader. You'd better watch your step."

The waitress arrived with their meal. Zellie picked up a forkful but stopped as she was lifting it to her mouth.

"I had a strange dream last night, Jack. I was near this big body of water, and there were creatures moving below the surface, roiling the water, but I couldn't see them. They were just large dark shapes. It was frightening."

Jack looked into her eyes.

"Interesting," he said,

Without thinking of what he was doing, he moved the statuette a few inches in her direction.

"Jack, I want to talk with Dr. Witner's assistant, Greta Carpenter. Do you know her?"

"Yes, and I think that's a great idea. She worked with Dr. Gavin for fifteen years or more. She'll give you some great insights."

"I definitely want to pick her brain about Dr. Witner."

"Even though your article is about Dr. Gavin?"

"I couldn't shake the sense, when I talked with Dr. Witner, that he was not unhappy about what happened."

"Witner's an opportunist, and he got lucky. Jim Gavin was the one person who might have kept him away from the permanent position. Now, the way's almost clear."

"Isn't that awfully convenient?"

"What do you mean?"

"I mean two and two equals four." She fixed him with her large eyes. "Hasn't anybody here thought of that yet? That Dr. Witner might be more than just an opportunist?"

"That's a pretty wild idea," he protested.

"I'm a fiction writer, remember? We sit by ourselves for hours and hours, rearrange things in our minds, thinking of all possible scenarios. I'm surprised you find it hard to imagine someone like Dr. Witner might be actively involved in securing his position. As a doctor, aren't you supposed to consider all possibilities when you're dealing with a mysterious symptom?"

"Sure," he said. "I know Witner's a manipulative, power-hungry SOB, but I can't wrap my mind around the idea of him trying to kill someone."

"Why not?"

"For one thing, he'd have needed help. He couldn't do it alone. I remember him saying he was on the phone with Debussy at the exact time Dr. Gavin was hurt. I don't think Witner has many friends outside of the hospital, much less someone who'd help him commit murder."

Nevertheless, a tingle traveled up his spine, though he couldn't pinpoint why.

"I hope you don't mind me rambling," Zellie said. "I'm just thinking out loud."

"Not at all. My friend Tim's got an even wilder theory. Tim suspects Dr. Gavin stumbled across a revolutionary anticancer medication down in the rain forest and that he was being stalked by a pharmaceutical consortium."

She laughed.

"Did I tell you about the letter Dr. Gavin received just before he came back?"

"No. What letter?"

Jack described the message from Dr. Zyman, and told her about his unsuccessful efforts to locate it.

"Wow. Finding that letter would be a good thing. You say the man who sent it to him died right after he'd sent it?"

"Yes. Gavin called it a message from the grave."

After dinner, they drove to the hospital in the Jaguar, which was running smoothly since he'd tinkered with the carburetor after work today. Three police cars and the Channel 11 News van were parked in front of the ED. Jack's chest tightened.

"Christmas, this looks too familiar. We'd better see what's up."

"I'm with you."

A moment later, they entered through the main entrance, and Jack spotted Susee Baker talking to a police officer. He quickly ushered Zellie into the registration area and found Darcy McFeely standing by the triage desk, a dazed look on her face.

"Jack, we tried to call you at home to let you know," she said when she saw him.

"Let me know what?"

"God, I still can't believe it."

"What?"

"Dr. Atwood just shot himself."

The ED was abnormally quiet. Ed Williams emerged from the trauma suite. He was one of the old-time staff emergency physicians, a short, brusque-looking man in his late-sixties. He was stripping off a pair of bloodied gloves. Jack went to intercept him.

"Ed, this is my friend Zellie Anderson. Listen, I just heard what happened."

Williams shook Zellie's hand then looked at Jack grimly.

"Unbelievable," he said, shaking his head. "They found him up in his office with a pistol wound in his head. He's got brainstem respiratory drive left, but otherwise he's an organ donor.

Jack was aware of Zellie taking his hand. He swallowed.

"Good God. Who found him?"

"Bryson Witner was still up in his office and heard the shot." Williams paused a moment, heaving a sigh. There was a splotch of blood on the toe of his white tennis shoe. "Jack, I'd better give you a heads-up about something."

Jack narrowed his eyes at the other man, who averted his, and Williams seemed suddenly reluctant to continue.

"Humphrey left a suicide note," he said after another pause.

"And?"

"Jack, the note blames what he did all on you." Williams heaved a deep sigh that seemed to lift his entire compact frame off the ground. "Listen, I need to go see how his wife is doing. That's her in the quiet room."

Jack could hear a woman crying. He watched Williams stride away, stethoscope dangling from his right hand, then turned to Zellie.

"I'm sorry I brought you into this."

"Please, no need to apologize," she said. "Are you going to be okay? You're as pale as a ghost."

"I've been through this before, but never someone I knew. I won't believe it until I see it for myself. I've got to see him."

"I'll wait here."

Humphrey Atwood lay on his back, a ventilator hissing next to the stretcher. Jack approached slowly. Atwood's eyelids were grotesquely swollen and purple. The entrance wound was visible on his right temple, a small hole surrounded by a dark powder burn. A trickle of blood still oozed from it. On the opposite side of his head, his scalp was matted with blood clots and flecks of brain tissue. It was the exit wound of a substantial bullet, probably a nine-millimeter.

He checked the monitor at the head of the stretcher. Atwood's vital signs were stable and within normal limits. Though his heart might go on beating for days, one thing was certain—the being that had been Humphrey Atwood no longer existed. Regardless of their previous conflicts, Jack felt tears prick his eyes, thinking of Atwood's wife and children.

It was then he noticed something that struck him as odd and incongruent. In Atwood's right ear canal was a small blood-soaked wad of what appeared to be cotton.

The ED staff wouldn't have put it there—there was no medical reason for it. Strange. It was as if, just before pulling the trigger, Atwood had wanted to protect his ear from the sound.

Then again, there was something "Atwood" about that little detail, something meticulous and beside the point.

Back in the hallway, a sight greeted him that made his entire body stiffen. Bryson Witner was standing next to Zellie, leaning toward her and talking. Seeing Jack, he straightened.

"Dr. Forester," he said as Jack slowed. "Ms. Andersen tells me you'd planned to give her a tour. I didn't realize the two of you were acquainted."

There was tension written in the look she gave him. He went and stood close beside her.

"That's right. We were going to pay Dr. Gavin a visit."

"I see. Bad timing, though." Witner tilted his head toward the trauma suite. "May this be our last tragedy. So, Ms. Andersen, you felt the need to talk with Dr. Forester to get information? I had hoped I'd supplied you with enough, but I can understand."

"One can never have too much information," Zellie said.

"Certainly, so long as it's reliable. Listen, Dr. Forester, could I have a private word with you?" He turned to Zellie. "I won't keep him long, and a pleasure to see you again. I'll be happy to talk with you tomorrow, if you'd care to stop by." He led Jack into a nearby empty cubicle and pulled the curtain closed. "Have you heard about Humphrey's suicide note?"

"Not in great detail."

"You will soon enough. I'm afraid it is going to make a great deal of negative feelings flow in your direction."

"What's your point, Witner?"

"You haven't given Nelson your decision with regard to resigning."

"I thought I had until tomorrow."

"That's right, but I wanted you to know the offer remains in force, but I don't know for how long. When the content of Humphrey's note becomes common knowledge, any political capital you may possess will evaporate."

"Thanks for the warning."

"Furthermore, the offer is contingent upon an amicable parting of the ways, free of negative comments made by either party. Please, keep that in mind when you talk to people like Ms. Andersen. Calumny is a two-way street. Just as the medical center would like to avoid being smeared, you, I'm sure, would not enjoy becoming unemployable."

Jack glared at him.

"So, pack my bags and don't say anything bad about you on the way out?"

Witner looked away for a moment, inhaled, his nostrils flaring, then shook his head.

"Dr. Forester, I gave you many opportunities to be collegial, but you keep beating your little drum."

"That's not the way it seems to me, Witner."

The interim dean started hard at him now, and Jack had never seen his eyes so focused or cold.

"You need to be careful about casting any aspersions you might regret. I'll let you get on with your tour."

Chapter 23

"If you've come to see Dr. Gavin, I'm afraid you're too late," said the nurse in the SICU, looking up from her desk at Jack and Zellie.

Too late! Good God, no.

Seeing Jack's look of horror, the nurse realized her poor choice of words.

"Oh, no, he's okay, Dr. Forester," she exclaimed. "I'm sorry. I meant that they decided to move him a few hours ago. He's fine. Or, at least, he's been the same all day. I'm sorry."

Jack let out a breath.

"No problem. Where is he now?"

"Up in a monitored suite on Seven East. He didn't need the SICU anymore, and all the visitors were getting underfoot."

"Is Dr. Hansen still his attending?"

"Dr. Witner is his attending now."

"Witner?" Jack and Zellie exchanged a look of surprise.

"Yes, they switched him from surgery to one of the medical teams."

His heart sagging, Jack took Zellie's arm and spun around, heading back down the corridor toward the elevators. On the seventh floor, an orderly directed them along a dim hallway. Close to the end, a desk had been placed crosswise, like a traffic barrier. A nurse sat there, and next to her stood a security guard with his arms folded. Jack didn't recognize either of them.

He introduced Zellie and himself.

"I'm sorry," the nurse said, "Dr. Witner says no more visitors tonight."

"I beg your pardon?"

"No more visitors," repeated the guard.

"Listen, I'm on the medical staff here, and I'm an old friend of Dr. Gavin's."

"It doesn't matter who you are," the guard stated. "It's the doctor's orders."

"Dr. Witner really did say no exceptions," the nurse confirmed.

Anger began stirring inside him. He stared at each of them in turn, glanced at Zellie, then looked back at the nurse.

"I'm like a family member. Couldn't you just look the other way for a few minutes? We won't disturb him."

"I'm very sorry."

"How would you feel in my shoes?"

"It's really out of my hands."

"This is not right," Jack said, his voice beginning to rise.

The security guard unfolded his arms.

"Jack," Zellie said softly, "I agree with you, but we can come back tomorrow."

The nurse's expression was sincere and regretful.

"Listen, if you like, I'll page Dr. Witner and ask him if it's okay."

Jack snorted.

"Never mind. Just tell me how he's doing."

"Everything's stable," she answered, glancing over at the remote cardiac monitor sitting on the desk.

In the car, Jack was unable to escape the image of Atwood lying on the stretcher, which mingled with the pain he felt at being denied access on the seventh floor.

Zellie broke the silence.

"Is your life always this interesting?"

"Not usually."

He turned toward her so she could see his face in the glow of the dashboard lights, which he had turned up high.

"Can you see me okay?"

"So-so, but I can hear you fairly well. Your voice must be in my best frequency zone."

He gripped the wheel hard.

"Zellie, I still can't believe Humphrey killed himself."

"I didn't know him like you did, but I understand what you mean. I remember him telling me about his children. He had one of each. Very proud of that."

"What's that old saying about a suicide? It kills more than one person?"

They drove in silence a while longer, then Zellie spoke again.

"You told me last night that Dr. Witner became the interim dean after Dr. McConnick—was that his name?—died in an accident."

"McCarthy. Bob McCarthy. He was a terrific guy."

"It was a scuba-diving accident, right?"

"Right. He was diving in Lake Stanwick, exploring an underwater cave, and he got lost, ran out of air. How did you know?"

"A nice old gentleman I met at the bookstore in town mentioned it. Was he diving alone? I thought they always went down in pairs."

"He had another diver with him, but McCarthy apparently went off on his own."

"The police definitely consider it an accident?"

He looked over at her. They were stopped at a light, and she was watching him, her eyes roaming his face.

"Yes, it was ruled an accident, not related to an equipment malfunction. He just took too many wrong turns. Why?"

"Think about it, Jack. Dr. McCarthy dies, and Bryson Witner becomes the interim dean. And then Dr. Gavin comes back, and now *he's* no longer a threat."

"Maybe Witner is mixed up with Tim Bonadonna's pharmaceutical consortium."

"Maybe it's just a conspiracy of one."

He looked at her. The light turned green, and he accelerated.

"I don't know, Zellie. It's just doesn't compute. He's definitely not my favorite person in the world, but he's an accomplished physician."

"So?"

"He's passed a lot of screening tests for character flaws, in a sense. You know what I mean? And he'd have so much to lose."

He found a parking spot close to the hotel entrance. He walked with her into the warmth of the lobby and over to the bank of elevators.

"Well," he said. "Listen, there was something I was going to ask you."

"Oh?"

"What do you think of New Canterbury in general?" he asked in a mock serious tone.

She laughed.

"That is not what you wanted to ask."

"All right. If you're so perspicacious, what was I going to ask you?"

"If I had any plans for tomorrow."

He looked into her eyes and smiled.

"I don't," she added.

"Listen, Zellie, I don't want to wear out my welcome."

"I'll let you know if that happens."

A knot was forming in Jack's throat.

"Good. Well. Good. I hope so."

Did anyone ever tell you how beautifully you smile?

"I'm a pretty basic chef," he said. "But I could put something on the grill at my place."

"Isn't it a little cold for barbecuing?"

"Not until January, in my book."

"Will your dog be there?"

"With bells on."

"Alright. Count me in," she said.

The elevator dinged, and the door slid open. Jack held it.

"Goodnight, Zellie, and thank you."

"Thank me for what?"

The power to respond left him, and he looked deeper into her eyes. She stepped to him and kissed him on the lips, and before he could react, she swung away and stepped inside.

"Does that mean we're friends?" he asked.

"Of course not. Maybe. Have you made a decision about resigning yet?"

"I don't know. Think I'm might stick around and see what happens."

She smiled, and he released the door. After she vanished, he remained there a few moments more, wondering if it had really happened.

Back home, he found Tony leaning against the railing out on the front deck, looking out over the valley where New Canterbury sparkled through the trees. Vapor rose with his breath.

"Hey, brother," Jack said.

Tony looked at him. He had showered, and his long black hair was wet and combed, his beard dripping.

"Hi, Jack," he said. "I bathed."

"I can see. Listen, I'm glad you're in. I wanted to tell you something. Wait here. I'll be back in a minute."

He returned with Zellie's book, a stocking cap—which he ordered Tony to put on—and two cigars, which were the last from the box of Cohiba's Tim Bonadonna had given him for Christmas last year. Clipping off the ends, he handed one to Tony, lit his own and passed the lighter to his brother.

He leaned against the rail next to Tony and puffed silently.

"Humphrey Atwood committed suicide tonight," he said, blowing out a gray cloud, looking at his brother, who continued to stare out over the valley.

Tony's expression was hard to read, as always. It held only a sort of distant and vague curiosity, a sense that he was only semi-engaged; and Jack doubted even someone like Zellie could break through that reserve.

"Why?" Tony said abruptly.

Jack thought about his answer before speaking.

"Well, he was feeling guilt and remorse, apparently. It was painful for him, and he wanted to escape it."

"Why was he feeling guilt and remorse?"

"He'd made a mistake and hurt someone."

Tony drew on the cigar, and it glowed, highlighting his eyebrows.

"The guy was always something of a jerk, Tony, but I never imagined he'd do something like that to himself and his family. I'm totally stunned."

"Are you sad?"

"That, too."

"Why was he a jerk?"

Jack puffed the cigar. He shook his head.

"I don't know, Tony. He was too self-important. It's just bad business any way you cut it."

"He cut himself?"

"No. A pistol." Jack decided to move on. "Hey, man, there's something else I need to tell you. I've met a very lovely woman—an incredible person—and I think I'm falling in love with her."

Tony glanced at him, making only the most fleeting eye contact before gazing away.

"I've never met anyone like her," Jack continued. "I've invited her here for dinner tomorrow. I want to show you something." He held up Zellie's book. "She wrote this, and that's her picture on the back. You probably can't see it very well now."

Tony took Jack's cigar lighter from his pocket and thumbed it on, playing the light over the photo.

"She looks awful young."

Jack was just drawing on the cigar and laughed, choking on the smoke.

"The picture's almost ten years old, Tony."

"She's pretty, Jack."

"She's beautiful, brother. She's very lovely. I'd like you to meet her."

Tony gave him another fleeting glance.

"Like I said, she's coming to dinner tomorrow night. Would you like to join us?"

"No, I don't think so."

"Come on, why not? She won't mind if you're quiet. You'd feel comfortable, trust me."

"It's not that."

"What is it, then?"

"Jack, if I had a date, I wouldn't want *you* to come."

Jack smiled and patted his brother's shoulder.

"That's thoughtful of you, Tony, but I'd really like you to meet her."

"I'll come up later, maybe."

"Not maybe. You come. Please."

"She's nice?"

"Very nice. Mom and Dad would have fallen in love with her instantly."

"Can I read the book?"

"Sure, but just don't get it wet or dirty."

"I won't."

Tony gave him a rare smile and wandered off down the steps toward the barn, the cigar clamped between his teeth, smoke trailing him in the chill night air.

Jack smoked a while longer and, growing cold, went back into the house. His cell phone buzzed, and he opened it to a text message from Tim.

> SORRY FOR DELAY IN GETTING BACK ABT LETTER. COULD NOT FIND IT W G'S BELONGINGS. WILL KEEP LOOKIN. YOU'VE NEVER KNOWN ME TO FAIL, HAVE YOU? LOL.

The phone buzzed. and a continuation message appeared.

> THOUGHT MORE ABT BIG PHARM BIZ AND DECIDED BEST TO SHARE W POLICE. STRANGENESS AFOOT ACROSS THE LAND. WE MUST TALK SOON.

Then came a third.

> WAS THAT WOMAN LAST NIGHT THE ONE YOU MENTIONED? NOT BAD, YOU DOG. SONIA CURIOUS. WE WANT DETAILS. WILL CALL TOMORROW. LOVE, T.

Jack then noticed another text message from earlier that evening he must have missed. He opened the screen. It was from Greta Carpenter.

> DR F—NEED TO SPEAK WITH YOU ASAP. DO NOT CALL ME AT WORK.

James Gavin grew aware first of pain on the left side of his chest that came and went rhythmically. How long he existed in this state of awareness, he couldn't be certain, but in the haziness, memories came—of being on an airplane, of being in a meeting, and then of fear, of seeing a man in a hooded jacket approaching, of being dragged, and of being lifted and of falling.

He tried to open his eyes. Or maybe they were open, and he was in a place of pure darkness. He could moving nothing, or at least was not aware of being able to move—no sensation of movement came to him.

Was he buried? Was he in a coffin? He couldn't move no matter how hard he tried.

He became more conscious of the pain now. His chest rose and fell, apparently of its own accord, for he was not aware of trying to breath. He was not in control of anything, but he felt the air come into his lungs, and when it did, a violent burning sensation stabbed his chest.

Was he on a ventilator? Yes. He had fallen, and he must have broken some ribs. What in the name of God was happening? Why was he unable to move a muscle, not even lift his eyelids? Was he paralyzed? Had he broken his neck? He could hear the hiss and click of the ventilator, and began to feel the pressure of a mattress against his back.

Then came the sound of footsteps, followed by a voice. It was like the bumbling of a bee at first, but it grew louder and more distinct. It was familiar, but as recognition came, he realized it was the last human voice on earth he wanted to hear.

What does this all mean?

Before he could puzzle it out, before the world could make sense, the void enveloped him again.

CHAPTER 24

Palm Springs, California

Daphne Gavin lay tanning on the patio of her penthouse, staring from behind her sunglasses at a contrail inching across the stratosphere and wondering how she was going to hold on to all of this until the new ship arrived.

She took a swallow of vodka-laced iced tea, and a drop of condensation fell between her naked breasts, sending a shiver through her. Something very good was about to happen, a new partnership opportunity of sorts, the best thing that had ever come her way; but it was at least several months off, and she was going broke in the meantime. There was no way to avoid it any longer—she needed to tighten her belt.

She stood, resolute, and pulled on a blue terrycloth robe. The vacuum cleaner whined faintly beyond the sliding glass doors. She might as well get it over with.

"Emelita," she called, rapping on the glass.

Daphne had bought the condo several years earlier when her bank account was fat from the sale of her house back in New Canterbury and the liquidation of some other assets, including Colin's share of the racehorse. There should have been three million in life insurance when Colin died, but his father—behind her back—had made sure the policy was allowed to lapse.

Bryson Witner had called her with the news, though, so she knew the mean-spirited old bastard was finally getting his due

She had sacrificed a lot as Colin's wife, spent most of her married life waiting for him to come home from the hospital. Then, after he'd gotten sick, she'd done her best until the very end. Now the old man was lying in a hospital bed, broken and comatose, a step shy of death's welcome mat.

She rapped again.

"Emelita!"

She heard the vacuum cleaner die.

Not long after moving to Palm Springs, Daphne had driven out to a crossroads in the desert and handed three thousand dollars to a man with carbuncles on his neck. She returned with Emelita, marching her straight into the shower. Fortunately, the girl had learned English in El Salvador and was as bright as Daphne had guessed by her eyes.

"Yes, señora?"

"Come here, and close the door so we keep the air conditioning in."

Emelita sat on the tiles next to Daphne, drawing her knees up and hugging them like a schoolgirl, though she was now sixteen.

"Emelita, you're going to have to leave."

Emelita had known things were bad financially, and she'd probably feared something like this was coming. Her eyes instantly overflowed, and she looked away. The trauma she'd been through in Central America hadn't toughened her up. She should probably be in a convent.

"But, señora..."

Daphne held up her hand.

"Emelita, I don't have as much money as I used to. I must conserve. *No puedo pagarte.* Do you understand?"

"I do something wrong, señora?"

"Stop it, Emelita. Stop it." Daphne handed her a tissue. "Wipe your nose. That's disgusting."

"But I like to stay with you."

"It's probably time you were out on your own, anyway."

Daphne had tried to discourage Emelita from becoming emotionally attached to her. You destroyed people by coddling them. That's why Daphne was a survivor. True, she hadn't had to watch her mother and sisters get raped and her father machine-gunned, but she had been abandoned by her mother the year before she started kindergarten. When she was fourteen, her alcoholic father had kicked her out, leaving her to make her own way in the condo-jungle of Fort Lauderdale. Before the age of eighteen, she'd seen a bit of everything and done a bit of everything, from running hot cars to porn.

But she'd survived, with her health intact and no prison record; and she'd had enough sense to get out when she could, never losing the determination to make something of herself. She'd fled to California with a new identity, attended college and discovered she had a talent for managing other talent. As a result, she'd ended up working in the back office of a major studio in Hollywood until she'd met and married a dashing young plastic surgeon with a taste for the fast life.

Colin Gavin had been a very beautiful man.

Did she crumble when he died? No, she did not. And even greater things were just around the corner. She could still look forward to the day when she'd be able to dump shovelfuls of steaming shit on the heads of those relatives who'd turned their backs on her all those years ago.

But Emelita didn't have the same fighter's instincts. According to Mr. Carbuncle, after the girl's family was slaughtered, a photographer found her sitting in a field wearing a bloodstained dress, waiting for the wild dogs to eat her.

"You don't have to pay me, señora. I want just to stay with you."

"Of course, you want to stay. You've got it made in the shade here."

"Señora Daphne, I need no money."

Daphne studied the mountaintops in the distance.

"So, you'd stay and not want to get paid?"

The girl nodded, ignoring the tissue and swiping her nose with her hand.

Daphne considered this. Emelita had turned into a decent little chef.

"I'll tell you what, young lady. Until my ship comes in, you can stay. But as of today, you work only for room and board, *entiende*?"

A fresh wave of tears came, but the girl smiled.

"Thank you, señora."

"Leave me alone now. Go—get back to work. And, Emelita, tell no one about this, especially not Mrs. Granger or Mrs. Erhenberg, do you understand?"

The girl rose, bowed and darted back inside. The vacuum cleaner whined to life.

That would mean five hundred a month saved, and the kid ate like a bird. Daphne slipped off the robe and stretched back out, but there were clouds moving in. The vacuum suddenly fell silent again, and a moment later, Emelita slid open the door,

"Señora, is a man here for you."

Daphne looked at her and flexed her ankles.

"Who is he?"

Emelita handed her a business card. She lifted up the sunglasses and read "Auren Mitchell, Esq., Attorney at Law, Conrad, Victorio and Dubendorf."

"I don't know him, Emelita. Ask what he wants."

Emelita returned in a flash.

"He say he a lawyer."

"Is that all he said?"

"He say he a friend of Mr. Victorio. He want to talk about Dr. Gavin. He say you would know."

He looks like a baby, Daphne thought as him slid one of her wicker chairs over and sat. She tightened the robe belt around her waist. *Couldn't be much over thirty, but he's balding a little. Nice build, though, tall,*

probably works out, like they all do around here. Those gyms are like stud farms.

"Mr. Mitchell, would you like something to drink?"

"A Diet Coke would be fine."

He had a good tan, but his suit and shoes were off the shelf, and his socks didn't match.

"Emelita, bring out a Diet Coke for the gentleman and a Southern Comfort Manhattan for me."

"Actually, if that's what you're having, Mrs. Gavin, I'll take the same," Mitchell said.

He's an underling. Why are they sending out an underling?

"Emelita, make that two Southern Comfort Manhattans."

Mitchell cleared his throat.

"Mrs. Gavin, it's awesome of you to see me without notice. Great view of the mountains here."

"So, how well do you know Sal Victorio?"

"He's one of my mentors."

Sal Victorio was one of the biggest legal names in Palm Springs, and was now semiretired. He'd made a fortune suing doctors and hospitals, and had been married for a while to the actress Susan Terwilliger. Daphne had known him quite well in Los Angeles before she'd married Colin, and she still maintained the connection. A good friend to have in a place like this.

"Well, I'm sure Sal makes a good mentor, but please don't call me Mrs. Gavin. Or do I look old to you?"

"You know that's not true. What would you like me to call you?"

"I don't know yet. Why don't you tell me what brings you here?"

Mitchell drew a newspaper clipping from his pocket and handed it to her. It was from the *New York Times*:

Nobel Laureate in Coma from Intern's Mistake

"I already know this," she said. "They called me. What do you people do—scour the papers for tidbits like this?"

"Actually, we have a college student that—"

Daphne cut him off with a laugh.

"My God. You really are ambulance chasers. How in the hell did this article lead you to me?"

"We have Sal to thank for that," he said. "It was blind luck. Sal happened to be in the office yesterday before going on a trip, and remembered that this Dr. Gavin was your father-in-law."

"Great memory."

"Our research people took the ball from here. We found out you are apparently his sole next-of-kin."

"You're wrong. He has a cousin or two in Nova Scotia."

"Not anymore. From what we could discover, they're all gone."

Daphne sipped the Manhattan, which was very good, and thought of the time she and Colin took a road trip to Canada. They had stopped at an old house at the end of a gravel road by a lake, where an old woman lived. She wore a blue linen dress, was very opinionated, and her fingers were stained with cigarette smoke. That was Colin's Aunt Louise. She must have been the end of the line.

"Why didn't Sal come to see me about this himself?" she said, lighting a cigarette.

"Because he's halfway to Australia right now," Mitchell said.

She stared at him.

"So, he sends me somebody fresh out of law school. Thanks for the favor, Sal."

"He sent me, Mrs. Gavin, because he knows I'll work my heart out to help you. I won't rest till you get what you deserve. I'm backed up by the resources of Conrad, Victorio and Dubendorf. Those doctors screwed up, and we can make them pay."

Daphne took another sip, and caught him glancing at her legs.

"You're wasting your time, Mr. Mitchell," she said, lifting one of her knees.

"Beg your pardon?"

"I have no interest in suing anyone just because they hurt my ex-father-in-law. I feel more like congratulating them."

"So, you and he weren't close?"

"You have the gift of understatement."

"I'm just trying to understand."

"Listen, there were many things my father-in-law didn't approve of, and I was at the top of the list. After he found out Colin and I had eloped, he hired a private detective. Fortunately, Colin was already well aware of the fact I hadn't been born with a silver spoon in my mouth. That's one of the things he liked."

"Your husband was a plastic surgeon?"

"A very successful one."

"I understand he died of ALS?"

Daphne slammed the glass down.

"Dammit, what *didn't* Sal tell you about me? It's true, Colin died a wasting death that took about three years, and toward the end, when I was very vulnerable, his father believed the worst about me, and he made sure I got turned out. I was not even allowed at the bedside to hold my husband's hand when he died."

For a moment, she felt as if she might cry, but the sensation quickly passed.

Mitchell had paused and was adjusting his tie.

"I'm very sorry to hear that."

"I'm not asking for pity. It's history."

"I didn't come to offer you pity. But maybe I can help you balance the scales."

"Money can't balance the scales, Mr. Mitchell." She drank the remaining liquid in the glass. "But I see what you mean. I'm not stupid."

"Mrs. Gavin—Daphne—the hospital released a press statement just this morning acknowledging one of their interns made a serious mistake, which led directly to the damage in question. That means the hospital's insurance carrier has already set aside money for a settlement if someone files a claim. A legitimate claimant simply needs to file suit. Essentially, all you'll need to do is show up and hold out your hand, Mrs. Gavin. Daphne. It's a slam dunk."

"Just how big of a dunk?"

"Sal estimated somewhere between one and one-point-five million."

Daphne looked up at the sky, where a thunderhead was building over the mountains. She glanced at Mitchell. He had beads of perspiration on his forehead.

"I like money as much as anybody," she said, "and I could certainly use some right now. But it's not quite that simple. I'm on the threshold of something better, and I don't want this to get in the way."

"You can always give it to charity, Daphne."

"You mean after I give you a thirty-three-percent contingency fee."

Mitchell shrugged.

"That's the standard arrangement."

Daphne Gavin looked back toward the mountains for a moment.

"What would I have to do?" she said.

"You and I will fly to New Canterbury and meet with their lawyers. The firm will handle all the arrangements—travel, lodging, meals."

"When would we go?"

A Cheshire cat smile spread across his face.

"There are two tickets waiting for us on a flight leaving in about three hours."

She sighed and stood.

"Let me go inside and think. You want to wait out here, or inside?"

"Here would be fine."

"Then at least take your jacket off. You're soaking."

She slid open the door and entered the coolness of the apartment. Emelita was at the counter cutting up vegetables. She looked up and smiled.

"Emelita, go out there and see if he wants anything else to drink. And don't flirt. I saw the way you stared at him, you bad girl."

The girl nodded, blushing.

In the bathroom, Daphne dropped the robe and got into the shower. What would be the harm of an unexpected visit to New Canterbury? Especially if it would dramatically ease the strain on her finances? How could it possibly compromise the new venture? What could be the harm?

Nothing.

She might even be there in time to see the old man buried.

CHAPTER 25

The sudden ringing of the telephone sliced through Jack's reverie. He'd been staring out the window into the predawn gray after a night of little sleep, the image of Atwood lying on the stretcher never far from his consciousness. Steeling himself against more bad news, he reached for the phone.

It was Greta Carpenter.

"I apologize for calling this early, Dr. Forester."

"Not a problem, Greta. What's up?"

"Did you get my message?"

Arbus padded in, sat in front of him and stared.

"Yes, right. You wanted to talk?"

"I was concerned you might try to contact me at the hospital, and that's why I called so early. I really don't feel comfortable there anymore. I know that sounds crazy, but what isn't these days?"

"Agreed."

"Could we meet somewhere today?"

"Certainly. Before I forget, the writer, Zellie Andersen, from *Coast-to-Coast* wants to interview you. I believe you met her already?"

"I did, yes. But that's strange. Dr. Witner told me she wasn't interested in talking with me."

"No, just the opposite."

"Why am I not surprised? You can give me her number when we meet."

They settled on lunch at a Chinese place a few blocks from the medical center called the Flying Duck. Jack said goodbye, then turned his attention to Arbus.

"You, my friend, do not smell good. You're getting a bath today. We've got company coming."

He opened the side door and watched the dog bolt for the woods. He also noticed the entryway floor was crusted with layers of paw and shoe prints. Arbus wasn't the only thing that needed cleaning.

He strolled around, appalled at how far he'd let things go. Dog hair covered the carpets. Cobwebs festooned the open-ceiling beams. Everywhere he looked, the list grew—windows opaque with grime, furniture strewn with magazines and papers, dishes filling the sink and overflowing onto the counters, and when he ran a finger over the top of the refrigerator, it came away black and sticky.

"An unsung mystery of the universe—how grease finds it way to the top of a refrigerator."

He jotted down the things he'd need to get at the store then pulled on a pair of old jeans and a sweatshirt and took his jacket from the closet. On the way to the barn, he dialed the hospital number.

"Yes, I'm sure, Dr. Forester," said the nurse. "There's been no change in Dr. Gavin's condition."

"One more thing," he said. "Dr. Atwood?"

The nurse picked up on his hesitation.

"I'm sorry," she said. "They discontinued the ventilator about half an hour ago and pronounced him dead."

Jack held the phone to his ear for a moment or two after the nurse hung up, feeling a mix of emotions—anger mixed with grief. Suicide was a stupid thing to do—stupid, horrible, destructive. He shook his head, put the phone back in his pocket and went in to the check the barn. Tony wasn't there. It was an open question whether he'd come in tonight to meet Zellie. Jack suspected he would.

Arriving in town before the stores opened, he found an empty table in a little café near the butcher shop on River Street and ordered coffee. It was a shame he didn't have Zellie's book, but someone had left a copy of the morning paper on a nearby chair. As soon as he opened it, the headline story jumped out and grabbed him by the throat.

Suicide Strikes Medical Center Again

Death note blames former ER Director Jack Forester

Pulse pounding in his temples, he read:

> *New Canterbury* — A second physician lies in critical condition at the medical center after a suicide attempt last night.
>
> Hospital officials announced at 11 p.m. that Dr. Humphrey Atwood, the assistant ER direc-

> tor, shot himself in his office at the hospital earlier and was rushed to the emergency room.
>
> According to hospital sources, Dr. Atwood had been increasingly depressed over his role in a medical error that occurred after the medical center's former dean, Dr. James Gavin allegedly jumped from the Beech Avenue footbridge several days ago.
>
> Gavin, a Nobel Laureate and well-known local physician, remains in a coma.

Jack's eyes flew down the text, his jaw muscles tight.

> A note found on Atwood's desk expressed dismay and rage over the failure of ER director, Dr. Jack Forester, to institute measures that would have prevented the medical error. Forester has since been suspended.

"Jesus Christ," he hissed.

He became aware of someone standing next to him.

"Hello, Jack." It was Armand Bedford, chief of the city police, a white coffee mug in his hand. "I was meaning to give you a call today, but I saw your car out front. It's hard to miss."

Jack started to rise. Bedford had been a close friend of his father's.

"Don't get up," the chief said, placing a hand on Jack's shoulder. "Let me take a seat." He eased his broad frame into the chair gingerly, like a man whose back was sore. "I know one thing." He pointed to the article. "Somebody at the medical center has loose lips. There's way more information there than the public needs to know right now." He continued in a softer tone, "Are you okay?"

Jack took a deep breath. He noticed his hands were shaking slightly.

"Jack, I've always felt like an uncle toward you," Bedford went on. "Do you want to talk?"

"I guess there's not much to say."

"How close were you with this guy Atwood?"

"We worked together, but that was about it."

Bedford nodded, stirring sugar into his cup.

"No love lost, then, I take it?" He set the spoon down and gave Jack a penetrating look.

"No."

"I read his suicide note last night. Anybody who would hang that kind of weight on another person—enemy or not—is a sick bastard in my book. I'm sure there are two sides to the story. I have no sympathy for him, not to mention what he's putting his family through. "

Jack felt a lump growing in his throat as Bedford continued.

"Listen, what Atwood did wasn't your fault. He pulled the trigger. You have every right to feel pissed off about the note, but not guilty about the act that followed. Do you read me?"

Jack's attention was drawn to a woman passing by on the sidewalk. For a moment, he thought it was Zellie, and his senses sharpened, but the hair color was too dark.

"I appreciate the kind words, Chief," he said, turning back to face Bedford.

"Jack, what's this I hear about you leaving town?"

He stared at the man with mingled surprise and irritation.

"Everybody seems to know about me leaving but me. Where did *you* hear it?"

"Someone at the hospital. I know this has got to be a tough time for you—not just with this business, but with Jim Gavin, too. But I hope you aren't thinking about it seriously."

"I haven't decided yet."

"Jack, let me tell you something. I still think of your folks every day. They were fine people, and I'm sure they'd want you to tough this out." After a moment of silence, the chief said, "Not to change the subject, but I wanted to ask you something about Jim Gavin. Before the accident, he called me, but I was out of town."

"He did?"

"I was at a damn budget conference in Albany," Bedford went on, as if he hadn't heard. "Every time I leave town something bad happens—a tree falls down in my yard or my wife's cat goes missing. It never fails. This time, an old friend throws himself off a bridge."

"I still can't believe he tried to commit suicide, Chief."

"I don't want to believe it myself, Jack. But Witner and Debussy claim he was acting depressed. People do these things, even great men like Jim Gavin. You're a doctor, I don't have to tell you that."

"So, you weren't able to talk to him?"

"No, and it's been a real weight on my soul. I wish Arlene had given him my cell number. In any case, she set him up to see me on Saturday morning, but by then, it was too late. Who knows—I might have been able to help him. But he left an odd message. I don't know. Maybe it fits with him being depressed."

"What was that?"

"He told Arlene he wanted to talk about the deaths of Robert McCarthy and Lester Zyman."

"That's what he told her?"

"I was wondering if you'd had a chance to talk with him at all?"

"Well, I did run into him just before a meeting the day he got back."

"How did he seem?"

"He was upset but not depressed. He was angry over the way things had been drifting at the medical center since he'd left."

"What, exactly, did he tell you?"

"That he wasn't pleased with Dr. Witner's leadership. He listened to me complain about how Witner had been making my job difficult and seemed to be sympathetic."

Bedford hesitated, his expression puzzled.

"I'm very surprised to hear that, Jack."

"Why?"

"I've talking with Bryson Witner a couple of times over the past few days, and you came up more than once. I mentioned our connection, and Dr. Witner had nothing but good things to say about you."

Jack's jaw fell open.

"You're kidding me."

"I first met Bryson at a reception last spring, and he's a very impressive guy. Old Abe Delancy thinks he's the top monkey, the way he's been whipping things into shape over there."

"That depends on your point of view."

"You're saying Jim Gavin didn't like him?"

"He said he was going to make sure things got better, and I took it to mean he was going to work against Witner becoming the permanent dean."

"Interesting. I'm very surprised. What else did he say? Did he mention McCarthy or Zyman?"

"Not McCarthy, but he said he'd gotten a letter from Dr. Zyman that Zyman wrote the day before he died."

Bedford cocked an eyebrow.

"Really? What did he say about it?"

"He wouldn't go into it. He said he had to do some research first."

Bedford rubbed his chin.

"A letter from Zyman," he repeated thoughtfully.

"Chief, I've tried to find that letter. He had it with him the day I saw him."

"No luck?"

"I checked his clothes at the hospital, and I even searched the accident site, and asked security to check his belongings. Nothing so far."

"Jack, I wish you'd given me a call."

Jack focused on his coffee, blushing.

"Sorry. I guess I should have."

"Yes, you should have, but don't worry about it. I think it's unlikely the letter would shed any new light on this mess. Actually, it fits with what we know—that Jim was depressed over the deaths of Zyman and McCarthy."

"I still don't buy he tried to kill himself. I think he was mugged."

Bedford sipped his coffee and gazed out the window.

"A mugging with no missing valuables. I don't know. It's funny, but suicides in a community often come in threes, and Atwood, I hope, puts an end to it."

A chill went down Jack's spine.

"Gavin and Atwood are two. Who's the third?"

"Well, I was thinking of the way Dr. McCarthy died in the lake last summer. Here's this very smart man who goes off into a cave without telling his diving partner. That's suicidal, if you ask me. He was diving with Fred Hinkle, the only guy in Peterskill County who knows much about those caves, but he goes off on his own like a five-year-old with a death wish. I'd just as soon dynamite those damn things shut."

Jack straightened.

"Who did you say his diving partner was?"

"Hinkle, the guy that runs the marina at the south end of the lake—Fred Hinkle. He's an ex-Navy SEAL, probably the safest diving partner a man could have. You're looking at me strangely, Jack. Do you know him?"

The background noise of the café grew loud in Jack's ears. When the front door slammed shut, he started. In his mind, he heard the voice of Katrina Hinkle. *My father and Dr. Witner are friends, but I don't like him. His hands are like ice.*

"Can I share a thought with you, Jack?" Bedford said.

"What's that?"

"If I were you, I'd consider making my peace with Bryson Witner. Like I said, he thinks highly of you. He's a mover and a shaker. I'm sure he can help things get back on track."

"You don't know the whole story," Jack told him. "And I doubt you'd believe me at this point.

"How's your brother getting along, by the way?"

"Fine. Thanks for asking."

"I can't tell you how impressed I am, Jack, at the way you look out for him. Again, you'd have made your parents proud."

"That's good," Jack replied, so distracted by his thoughts he barely heard the compliment. "So, Dr. Gavin's case is being officially ruled an attempted suicide?"

"Yes."

"What about that missing letter?"

"I'll put out the word to our people to keep an eye out for it. But I think I know pretty much what it'll tell us. Jim got a letter from a dead friend along with a notice of that friend's death. It must have been a huge shock. We can't wish bad things away.

"Listen, it was good to see you, bud." Bedford drained his mug and stood. "I'd better be getting on to the office By the way, that nutty security guard actor friend of yours—what's his name?"

"Tim Bonadonna."

"Yeah, Bonadonna. He's called the department three times demanding that we investigate the possibility a drug company tried to murder Gavin."

"He means well, Chief."

"I'm sure he does, but if you see him, please ask him to put a lid on it. What's up with that guy?"

"He goes off on tangents sometimes, but he's a great friend. A little too much imagination for a small town, maybe."

"Well, tell him to stick to Shakespeare."

Jack came out of the supermarket with two handfuls of shopping bags and loaded them into the Jaguar's trunk. With a couple of hours remaining until his rendezvous with Greta, he drove by the medical center then crossed the Seneca River Bridge under a steel-gray overcast. There were no other cars in sight. He jammed the gas pedal down and accelerated through the winding curves of Route 19 toward Lake Stanwick.

Twenty minutes later, he pulled into the gravel parking lot of the Deepwater Marina. It was just past the wooden bridge over the Miller Creek Inlet, a small white frame building with a poster near the entrance listing boat rental fees. A red-and-white diving symbol hung by the front door.

To the right of the marina, a concrete boat ramp angled down, and two wooden docks extended into the water. The slips were empty except for a single vessel, an old cabin cruiser.

Jack killed the engine. A sharp wind from the north was whipping up whitecaps and sending scraps of paper and plastic skipping across the lot. He'd used to fish here on the lake's shallow south end when he was a boy, catching perch and bullheads. There had been a little bait shop on the spot where the marina now stood and no concrete boat ramp, just a muddy bank. The storage lot for boats and trailers across the road had been a cattail marsh.

Just west of the storage lot rose a tiny hill, and on top of it sat a small blue ranch house, which also hadn't been there when he was a boy. It was Fred Hinkle's house.

He took his time crossing the lot to the door of the marina building. The windows were dark, but there was an "Open" sign in the window. When he tried the door, it gave with the tinkle of a little bell.

The place appeared deserted. Beyond several display racks of fishing tackle, three galvanized minnow tanks ran the length of one wall. Other shelves were devoted to boating and diving equipment, and against one wall leaned a row of yellow scuba tanks.

A door opened behind the counter, and a man strode out, wiping his hands on a greasy rag. As if surprised to see a customer, he stared at Jack for a moment.

"Good morning," Jack said.

He was a wide-chested man about forty years old with close-cropped hair and prominent forehead and chin. He was broad in the shoulders, and his upper arms bulged with muscle.

"What can I do for you?" he said, tossing the rag on the counter.

"I'm looking for Fred Hinkle."

"You've found him."

"I'm Dr. Jack Forester from the New Canterbury emergency department. I treated your daughter Katrina yesterday. Just happened to be passing by and thought I'd stop and see how she's doing."

Hinkle's dark eyes were inscrutable.

"Well, I'm afraid you didn't cure her. She stayed home from school again today."

In the background, the filters in the minnow tanks hummed and gurgled.

"Sorry to hear that."

"My wife said you couldn't find anything wrong with her."

"Nothing showed up on the tests, but I gave your wife a referral to a pediatrician I'm sure could help."

"You gave her a referral?" A shadow passed over his eyes. "I didn't hear about that."

"I could give you the doctor's name again, if you'd like."

"Do that."

He handed Jack a sheet of paper. Jack consulted his cell phone for Virginia Sortelli's office number, and as he was writing, he heard the bell above the door tinkle.

"Speak of the devil," Hinkle said. "You're not supposed to leave the house if you didn't go to school."

Katrina was dressed in a baggy gray sweatshirt and a pair of jeans.

"I'm feeling better. Did you need some help? I'm bored."

"You need to go back up to the house. The doc here stopped by to see how you're doing."

"Hi, Katrina," Jack said.

She stared at him.

"Hi."

He turned away to give Hinkle the sheet of paper, and when he did he heard the bell tinkle again. When he looked, Katrina had disappeared.

"She's a good kid," Hinkle said, "but she's been through some tough times."

"Dr. Sortelli can help her."

"I'll give her a call."

"I understand Katrina's seen Dr. Witner."

Hinkle shrugged and stuck the paper in his shirt pocket.

"For what it's worth," he said. "Is there anything else you need? I'm pretty busy today."

"I understand you offer diving classes here."

"Do you have a card?"

"No."

"Then start with the course at the YMCA. Stop back after, and I'll set up your open-water dives. That's about it."

"Sounds great. I'd love to see Lake Stanwick under the surface—anywhere but the caves. I'm not sure I'd care for that, especially after what happened to Dr. McCarthy this summer."

"It doesn't have to be unsafe."

"What, actually, happened to him?"

Hinkle picked up the rag.

"What did you say your name was?"

"Forester. Jack Forester."

"It's a funny thing about doctors," Hinkle mused, twisting the rag. "Must be the education. They think they can't get hurt."

"But Bob McCarthy was highly experienced, wasn't he?"

"Anybody can find themselves in the wrong place at the wrong time."

As Jack descended the steps of the marina and crossed the parking lot to his car, the back of his neck tingled. He looked, but couldn't see Hinkle.

Then he spotted Katrina standing on the bluff by the little blue house, staring down at him.

Jack took a table near the door of the Flying Duck and waited for Greta to arrive. Twelve-fifteen came and went, then twelve-thirty. He'd nearly given up hope when he finally saw her walk in the door.

"Jack, I don't have much time," she said, surveying the room as she sat. "Let me jump to the point. There is something strange about Dr. Witner—and I mean more than just that he's a far cry from Dr. Gavin in terms of human kindness."

"No disagreement, Greta."

"Have you ever heard of something called the Society Carnivalis?"

"No."

"Neither has anyone else, and Google couldn't help me, either."

"Where did you run across it?"

Greta scanned the restaurant again, then leaned closer.

"A few weeks ago, Dr. Witner was called out on an emergency. He locked the office door like he always does, but I could see it was still ajar. It wasn't closed when he turned the bolt.

"I know it wasn't right, but I went in. I saw a book lying on his desk with the words *Society Carnivalis* on the front. I probably should have just walked away..."

"What did you see in it?" Jack encouraged her.

"I was shaking like a leaf. I just flipped through it very quickly. There were a lot of lists and what looked like meeting minutes, and some kind of manifesto."

"Manifesto?"

"Yes, you know, like a statement of purpose?"

"What did it say?"

"It looked like, I don't know, plans to fight against something. Whatever, it sounded very strange. And then there were lists and lists of names—it looked like almost everybody who works at the medical center and descriptions after their names in some kind of code. Some of them were checked off."

"Did you see any names in particular, Greta?"

"No, my heart was in my throat. I've always wondered why he's so secretive. It just isn't normal. He had a private secure phone line installed in there. Why? Do you know what else was on his desk? A row of marbles. Why would a grown man be playing with marbles?"

"I have no idea."

"Maybe I'm going nuts, Jack, but I think he's connected with some kind of criminal organization. I think..."

She stopped, and her face went blank as she stared out the restaurant's front window. Jack followed the direction of her gaze; Witner was walking by. He didn't turn his head in their direction, but a slight smile formed on his lips as he passed. Then he was out of sight.

Greta turned to Jack and was undeniably frightened.

"I'm not an alarmist, Jack, but something isn't right. You just saw that. How did he know?"

"Might just have been a coincidence, Greta," he said, trying and failing to sound convinced.

"Should I go to the police? I mean, I've thought about it, but all I've mainly got is this feeling. That, and a book I was looking at without permission."

"I agree, Greta. At this point, given the friends Dr. Witner has, I don't think the police would listen to you."

"But you understand what I'm saying, don't you? You don't think I'm crazy?"

Jack shook his head. "No. And I'm glad you shared this. I've got some real concerns about him, too, Greta, and I'm going to be checking up on some things."

"Good," she said, sounding as though a great burden had been lifted. "Please let me know if there's anything I can do to help."

"I will."

"One more thing—be careful," she warned. "We don't need any more tragedies."

Chapter 26

What a pleasant feeling, Jack reflected, to be standing by the sink in the kitchen of his house, cleaning up after a meal and talking with an interesting and very attractive woman. Ordinarily, he would have left things on the table or the kitchen counters and worried about it later. But she'd laughed at this suggestion and, in a firm but friendly way, gone to work, handing him a towel.

So, they'd cleaned and talked; and before Jack realized it, the kitchen was back in order, and he'd enjoyed the experience. After that, he found her a pair of gloves and a heavy sweater and gave her a down vest to put on over the sweater, and they took wine glasses out onto the deck, where the stars had come out. Distant lights from the city glittered through the trees.

"This was just what I needed," she said. "As much as I love New York, I'm still a country girl. And here comes my friend. Hello, sweetie."

Arbus trotted up to her.

"He hasn't left you alone all night," Jack said.

"I'm sorry your brother didn't join us for supper."

"He might still come."

During the meal, they'd talked a lot about his brother.

"He must be extremely resourceful to get along out there all by himself day after day. Does he ever seem lonely?"

"Sometimes I think he's the one who feels sorry for me."

She looked off into the darkness for a moment, and then turned to him.

"Jack, in case no one's ever told you—you're a very generous person."

"What makes you say that?"

"For one thing, the way you've shaped your life around your brother's."

"I can't take credit for that. It just happens to work out."

"You understand what he needs, and you take care of him. That's nice. It's more than nice—it's good."

Looking at her, Jack's heart swelled. She raised her wine glass and clinked it against his.

"And you grill a mean chicken in subfreezing weather," she added.

"It's actually thirty-six degrees," he corrected, grinning. "This is a heat wave by New Canterbury standards."

She laughed, but Jack had noticed a shiver in her voice. He led her back inside, kindled the fire he'd already laid in the wood stove and pulled a couple of chairs up close to it.

"So," she said, "we've managed to avoid talking about the medical center for almost two hours."

"Which has been a good thing."

"But where do we go with this mystery from here?"

"I need to tell you some things."

Jack described running into Armand Bedford, and how he'd learned about the connection between Witner and Hinkle, and then how he'd driven out to Hinkle's marina. She listened raptly as he described his lunchtime meeting with Greta Carpenter, and of the eerie passage of Witner by the window as he and Greta were talking.

She swirled the wine in her glass, lost in thought. An idea had been edging into Jack's mind all evening, and he decided to confess it.

"Zellie, I'm starting to feel like I may be dragging you into danger."

"You're not dragging me anywhere," she said, glancing up and smiling.

"I know that. But I'm getting this ominous feeling. I don't like it."

"Tell me more."

"I'm not sure what to tell you. I do know I've got no choice but to keep digging, keep trying to find out what's going on. My whole life is at stake here."

"I understand that, but I can't write the story unless I know the truth," she pointed out. "I want to see this through as much as you do."

"All of this might still be a pack of coincidences."

"Two minds would be better at figuring that out, don't you think?"

"Holmes and Watson, huh?" he said.

"And I'm a big girl—please remember that. I've been taking care of myself for a long time."

He nodded.

"I'll be Holmes, by the way," she added. "You're the doctor, so you can be the straight man."

"You cut a tough bargain. But, onward, Holmes."

"Okay, let's review the facts. What do we know for sure at this point?"

"We know that Fred Hinkle and Bryson Witner have a relationship, and that Hinkle was the only witness to Bob McCarthy's death in the underwater cave."

"And because McCarthy died, Witner became the acting dean," Zellie put in.

"And Lester Zyman died unexpectedly right after he posted a letter to Dr. Gavin," Jack continued.

"And something in that letter made Dr. Gavin fly all the way back here."

"And we know now he wanted to talk to the police about the deaths of Zyman and McCarthy."

"But before that could happen, Dr. Gavin allegedly tried to commit suicide, which goes against everything you know about the man."

"Then Bryson Witner starts telling everyone Dr. Gavin was showing signs of depression, even convincing the chief of police."

"But when you talked to Gavin, you didn't get that impression at all."

"Witner wanted you to believe he and Gavin were on good terms."

"Which I would have bought if you and I hadn't become acquainted—and Dr. Witner last night was obviously not pleased we know each other."

"Right. If someone tried to kill Dr. Gavin and make it look like suicide, things didn't go as planned. Thanks to some shrubbery, he survived. But when he gets to the ED, a mistake nearly kills him."

"Jack, is there any possible way Witner could have arranged for things to happen the way they did in the ED?"

Jack shook his head.

"I can't see how. Atwood was one of Witner's disciples, no doubt about it, but there would have been too many variables. Instead of screwing up, that poor intern might have done the right thing and saved Gavin. So, the medical error in the ED had to have been chance."

"But then Atwood commits suicide," Zellie mused. "How does that fit? Or does it?"

Jack shook his head.

"I can't believe we're thinking seriously there's some huge conspiracy going on. Tim must be wearing off on me."

"Don't drop the thread, Watson. Let's keep brainstorming."

"I'm with you, Holmes. By the way, Tim texted me this afternoon. He and Sonia have invited us to their place for dinner tomorrow evening. Like I said before, I don't want to wear out my welcome."

"No, I'd like that."

"They have a place on Lake Stanwick. Beautiful country."

"I'll look forward to it. Where were we?"

"I was wondering whether Atwood's death was just another piece of good luck for Witner."

"Why would it be good luck for him?" she asked.

"Well, Humphrey would have taken a lot of heat for that error in the ED as time went on, and because they were close, Witner's reputation would have been tarnished. Witner stood up for him."

"So, Atwood's suicide focuses attention on *him* and, thanks to his suicide note, on you, Jack. This is wild, but is there any way Witner could have arranged for that suicide?"

Jack stared into the fire for a moment.

"Well, Witner *is* the one who claims to have heard the shot and found him."

"Good God."

"You see what I mean about the danger in all this?" he said, gazing directly into her eyes for a long moment. Then: "Would you like a cup of coffee?"

"I'd love one," she said. "I'd help, but your best friend's lying on my feet."

A few minutes later, coffee mugs in hand, they continued.

"Tell me again the name of that society Greta Carpenter told you about."

"The Society Carnivalis."

"What a weird name."

"Yeah, sounds like the cruise ship line from hell."

"So, there's another thing we know—that Dr. Witner belongs to an organization of some kind and keeps records in code. Lord knows that that could mean. Jack, do you have internet out here?"

"Just dial-up, and it's very slow."

"Then I'm going to research it first thing tomorrow."

"And I'm going to try to find that letter. That's something concrete I could take to Armand Bedford. Right now, like I told you, he thinks Witner's the greatest thing since light beer. If I go to him with nothing but these suspicions, he'd have me committed. There's just nothing solid to go on. You're the writer, Zellie—what would a fictional detective do now?"

"Good question. One of my favorites is Maigret. He was created by the Belgian writer, Georges Simenon."

Jack shook his head. "Never heard of him."

"Maigret is very low-key. He follows hunches and asks a lot of questions and looks at things more than once. And he keeps an open mind. Like Columbo."

Jack heard the side door into the kitchen creak open. Zellie's back was to the door, and she hadn't heard it.

"Tony's here," he told her.

She smiled and turned to see. Tony stopped, hesitating.

"Tony, thanks for coming," Jack said. "This is Zellie Andersen, the friend I told you about. She's looking forward to meeting you. Come on in."

Tony closed the door, but he didn't come any farther than the entryway. Zellie stood. She looked at Jack, who nodded, and they both approached him one step at a time. When they came to within about six feet, Tony inched back, and they stopped.

"Hello, Tony. I'm Zellie."

Tony smiled at her then glanced at Jack.

"We saved a plate for you," Jack said. "It's in the fridge."

Tony nodded then brought out a thin tube of brass about a foot long, age-tarnished, with holes along the length and a green plastic mouthpiece. Jack recognized the pennywhistle his father had brought back for Tony from a trip to Ireland.

"Do you play, Tony?" Zellie asked.

Tony nodded. He brought the instrument to his lips and answered with music.

"Can you hear it, Zellie," Jack asked, turning toward her.

Fairly well," she said. "It's lovely."

It *was* lovely, a Celtic melody in a minor key, full of lilting trills and graceful shifts. Into Jack's mind came the image of an ancient green forest. He looked at Zellie. Her gaze was rapt, and her eyes slightly dim with unshed tears.

The song ended, and Tony lowered the flute. He had not taken his eyes from Zellie, which was highly unusual for him, and now he blinked several times—and smiled.

"Thank you, Tony Forester," Zellie said. "I hope we're going to be friends."

"I liked your book," he responded.

Zellie beamed and glanced at Jack.

"Is this a plot?"

"I gave it to him last night. Tony, have you really finished it already?"

Tony reached into the large side pocket of his parka and brought out the book, safe inside a plastic freezer bag. He handed it to Jack, picture side up, and nodded.

Chapter 27

"Listen, this is getting more than a little frustrating," Jack said, struggling to keep his tone polite.

It was early the next morning, Monday, and he stood before the desk that blocked the corridor beyond which lay Jim Gavin's room.

"I'm sorry," said the new nurse, whose name tag read "Lillian Blockman," an appropriate name if ever there was one, Jack noted.

"He's been here since Saturday night. Do I have to file a written request or something, Ms. Blockman?"

"Please don't be angry with me, Dr. Forester. I have no control. Per Dr. Witner, I can only admit staff directly caring for him."

Once again, another unfamiliar security guard stood nearby, and his expression was bored and unfriendly. He was going to have to talk to Tim about this.

"I'm not angry with you, Lillian, but this is absurd."

"I understand how you must feel, sir," the nurse said. "It's just that all sorts of people were trying to get in. We even had medical students trying to take pictures with their cell phones. And the press, of course."

"What does that have to do with me?"

"Would you like me to page Dr. Witner?"

"All right," he said. "Why not?"

While she dialed, he studied her desk. The monitor crouching on the right side was ICU-quality, giving a continuous display of Gavin's cardiac rhythm, pulse, respiratory rates and blood pressure. In front of her lay a blue plastic notebook, where she was keeping a record of those parameters.

Witner returned the page. She picked up the phone, and Jack listened to her relay his request. She nodded and hung up, her face coloring.

"I'm sorry, Dr. Forester, but Dr. Witner feels that Dr. Gavin should not be disturbed until later in the afternoon. He said he would meet you here about five p.m. if you'd like, or at nine tomorrow morning."

"That's insane."

"There's nothing else I can do."

"Yes, there is. You can let me in for a half a minute. Only you and I and our friend here will know."

Her face colored even deeper, but this time with anger.

"Maybe you don't care about my job," she snapped, "but I do, and so do my kids. I'm a single mother."

Jack accepted that he was wasting his time. He marched toward the elevators and, a few minutes later, bowled into Tim Bonadonna's basement office and slammed the door behind him.

"Son of a bitch!"

"Good morning to you, too," Tim said.

"According to Dr. Witner, I have to make an appointment at his convenience to visit Dr. Gavin."

"Hell's bells. Sit down before you pop a gasket."

Jack was too agitated to sit.

"Any luck finding the letter?" he demanded.

"Like I told you, I found his belongings, but no epistle. Ergo, he probably didn't have it on him. I bet he left it home."

"Great."

"But I did bring you a little present, Jackson. You owe me." Tim reached into his desk and handed Jack a ring of keys. "These are copies of the keys Dr. Gavin had on him. One of them has to be his house key. These are yours to keep. The originals are back in the box."

Jack took them, astonished.

"Tim, thank you. This is great."

"All in a day's illegitimate activity, my man." Tim's eyes darted from side to side as though scanning for potential eavesdroppers, despite the fact they were sitting in a closed office. He leaned close. "Listen, I'm certain he discovered something down there in the rain forest. Be extremely careful."

"You know, Tim, I have come to the conclusion that you're right about something going on behind the scenes."

"Yes!" The animation on Tim's face was soon replaced by a quizzical expression. "You do?"

"But not what you're thinking." Jack carefully led his friend into the web of connections he and Zellie had outlined the previous night. When he'd finished and leaned back, Tim's eyes were wide and his expression astonished.

"Jack, I know Witner is a pompous turd, but good God, this is hard to swallow."

Jack couldn't help but laugh.

"Harder to swallow than the cloak-and-dagger theory you've concocted?"

The big man stroked his beard, and after a moment he smiled.

"Well, maybe you've got a point. Don't forget dinner tonight."

Half an hour later, Jack pulled into the parking lot of the Jefferson County Coroner's Office, which occupied the basement of the Public Health Department on St. Vincent's Street. He found the coroner, Dr. Annabel Singh, in the breakroom drinking a cup of coffee and eating a cookie. In her late fifties, Dr. Singh was also a professor of pathology at the university, and had long gray-streaked hair pulled back in a ponytail.

"Very good to see you, Jack. You have been sending me too much business from the emergency department lately. You are not saving enough people. Do you like chocolate chip cookies?"

She nodded toward a platter on the table. When Jack declined, she took one and put it in his hand.

"Eat it, please, and tell me what you think. I have added cinnamon to the recipe. I made them for my new assistant because it is his birthday today. But who needs an excuse to enjoy a cookie. Tell me?"

Jack took a bite and told her it was wonderful.

"So, what brings you to see me?"

"Annabel, you did the autopsy on Bob McCarthy, didn't you?"

"I did."

"It was declared an accident, correct?"

"Yes, that is right."

"And there was no suggestion of foul play?"

"Of course not. We did all the usual toxicological studies and organ analyses, you know, and nothing unusual. Why do you ask?"

"Some questions have surfaced."

Her dark eyes pinned him.

"What sort of questions?"

"I don't really know yet."

"So, questions have surfaced you do not really know anything about yet?"

"I can't say anything more at this point."

"It is funny you should mention this."

"Why?"

"There *was* something about my findings that I could not easily explain, and it has been like a grain of sand in my shoe."

"What was that, Annabel?" Jack put down the half-eaten cookie on the table.

"It was not enough to change the final determination, but I always want to explain everything about a case, and it was something I could not completely understand. Here, let me get my report and I will show you"

She returned a minute later with a folder.

"The cause of death was asphyxia," she said. "But there were signs of what might represent a struggle before he died."

"How so?"

"His fingertips were deeply abraded. We could explain that easily, though, because he would have clawed at the walls of the cave, trying to find his way out. How awful those last minutes must have been."

A shiver crept up Jack's spine.

"No doubt."

"I found these linear contusions on his shoulders that did not quite make sense. Here, you can see what I mean for yourself."

The pathologist laid out a series of color photos, and the muscles in Jack's neck and shoulders tensed. McCarthy's face was frozen in a grimace, his eyes wide open in an expression of terror heightened by a rectangular indentation in his skin the shape of his diving mask.

"Now look at that," said Dr. Singh, pointing. "Do you see what I mean?"

Jack brought the photo closer. Across the top of each shoulder was a faint dark line in a nearly identical location on each side.

"Could that have been caused by the straps of his air tank?" he asked.

"That's what I thought, too, Jack, and perhaps that is what it is. But the straps were very wide, and padded by his wet suit. Logically, they should not have caused bruising like that."

"Do you have any other ideas?"

"No, but it reminded me of an autopsy I did many years ago on a young man who had died in a prison riot. He had put his head between the bars and was trying to break them loose with his shoulders. It left bruises not unlike those on Dr. McCarthy's shoulders."

"Strange," Jack agreed. "Did you tell the police about it?"

"Certainly. But it turned out he had been doing some yard work the day before and might have carried something on his shoulders. Nothing else made sense, so I just noted this on the autopsy report. Probably it means nothing, but it is still, as I said, a grain of sand in my shoe."

Gavin lived in a neighborhood of large houses dating back to the 1920s, many of which had been converted into flats. It was a favorite area now for med students and residents—quiet, safe, an easy walk to the hospital.

It was half-past four in the afternoon, and dusk was near, the sky thick with clouds and the temperature dropping. The radio had forecast snow that evening, and it sure looked like it to Jack as he slowed the Jaguar and eased by Gavin's home. There were no other cars and no people on the sidewalks. He checked his watch again. He was not due to meet Zellie for another hour.

It was an old two-and-a-half-story brick colonial with gables and a slate roof. The front lawn was blanketed with maple leaves. He turned left at the next cross street and parked a long way down the block. He got out of the Jaguar, locked it and strode casually back up the street—somebody just out for a little walk before dinner.

When he reached the house, he didn't slow at first. He walked by and waited for a car to glide past, then he doubled back, cut across the yard and went to the side door, which luckily was hidden from the street by an overgrown hedge. The fourth key on the ring Tim had given him opened the door. He looked around. Still no one in view.

Inside, the door closed and locked behind him, he climbed three steps to a landing that opened directly into the kitchen. The light outside was failing quickly, but he could still see well enough to make his way. Now, the question was—where would Gavin have left the letter? With any luck, it would be lying on a counter in plain view, and he could get the hell out of here. Prowling around the empty house was a creepier sensation than he'd expected.

He checked the kitchen first, then went into the dining room. Nothing. Then he climbed the stairs and found the master bedroom. A small carryon bag lay open and empty near the bed, and the bed itself was unmade. He scanned the bedside table and the chest of drawers, but they were clear of anything made of paper. It went against his grain, but he began opening drawers.

It was painful to see the clothing folded inside the dresser. There was even a drawer of things that had obviously belonged to Betty Gavin. He shut it quickly and check the nightstand drawer. There were a few coins and a bottle of nasal spray. Feeling increasingly like an intruder, he strode out of the room.

Descending, Jack entered the living room, where the furniture was still covered by sheets. Only a feeble light was filtering in the windows now. He checked the top of the coffee table, the end tables and the mantle. Then he noticed another, much larger suitcase by the entrance to the foyer, where Gavin must have set it when he'd gotten home.

Kneeling, he laid the suitcase flat and opened it. A familiar smell of clothing and aftershave wafted out, and for some reason, he thought of his parents, more intensely than he had for quite some time. It was a long moment before he could continue.

He closed the suitcase, coming to grips with the idea that he'd reached another dead end. Then he remembered Gavin's study. As he rose, a sudden cracking noise caused his heart to thump against his ribs. He froze. It came again—like a bone breaking, this time followed by a watery tinkling sound.

He breathed again. It was only the radiators. The boiler in the basement was coming to life with the fall of night, sending hot water into cool pipes.

Gavin's study was at the very back of the house. When he had guests over, Gavin would often invite them back there after dinner for a brandy and some shoptalk. Jack himself had spent more than a few hours there. The hallway was deep in shadow. He came to the door and tried it. It was unlocked. With the window shades down and the curtains pulled, it was pitch dark. Just as well. He shut the door and flipped the light switch.

The first thing he saw was a pile of sheets lying on the floor. Gavin must have uncovered the furniture in here and hadn't taken the time to put the covers away.

Jack looked at the desk, and his hopes surged. On the blotter lay several envelopes. Disappointment returned. There was a letter from the New Canterbury Municipal Orchestra, another from the National Wildlife Federation, and the last was a Southern Tier Gas and Electric bill. There was nothing else on the desktop, or on top of the file cabinets or bookshelves.

He sagged down into Gavin's chair and opened the top drawer. There was a photograph of Gavin and Betty, standing proudly on either side of Colin. Colin was wearing a cap and gown—probably his graduation from Stanford Medical. He replaced it then opened the lower right-hand drawer, which contained a number of hanging file folders, each with a name on the tab. Might he have filed the letter?

Sure enough, there was a folder labeled "Les Zyman." Jack opened it to find many letters, his spirits rising. There was correspondence dating all the way back to 1968, but nothing more recent that about three years. He checked it carefully again, then replaced it.

A thought occurred to him. What if there was a file on Witner? He looked again, and there it was—"Bryson Witner: Confidential."

He lifted the file out and set it on the desktop. He checked his watch—he'd been in there for twenty-five minutes now—and opened it.

It contained only three letters, all dated shortly before Bryson Witner had arrived in New Canterbury several years ago. One was from Witner to Gavin, inquiring about a position. Another was also from Witner to Gavin, thanking him for giving him the post and promising Gavin the decision would never be regretted. He scanned these quickly, then reached for the third.

It was a letter of reference written on the elegant letterhead of Magnus Schwartz, MD, Professor of Medicine at the Harvard Medical School and vice-chair of the Department of Internal Medicine, Massachusetts General Hospital.

Jack smoothed it out and read.

Dear Jim,

    I trust all is well with you and yours at New Canterbury and I look forward to seeing you again this fall at the Scientific Session in San Diego. To the point: I can understand your concerns about hiring Bryson, but am glad to hear you are leaning in that direction.

    I strongly believe his problems are behind him, and I think he would flourish in the nurturing environment you have created there for new faculty. He had risen so quickly and accomplished so much here in Boston that his breakdown didn't come entirely as a shock. In short, Jim, I believe the man overworked himself in the service of his calling.

    But I am happy to say that Bryson's six-month hospitalization at McLean led to a full recovery, and thanks to the ministrations of some very talented psychiatrists, I am convinced he learned how to prevent such an event from ever happening again.

    In truth, I wish he'd stay with us. His work in geriatric endocrinology—particularly the effects of aging on dopamine receptors—will provide fruitful research for decades. But breakdowns carry a stigma that can never be fully erased. He wants to start fresh.

    I cannot think of a better place for him to re-blossom than under your wing, my friend. I give Bryson Witner a hearty thumbs-up. I assure you, also, that the medication he now takes will not interfere with his clinical work, his research, or his teaching activities.

CHAPTER 28

Jack had first seen the Seneca Hotel many years earlier when his parents had taken him there for someone's wedding reception. As he waited for Zellie, he decided it looked much the same as he remembered, with the potted trees and the pink marble columns around a sunken central lounge, classical music playing in the background. He spotted her on the far side of the lobby, sitting in an alcove and talking to a woman whose face was hidden by a plant.

A maroon-jacketed porter came up to him.

"Can I help you, sir?"

"Thanks, no, I'm fine. I've found what I'm looking for."

The porter followed his line of sight and grinned.

Zellie hadn't noticed him yet, so he indulged the impulse to stare at her, surprised by how strongly the sight of her affected him.

She saw him, smiled, rose and approached. There was no doubt about it, she took his breath away. It was everything—the shape of her face and her smile, her curves, the way she moved. There was a perfection he would have found it hard to describe simply in words.

"Hello, there," she said. "Is everything all right?"

"Yes. Yes. Fine. Good to see you."

She tilted her head.

"You have a strange look on your face."

"Do I?" *I'm in love with you.* "I didn't realize it."

"Well, it's good to see you, too," she said. "How did things go today?"

"I had a very interesting meeting with the coroner, and I burgled a house for the first time."

"Did you now?"

"Yep. I had a look around Dr. Gavin's place."

"The letter?"

"No, unfortunately, no letter from Dr. Zyman, but I did come across an extremely interesting letter pertaining to the interim dean."

"Really? I want to hear all about it, but first you need to meet someone. Actually, you already know her."

She took his hand and led him toward the alcove. Able to see the woman now, Jack recognized her, and his heart sank a little. It was Daphne Gavin.

"Hello, Daphne," he said, extending his hand.

She beamed him a smile.

"And hello to you, too, Jack Forester. How nice to see you again."

"You the same."

In truth, Jack had never expected to see her again. Back when Colin was dying and the scandal erupted, he'd kept an open mind and avoided the gossip. True or not, the whole thing was tragic. Despite Jack's loyalty to Dr. Gavin, he'd always suspected that at least part of Jim's antipathy toward Daphne was related to the extreme grief he felt over his son's illness, as if Daphne were somehow to blame. The times Jack had met her at the Gavins', she'd been pleasant enough, but there was something world-weary and calculating about her that prevented a sincere connection.

Distracted by his thoughts, he missed what she had just said.

"Beg your pardon?"

"I said, the last time I saw you, Jack, was at Colin's funeral."

"I'm sure you're right."

"Aren't *you* looking well."

With a nod, Jack returned the compliment. Daphne had always been a stunning woman—it wasn't hard to understand why Colin had fallen for her. She had to be in her mid-forties now, but was more attractive than ever, dressed tonight in black stiletto heels and an off-white pantsuit that did justice to her athletic figure and tan. He glanced quickly from her to Zellie, and noted the differences. What Zellie may have lacked in the glitz department, she more than made up for in something he found more interesting and yet hard to describe, something genuine and serene.

Daphne was very talkative, and was obvious by the way Zellie looked at the older woman that she liked her. As they took seats back in the alcove, Daphne went on to describe how she'd gotten into town the day before, and that she'd heard from the porter there was a writer staying at the hotel doing an article on Jim, and so she'd taken the liberty of introducing herself.

"I assumed Zellie would want to talk to his next-of-kin."

"It was kind of you to go out of your way," Zellie added.

"My pleasure, sweetheart. It's strange, but I feel like we're old friends."

"It's true," Zellie said, smiling at Jack.

"And then, I was delighted when Zellie mentioned she knew you, Jack. I'm just amazed nobody's snatched you up yet. But what's your medical opinion about Jim? I saw him a little while ago, and he looked terrible. Is the old man going to pull through?"

"All we can do is hope," he said, then added in a darker tone, "I'm having trouble getting in to see him."

"Zellie mentioned that. Why is Dr. Witner being so harsh about visitation? I don't understand."

"That's a good question. Witner did say he'd meet me at five this evening and escort me into the room, but I was tied up with something."

Daphne's expression turned worried.

"Can I tell you two something about Dr. Witner?" she said, lowering her voice.

Jack and Zellie exchanged glances.

"Please do," said Zellie.

"I have deep concerns about him caring for my father-in-law."

"You're not the only one," Zellie said.

"Oh, really?"

"Yes."

"Interesting. But for me, it's more than just his medical skills," Daphne insisted, leaning forward. "He is so incredibly ambitious, and I think he may be unscrupulous. I'd lost touch with things around here for the past couple of years, but when they called me about Jim's accident and I learned that Bryson Witner was the acting dean, I was shocked."

"You say accident, Daphne," said Zellie. "You don't think he tried to commit suicide?"

"I have serious doubts about that," she said, her voice dropping even lower. "You, too?"

"Very definitely," Zellie agreed.

"Thank God, I'm not alone, then."

Zellie looked at Jack and held his eyes for a moment, as if asking him something. Then she turned back to the other woman.

"Daphne, I think we should share some things with you."

"Zellie," Jack said, "now might not be the best time."

"Oh, please," Daphne cried. "If you've got some information about what's going on, please give it to me. I am seriously worried."

"I think it would be okay," Zellie said, glancing again at Jack. "I really do. We could use some help."

Jack thought for a moment, then decided to set his misgivings aside. He smiled at her and nodded.

For the next several minutes, Zellie outlined what they knew and what they suspected. Daphne's expression grew increasingly solemn, her face draining of color.

"Good Lord," she finally whispered. "Are you thinking of going to the police?"

"Not quite yet," Jack said. "It would be easy if we could find the letter from Dr. Zyman."

Daphne eyed both of them in turn, her gaze fierce.

"I want to help. And I think I definitely *can* help. Believe me, I am so glad you told me. But I'm afraid we'll have to save anything more for later. That young fellow coming our way is my attorney."

Jack saw a dark-haired man wearing a light-gray suit striding toward them.

"Your attorney?" said Zellie.

Daphne flushed slightly.

"It's a long story, hon, but don't worry—I'll tell him nothing of this. I promise you, I'm going to try and have another physician be assigned to care for Jim. I'll do all in my power."

"There you are," said the man, coming up next to them.

He was young—Jack guessed him to be about twenty-nine or thirty. He couldn't have been a lawyer for long. Daphne introduced him only as Mr. Mitchell, and Mitchell energetically shook their hands.

"Nice to meet you, *very* nice to meet you. Dr. Forester what kind of a doctor are you?"

"Emergency medicine."

"Awesome. You even look like George Clooney. So, do you work at New Canterbury Hospital?"

Jack nodded. There was something about the man that made him want to step back for breathing space.

"By any chance were you working in the ER when Dr. Gavin was brought in?"

"Mr. Mitchell," said Daphne sternly, "not now."

Mitchell looked at her quizzically. Daphne picked up her purse.

"Zellie and Jack, I have to go now. I'll be in touch with you tomorrow morning. Mr. Mitchell, let's leave these nice people in peace."

As he drove through snow flurries to the Bonadonnas', Jack described his meeting with Annabel Singh, and the unexplained bruises on McCarthy's shoulders. Then he told Zellie about his visit to Gavin's house, and Witner's reference letter from Harvard.

She stared at him with an astonished smile.

"Watson, I'm impressed."

"Why, thank you, Holmes, but I don't think I've got the stomach to be a professional cat burglar. I just about stroked out when the radiator came on. Bang."

"I'm sure you underestimate yourself. I wish I'd been there. You had much more fun than I did."

"No luck with that Society of Carnivals business?"

"Society Carnivalis," she corrected. "Nada. No reference to anything remotely relevant came up in all the search engines. I even called my friend at the New York Public Library. Zilch."

"Sorry you stuck out."

"So it goes. Now we know Bryson Witner has a history of mental illness. I'm not surprised. Excellent work."

"What now?"

"I think we need some more details about this mental breakdown."

"I agree, Zellie. Listen, I've stayed close with a classmate of mine from med school who works at Harvard now. I'm going to call him when I get home."

The snow was coming down thicker now, the windshield wipers slapping furiously. He leaned forward and slowed.

"I'm curious about something," he said.

"What's that?"

Jack risked a glance over at her.

"What was your sense of Daphne?"

"Well, when she first knocked on my door, it was like—who is this woman? Then, when we sat down and really started talking, I liked her. I like her a lot."

"Interesting."

"She's been through some very tough times. She's a survivor."

"She told you about Colin and all that?"

"The whole thing. She broke down. I can't even imagine what it would be like—your husband dying, being accused of betraying him, being pushed away at the final hour."

"I remember it as being very ugly. Do you think she was innocent?"

"Jack," she said, reproachfully, "I'm not sure that's even the point. Whether she did or didn't, turning her away was not right."

"I don't disagree."

"Did you know Colin well?"

"Not really. He moved in very high circles."

"Daphne told me she's forgiven her father-in-law. She understands he was acting protectively."

"I give her high marks for that."

"The only thing that surprised me was the lawyer. She hadn't said anything about that earlier. I wonder if she's planning to sue the hospital."

"Wouldn't be unlikely, I guess. An act of gross negligence occurred. Somebody's going to get a settlement."

"Does that mean you'd get sued, too?"

"Probably.'

"No wonder she didn't want her attorney hanging around you."

"If I do, believe me, I won't take it personally."

She reached over and squeezed his arm.

"In any case," she said, "we've got another ally now, and that's good."

"What's the old saying—the enemy of my enemy is my friend?"

They were getting close now, the road winding downhill. The Jaguar broke into a skid, and Jack steered out of it.

"Sorry 'bout that," he said. "This baby is a little squirrely on ice. After Thanksgiving, she goes up on blocks till spring."

"I love your little car," she said. "My only complaint is the size. I'm a little claustrophobic. I wish we could put the top down."

"Now?"

"It might be fun."

"You're right. We're dressed warm enough for how fast we're going, and the snow would go over us in the slipstream."

"I'm game if you are," she said.

Jack found a wide shoulder, pulled off, fastened down the top and handed her a blanket and a stocking cap from the boot. Then they continued the drive, both with large grins, ignoring the stares from the few cars coming up the hill, snowflakes swirling overhead.

Five minutes later, they coasted into the hamlet of Stanwick Grove. During the summer season, Stanwick Grove had a thriving cottage rental business and hosted several music festivals, but now most of the buildings were dark.

"Almost there," he said, glancing at his watch. "We're a little early. I wanted to show you something first. One of my favorite places. It's on the way."

He stopped in front of an old stone church, got out and raised the top. Then he led Zellie to the church door and retrieved a key hidden under a flat stone to the right of the threshold.

"The pastor's an old friend of the family," he explained.

The air inside was cool but comfortable. Jack flipped on a light switch.

"It's beautiful," she said. "How old?"

"A hundred and fifty years. It was the first stone structure in the region. German settlers build it."

"I'll bet the stained glass is lovely in the light," she said. "Do you go here?"

"When I was a boy I did."

"But not anymore?"

"Not often, no. Someday, if I'm around long enough, I'll probably come back."

"You sound like me," she said.

He was standing barely a hand's-breadth from her. Her eyes sparkled in the dim light.

"I like things like this," she said.

"I thought you would. But there's more, unless you're getting cold."

"No, I'm fine."

He opened a door behind the altar and turned on another light. He let her go first, and they began climbing a stairway that ran along the inside walls of the steeple.

"Something you should know about me," she said over her shoulder. "I don't like bats."

"That's okay, I don't think more than a few thousand live up here."

"Thanks. I'll pretend I didn't hear that."

The stairs ended on a wide circular platform where a ladder continued up to the bells.

"You don't expect me to go up that, do you?" she said.

"No," Jack assured her. "This is the destination."

He went to a large rectangular window and slid open the wooden shutter. The lake was visible through the falling snow, a wide swath of darkness outlined by an irregular scattering of lights.

"If it were clear, we could see all the way up to the northern outlet," he said.

Stepping close to her right side, he pointed out the lights of Deepwater Marina to the south and indicated the area of the far shore where Witner's house lay.

"The cave where Bob McCarthy died is about three miles up in that direction, north of Witner's place. The Bonadonnas live on this side, just around that point."

"There aren't many lights on the far side, are there?"

"No, the western shore is pretty remote."

"So, Dr. Witner likes his privacy."

"And he's got plenty of it. The Bonadonnas' is where I keep my own little sailboat," he added, changing the subject.

"Do you sail a lot?"

"Never enough. I love it."

"Jack, this really is neat."

"Zellie," he said after a moment, turning to her, "I need to tell you something."

She wasn't watching his face. He touched her shoulder and waited for her to swing toward him.

"I want to say something to you," he repeated.

She studied him. "I heard you."

"I need to tell you...I'm in love with you."

He was not at all sure what response to expect. He hadn't planned to say this when he'd stopped at the church. Or had he? His heart pulsed as her gaze broke away. Then he noticed tears forming in her eyes.

"Hey, listen," he said, suddenly awkward. "I'm sorry."

She sniffed and turned farther away.

"Don't say you're sorry," she said.

He grabbed in his pocket for a handkerchief.

"It's clean," he said. "And okay, I'm not sorry."

"Thanks," she said, taking the handkerchief. "It's not you. I have a trust problem."

"I wouldn't say it if I didn't mean it. I can't imagine hurting you."

"You say that now," she said.

"I swear on my life."

"How many women have you made this confession to?" she demanded, looking back full into his eyes.

He opened his mouth to respond, but she put finger on his lips.

"No," she whispered. "Don't answer. That's not a fair question, and I don't care anyway." She stepped close and raised her face. "Kiss me instead."

CHAPTER 29

As she searched in a drawer for a misplaced stapler, the Surgical Intensive Care Unit ward clerk recognized something that didn't belong.

"Oh, shoot," she said. "So, that's where it went."

It was a much-folded envelope addressed to Dr. Gavin. Someone had handed it to her the night he was admitted, having found it in his overcoat pocket. She'd meant to give it to the security guard along with Gavin's wallet and keys, but she'd set it aside for safekeeping and forgotten about it. It had been a crazy night.

Rather than risk misplacing it again, she popped up to the seventh floor on her next break and handed it to the nurse sitting at the desk in the hallway, explaining what had happened. The nurse told her not to worry, that she'd handle it.

During dinner, Daphne Gavin and Auren Mitchell talked about the next day's meeting at the university, but Daphne's mind was elsewhere, pondering the story Jack Forester and Zellie Andersen had shared with her. That letter from Zyman to her father-in-law had huge implications. If it still existed, it had to be found. She brushed off Mitchell's offer to go out for drinks. He was getting way too friendly, anyway.

She called a cab directly from the restaurant, leaving him high-and-dry, and went to the hospital, where she'd been given carte blanche to see the old man whenever she wanted. Striding down the seventh-floor corridor, she said hello to the nurse and was about to pass by when the young woman held up something.

"I'm afraid this got misplaced, Mrs. Gavin."

"What is it?"

"It's a letter Dr. Gavin had with him when he got hurt."

Daphne halted and stared at her.

"What did you say?"

The nurse repeated her words.

Daphne stepped up to the desk, her heart beginning to beat faster.

"Are you certain?" she said.

"Yes. The SICU clerk just brought it up. Should I have security put it with his other things?"

"For heaven's sake, no," she said. "I'm mean, I'll be glad to take it. I'm sure Dr. Gavin would want me to keep it for him. Thank you."

It was all she could do to keep from snatching it out of the woman's hand.

"Our apologies," said the nurse, passing the letter over.

"Not a problem," Daphne said, smiling. "These things happen."

She took a few steps toward Gavin's room and studied the envelope. The name on the return address was Lester Zyman, MD, PhD. The envelope had been cut open along the top edge then taped shut.

"Do you know what it's about?" she asked, glancing back at the nurse.

"What—the letter?" said the nurse. "No, of course not, Mrs. Gavin."

"I'm sorry," said Daphne. "I didn't mean to imply you were a mail snoop. It's been a long few days."

"I understand."

"Oh, by the way, any change in his condition?"

After being assured there was none, Daphne thanked her again—*If you only knew how thankful I really am*—said good evening to the hospital security guard sitting in a chair by Gavin's door, reading a magazine and trying to stay awake. The guard returned her greeting, and she entered the room.

The light was dim, and the acrid-sweet smell of a sickroom made her throat tighten. It was exactly how Colin's room had smelled when he could barely lift his hand off the sheet anymore.

She went to the bedside and stared down at the father of her dead husband, so very close to death himself; it was the first time she'd laid eyes on him in three years. The change was shocking. He had lost weight, was almost skeletal, the outline of his skull visible, and something uncomfortable stirred in her. He looked more than ever like his son.

She spun away, draped her coat over a chair and switched on the overhead lights. Using her long fingernail, she peeled away the tape and yanked the letter out.

"My God," she whispered, her heart pounding.

There was no question this would get the police interested. It was the smoking gun. Zyman had seen Witner and Hinkle together the day before McCarthy died, and he speculated how and why Hinkle might have caused McCarthy's death. He also suspected that Witner was planning something for him. He had seen Hinkle lurking near his home that morning.

She heard footsteps approaching the door, followed by the security guard's voice. She didn't have time to put the letter back in the envelope, so she crumpled them together and tucked them between her breasts just as the latch clicked and the door swung open.

Bryson Witner closed the door solidly behind him.

"Hello, Daphne," he said.

"May I flatter myself and think you're here early because you couldn't wait to see me? Or is it just your compulsive nature."

"Maybe a little of both," he said, approaching.

She closed the distance, took his head with both hands and kissed him, hard. They stood glued together for a long moment.

"You don't know lonely I've been, Bryson," she said. "I hope you're not still angry with me for coming like this."

He stepped back to arm's-length.

"I don't like surprises, Daphne. You should know that by now."

"Oh, Bryson, you just would have told me to stay away," she said with a pout. "Like you always do.

"Maybe not."

"We've been extremely careful. We deserve some time together."

"And will have it. But you must be patient."

"I *have* been patient. I called you the minute the plane landed."

"In any case, I think this is going to work out for the best. Do you have any news for me. Did you approach the Andersen woman at the hotel like I suggested?"

"Of course, I did, for God's sake. Do you take me for a bimbo?"

"What did you find out?"

"I talked with both with her and Jack Forester. At length."

"Well?"

"Well, you'd better thank your lucky stars I came."

"We're running out of time."

"Don't give me that look, Bryson."

"Please, my love. Share it now."

She leveled a stare at him, her face turning grave.

"You were absolutely right to be concerned, Bryson. They are putting things together."

"I want to know every detail."

Her words tumbled out as she gave him every word of the conversation. His face grew tight and pale.

"How the devil did they connect me with Hinkle?"

"I'm not sure. But it doesn't matter how. The fact is, they did."

"Of course, it matters how."

"This is not good, Bryson."

"Be quiet, I'm thinking."

"Thinking what? Don't shut me out."

Witner went on rubbing his chin, staring at the corner of the room.

"Say something," she insisted, rubbing his shoulder.

He looked at her, distractedly at first. Then his eyes relaxed, and something approaching a smile came to his mouth. He reached up and traced the outline of her face with his finger.

"Daphne. You are among the..." He paused, as if searching for the right adjective. "Among the most competent people I've ever known."

She grimaced.

"For God's sake, is that the best you can do?"

He smiled, almost teasingly.

"And wonderful and resourceful," he added. "And beautiful." He pulled her close and kissed her.

"That's better, Bryson. Much better."

"The end is in sight," he said, breaking away and pecking her forehead.

"I hope so. This hasn't been easy. All these damn games."

"But how well you've worked behind the scenes, Daphne. The *Medical Media* program would have been impossible without your help. I only wish I could have acknowledged you. But...in time."

"I can deal with delayed gratification, for God's sake, but things are getting very tight for me financially. I know you don't like to talk about it, but that's one of the reasons I did this. Along with seeing you, of course. I just hate asking you for money, but my attorney says, given what happened here, the obvious mistake and all, I just have to hold out my hand."

"And I'm sure he's right in that regard."

"I hate sponging off you like some mistress. This was a clever and thrifty way of getting to see you, so please don't be angry with me. Look how much I've helped already." She kissed him again. "Now, after you become the dean and I'm your wife, buster, watch out," she added. "You'll need to hide the checkbook. You're not jealous of my young lawyer, are you?"

He brushed off the flirtation.

"Daphne, don't get careless. We cannot take the slightest chance of being revealed."

"I've saved the best for last, Bryson," she said, nuzzling his cheek. "I've got a little present for you."

"Daphne, this isn't the time or place for fooling around."

"No, not that, silly. This." She pulled the letter from her cleavage and waved it in his face. "This is the letter Jack Forester was looking for, Bryson. He was right. The old man had it on him when he bit the dust. The nurse out front just handed it to me. They mislaid it when he was admitted."

"Are you serious?"

"You'd better read it."

"Has anyone else opened this?" he demanded when he'd finished, glaring at her.

"Don't be crazy. If anyone read it, do you think they'd have simply turned it over to me? Of course not, Bryson."

"No, you're right." He shook his head and his face relaxed, a smile returning. "You are a clever creature. We are following a path laid out in advance. We cannot fail."

"Bryson, do us both a favor, and keep those predestination ideas to yourself. It creeps me out when you talk like that. You've been taking your medications?"

"Of course." He strode into the bathroom, and she heard the sound of paper ripping and the toilet flushing.

When he returned, he put his hands on her shoulders and gazed into her eyes.

"You say they are putting the details together?"

"They are. But without the letter, I don't see what more they can do."

"Nonetheless, Daphne, I believe I'm going to need Hinkle's help again."

She sighed and turned away.

"Bryson, I don't like that man. I don't trust him."

"You trust me, don't you?"

She looked back up at him.

"Not completely, but enough. Hinkle is the only one who can implicate us."

Witner's eyebrows arched, and he crooked one corner of his mouth.

"Actually, he's not the only one now who knows everything."

"What are you talking about?"

He nodded in the direction of the bed.

"Your father-in-law knows," he said.

"How? He's in a coma."

"No, he just appears to be in a coma, Daphne. He is under the influence of two medications—a sedative and a paralytic agent. Otherwise, he's recovering quite well. You see, toward the end of a dosing cycle of the sedative, such as right now, he's capable of sensing the outside world, though thanks to the paralytic, which is longer-acting, he can't move a muscle. It's possible he's overheard this conversation."

She frowned and stepped away.

"You mean you're keeping him alive, but out of it?"

He nodded.

"Bryson, that's not funny. Why don't you just put him out of his misery?"

"The time's not right, Daphne. But I do need to medicate him now."

He removed two syringes from the pocket of his lab coat. Ripping open an alcohol swab, he cleaned the IV injection port and injected the contents of each.

"Bryson, this is not only weird it's risky. Seriously, why don't you just finish him off?"

"Because, obviously, I've got a reputation to protect. I can't have my star patient die this soon after I've assumed his care."

Chapter 30

Fred Hinkle drove up an old timber road out of sight of the main highway, then killed the lights, drove a little farther and shut off the engine. Before getting out, he rolled down the window and smoked a cigarette. The occasional hiss of cars passing on the highway was muffled by the trees and the snow that continued to fall. It was almost midnight. He thought of the warm bed where he'd left Martine, and he flicked the butt out into the snow and opened his pack.

Having no specific plan, he'd stuffed it with everything—knife, pistol, pepper spray, rope, flashlight, tool kit, garrote, duct tape, matches, hatchet. At the last moment, he'd even stuck some C4 into a plastic sandwich bag and put it in one of Martine's Tupperware containers, along with a blasting cap, wire and timer. But after driving around for the past hour, thinking hard as he reconnoitered, a good scenario had finally materialized. He knew the way forward now. It was almost certain to work, and would be fairly easy to accomplish.

He had to hike nearly two miles up the narrow road until he reached a point from which he could see Forester's house. It was still snowing, and that was good. His tracks would be covered. On the way back, though, it would be safer to return through the woods and avoid the road entirely.

Breathing heavily, he gazed at the house and calculated the distance between it and the garage. There was a barn out back, but the driveway led to the garage. That's where the vehicles had to be.

Everything was dark. Very dark. That was good. Now, a little break before the assault.

He stepped from the shoulder well back into the trees. Reaching around to the pack, he removed a handful of M&Ms from a side pocket. He popped them into his mouth. Then he lit a cigarette.

If life were fair, and he could do as he pleased, he'd far rather be targeting Witner. The more Witner got his hooks into him, the more he realized the man was a genuine maniac. If anything, Hinkle had a soft spot for Jack Forester, a guy who had gone out of his way to help Katrina. But, at least for now, he couldn't cross Witner and hope to survive. There was no other choice, and there was also no doubt that someday Witner would get what he deserved. In the meantime, life just wasn't fair.

He'd been tempted to invite Witner along this evening, just to fuck with him, but in truth, he'd much rather be working alone. And he much preferred to do the planning himself. Granted, the Gavin hit could have come off better, but few missions went as smoothly as the first one—Dr. McCarthy. Witner, discovering McCarthy was an avid underwater cave diver, had steered him Hinkle's way; but the idea to trap him in a cave had been one hundred-percent Hinkle's, and it had gone off without a hitch.

They'd made the descent, and Hinkle led him to the cave, telling him to check it out first. After McCarthy went in, Hinkle wedged four beam jacks he'd planted behind a boulder into the rock at the entrance, and there was no way anyone larger than a muskrat was getting out. All he had to do was wait until McCarthy's air ran out and dispose of the jacks. Clean as could be.

But he'd taken no pleasure in it. It would have been a shitty way to go—trying to squeeze though the bars and seeing the light bouncing off the surface only seventy-five feet up. McCarthy might even have been able to see the bottom of the boat where his wife and son were waiting for him. How could you not feel sorry for the poor son of a bitch? It was one thing shooting someone who was trying to kill you, but there was no satisfaction in this sort of thing.

And Witner—where had he been? Sitting in his office safe as a bug in a rug, just like he was probably snoring in the sack right now.

Hinkle shook off thoughts of McCarthy and Witner and went back to this evening's task. He'd gone through a hell of a lot of options, but most of them were lousy. Forester was too young for a heart attack, like they'd staged with Zyman, and there had already been too many suicides. It was going to have to be an accident, and after weighing many possibilities, he'd settled on good old-fashioned brake failure.

During his trek up the hill, he'd confirmed the road made a ninety-degree turn shortly before intersecting the main highway and that, above the turn, was a steep, straight stretch of road a tenth of a mile long. A vehicle coming down that stretch without the benefit of brakes would hit the curve doing sixty or better. At that speed, there'd be no way to negotiate the bend, especially if the road were wet or icy, as would be the case tomorrow morning. It would sail through the rail and plummet fifty feet down into a streambed strewn with boulders. If Forester tried to pull off onto the shoulder, the ditch was deep and rocky; the vehicle would be very hard to control. It would roll and slam into the woods.

Either way, Hinkle would be waiting in the trees with a blunt object to perform a coup de grace if needed.

He stubbed the cigarette against a tree and tore the butt into filaments of paper and filter. Then, making his final approach through the trees, he inched forward, keeping the garage between him and the house, all senses alert. The side entrance to the garage was on the wall facing the house. It was unlocked.

He closed the door and flicked on his penlight. There were two vehicles—the Jaguar, the one Forester'd driven to the marina, and an old Ford pickup. Given the snow, Forester would probably opt for the truck. Poking around the underside of an F-150 was like playing in his own back yard. Nonetheless, he needed to make sure Forester would take it.

Using a rubber mallet padded with a rag, he drove a couple of roofing nails into the left front tire on the Jag. He unscrewed the valve stem then, when the hissing stopped, screwed it back in. He did the same to the left rear tire. The Jag was going nowhere, which was good. Forester had done a decent job restoring it.

That done, he slipped underneath the Ford, dragging the pack next to him. The trick would be to leave enough pressure in the system so the brakes would feel reasonably normal for a few minutes. Not hard to do at all. Taking a set of vise grips and a rag to pad the fitting and prevent the appearance of fresh marks, he stuck the penlight between his teeth.

He was poised to grab the fitting with the pliers when he heard movement. He doused the light and listened. Shit. The damn door was opening. As quietly as possible, he reached into the bag and pulled out the nine-millimeter, simultaneously tucking his legs under the truck so he was completely hidden.

The garage light came on, and he heard footfalls on the cement. *Witner, I wish you were here to enjoy this.*

The Jaguar was between him and the intruder. From his vantage under the truck, however, Hinkle could see the intruder's boots on the far side of the Jag. They were old and mud-caked, and the pant legs were ragged and filthy. Was this the brother? Probably so.

Though he tried to muffle it with his palm, the click made by the nine-millimeter's safety was loud. Crap. He hadn't oiled it in months. The boots stopped shuffling. Then they turned and began coming around the front of the Jag toward the pickup.

But wait. If he could just incapacitate him, all might not be lost, and he might still salvage the mission. Or at least there wouldn't be a murder investigation to make future missions more difficult. Hinkle set down the pistol and got out the can of pepper spray. Just let the bastard get his face down here. One good long spritz, and he'll be outside rolling in the snow.

The boots stopped no more than three feet away. He watched as a pair of knees eased down onto the floor. Hinkle extended his hand, finger poised on the button.

Come on, let me see your face.

There it was—a beard and long hair. The brother. Hinkle pressed the button but nothing happened. The canister was dead. Dammit. He grabbed the pistol and saw the brother start back and dart away so fast he didn't have a chance to aim.

Cursing, he stuffed the pepper spray can and tools into the pack, rolled out and jumped to his feet, gun extended in one hand, pack in the other. The damned brother was nowhere to be seen, and the door was open. The mission was blown. His only priority now was getting the hell out.

Hinkle hit the door running and had almost made the tree line when he felt something hit the back of his left thigh, followed by searing pain. He hadn't heard a shot, but obviously he'd been hit. It didn't slow him, so it couldn't be that bad.

He reached the edge of the woods and kept going as quickly as the darkness would allow, his hands outstretched to feel for trees, stopping every few minutes to listen for pursuit. After ten minutes, he slipped behind a huge tree and reached down to check the wound. He was startled to discover a shaft protruding from the back of his leg.

What the fuck?

It had to be an arrow. A gentle wiggle confirmed, thank God, that it was not lodged firmly. It was just in muscle, not bone, the penetration depth probably about two inches, the best he could tell. The weirdness of it almost made him laugh out loud.

Unbelievable. That son of a bitch can shoot, or he was awful lucky.

He removed his right glove with his teeth, took a deep breath and, at the count of three, jerked the shaft rearward. The arrow came free with an explosion of pain. It was a hunting broad tip. Jesus Christ.

Head spinning, he sank down and concentrated on breathing as quietly as possible while he sliced a rag into strips with his knife and bound the wound tightly until the bleeding stopped, all the while listening.

Nothing but the hiss of snow on branches and dead leaves.

He rose unsteadily to his feet, the arrow gripped in his hand. The mission may have failed, but he sure as hell wasn't going to leave them a source of DNA.

CHAPTER 31

Jack met Zellie in the hotel restaurant. The previous night, when they'd driven home from the Bonadonnas', she'd gone quiet. By the time they said goodnight, with just a perfunctory kiss at the elevator this time, she seemed to be avoiding his eyes. Though she smiled this morning as he approached, he could sense she was still reserved.

"Morning," he said, beaming her a smile and sitting.

"I ordered you some coffee," she said, leaning back in her chair.

Jack was certain it had nothing to do with the evening they'd spent with Tim and Sonia's. She had obviously enjoyed their company, talking as much as anyone, laughing and telling stories.

"Coffee," he said gratefully. "You're a genius. Thank you."

No, her reserve had to be related to that long kiss in the steeple, the kiss he had been re-imagining almost continuously since it had taken place.

"Sleep well?" he asked her.

"So-so. How about you?"

"Like a log." It was only partly a lie. He'd tossed fitfully for an hour or so before sleep finally hit him.

That had to be it. The steeple. She was being cautious.

The waitress came up.

"My Lord, can you believe this weather?" she said. "So much for global warming. What can I get you two this morning?"

She didn't want to leap into a relationship with someone she'd only known a few days.

"An English muffin for me," Zellie said. "And a glass of grapefruit juice. You wouldn't happen to have to have any grits, would you?"

Caution was something he could understand and respect. It would be like her.

"Darlin', I'm not even sure what grits are. Pink or regular?"

She was smart. He wanted to reassure her it was alright.

"Pink or regular?" Zellie repeated.

"The grapefruit."

"Ah—pink, please."

She could set her own pace, and he would wait for her until hell froze over.

"And you, sir?"

The question was how to tell her without sounding aggressive and driving her further away.

"Let's see," Jack said, scanning the menu. "I think I'll go for the the Lumberjack Special with bacon and home fries, please. And orange juice."

"You got it. Over easy for the eggs?"

"Yes, thank you."

"Maple syrup?"

"Sure."

Jack handed over the menu and saw Zellie watching him, her eyes glowing with amusement.

"What are you smiling at?" he said.

"Picturing you as a lumberjack. You look preoccupied this morning."

"Can't imagine why."

Her hand strayed over to rest on his, causing Jack's heart to suddenly roil with confusion and happiness. He wanted to lift it to his mouth and kiss it, but he checked himself.

"How's Dr. Gavin doing this morning, by the way?" she said.

"Dr. Gavin? Oh, he was status quo when I called."

"I guess that's better than worse."

"Listen, Zellie, I was able to reach George Spengler in Boston this morning."

"Great. Can he help?"

"He thinks so, and he really wants to. George was very close to Dr. Gavin, too."

"How much did you tell him?"

"Not much, at this point. That I needed to see Bryson Witner's Harvard personnel file because of some strange behavior cropping up here. George said he knows somebody in the right place. I think we're in luck."

"Excellent, Jack. When will he call back?"

"As it happens, Sherlock, he's invited us to Boston today."

Her hand slid off his.

"Us?"

"You think I wouldn't tell him about my partner in crime?"

"But...today?"

"Did you have something else going on?"

"I don't know, Jack. What is it—a four-hour drive?"

"Closer to five, but I promise you'll love them. Leah's a cellist, and they have a four-year-old daughter."

"It's tempting," she admitted, stirring her coffee.

"But...?"

"I don't know, Jack, it's..." Her voice trailed off, and she gazed out the window.

"Let me guess. You're thinking this is too much, too fast."

"What—you mean with you and me?"

He looked around in mock surprise. "Is there anyone else here?"

"Don't tease. I'd just hate to barge in on your friends."

"You can be honest."

"Okay, I feel a little upside-down—I don't know. I'd like some time to think. And I've got a lot of writing to get caught up on. I've been slacking off terribly. I have a lazy streak a mile wide, and you've been enabling it."

Jack smiled and shook his head.

"You can write in the car."

"I really don't feel like going. If you think you need to, it's alright. When will you be back?"

"Tomorrow. It'll just be overnight."

"Then I'll see you tomorrow. Are you afraid I might run away or something?"

As the waitress came and set down their plates, Jack thought about that comment. There was some truth in it. He *was* half-afraid this whole thing would turn out to be an illusion, that she'd suddenly vanish from his life. His heart clenched at the thought. But that wasn't the only reason.

"Freshen your coffee?"

"Please," Jack said. When she'd left, he leaned forward. "Listen, I've got to tell you something, Zellie. The Jag had two flats this morning. There were nails in the tires, and the side door to the garage was wide open. What really got my attention was Tony. He looked upset, and he followed me around like a puppy before I left. I couldn't get him to talk to me. This is very weird."

"You think somebody broke in?"

"This is the first time I've had any problems like this."

"You didn't hear anything?"

"No, but Arbus is the opposite of a watchdog."

"Jack, you should call the police."

"I haven't yet. It won't do any good, but I will."

"Don't be like that."

"Zellie, I don't like the thought of you staying here alone."

She frowned, grabbed up a muffin half and began spreading jam.

"You should know something," she said, glancing up at him. "Just because we shared a kiss doesn't mean you need to start hovering over me like my lord protector."

He sat up straighter.

"I know that."

"I really can take care of myself."

"I wasn't suggesting you can't, Zellie."

She dropped her muffin and took his hand again.

"Oh, Jack, I've hurt your feelings. I didn't mean to. I appreciate your concern."

"No, no, I understand."

"Do you?"

"I do. I'll just stay here."

She let go of his hand and went back to her breakfast.

"No, Jack, you go. I mean it. I've got things to do."

"I can just as easily do it over the phone. George won't mind."

"Jack, obviously, you thought it was important to see him personally."

"Well, it might help."

"Then do it, Watson. I'll be fine."

"But..."

"You'll be back tomorrow?"

"Definitely."

"When?"

"I'll leave at noon, be here by five."

"Then, if you like, we can go out to your place when you get back, and I'll cook dinner this time. What do you say?"

Jack stared at her.

"Okay. I'll shovel off the grill."

"You're very funny. Just do me a favor."

"Which is?"

"Don't stay away too long."

She said that with a sincere smile, and he felt her reserve drop away. This time he obeyed the impulse, lifted her hand and gave it a kiss.

After Jack left, Zellie stayed in the restaurant to have another coffee and write in her journal. He hadn't been gone five minutes when Daphne Gavin marched up.

"There you are," she said. "Mind if I join you?"

Zellie closed the notebook and smiled.

"Please. I was just thinking of you. I was going to call you in a little while."

"I'm going out, so I'm glad I caught you." Daphne glanced down at the egg-stained plate across from Zellie. "Is Jack here?"

"We just had breakfast, but he had to leave."

"I see. He's such a lovely man."

"I think so, too."

Daphne gave her a conspiratorial grin.

"I'm sorry I missed him. But let me catch you up on what's going on. Unfortunately, I haven't had any luck getting my father-in-law assigned to a new doctor yet, but I'm working on it. The most exciting thing is that I talked with an old friend of mine who lives not far from Dr. Witner. She used to be an obstetrics nurse. She told me she's seen some strange things going on at his place."

Zellie pulse increased.

"Like what?"

"Things like that Mr. Fred Hinkle has been visiting Witner a lot recently. And I mean *a lot*. She and I only talked for a few minutes, Zellie, but she's invited all of us out to her house tonight. You and me and Jack."

"Darn it. I'm afraid tonight won't work, Daphne."

"Why not? This could be very important."

"Jack's driving to Boston."

"Boston?"

Zellie looked around, then leaned closer.

"Jack discovered something else about Dr. Witner yesterday."

"For God's sake, tell me."

"He found a reference letter in your father-in-law's house."

"You mean he broke in?"

"He had a key."

"That's pretty gutsy. Good for him."

Zellie went on to explain the contents of the letter, and that Jack had a friend at Harvard who could help him get more details.

"Oh, my God, Zellie," the older woman cried. "This is excellent. This is just incredible. But does he have to leave today? Can't you tell him to hold off until tomorrow?"

Zellie paused, studying the tablecloth and thinking. Why did she and Jack have to walk lockstep on this? It would be terrific to have Jack there, of course, but there was no reason she couldn't gather information while he was gone.

"Daphne, he needs to follow up on this right away. I want him to go. But there's no reason I can't go with you tonight to visit your friend. Both of us don't have to be there."

Daphne pondered.

"I think you should call him and tell him to stay."

"I really don't see why."

Daphne was silent for another moment, then shrugged and smiled.

"Okay, if that's the way it has to be," she said, patting Zellie's arm. "We should strike while the iron's hot."

"That's what I think, too."

"Then, I'll hook up with you later this afternoon, Zellie. Meanwhile, I've got to head over to the university. Mr. Mitchell and I have a little meeting with the president about my father-in-law's accident. Mitchell says he's come down with the flu, but I'm hauling him over there anyway. It's probably just a hangover. I'll call you, sweetie."

Chapter 32

It was mid-afternoon when Jack climbed the front steps of a two-story brick townhouse in Cambridge. He didn't have a chance to touch the buzzer before the door swung open and a tall man with a shock of blond hair greeted him with a hug.

He followed his old friend into the kitchen, where Spengler proceeded to brew a pot of coffee from fresh beans, pulling containers and devices out of cupboards with a dexterity that suggested why he had become one of the most productive interventional cardiologists at the city, threading catheters into a dozen hearts a day and spinning off a research paper every month or two.

As they were catching up, Leah Spengler came into the kitchen and gave Jack a kiss. A small and beautiful dark-haired woman, Leah spoke with a Ukrainian accent.

"So, where is the girlfriend George said you were going to bring with you? He said you raved."

"I said *might* be bringing with him," Spengler protested.

"Was I really raving, George?"

"For you, yes."

"She must be very special," Leah added.

"And very independent," Jack told her. "I couldn't talk her into coming today. She wanted to stay close to the situation in New Canterbury."

"Speaking of which," Spengler said, "I've got a lot to tell you, my friend."

"Listen, you two can have the solarium all to yourselves," Leah said. "I've got to get Maria up from her nap. Jack, I want you to tell me all about her over dinner."

Spengler led him to the rear of the house, where a hallway opened up into a new room with arching Plexiglas panels. Plants and orchids hung above, and the air was fresh and smelled of leaves and humus.

"Very nice," Jack said.

"Leah's idea—as are most of the good things around here. She calls it the oxygen factory." He arranged a couple of chairs so they could face each other. "Jack, I was able to find out a lot more about this Bryson Witner character, and much faster than I'd expected. I was afraid you and I would be up half the night engaged in some unorthodox file searching, but I got very lucky. I probably could have given you all this on the phone and saved you the trip."

Jack felt a pang when he heard this. He hadn't been able to shake off a sense of foreboding, mainly about Zellie staying back in New Canterbury.

"I'm glad you could visit, anyway," Spengler continued. "I was able to slip away from the cath lab this morning, and the first person I talked to was Mel Vincent, who's on the staff at McLean and knows how to access the records, and who owed me some favors. What I couldn't find out there, I was able to learn from a peek at Witner's old personnel records at Mass General."

"I won't ask how you managed to do that," Jack said.

"I'm a nice guy—that's all you need to know. In any case, here's the lowdown. First of all, Witner was a prodigy. He entered Williams College when he was fifteen and graduated summa cum laude with a double major in biochemistry and psychology and a minor in drama."

"Not bad."

"After Williams, it was Harvard Med, where he made Alpha Omega Alpha, was third in his class and got a paper published in *Science* on nuclear magnetic resonance spectrometry before he graduated. This guy's academic record makes the rest of us look like morons. There's only one little blemish during his career as a medical student."

"What was that?"

"He killed somebody."

"Oh, really?"

"He was on the Harvard boxing club and gave one of his opponents an epidural hematoma. It must have been one hell of a punch. In any case, he wasn't charged with anything, and it didn't seem to slow him down.

"After getting his Harvard MD, he did an internal medicine residency at Hopkins, then a two-year geriatrics fellowship at Baylor, followed by a second fellowship in geriatric endocrinology at the University of Vienna. During those years, the man wrote no fewer than twenty-three papers."

"He's a machine."

"So, it's not surprising that Harvard recruited him back to join the endocrinology division. But something weird happened when he got back to Boston."

"What?"

"His academic output dried up after a year or two. He stopped writing papers. The personnel file records he was counseled about this numerous times, and about other things, too, like failing to attend committee meetings and rudeness to his supervisors. Also, he was not a popular teacher. The student evaluations I saw were pretty consistent—he was uninterested in teaching, arrogant, cold, went off on tangents."

"Sounds like he wasn't long for Harvard."

"Exactly, and on the brink of getting fired, he totally decompensated and ended up being involuntarily committed to McLean."

"I knew from the reference letter he'd spent six months there."

"I bet you didn't know that one of his patients died unexpectedly just before his breakdown."

"I don't like the sound of that."

"Criminal charges were never brought against him, but the records discuss a concern that Witner had overmedicated a man on his service. Then things get even weirder, Jack."

"Please continue."

"Witner didn't have a simple stress-related breakdown. We're talking about a major schizophrenic break—auditory hallucinations, a complex system of delusions and homicidal ideation. Second day at McLean, he assaulted a security guard with a broken bottle."

At this point, a little girl ran into the room and hopped on Spengler's lap.

"Maria, do you remember Dr. Forester? He was here at Christmastime last year."

"Hi, Dr. Forester."

"Hi, kiddo."

"Listen, Dr. Forester and I need to talk some more, sweetie. We'll all get together for supper in a little while."

After his daughter had darted back out of the solarium, Spengler continued.

"Witner's discharge summary from his stay at McLean reads like a classic study of what happens when an individual with a very powerful intellect develops paranoid schizophrenia. He had created an elaborate delusional universe with its own internal logic."

"The smarter they are, the stranger it gets."

"It revolved around the belief that most humans have been infected with a virus-like particle that incorporates them into a super-organism with a single mind."

"Like the Borg."

"Witner believed he was the select leader of a secret organization dedicated to restoring humanity."

Jack looked up from the flower he'd been staring at.

"Did the record mention what Witner called this secret organization?"

"Those guys are very thorough in their write-ups. It doesn't come right to mind, but I think it did."

"The Society Carnivalis?"

"Yes! That was it. I guess that must mean there's a chapter in New Canterbury."

Jack rose to his feet. "George, I need to make a call."

Returning from the hotel's exercise room where she'd spent half an hour on the stationary bicycle, Zellie unlocked her door and entered her room. Late-afternoon sunlight was flooding in the windows from a pale sky. Pulling the curtains, she undressed and turned on the shower. Before stepping in, she slipped off the hearing aid and set it on the sink.

Luxuriating in the warm water, she thought of what she'd accomplished that day. As it turned out, Daphne had been away most of the time, so she'd stayed in the room and written, mainly sketching out ideas for a new novel that had begun taking shape in her mind several days ago. A large part of her wished she'd gone with Jack.

But that's why she'd turned him down, wasn't it? Although this new relationship felt good—very good and very right, maybe the most right she'd ever known—she still feared it could be half-illusory. She'd wanted some time alone to let her feelings settle.

And they had. It still felt perfectly sensible and even wonderful, and she was eager to see him again.

She finally turned off the water and reached for a towel. After she hung up the towel and put the hearing aid back in, she realized the phone was ringing. It wasn't her cell, it was the hotel phone.

"I'm coming. Don't hang up." Naked, she strode to the far side of the bed and picked it up. "Hello?"

"Well, hello, there, stranger." It was Muriel Gillman. "You haven't called in almost three days, Zellie. Is everything all right?"

"All's well, Mommy."

"I've been trying to reach you by cell phone all day."

The battery's dead, and I can't find my charger, for some reason."

"Shame on you. In any case, you sound well. How's the story coming?"

"The deeper I dig, the darker it gets."

"Why? What are you turning up?"

"Maybe some serious skullduggery, Muriel. It's too early to say more."

"Oh, come on—give me some details."

"You'd think I was crazy. Not for a few days. Can you extend my deadline? We've got some more work to do."

"How long?"

"Five more days, maybe a week."

"I can do that, I think. Who's we?"

"I'm working with one of the doctors here. His name's Jack Forester."

Muriel was silent for a moment. Smiling, Zellie carried the phone to where she could view herself in the mirror.

"I see," said Muriel. "So, is he cute?"

"We've become good friends, Muriel."

"Good friends. Uh-huh. God help us. What about smart? The older I get the more I like smart. Just because he's a doctor, doesn't mean he's smart."

"Muriel, you won't believe it. He recognized me from my old jacket photo on *Burning Down the Boardwalk*. He still had a copy."

"Oh, please."

"I'm serious."

"Are you sure he wasn't putting you on?"

"Positive."

"Does he have a sense of humor? Some doctors never laugh. All they do is work. Work and die young. Of course, they're usually well-insured."

"Muriel, stop it. You'll just have to see for yourself."

"You live in New York for ten years and can't find anybody who isn't a loser, then one week in the boondocks and you meet Prince Charming. You be extremely careful—please. You wouldn't be the first clever woman to get taken for a ride on the hormone roller-coaster. The world is loaded with cads and bounders, remember that. Just pack your parachute and—"

"Cads and bounders, Muriel?" Zellie broke in, laughing. "You've been reading too much Dickens."

"But it's true, and you never know where you'll find them."

Jack stood in the Spengler's kitchen with the phone pressed against his ear. Her cell phone was going straight to voice mail, and the voice mail was full. The smell of food filled his nose. Leah was an excellent cook. He hung up and dialed the hotel number, asking the clerk to connect him with her room.

It was busy. Blast. He had to let her know about this. She should avoid going out alone and under no circumstance get close to Witner. He hung up, tried again—still busy—so he asked the desk to connect him with Daphne Gavin's room.

"Hello, Jack," she said. "Are you still in Boston?"

"How did you know I was in Boston?"

"Zellie, of course."

"Have you seen her?"

"Certainly. She went down to the exercise room a little while ago, but she and I will be going out in about an hour. Are you having any success there?"

"Yes."

"That's very good. Very good. Do you still plan on being back tomorrow afternoon?"

"Yes, but I really would like to talk to Zellie."

"You sound concerned. But, I understand. You can relax, Jack. I'll look forward to seeing you tomorrow. She's fine, and I'll pass the message to her. She'll be safe and sound. She'll be with me."

Why didn't that make him feel better?

Chapter 33

They were eating supper when Spengler got paged by the cath lab.

"Jack, I'm really sorry," he said, returning to the dining room. "They've got two acute MIs coming in. I should be back in a couple of hours."

"That usually means about five hours," Leah translated.

"No need to apologize, I understand."

"Stay up for me, okay?"

"Maria and I will keep him entertained," Leah said.

A little while later, she and Jack carried cups of coffee into the living room.

Maria came up to him. "Dr. Forester, would you like to read me a book?"

"I was hoping you'd ask."

She brought over an armload of them. Then she dragged over a little wooden rocking chair and sat down in front of him.

"You won't be able to see the pictures sitting there," he pointed out.

"It's okay—I know them all."

"I'll bet you do. Your daddy has a photographic memory, too."

"What's a phographic memory?"

Jack told her. His answer, however, led to another question, and his answer raised yet another question, and so it went for the next half-hour until they arrived at the subject of pets.

"Do you have a cat?" she asked him.

"No, but I have a very nice dog."

"What's her name?"

"He's a boy, and his name is Arbus."

"Arbus? Why is that his name?"

"I'll explain, but you'll have to promise not to ask any questions until I'm done telling you, okay?"

"Okay."

"Well, I got Arbus when he was just a puppy, and I thought of all sorts of names. I thought of calling him Bill, or Bentley, or even Baxter."

"And Red?"

"Yes, Red, too," he agreed.

"Rodney?"

"No, not that one. I just couldn't seem to find the right name. So, for many days, I just called him *boy*. Then one day, I woke up and saw him sitting next to the bed, and without thinking, I said, 'Hello, Arbus.' As soon as I said it, he lifted his head and tilted it, like this, and he smiled. So, there it was. It was like he'd been waiting for me to figure it out."

"He knew all along."

"Now," Jack said, looking at his watch, "which book would you like?"

"I think I want watch a movie now."

"Me, too."

"*Snow White* or *Shrek*? I like *Snow White*, but Mommy doesn't."

"Why's that?" Jack asked. He glanced at Leah, who was smiling and shaking her head.

"Because," the little girl recited, "it shows a woman keeping house for seven little men who are old enough to take care of themselves."

"Maria," cautioned Leah.

"I see," said Jack. "Your mom's got a point."

Maria opened a cabinet under the TV set, inserted a DVD and pulled her chair up next to Jack's.

"But the dwarfs aren't mean or anything," she added. "They don't know any better, right?"

As the movie went on, she provided him with scene-by-scene narration.

"This is where Snow White does something really dumb," she noted as Snow White was offered a poisoned apple by the wicked queen disguised as an old hag. "Look—she's going to take it. I'd never do that. You wouldn't, would you, Mommy?"

Sunk deep in a magic sleep, Snow White lay on a table in a drug-induced coma, surrounded by seven tearful little woman-exploiters. A tingle went over Jack's scalp. An image of Jim Gavin lying in the hospital floated through his mind. A drug-induced coma? Could it be? He rose to his feet.

"What's the matter?" asked Leah.

"I don't know for certain, but a friend of mine may be in more trouble than I thought. Leah, I'd better head home. Please tell George I'll call him."

Zellie couldn't put a finger on it as she and Daphne drove westward away from New Canterbury, following the same road she and Jack had taken the evening before. Something was different about Daphne tonight. She seemed nervous and kept glancing at the rearview mirror even though the road was nearly deserted.

Zellie cleared her throat.

"So, how did your meeting at the university go, Daphne?"

"Not very productive."

"How so?"

By concentrating on Daphne's lips and turning so her right ear was in play, Zellie could manage to make out her response fairly well.

"Well, Zellie, it's not easy to have a meeting when my legal counsel grabs his stomach, vomits and faints on the floor."

"Oh, no. So, he really did have the flu?"

Daphne didn't answer for a moment, a bored expression on her face. She concentrated on the road.

"Is he alright?" Zellie prompted.

"Oh, I think he'll be fine. Debussy wanted to send him over to the emergency room, but Auren pulled himself together and went back to the hotel. He looked like death warmed over."

"I hope he does okay."

Daphne muttered something she couldn't make out, and Zellie decided it wasn't worth pursuing.

"So, where, exactly, does your friend live, Daphne?"

"Not too far now. What's the matter?"

"Nothing. Just curious."

"I don't know about you, but I'm starving," Daphne added in a lighter tone.

The night was clear and stars were out, but there was no moon. They passed over a small bridge, and a bright light came into view. It was a single mercury-vapor floodlamp in front of a building on the lake side of the road. A sign said *Deepwater Marina*, and she saw the name Hinkle below it. A shiver played between her shoulder blades.

After the marina, the road curved to the right and veered northwards up the western shore of the lake. They passed a dozen or so houses, most of them dark. After that, they entered an area of woods, and the road began climbing away from the water.

In a few minutes, they were on the top of a ridge, and Zellie could see a cluster of lights on the far side of the lake. Her sense of geography was good, and she judged correctly those lights were the town of Stanwick Grove. She thought of last night in the church tower, and a warm, pleasant sensation washed over her. She wondered what he was doing now.

Then they were back in trees.

"Your friend must like her privacy as much as Bryson Witner."

"Don't we all?" Daphne said.

Zellie felt her brake the car. A black mailbox with phosphorescent numbers flashed briefly in the headlights.

"And here we are," Daphne announced. She swung the wheel hard and turned rather fast into a gravel driveway, and they descended in switchbacks down toward the water. She seemed to know the way well.

Finally, Zellie could see the silhouette of a large house growing more distinct though the trees. It was two-and-a-half stories, and sheathed in gray wooden shingles, the roof broken by four large gables, with an attached garage. Light poured from the first-floor windows. It was a lovely place.

The driveway had a turnaround that curved by a screened front porch on the uphill side, The lake was invisible somewhere to the rear of place, but it couldn't be far away. Daphne stopped in front of the porch and turned off the engine.

"There," she said. "I can almost smell supper."

Zellie opened the door and stepped out. Gravel crunched under her shoes, and the air was colder than she'd expected, chillier than back in town. She looked up and saw stars twinkling through pine boughs.

"After you," Daphne said.

Zellie went up the steps and opened the door to the porch. She stepped in and Daphne followed her. The door clapped shut behind them.

"Hello!" Daphne yelled. "It's us."

Zellie went to the heavy-looking main door and knocked.

"It's okay," Daphne said. "They know it's me."

Zellie hesitated, so Daphne opened the door and ushered her in. They were now in a large foyer. Off to the right was a living room with an oriental carpet. A kitchen lay at the far end of the hallway, and to the right rose a broad staircase with an oak bannister. It reminded her of a bed-and-breakfast one might find in the Smoky Mountains, the kind she could imagine her and Jack staying in someday.

Did I really just think that?

Something struck her as strange, but it took her a few seconds to realize there was no smell of food cooking. Instead, she became aware of a faint animal smell that was vaguely feline but sharper, and not particularly pleasant. She turned to Daphne, who was unbuttoning her coat.

"Where are they?"

Daphne laughed. "My guess would be down in the wine cellar arguing about the right bottle. Either that, or they're upstairs making whoopee."

"What?"

"Oh, don't act like a prude. Here, let me take your coat."

Then Zellie saw a small animal crouched halfway up the stairs, and a shock went through her. Its two inky black eyes were glued to her. Weasel, she thought. No, it's a ferret.

The creature turned and darted up the stairs with a strangely repulsive, undulating movement. Now she understood the smell.

"Daphne," she said, "did you see that thing?"

There was movement in the semi-darkened room on her left. A man was approaching them from the shadows.

"Welcome, Ms. Andersen," Bryson Witner said as he stepped into the light. "I was beginning to think you'd gotten lost."

Zellie's breath froze. She stepped back. She turned to Daphne, but Daphne didn't look at all surprised. She was smiling.

How could she had been so stupid? This had all been a game. All of it. The woman *was* an actress.

Daphne removed a pistol from her purse and leveled it at Zellie's chest. Zellie could only shake her head in numb disbelief as Witner grabbed her arms and yanked them behind her back. Cold metal snapped shut around her wrists.

Chapter 34

Jack sped westward on I-90, his foot hard on the pickup's accelerator pedal, his thoughts unsettled and growing more so. Facts swirled though his mind—the way Gavin had been moved to a private suite, Witner his attending; the rigid visitation rules, the realization Witner may have kept a patient comatose with medications.

There was only one way to find out. He had to get home. Above everything else, he couldn't shake the sense Zellie was in danger. Something wasn't right. He was certain of it. Why had she been so stubborn about coming? He should have pressed the issue harder.

The lights of Boston faded behind him but not fast enough. He really did need to get a real car one of these days. He passed through Wooster, then Springfield and finally approached the New York state line. It was eleven p.m., and he still had more than half the way to go.

He pulled into a truck stop for gas. The lot was crowded with idling tractor-trailers. As he stood filling the tank, their rumble sounded like vast subterranean machinery. He dashed inside to grab a cup of coffee, and called the Seneca Hotel and asked for Zellie's room again.

He wanted nothing more in the world than to hear her voice. He had the clerk try Daphne's room, but still nothing. Might the two of them be down in the bar having drinks or a late dinner or something? The waitress handed him the coffee, and he paid while a country singer crooned in the background that when he'd come back home all he'd found was a little note on the fridge.

As he jogged back to the truck, he called the front desk again and asked the clerk to check the bar. She was reluctant but agreed, and came up empty-handed, though he wondered how aggressively she'd looked.

A few minutes later, he crossed the border into New York, and soon after that he turned off the interstate. The rest of the way to New Canterbury was on two-lane roads, through one small town after another, with long stretches of dark countryside in between.

Zellie lay alone on a bed in darkness leavened only by the green glow of an alarm clock on a dresser. Before leaving her, Witner had moved the handcuffs to the front so she could lie on her back but had added shackles around her ankles.

I'm going to die.

Images of her loved ones flashed through her mind in a self-torture she had no control over, and she wept. The thought of Jack Forester and the love they had possibly just discovered made it worse, mocking her with a promise of happiness.

But as the hours passed and nothing happened, the aching terror abated, and her eyes dried. She listened...and thought.

She didn't know exactly what their plans were. Could this all be a mistake? Could it be that Witner was not what he seemed—that this was being done somehow for her protection? No, that was insane. All she had to do was feel the weight and coldness of her bonds. This could not end well. *But don't give up yet.*

How could she have trusted Daphne Gavin? Why had her powers of perception deserted her so thoroughly? For some reason, it had always been that way with women. Her heart swelled with anger at the betrayal, at her own gullibility. She raised her head and looked at the clock. Eleven p.m.

Not long afterwards, she heard a creaking sound—they had left her hearing aid in. The room flooded with light, and dread washed over her. Somebody was approaching. Daphne came into her field of vision, wearing a purple bathrobe.

"Time to get up," she ordered.

Zellie wasn't sure she could control her voice. She made no reply, didn't move.

"Come on, just swing your legs off and stand up. We're just going out to the next room to talk. Listen—don't make me have to go get him, all right? You can still walk with the chains on, so let's go."

Zellie shook her head.

"It's your own fault. No one invited you to meddle. I suggest you make it easy on yourself. I don't have anything personal against you."

She grabbed Zellie's arm and pulled her into a sitting position, then helped her to her feet. Without thinking, Zellie laced her fingers together into a two-handed fist and propelled it straight into the other woman's face. As Daphne screamed and stumbled, Zellie tried to make the door, but the chains tripped her and she sprawled headfirst, the odor of dusty carpet in her nostrils.

Witner's shoes appeared in the doorway. Out of the corner of her eye, she saw Daphne stomping toward her. Pain blossomed in her side—Daphne had kicked her.

"Stupid little whore! Look at what she did, Bryson. My nose is broken."

"Daphne, mind your temper."

"You mind your own temper," she cried. "Where's the gun? Let's just get this over with."

"I said, calm yourself."

Zellie felt another kick, but this time Daphne's toes—her feet were bare—connected with Zellie's hipbone. It hurt, but Daphne's cry of pain suggested her foot had gotten the worst of it.

"All right, now, that's enough," Witner ordered. "Stand up, Ms. Andersen. It's conversation time."

He reached under her shoulders and lifted. In a moment, she was up, swaying, facing Witner, who wore a bathrobe that matched Daphne's. Two lines of blood ran down Daphne's upper lip, and the bridge of her nose was swelling, her expression furious. Good.

Witner gripped Zellie's upper arm and forced her to hobble forward. He steered her into the dining room, where there was a long table that could have seated fifteen people.

They weren't alone.

Two men sat at the far end of the table, staring straight ahead, stiff and unmoving. Zellie blinked and swallowed. Something wasn't right. Both of them wore old-fashioned suits. One had a gray beard, and the other had muttonchop sideburns. Their skin was dull and waxy, and their hands on the table were in identical prayer-like positions.

They were mannequins.

Witner laughed as he guided her into a chair at the end of the table opposite the mannequins and forced her down. He then he pulled up a chair and sat next to her. Zellie looked around. Daphne had disappeared. Chills crawled up and down her neck.

"So, once again we sit to talk, Ms. Andersen. But I'm being rude." He motioned toward the dummies. "Allow me to introduce Dr. Benjamin Rush on the left, and across from him, the Honorable Sir William Osler. They're sound-actived."

He rapped the table with his knuckles, in a "shave and a haircut" rhythm—*ra-ta-ta ta ta*—and the mannequins' lower jaws began bobbing. A tinny-voiced cacophony broke out:

Good morning, Sir William.

Good morning, Rush, you revolutionary scoundrel.

Laughter.

Why did the egg cross the road?

Because it lost the fallopian way?

No, because it was so inclined.
Laughter.
My gallstone lies over the liver, my gallstone lies over the spleen.
"Enough, please," Daphne yelled from the kitchen.
Witner rapped the table again and the noise stopped. The weirdness of it redoubled Zellie's sense of horror.

"That's just a silly little test program, Ms. Anderson," Witner explained. "They also contain digitized recordings of medical lectures. I've always been interested in puppets, you see. The rest are down in the basement."

He laughed again, louder, a deep resonant murmuring sound that trailed off then abruptly stopped as he turned from them to her.

"You're quiet tonight, Ms. Andersen. I understand you and Dr. Forester have made some discoveries, though it's obvious you didn't see through dear Daphne. She's a very good actress, don't you agree?"

Zellie looked away.

"In any case," he continued, his voice dropping so low she could hardly hear, "it's a pity you're Infected.

She glared at him.

"What do you mean?"

"Oh, you know exactly what I mean." His voice fell even lower as he leaned toward her. "You don't have to hide it anymore. You know who I am, and you know exactly what I mean by Infected."

"I don't have any idea what you're talking about."

Daphne called from the kitchen again, "Bryson! If you're saying what I think you're saying, please stop that business," she demanded. "For the love of God, remember what we talked about."

Zellie noticed with surprise that Daphne's words made Witner sit upright and blush. She'd never seen him display anything but complete self-confidence before.

She was wondering what it meant when something brushed against her left ankle, and she started so badly it nearly toppled her chair. Witner steadied it, and seemed to recover his poise. Two ferrets darted from beneath the table, one chasing the other into the kitchen.

"Nothing to fear," he informed her. "They're pets."

A barefoot and angry-looking Daphne marched from the same room, sidestepping the animals, an ice-pack pressed to her nose and a cup of yogurt in her other hand. She came up to Witner and lifted her foot.

"I think my toe's broken, too, Bryson."

Witner touched it.

"Ouch, be careful!"

"It doesn't look fractured to me," he said. "It'll be fine. Don't be a hypochondriac."

"It hurts like Hades."

"Then take some ibuprofen—and be more careful."

She lowered her foot and sat next to him. She put down the ice pack and began spooning up the yogurt, stopping to glare at Zellie, her eyes dark with hatred.

"He's not insane," she hissed.

"Oh, really?" Zellie said, forcing her voice to be calm, looking back and forth between the two of them. "Why would I think that? Just because he tells me I'm 'infected.'"

Witner glanced at Daphne, and shrugged. "All will be fine," he said. "I know exactly what I'm doing."

Zellie looked at both of them in turn again.

"What happened when you got sick in Boston, Dr. Witner?"

"What?"

"Was Daphne with you then? Does she know all about it?"

Witner leaned closer, so close she felt his breath. She closed her eyes.

"I was not sick," he growled. "Daphne understands. No one else but her."

"Bryson, for God's sake, don't let her get under your skin," Daphne scolded. "That's what she's trying to do."

"I can handle this, Daphne," he replied evenly.

"Bryson, please."

Zellie's breath was coming fast, her head feeling light.

"She's worried, isn't she, Dr. Witner. She knows how crazy you really are."

Witner fixed his eyes on her again, and leaned still closer.

"You told me I'm infected with something. You're a lunatic."

"Zellie," Daphne warned, "I'd advise you to watch what you're saying."

"Ms. Andersen, there is a purpose at work here of which you have no idea, and if you did—"

Zellie inhaled sharply and shouted. "Before long everyone's going to know what you are."

Daphne threw the yogurt cup on the table so hard it bounced over Zellie's head. She stood and leaned toward her, her face contorting.

"Shut up! You're looking at a man who's got the brains of ten thousand like Jack Forester! Neither you nor anyone else is going to push him over the edge. It's my job to keep him poised there where his energies are focused and where he will continue to do amazing things. So, shut your stupid little mouth, or I'll make sure you'll be begging for me to blow your head off before this is over."

Zellie blinked and decided to push on. She had nothing to lose.

"What's the Society Carnivalis, Dr. Witner? Everybody knows about it now."

"You want to see the Society?" Daphne answered for him, pointing at the mannequins. "If there's any Society, that's it right there."

A visible tremor passed though Witner. He half-rose, then sat back down, and appeared to relax, though he continued staring at the mannequins as if expecting them to enter the conversation. But it was Daphne who, stroking his shoulder, finally broke the silence.

"So, what's next, Bryson? It's getting late."

"I don't think Ms. Andersen has any useful information, so we're going to sedate her for the rest of the night."

"Why not just end it? I really don't like this playing around."

"Because I do not yet have a definite plan that will tie up all the loose ends. She may be useful. Forester is still out there. He'll want to find her."

"Damn it. That trip of his was bad luck."

"Everything presents an opportunity. You just have to trust me."

"So, when *are* you going to have a plan?"

"By the morning, I'm sure. Like Frederick Kekule, some of my best ideas come late at night."

"I hate it when you get esoteric on me, Bryson. What are you talking about?"

"Kekule was the father of organic chemistry, best remembered for discovering the structure of benzene. The old chemists knew it contained six carbon atoms, but its structure remained a mystery. One night Kekule dreamed of a snake biting its tail. That was it. It's a ring."

"Too much information," Daphne replied, glaring again at Zellie.

It was not exactly a sense of relief Zellie felt knowing she wouldn't die tonight. As long as there was time, something inside her wouldn't give up hope.

Chapter 35

It was still well before dawn when Jack pulled into his driveway and skidded to a stop in front of the garage, sending up a plume of slush. He'd reached New Canterbury an hour or so earlier but had gone directly to the hospital. The nurse refused to let him see Gavin, as he'd expected, but she also wouldn't let him near the medical chart—not even so much as a quick glance at the medication or the vital sign record.

He wasn't sure if he'd find anything relevant, but it was a good place to start. She was "under orders." He tried reasoning with her, at which point the hospital security guard marched over and asked what the problem was. Again it was someone he didn't know.

"Just call Tim Bonadonna, and he'll vouch for me."

"I'm not calling anybody this time of night," the guard said. "Stop harassing the nurse and move on, Doctor."

He would need to find another way. Fortunately, Tim didn't mind bending rules for a good cause.

He jumped out of the truck, his leg muscles stiff and tight. As he reached for his overnight bag from the passenger side, a piercing whistle stopped him. What the heck was that? It hit his ears again, sending a chill up his back. It came a third time, sharp and high-pitched, a single note. No bird ever made a song like that. It was coming from overhead.

Cautiously, Jack stepped away from the garage until he could see over the eaves to the roof. In the predawn darkness, he could just make out someone sitting on the peak. The sound came again, softer and now with a trill at the end. It was a pennywhistle.

"Tony?"

"It's me, Jack."

"What are you doing up there?"

Tony lifted something. It took a moment for Jack to realize it was his bow.

"Looking out," Tony said.

"What?"

"Just looking out."

Jack remembered the night before.

"Have you seen anything, Tony?"

Tony lifted the whistle to his mouth and blew a three-note minor melody.

"Alright, just watch yourself up there," Jack said. "You could break your neck if you fall. Are you warm enough?"

"Yeah."

He found Arbus lying on the kitchen floor. The dog lifted his head and yawned, making a groaning sound. Jack knelt and petted him.

"It's okay. Just me. Pissed and worried."

In his study, the answering machine's red light was blinking. It had to be from Zellie. He jabbed the listen button.

"Hi, Dr. Forester, Randy Delancy here. Hope all is well. I wanted to remind you that you're on clinical duty next Saturday, and to see if I could ask you some questions regarding the schedule for next month. So, maybe you could give me a call when you have a moment? I'll try again tomorrow."

That was it. Nothing more.

Jack started to call the Seneca Hotel, but he stopped and hung up. What was the point in waking her just to tell her he'd gotten back sooner than expected? She might not hear the phone anyway. He wasn't thinking clearly. If she answered, it would only disturb her sleep. If she didn't answer, on the other hand, it would increase his level of worry to no good end. He'd be over there in just a couple of hours to see her in person.

So, he called Tim Bonadonna instead. Tim's cell phone went directly to voice mail, so he called their land line. Tim kept odd hours and might be up.

After several rings, it went to the answering machine. The canned message was Tim mimicking the sound of a computer-generated voice: *The party or parties you are trying to reach is or are currently unavailable. Messages that do not include the caller's name, phone number, and date and will be discarded. Caveat vendor. Thank you. This is a recording.*

Jack shook his head and spoke into the receiver.

"Tim, it's me. If you can hear this, please pick up—if not, it's about four-thirty a.m., and things are reaching a critical point. I have to see Dr. Gavin's medical records, and I'm getting blocked. This is of extreme urgency. I'm going to grab a little sleep, but the phone will be right next to me. Call, amigo."

Setting his alarm for six, Jack flopped onto the bed, not bothering to undress.

CHAPTER 36

For some reason—or for no reason—they had left the window cracked open and the blinds up so that Zellie woke to the sound of wind gusting against the wooden shingles and whistling around the corners of the house.

At first her mind played tricks with her; she thought she was on a camping trip and the wind was trying to get in the tent. But when she attempted roll away from it, her wrists and ankles felt the cuffs and soon the living nightmare she was in returned full force.

They had drugged her last night. The last thing she remembered was a needle entering the fold of her left elbow. Why didn't they just kill her then? She wept as she watched the sky turn gray outside, pine boughs bending and pulsating in the wind.

Finally, the door opened. Moments later, he forced her toward a set of stairs that led to the basement. When he switched on the light, she saw how steep and long the flight of steps was, and she thought of wrenching away and diving head-first, ending it herself. Then the moment was gone, and the gesture too much against her nature in any case.

Ice filled her mind as she came to the bottom step, every cell within her crying out against the thought of being extinguished. The sole of one foot touched the cold concrete, then the other; and with his hand tight on her arm, he made her shuffle along a cleared path through the clutter, the leg shackles biting into her ankle bones with each step.

They passed the two mannequins that had sat at the table the night before, now propped on boxes near the foot of the staircase, leaning against each other mute and lifeless, their eyes seeming to follow her.

She knew it could come at any moment—a blow to the head or a wire wrapped around her neck. She tried to find some neutral object to focus her attention on, tried to empty her soul of memory and grief. She must pray and not give in to terror. It would soon be over. And maybe there was a way out.

Suddenly the pressure on her arm was gone. She gasped involuntarily, her neck tensing.

"Here we are, Ms. Andersen," he said.

Her throat too tight to form a word, she flinched as his arm moved upwards. But he only pulled on a light-string, and two long fluorescent bulbs flickered to life. Witner was still wearing his bathrobe. He cupped his hand around his mouth and shouted back toward the stairs.

"Daphne, come down. I need you."

Zellie's gaze careened around the room, bouncing off an old green overstuffed chair with badly frayed arms to a bookcase full of magazines, then a dusty cupboard, then over near the wall to a large chest freezer. The two ferrets scurried past her feet. Like sports fans trying to find a good seat, one hopped up on the old chair and the other onto the top of the freezer, where it skidded off the far end.

Trembling, she looked at Witner.

"I have to use the bathroom," she said.

"Oh, I think that can wait. Daphne, where the devil are you?"

Daphne's legs appeared on the stairway. She was still in her bathrobe and moving slowly, one step at a time. As she came toward them, Zellie saw that her face was pale, and her right hand was clutching her stomach.

"You've finished breakfast, I see," Witner said.

"I think I'm coming down with what Mitchell had. I do *not* feel well." Passing Zellie without a glance, she swatted the ferret off the chair and sank down. "I'm feeling nauseous, Bryson. Do you have any medicine upstairs?"

"A nauseous person is one who induces nausea in others, Daphne. A person who is experiencing the symptom of nausea is feeling nauseated."

"Thank you for the fucking grammar lesson. You're such a sympathetic person. So, what's the plan?"

"Everything has fallen neatly into place. We have a perfect plan"

"Bully for us," she said. "I'm getting a headache, too. Damn that lawyer. I'm going back to bed."

"Would you please let me use the bathroom?" Zellie murmured.

"*You* need the bathroom?" said Daphne. "Not before me—I feel the runs coming on."

"I'd always intended to build a lavatory down here," said Witner. "Never got around to it, though, so I'm afraid both of you are out of luck."

"Then hurry up," said Daphne. "What's your plan?"

"Simply this. When Dr. Forester returns to New Canterbury from Boston this afternoon, the hotel will have an important message for him, ostensibly from Ms. Andersen. This letter will reassure him that all is well, but that he must meet Ms. Anderson and yourself, Daphne, at Hinkle's marina this evening."

"All right. Then what?"

"Once there, the ever-impetuous Dr. Forester will make the ill-advised decision to take a boat out for a brief cruise designed to impress you two ladies. Unfortunately, he will not have reckoned upon just how foul the weather is. And, against Hinkle's advice, out you all will go."

Daphne looked up at him. "And?"

"Why, the boat will capsize, of course, and all will drown."

Zellie squeezed her eyes shut.

"Bryson?" said Daphne.

Something in the woman's voice made Zellie open her eyes and look at her.

Daphne was slouching forward, her face gray and glistening with sweat. A thick golden chain had slipped from beneath her robe and now dangled in front of her, swaying as her chest rose and fell. Without warning, her back arched, and she vomited onto her feet.

Zellie looked at Witner. He wasn't in the slightest concerned. In fact, a faint smile was playing on his lips.

"You have every right to feel ill, Daphne. You're dying."

Daphne gasped, and more vomit splattered on the concrete.

"Within several minutes, you will be dead, and the Infection you carry will be neutralized."

She looked up, eyes blinking rapidly, not comprehending.

"I might as well tell you while you can still hear me," Witner continued. "First of all, when that ridiculous plastic surgeon you married was dying, it was I who made sure your father-in-law believed you were having affairs, even though you weren't."

Daphne's head sagged, and she vomited again.

"It was an experiment at first. I was curious to see how it would affect the general situation, and I had always been interested in wearing down Dr. Gavin's ego."

Daphne's mouth opened, but she was clearly too weak to say anything.

"So, I befriended you. That was fate, Daphne. It didn't take me long to discovered your intense ambition to rise in the world, and once I realized you would stop at absolutely nothing, that you were, in essence, an amoral creature, it became obvious you would be useful. I was not mistaken. They sent you into my life for a purpose."

Daphne eye's closed.

"Behind the scenes, you helped me initiate the *Medical Media* program and last night you brought Ms. Andersen. But your usefulness to us has ended. Yes, that's right, Us. The Society and I, the Society you mock."

More vomit trickled off her chin.

"The orange juice I gave you this morning contained cyanide, which, by the way, is not checked for in routine autopsies. Your body will be dragged from the lake as a drowning victim, along with the corpses of Dr. Forester and Ms. Andersen. And Fred Hinkle, too. After your boat capsizes, he and I will attempt a rescue, but alas, the only survivor will be me."

Daphne slid from the chair, rolled onto her back and began convulsing, her legs and arms thrashing, weaker and weaker.

Witner turned to Zellie.

"Once one is Infected, Ms. Andersen, there is no cure. This is the final mercy for you all."

Daphne's body went limp; vomit filled her mouth and ran down her cheeks. But the horror wasn't over yet. Her right arm rose several inches then fell. As if making a final comment on the state of affairs, her sphincters relaxed; and from between her sprawled legs a pool of urine spread, darkening the cement as the stench of feces filled Zellie's nose.

The next moments were a blur. Witner dragged Daphne's body to the freezer. Zellie stumbled and sank to her knees, watching him open the lid. A single thought erupted in her mind—*I've got to warn Jack.*

Witner worked the limp corpse into the freezer.

"The interesting thing about the imagination, Ms. Andersen, is that I did not realize I needed to kill Daphne until this morning. But this is perfect, and the need so obvious. By midnight tonight, there will be no one left who knows the true nature of my mission. Now, in you go. I'm going to be late for rounds at the hospital."

He tried to heft her to her feet, but her legs would not cooperate. So, he dragged her. She grabbed the edge of the freezer and pushed away, but he grabbed her hair near the scalp and pulled her neck back until she could barely breathe.

She felt the cold breath of the freezer on her face and despite the pain fought to turn away. She clawed at his eyes as he lifted her inside, feeling one of her nails dig the skin of his cheek. She felt Daphne Gavin's body beneath her as the lid began closing. She screamed.

There was a soft *clunk,* and she lay in the foetid darkness with only a dead woman for company.

CHAPTER 37

Jack's eyes shot open. It was eight o'clock—he'd overslept by two hours. Jumping out of bed, he immediately called the hotel.

"Good morning. Please connect me to Zellie Andersen's room."

"Are you Dr. Forester?"

"Yes, why?"

"There's a message here for you from Ms. Andersen."

His heart surged. "Excellent! What is it?"

"It's a letter."

"Friend, I don't care whether it's a letter or a smoke signal, just read it to me."

"It says 'Personal and Confidential—for Dr. Jack Forester's eyes only.'"

"I'm Jack Forester, and I'm asking you to open it and read it, please."

"I'm going to have to ask my manager."

"You remind me of a nurse I know."

"Beg your pardon?"

"Never mind. Go ask you manager, if you have to."

"Let me put you on hold." He came back a minute or so later. "I'm sorry, sir. It has to be hand-delivered."

"Give me a break."

"Do you want to talk to the manager, sir?"

"Never mind, I'll be there in ten minutes. Put me through to Ms. Andersen's room."

He let it ring for a full minute before hanging up. Dressing quickly, he was heading for the door when the phone rang.

"Zellie?"

"Don't you wish," said Tim. "Hey, got your message. What the hell's up?"

"Dr. Gavin's medical records—I need to see his medical records, Tim. Can you get them for me?"

"Can I get you his records?"

"The nurse and the guard up there keep putting up barricades. This is essential."

"Tell you what, I'm about to enter the morning meeting. I'll arrange for myself to be assigned the Gavin security slot today. Seeing as I'm going to put my livelihood at risk for you, may I ask why you need his records?"

"Because I watched *Snow White* last night."

"Oh, well, why didn't you say that."

"Tim, there's no time to explain."

It was getting harder and harder to draw breath, and her chest felt like it was being crushed in a vise and pierced with needles. Her face had begun to tingle.

It had only been several minutes since the lid was closed; there had to be plenty of oxygen left. This must be hyperventilation. To make it go away, she held her breath. Even doing that, however, she nearly choked as her gorge rose. Fighting it, she focused on thinking of a way out of here.

When she was a child, she'd heard of kids getting locked in old refrigerators or freezers and suffocating. Once, when she was a teenager, she'd found an old abandoned fridge in a field near her house, and she had taken a rock and smashed off the latch so it would never trap anyone. It would take someone with a twisted mind like Witner to do something like replace a safety latch with an old, dangerous one.

She made her next few breaths slow and measured, and sure enough, the sense of suffocation lessened. She reached up and began examining the locking mechanism with her fingers. Thank God her hands were shackled in front rather than behind.

She felt a metal rod not much thicker than a pencil protruding down from the lid where it met the front wall of the freezer. She jiggled it and discovered a small amount of play. The sense of chest tightness was returning, and she forced her breathing to slow. *Think! And don't make any sudden movements.* Too much activity, she realized, might cause her to slip from on top of the dead woman and become wedged in beside her. The thought of that made her nearly retch again. *Stop. Think.*

She lay still for moment, letting her breathing settle. She could feel the bones of Daphne's face under her head. The cold was intense, and she began to shiver.

Examine the lock again. You've got to warn Jack. Don't give up yet.

Her fingers relocated the prong. It was cold and smooth. It had to be part of the locking mechanism, hooked into a little ridge inside the wall. If she could get her finger behind it and pull hard enough...

"I'll need to see ID first," the clerk said.

Jack glanced down at the young man's name tag.

"Listen, Jim, I was in such a hurry to get here I forgot my wallet."

"Sorry, sir, I'll need to see some identification before I can give you the letter. That's hotel policy for confidential messages."

"Yeah, but it's not like I'm a stranger or something."

"You are to me."

"Listen—" Jack began.

"*You* listen, sir. I don't make the rules. Most people I know carry IDs."

Something in Jack snapped. He grabbed the clerk's tie and yanked him halfway over the counter.

"You'd better take that smug look off your face, Jim. I haven't had all that much sleep in the last couple of days, and I'm worried about my friend. So, give me my letter or I'm going to climb in there with you."

The young man's face went white. At that moment, an Asian woman emerged from the back office and did a double-take. She marched over.

"What's the problem here?"

He released the clerk's tie.

"I'm Dr. Forester. The problem is that Jim, here, won't give me a letter that belongs to me, and this is urgent."

"Jim, why didn't you give the gentleman his letter?"

"Because it's marked confidential, and he doesn't have ID."

"I see," she said. "Good work." The woman turned icy eyes on Forester. "Sir, I cannot release the message from the safe without a copy of your ID. I'd be happy to call the police to help us straighten this out."

"Forget it. I can get some ID at the hospital. I'll be right back." He looked over at the clerk. "Sorry, kid."

Zellie couldn't get her finger behind the prong—there wasn't enough room. She needed something to work behind it. Anything. A strip of cloth would do.

She tried to tear the hem of her skirt, but her fingers slipped off and the cuffs brought her wrists up painfully short. She then attacked her blouse, but the fabric was heavy and the seams oversewn. Tears of frustration running down her cheeks and pooling in her ears, she unbuttoned it and tried shearing it with her teeth. If she could only get it started!

Frustrated she sank back. She was going to run out of oxygen. She had to think of something else.

A mental picture came to her—Daphne's necklace. Swallowing hard and steeling herself, she rolled over, working her arms around, feeling the springy give of Daphne's ribs as she moved. She must have forced gas out of the dead woman's stomach because an awful, rotten odor suddenly ravaged her nose. She gagged and turned her head away.

No! Don't vomit. You'll just make it smell worse.

She continued turning, her shivering intensifying, until finally she was facing the corpse. She felt for the necklace. It was slimy. She tugged on the chain, sliding it around Daphne's neck until she felt the clasp. Her fingers were so numb with cold she could barely feel it.

Willing all of her dexterity into the tips of her fingers, after several minutes of effort, she felt the ends of the necklace part. She pulled it carefully from around the dead woman's neck. Fighting against a renewed wave of shivering, Zellie reversed the process and was soon lying face-up again.

The work had been exhausting. Her arms and legs felt like bars of lead, and a different tightness was closing around her chest now. The air she drew in felt lifeless and stale. Taking no time to rest, she said a prayer and set to work.

It was more difficult now to find the prong because her arms felt so heavy. But she did, and managed to gradually work the chain of the necklace behind it. Though the chain was fairly thick, there was a risk the links would rupture. If it broke, there would be no other chance. What if she doubled it to made it stronger? *Yes.*

She set to work again, rethreading one end of the chain back through the narrow space behind the prong. It took four or five tries, but she succeeded.

Saying another prayer, she wrapped the loose ends around her fingers and pulled. To her astonishment, the prong immediately moved a full inch. She felt rather than heard a click, but the lid didn't rise. She released the pressure, and the prong sprang back to its original position. What was going on?

Of course—she needed to push against the lid for it to open when the prong was disengaged. She brought her knees up against the undersurface and again pulled on the necklace.

To her utter delight and relief, a crack of light appeared. It was very dim—Witner must have switched off the light. She raised her knees and a little more light appeared. But the most magical thing was the air—its sweetness and warmth. She could feel strength flowing into her muscles with each breath.

Witner had said he was leaving for the hospital, but he would have to shower and dress first. He might decide to come back to check on her. She gripped the now completely exposed prong in the fingers of her right hand and pulled the lid down so that only the slightest sliver of light remained. If only she had normal hearing.

She saw a flash of movement and felt the lid press against her hand. *Oh, please, no.* Someone was pushing it shut again! The prong started to ease back into its hole. Her fingers tightened around it.

But the pressure on the lid, for some reason, grew no heavier. She saw another flash of motion through the crack, and the pressure grew slightly heavier; but now she could hear a faint scratching on the lid.

The ferrets. They had seen the lid move and were investigating. A groan of relief escaped her, but she didn't dare relax yet. She must wait before emerging—make completely certain he had left. How long? Ten minutes? Twenty?

Holding the prong so it couldn't latch, she rested her head on her arm and endured the shivering, maintaining a crack of about a quarter-inch, just enough to let in air. She must find a telephone and reach Jack. *By now, he must know something's wrong.* He would be worried for her, she knew it, and he was in personal danger as long as Witner was out there somewhere. Then she had to get away from this place. Daphne's car keys shouldn't be hard to find. Even with the cuffs and leg shackles, she could drive.

She began counting, her body increasingly racked by shivering. When she'd reached thirty-two hundred seconds—twenty minutes—she opened the lid, grabbed the edge and raised herself just enough to peer out.

From overhead she heard, very faintly, the sound of footsteps. She was just about to duck back inside when she realized they were moving toward the front of the house. Then she heard the sound of a door shutting. If only she could hear well enough from here to know when—and if—he drove away. She would just have to rely on hope.

She counted to five hundred and sat up. Her legs were numb and all but useless at first, but she managed to maneuver them until she could perch on the rim of the freezer, How good it felt to breath clean air and feel the warmth. She didn't look back inside.

Gradually, so as not to lose her balance, she swung her legs, flexing her knees and ankles until she could feel them again, then eased to the floor, swaying, leaning back against the freezer until she felt steady enough to move.

She would have to go back upstairs, but the thought she might have misheard, that Witner could still be there, caused a wave of panic to flow through her chest. She began counting again, straining her ears to hear. She reached five hundred again—nothing.

By now, the urge to warn Jack and then flee this place forever had finally overcome her terror. Anyway, she had no choice. She would go upstairs, call Jack Forester and search for Daphne's purse. Maybe the gun was still there, too. That thought energized her.

She was hobbling toward the stairs when her eyes lit on a ball peen hammer lying on top of a cabinet. She thought crazily for a moment of using it to destroy the lock on the freezer, but...was she losing her mind? That would be noisy and pointless.

Then she noticed something else, something she'd seen earlier that morning that hadn't registered when Witner brought her down here. It was a door. What now drew her attention was that she could see light filtering though a dark-orange curtain snugged to the top half. It had a window, so the basement must be above ground level at that side of the house.

She had noticed as they'd arrived—could it only have been last evening?—that the grounds sloped sharply down to the lake. This would be the back of the house, then. It might it be another way out, and she decided to have a look.

She moved the curtain aside. A lawn outside sloped down to the water about a hundred feet away. The lake was gray, and churning with whitecaps under an overcast sky. She could just make out the far shore. A brick path led down the lawn to a little boathouse and a dock, where an old-fashioned-looking speedboat was moored. A driveway ran down toward the boathouse.

A key hung from a nail driven into the door frame. It was too small for a car key, and was attached by a beaded chain to a little red-and-white plastic float. It had to be for the boat. If she couldn't find a car key, she might be able to use this. So, there were multiple potential ways of escape, and with that realization, her confidence rose.

As she was letting the curtain close she noticed a blur of movement out the window, and her heart pounded. A car came down the driveway and eased toward the boathouse. For a moment, she fantasized that it might be Jack. It was a large black SUV, and there was lettering on the door. Straining to read, she made out the words *Deepwater Marina*.

It was Fred Hinkle.

Her mind raced, and again she willed herself not to panic. He got out of the truck and headed up the slope directly toward this part of the house. He must intend coming in this back door. She dropped the curtain and spun around. She had to hide. It was okay. He would come, he would go. She could still get out. All wasn't over. If only she had that gun. But there was no time to look now.

She remembered the hammer, and she hobbled over and grasped it by the handle. It was heavier than she'd expected. She spied a bunch of winter coats hanging from a wire beneath the staircase. She had just managed to stagger over and slide behind them when she heard the sound of someone working the doorknob—a clicking, as if he were trying keys. Trembling, she worked herself farther back into the garments and the shadows, inhaling the odor of Witner's aftershave, the same smell that permeated his office.

The door swung open. Footsteps. The door banged shut. She heard him wander around, stopping where Daphne had died and cursing. The footsteps went to the freezer. She could faintly hear the lid cracking open, then another curse.

Did he know she was supposed to be there, too?

She parted the coats just enough to see. He was closing the lid. Then he turned and sat on top of it, taking a cell phone out of his pocket and opening it. He was a short, very muscular man with short hair. He hadn't turned on the overhead light, so she couldn't make out his features.

He punched in some numbers then set the phone next to him on the freezer and folded his arms. Time passed achingly slow, during which she could hear and feel every beat of her heart. Finally, his phone rang, and he opened it.

"Witner, you said there were two in the freezer...Well, there's only one. Nice work, Dr. Death." He laughed. "Don't get angry with me, Witner. I'm just telling you what I found. You asked me to come clean up, and that's what I'm doing...How the hell should I know? She probably went out the back door. That's what I'd do. Are there any guns around here she could get her hands on?...Where is it?...Alright, I'm going to check that out...No, the other car is still here...I'll secure the gun, then I'll take a look around. I don't want anyone sneaking up on me."

He hung up.

She heard him stroll around the basement, stopping every few steps. She willed her trembling to cease and her breathing to slow as he passed by her sanctuary. In a moment, he was climbing the stairs.

Did she have enough time to make the door? She leaned out and looked, her mind spinning, trying to judge the distance. It wasn't far. It might be her only chance. But there'd be the run across the lawn, down to the lake. Maybe she could steal his truck? Or take the boat. *Don't be a coward. Do something.* If only she didn't have the shackles on.

Across from her sat the two mannequins, glaring stupidly at her, as if mocking her hesitation.

She heard his footsteps on the stairs, coming back down. She squeezed her eyes shut in an agony of self-castigation and fear. *Don't lose it. Don't lose it. Wait it out. He's going to search the basement. He'll find me.*

He'd reached the bottom of the steps, and he was definitely searching, going very slowly, stopping, moving things. She gritted her teeth and gripped the handle of the hammer. He was coming toward her hiding spot. Any fool would know to check behind the clothes. All he'd have to do was bend down and he'd see her legs in the shadows.

He was almost there.

She knew suddenly what to do.

Reaching up with the hammer, she rapped the bottom of one of the wooden steps—*ra-ta-ta ta ta*—and held her breath. In response came a burst of mechanical voices and a gale of crazy laughter.

This was it.

She slipped out between the coats. He was just a few feet away, his back to her, staring at the puppets.

"What the hell?" she heard him say as she raised the hammer.

Chapter 38

Jack pulled into a handicapped spot near the emergency department, jogged inside, went to his locker and grabbed the ID badge off one of the lab coats he kept there. He was already halfway out the door when Tim hailed him.

"Hey, where you going? I thought we were supposed to meet?"

Jack glanced at this watch.

"Sorry, Tim, a little complication came up. I've got to pick up a letter at the Seneca Hotel. I'll be back in ten minutes. I was going to call you."

"This can't wait." Tim's voice dropped to a whisper as a nurse strode by pushing a patient in a wheelchair. "I've got what you wanted, Jack." He held up a plastic bag. "But I need to get it back pronto, or I'm a dead man. I'm technically on a coffee break."

Jack pursed his lips and looked around.

"Okay, let's go into the family grieving room. This shouldn't take long."

Luckily, it was empty. Jack ushered him inside and shut the door.

"My friend, you're an unscrupulous genius."

"Thanks. Will you feed me if I get fired?"

Jack pulled out the blue binder and began flipping pages, Tim peering over his shoulder.

"What do you see?"

Running his finger across rows of numbers on a sheet of graph paper, Jack turned to the next page, then the next.

"Interesting."

"How so?"

"Well, look, Tim, there's a recurrent variation in his vital signs, but it's not diurnal."

"Talk English. What's diurnal?"

"Diurnal means daily. There's a normal daily fluctuation in the body's physiologic parameters. It's regulated by the brainstem and various hormone levels. Our core temperature and blood pressure rise during the daylight hours, for example, then fall to a low point just before we wake up."

"You mean his pattern is off?"

"If Gavin were brain-dead, we'd expect the cycle to be chaotic, or even absent completely. But look—every eight hours his blood pressure eases down then slowly rises again. It's like clockwork. It's too perfect."

"Alright, but what's it mean?"

"It's got to be medication-related."

"What kind of medication?"

"Let's see what's on the list." Jack flipped to the drug chart. "It's a shame this hospital doesn't have a fully integrated computer information system yet. This would have been a lot easier, and you wouldn't have had to steal his chart."

"Speaking of that, I hate to rush you, pal."

"I know. Okay, here's the med chart."

"Do you see any connections?"

Jack ran down the list.

"None whatsoever. There's nothing here that would explain it."

"You mean this is a dead end?"

Jack stared up.

"Just the opposite. It means I'm right. Witner has been slipping him something."

"Such as?"

"It could be all sorts of things. The combination of a paralytic and a sedative would do it." He flipped back to the vital sign record and pointed. "And it looks like Dr. Gavin is due for another dose."

"Shall we call the police?"

"And have them question Witner, the psychopath with the silver tongue? No, I don't think we have the time."

"Speaking of time, I've got to get these back."

"I'm coming with you."

"What about the letter you had to pick up?"

"It'll have to wait." Jack faced his friend, handing him back the bag. "Listen, Tim, a shit storm is about to hit this place. I won't hold it against you if you don't want to be involved, my friend. You've already helped way beyond the call of duty."

"Are you fucking crazy? No way." Tim punched Jack's shoulder. "You know me better than that."

Jim Gavin was waking, aware of cool air against his skin and of the ventilator's methodical hissing. He heard the door open and steeled himself, but instead of Witner's taunting words, he heard the nurse's soft-soled shoes. She came closer, humming, was so close now, right above his head. So close. He could almost make out the tune. If only he could signal her.

He heard her pressing buttons on the monitor.

Don't go away. Look at me.

He tried to open his mouth, but his muscles were still in the paralytic's grip and wouldn't cooperate. Frustration crested inside him, almost physically painful.

The nurse moved away, and the door closed.

The medication wearing off meant Witner would arrive soon. That was the only certainty in his life—whenever he neared consciousness, Witner appeared to prevent it. Now, he knew why.

He had heard the entire conversation between Daphne and Witner, and no longer had to wonder what in God's name had happened to him. He understood only too well.

Daphne. That had been the most shocking of all, to learn of her involvement. He'd always had many doubts about her character, from the first time Colin had brought her home. Poor reckless boy, always drawn to danger. Yet never would he have believed Daphne capable of being in league with the devil himself.

And he completely powerless in the face of it. Another a wave of frustration surged through him.

But wait. What's this?

He wasn't imagining it—he could move his eyelids. He could see light. The paralytic was wearing off. Was it possible justice had finally caught up with the lunatic, that Witner was late because he'd been found out?

Fingering the syringes in his pocket, Bryson Witner waited impatiently for the elevator to reach the seventh floor. This had been a day full of complications. He'd been late leaving the house and, because of that, was tardy for rounds, which lasted longer than usual, thanks to several new patients. It was the one time he wished Randy Delancy hadn't been so scrupulous about grabbing good cases. All this had thrown his routine well behind schedule, but it couldn't be helped.

How in the blazes had Zellie Andersen gotten out of the freezer? It should never have happened. Never. Thank God he'd ordered Hinkle to go clean up. Hinkle was a born man-hunter. He'd find her.

The elevator door slid open. Directly in front of him stood a dumpy black-haired nurse, staring at him. It was an odd occurrence, and it unsettled him. *Beware the unexpected.* She was patently Infected.

Composing himself, he brushed past, avoiding physical contact, and strode down the hallway toward Gavin's suite. Why was she staring at him? Why had she picked that particular elevator to wait for? Might there be a meaning of some kind there?

One cure for his anxiety would be to reach Hinkle again and receive reassurance no more complications had arisen. *Yes.* He slowed. Such a call was in order. It should probably be, come to think of it, the very next order of business. He was already late to medicate Gavin, but the old man wasn't going anywhere. That could wait a few more minutes.

Where was the closest phone? At the nurse's desk, of course. No, that wouldn't do. He had already committed the indiscretion this morning of speaking to Hinkle from a phone in the public purview. No, he needed to get back to his office. It would be worth the delay. He would still be back in a jiffy.

Turning on his heel, he headed back for the elevators at a jog, and a short while later strode by Greta Carpenter at her desk in the anteroom. He ignored the look she gave him and went directly inside. Goodness, he was feeling a little out of breath. He must get back to regular workouts at the faculty club. They were much more satisfying now he'd stopped the infernal medications, which were part of the plot against him, after all, designed to rob him of strength. Daphne was in on that, and she'd paid the price. After today...after today...

Locking the door behind him, he dialed his home number. No answer. Damn!

A tingle worked its way across his scalp. Who was the nincompoop who'd said no news is good news? He hung up and tried Fred's cell. No answer there, either. So, he called the marina. No one picked up.

Finally, he phoned Hinkle's house, where Frau Hinkle greeted him with a snotty "How should I know where he is? I'm not his mother."

Hinkle was unreachable, but that didn't necessarily indicate a problem. He was probably in transit, or had stopped in a bar. Maybe he had a girlfriend on the side.

In any case, Witner decided he would have to drive home at lunchtime to check on things. So be it. No disaster. He'd forgotten to leave out food for the ferrets anyway. Two birds with one stone.

The intercom buzzed, startling him. Greta's voice, even colder than usual.

"Can you take a call from Mr. Debussy on line three?"

Should he or shouldn't he? He hadn't spoken to Debussy in more than twenty-four hours, which was a record of some kind. There might be significant developments. He'd make it quick.

"Hello, Nelson, my friend."

"Good morning, Bryson. Listen, we haven't had a chance to catch up on things recently. Did you know Daphne Gavin brought her lawyer by yesterday and suggested I offer her a settlement! The cheek! The old doctor hasn't even passed to the other side yet, and they've got their hands out. Lawyers. I agree with Shakespeare. Kill 'em all."

Witner rolled his eyes.

"A settlement," he agreed. "My Lord, such gall."

They hung up, but just as one dust mote attracts more, the delays impeding him began to accumulate. Thirty seconds after he hung up, a producer from Viacom called with some inane question about the procedure scheduled two weeks away. Witner slumped in his chair and forced himself to chat for a moment.

Then, as he was opening the office door to leave, Jacob Hansen barged in, his face red, complaining about a shortage of staff in the operating room. They'd had to cancel three procedures.

"Why are you coming to me? Can't you handle this yourself?"

Hansen was taken aback.

"What?"

Witner saw anger rising in the other man's face. He needed to get back to the seventh floor and dose the old man, for God's sake, before Gavin started moving.

Still, he couldn't alienate the chief of surgery. *Smile, now, be charming.*

"Only kidding, Jacob. How can I be of service?" Summoning all his patience, he listened to Hansen snivel.

He never should have come back to his office. Upwards of a quarter-hour had now been wasted. Why was this happening?

By the time Hansen had his say and left, Witner was nearly trembling with frustration. All these brambles sprouting in his path had the feel of something more than coincidence.

Is there a message for me in all this?

He suddenly understood. It was time to wrap things up with the old man. Yes. On this day of final mercy for all the others, the *danse macabre* with Gavin must end as well.

He dashed into his office bathroom and locked the door. The scratch Zellie Andersen had left on his cheek was looking angrier than when he'd left home, damn her. He took a box from the cabinet, removed a syringe and a bottle containing concentrated potassium chloride. Filling the syringe with enough of the potassium to kill an elephant, he recapped the needle.

But no sooner was that done than Greta's voice came over the intercom again. He cursed and put the syringe into his lab coat pocket, where it made a plastic click against the ones already there.

"Dr. Delancy is here. Do you have a moment for him?"

"Tell him I'm busy."

"He says it will only take a minute."

Greta, you meddling fool!

Yes, Greta, too, would need to be dealt with in due time. That would be a pleasure. No more sneaking off at lunchtime for meetings with his enemies. Meanwhile, he could not appear stressed. Everything must seem normal. This was all for a purpose—he had to remember that. He took a deep breath and buttoned his coat.

"All right, send him in."

He made the appearance of listening as Delancy complained about the ER schedule. He was starting to sound like Atwood.

Witner thrust up his palm.

"Enough, Randy. I'm sorry, but you're going to have to work this out for yourself. That's your job now. I don't know what the devil else I can do to help you."

Delancy looked wounded.

"Sir, are you all right?"

He made his expression soften.

"Why, of course, I'm alright. I'll be happy to help you, but I'm a little overwhelmed today."

"I can imagine you are, sir, with all the responsibilities you've taken on. Is there any progress with Dr. Gavin yet?"

"None, I'm afraid."

"Has there been a decision made about taking him off life support yet?"

"As long as there's a thread of hope, Randy, we'll cling to it. Now, I'm sorry, but I must attend to other things."

A few minutes later, he was finally back on the seventh floor. He strode past the nurse's desk, nodding to her and to the security guard sitting by the door, a new man since yesterday—tall, stocky and bearded.

He entered Gavin's room, took a deep breath, and a sense of calm returned. Stepping up to the bedside, he gazed down.

"Hello, Jim."

Deep inside that old carcass, Infection was festering. As he stared, he could almost hear whispering as the viruses tried to establish communication with their kind. It seemed to be growing louder. Of course. They sensed what was going to happen next.

"Sorry I'm running a little late today. You're probably starting to feel almost sprightly. In case you've wondered, I've been using pancuronium bromide, along with chlordiazepoxide, but today, it's time to change the routine."

Gavin's eyelids fluttered. From his lab coat pocket, Witner took out the syringe.

"Today, you'll be getting potassium chloride, which will stop your heart in a minute or two. Potash, as the ancients called it." He held the syringe up to the light and tapped it. "This room has a wonderful view of the Mt. Seneca Cemetery. I never noticed before how the tombstones march up the hill like a militia. You'll be the newest recruit."

He leaned over the gaunt face.

"You hired me out of pity, Jim, I know that very well. You thought you were getting a great bargain—my talents at a fire sale price. But you got Charon, and I'm here to row you across the Styx." He removed the cap from the needle and lifted Gavin's IV line. "I'm actually freeing you from something, and you'd thank me if you could understand."

Gavin's eyelids were now open, the pupils rolling, his cheeks twitching slightly, his lips trying to form a word. Witner had arrived not a second too soon.

"Joining you today on the opposite shore will be the Andersen woman, along with your duplicitous daughter-in-law, Mr. Hinkle and, last but not least, Dr. Forester. Your attempt to join forces against my mission was always doomed. I'll be named dean within two months, and if you think my rise here was rapid, you just wait. I will not stop until this blight is erased."

Witner located the rubber injection port on the IV line.

"Potassium is a marvelous weapon, you'll have to agree—completely undetectable postmortem because dead cells release vast amounts. This is how Lester Zyman died. Hinkle held him, and I injected though a vein in his foot."

Witner was about to insert the needle into the port when he realized something. He had not sterilized the injection port by swabbing it with an alcohol pad. Since medical school, this was a ritual he'd never broken. Never.

Swab then stick. Swab then stick. That ritual had been hammered into his brain. Why in God's name should he worry about it now? He stood frozen, his jaws tight, a drop of sweat percolating down his back.

"Oh, all right," he said. "Why fight it?" He recapped the needle and dropped the syringe back into his pocket. "Jim, the human mind is a strange thing."

Opening the bedside drawer, he found an alcohol swab, tore it open and was about to wipe the port when a sound from outside made him stop and cock his head. There were footsteps in the hallway, coming closer—multiple footsteps. Now someone was talking to the security guard.

In one swift movement, Witner fished the syringe from his pocket, jabbed the needle into the port and squeezed, finishing just as the door swung open. What was that damn security guard doing? He yanked the needle out—there was no time to recap it—and dropped the syringe back into his pocket, all while swiveling toward the door and arranging a grave look on his face.

He felt his heart skip a beat, and his face suffused with heat. There, staring at him insolently, was the one person he least expected to see at that moment. Forester was supposed to be in Boston, according to Daphne, not due back till this afternoon.

But you're a few seconds too late.

"Dr. Forester, who gave you permission to be here?"

Forester didn't answer, and he wasn't alone. Beside him was an old woman Witner recognized as one of the volunteers—Eleanor somebody. He cleared his throat as the she stepped toward him, beaming, her hand outstretched.

"Why, hello, Dr. Witner. How wonderful to see you. I ran into Dr. Forester in the elevator, and he escorted me here. He's always so kind, isn't he? So, is our patient doing any better today? Jim is my neighbor, you know. I could tell you so many stories."

Witner modulated the expression, letting his expression fade deeper into somberness and grief. He took her hand and pressed it in both of his.

"Eleanor, I'm afraid..."

"What's the matter, Dr. Witner?" Her voice fell.

"Things did not work out as we'd hoped."

Eleanor's hand went to her mouth.

"Oh, my God, he isn't...?"

Witner moved his gaze to Forester and shook his head sadly. More than a minute had passed since he'd injected the potassium. The game would be over now. He drew a breath and released it slowly. He brought moisture to his eyes by remembering the day his father had killed himself.

"I'm afraid so," he said softly. "Not unexpected, but never easy."

"That's strange, Witner," said Forester. "He appears to be in normal sinus rhythm up on the monitor."

Witner's eyes darted to the screen, and shock coursed through him. This could not be! Even if Gavin's heart hadn't stopped, a dosage of that much potassium should be causing some dramatic pre-terminal changes in the heart rhythm. Had he taken the wrong syringe out of his pocket? That was the only explanation.

Gavin's eyes were closed again, and his face utterly relaxed. That was it. He had given him the wrong medication, the paralytic.

Forester pushed past him and reached down to feel Gavin's wrist.

"Dr. Forester, you're not supposed to be here. This is inappropriate."

"Yet, here I am, and I'm not going anywhere."

The old woman looked at both of them with an astonished expression.

"Security!" yelled Witner.

"He's got a normal pulse, too," Forester noted. "What made you think he'd died?"

"I was speaking figuratively, of course. You understood my meaning, didn't you, Eleanor?"

"I must admit you certainly had me scared," she said, her expression growing increasingly puzzled.

"I'm going to examine him," Forester said.

"No, you're not. Guard, dammit!"

"What on earth is going on?" Eleanor asked. "Why shouldn't Dr. Forester be here?"

"Dr. Forester no longer has hospital privileges."

"Since when?" Jack demanded, whirling on him.

"Since this morning," Witner improvised. "It was a decision I regretted having to make, but circumstances forced my hand."

"What circumstances?"

"That will all come out at the hearing."

"Listen, Witner, I know all about your problems at Harvard."

Witner felt his color rise, but he controlled his expression.

"And I know about the Society Carnivalis."

Witner exhaled sharply.

"Now is neither the time nor place for this discussion." He nodded in Eleanor's direction. "I have no desire to embarrass you, Dr. Forester."

At that moment, his pager beeped. He looked, and an electric charge coursed through him. It was Humphrey Atwood's number. He stared at it. What did this mean?

"Guard!" he cried again.

The door flew open.

"Yes, sir? How can I help?"

"Why did you let this man in here?"

Tim Bonadonna shrugged.

"He told me he was your son, sir."

"My son!"

"I'm sorry, sir, I was—"

"Just escort Dr. Forester out of the building immediately. If he resists, call the police."

"It'll be my pleasure, sir." Tim stepped aside to let the interim dean march out. "I'll take care of it right away."

"My son," Witner muttered, casting a withering glance at Forester before he went through the doorway.

Once in the corridor, he trotted for the nearest flight of stairs. There was no time for elevators. He'd waited too long, let himself be distracted by a parade of Infected idiots. It was his own fault. He'd made a mistake. *I'm sorry.* There must be a reason for it. He could still finish the job. *I'm sorry.* He bounded down to the accompanying echo of footfalls in the old stairwell.

Greta looked up in amazement up as he rushed past.

"No interruptions," he commanded. *You'll be next.*

Locking the door, he took out his cellphone and dialed. Humphrey Atwood's number? What the blazes was going on. It had to be a message of some kind. After half a dozen rings, someone answered.

"Hello?"

The voice was that of a boy, no older than ten, surely.
What in the name of Moses...?
"Hello?" repeated the voice.
"Is this five-five-five-zero-zero-one-two?"
"Yes."
"Listen, did someone from that number just page someone?"
"I did."
"You did? And who the devil are you?"
"Are you my dad's friend, Dr. Witner?"
"I asked who you are."
"I'm Jeremy Atwood."

It felt like a glass of ice water had just been poured down his spine. He saw Atwood standing, his eyes closed, holding the pistol against his temple.

Now, Humphrey, I'm going to help you angle it so the bullet will only crease your scalp, but you'll have to relax your wrist more, yes, that's right, that's just my hand over yours, relax, relax, it'll all be over in a sec. Then the sharp report, blood and gray matter spraying the wall.

Witner waited a moment before speaking. He heard nasal breathing on the end of the line, a sniffle.

"Why are you calling me?"

"I found my dad's address book, and it had this number. It was in red, and it said for emergencies."

Witner said nothing. He heard whispering.

"Nobody wants to talk about him now, especially Mom. He was supposed to take me to my hockey tournament today."

"Do not call this number ever again—ever, do you hear? Throw that book away immediately. That's what your father would have wanted."

"Okay," said the boy, his voice now quivering. Another sniffle. "Do you know what happened to my dad?"

"Of course, I don't," he snapped. "Why would I know what happened to him? Listen, how old are you?"

"Nine."

"Your father was a well-meaning sort of person. You'll forget all of this soon enough, and someday the world will be a better place."

If you're not Infected.

Witner heard the sound of a woman's voice in the background, approaching.

"Jeremy–? Why are you crying? Who are you talking to, honey? Give it to me."

Witner slammed the phone down and felt an odd urge to piss. He dashed into the bathroom and yanked down his fly, the sound of his water mingled with a wave of whispered words he could not quite make out.

Talk to me. What do you mean by these things?

Chapter 39

Jack stood at Gavin's bedside and listened to Witner's footsteps recede up the hallway.

"What on earth is going on?" said Eleanor. "I've never seen Dr. Witner like this before."

"It's a very long story."

"Jack," Tim warned, hovering in the doorway, "he'll be back soon. I'm supposed to call the cops on you."

"We've got to get Dr. Gavin out of here."

"Would somebody please tell me what's happening?"

"And how are we going to accomplish that, amigo?" Tim said. "The nurse out there is Gestapo-trained."

"I've got an idea," said Jack. He turned to Eleanor. "Listen carefully, I'm going to tell you something you may find hard to believe. But I need your help, and Dr. Gavin needs your help." He swiveled back to his friend. "Tim, go tell the nurse Eleanor just fainted, and we need to take her to the ED. There's a stretcher down by the elevators. Bring it here."

"Jesus and Mary, I need to change jobs anyways," Tim said, shaking his head. "Oh, yes, I do."

Tim returned with the gurney, wheeled it into Gavin's room; and a short while later, Jack pushed it back out into the hallway, headed for the elevators.

The nurse looked up. When Tim told her Eleanor had fainted, she'd come running in and found her on the floor, with Jack kneeling at her side.

"It's probably just a vasovagal episode," Jack told her. "But I know her well and she's got a cardiac history. I'd like to take her down to the ED and check her out."

The nurse had agreed then returned to her post in the corridor.

"How's she doing?" she asked as they moved past.

"She's starting to come around. Thanks for your help."

"You bet."

"By the way, Dr. Witner told the security guard to stay in Dr. Gavin's room. Don't know why, but that's where he is."

"Okay. Do you need some extra help with the gurney? I could call an orderly."

"Nope, I need the exercise."

The elevator's descent seemed to take forever.

"How you doing, Eleanor?" he asked.

"I'm frightened."

Jack lifted the blanket. On his side, pressed against Eleanor, lay a motionless James Gavin. Jack had fastened a plastic hose to the the endotracheal tube so Eleanor could breathe for him.

"Tell me again how often I'm supposed to do this?"

"Every three seconds. That's perfect—just blow slowly and deeply into the tube."

"It's lucky I'm so skinny," she said. "Are you sure my breath has enough oxygen for him?"

"More than enough until we get to the emergency department," Jack assured her, placing the blanket so only her head was visible.

"Dr. Witner is going to be hopping mad," she said. "But if you're correct, Jack, it only serves him right. How could he do such a thing?"

"Just imagine the story you'll have."

The elevator bumped to a stop, and the doors slid open. Jack guided the stretcher into the corridor, then pushed it toward the ED's back door several hundred feet away. His heart was pounding. Things were going too easily. This was a piece of cake so far. It couldn't last.

Suddenly, a man in a long white lab coat rounded the corner in front of him. It was Norman Scales. Of all the people he cared not to meet now, the Chief of Internal Medicine was high on the list.

As they drew close, Scales recognized him and nodded.

"Hello, Norman," Jack said, pushing faster. The ED was only fifty feet away now.

"Dr. Forester? What—have they got you doing orderly work now?"

"Nothing like a little manual labor to clear the mind."

"If you say so," Scales said, his lips curling into a supercilious smile. "Looks like you're adept at it. Maybe you've finally found your métier. Feel free to sweep my office when you're done."

"Good one, Norman."

Screw you.

Scales chuckled at his own joke as the stretcher glided by. Though Jack breathed with relief and winked at Eleanor, the back of his neck was tingling with tension. The ruse back up on the seventh floor wasn't going to last long. Somebody—either the nurse or Witner—would enter Gavin's room and find Tim lying there reading a magazine with the monitor leads on his chest. Maybe they already had. Any second, there might come a sudden stampede of footfalls behind him and a burst of shouts. But once inside the ED, he'd be on home turf.

"Here we are, Eleanor." He yanked open the door and wheeled the stretcher in. At the central station, he stopped in front of Kathy.

"Jack?" she said, half-standing. "What the heck's up? Who's this?"

"Don't ask—extreme emergency. Find out if Suite X is clear."

Like the fine person she was, Kathy sprang to the other side of the station and checked the locator board.

"It's clear," she told him. "Do you need any help?"

"Please call the respiratory tech and have him meet me there with a ventilator, super stat. And please page Dr. Wick, the toxicologist."

He turned the corner to the left, where he ran straight into Randy Delancy.

"Dr. Forester? You're not supposed to be here today."

"Too busy to talk, Randy. Out of my way, please."

"Who's this?" Delancy leaned over the stretcher. "Why is she breathing into that tube?"

"We can continue this discussion later. Step aside. Don't do that, Randy."

It was too late. Delancy had lifted up the blanket. A look of dismay blossomed on his face.

"Is that Dr. Gavin?"

"That's right." Jack began pushing again, forcing the younger man to jump aside.

"What's going on?"

Jack didn't answer. He rounded the corner into the side corridor. Another voice hailed him. Steve Brasio came toward him carrying an x-ray film.

"Dr. Forester, have you got a minute?" he said, coming up alongside Jack and keeping pace. "Are you coming on duty?"

"No time to talk now, Steve. Listen, help me get this stretcher into Suite X, would you?"

The intern grabbed one of the side rails and leaned into pushing.

"Sir, could you give me a hand with a weird case I'm seeing?"

"Isn't Sue Redwater your attending today?"

"She is, but this patient is demanding that all his physicians be male. He won't even let a female nurse in the room."

"I'd love to help, but I can't let go of this case right now," Jack said. "Give him another breath, Eleanor. We're almost there. Tell you what, Steve—you help me, and I'll help you."

They reached the wide entrance to Suite X. All three curtained cubicles were empty.

"Steve, move out one of those stretchers so we can fit this one in. We'll put it there in the corner."

Once the old stretcher was out, Jack slid in the one carrying Eleanor and Gavin. He closed the curtain and looked at Brasio.

"Brace yourself, Steve." And he pulled the blanket down.

Brasio's eyes bulged. Before he had a chance to ask a question, however, John Kellogg, the respiratory tech, slipped in through the curtains.

"What's up, Dr. F?" he said. "Kathy said there was a super stat emergency here. You needed a ventilator?" Kellogg then looked down at the stretcher and gaped. "Holy shit."

"You're not kidding," said Brasio. "That's Dr. Gavin, isn't it?"

"Yes, it is," said Eleanor, sitting up. "And I'm breathing for him."

Jack flew through an explanation, telling them as concisely as possible why he believed Gavin's coma was due to intentional overmedication.

"Just trust me for now. We need to get him back on a ventilator. Could you do that for us, John?"

"You bet."

"Great. And listen, there's going to be some political chaos hitting this place real soon. Let me handle that end of things."

"You got it," Kellogg said.

"One more thing—do *not* leave him alone with anyone else. Especially not Dr. Witner, do you understand?"

Jack helped Eleanor off the stretcher while Kellogg hooked up the ventilator and Steve Brasio, still carrying the x-ray film, attached monitor leads to Gavin's chest. With that done, Jack turned to the surgical intern.

"Steve, I don't have much time, but what's the story with this weird case you've got there?"

"Thanks, Dr. Forester. This guy came in a little while ago with belly pain and vomiting." Brasio handed him the film. "Take a look."

Forester held it up to the ceiling light. "No wonder he doesn't want a female physician. He's got a vibrator in his rectum."

"He says it was an accident," said Brasio.

"It's always accidental.

"What do I do?" asked the intern. "I've never dealt with anything like before. Does he need to go to the OR?"

"No. Put him on a pelvic table in stirrups and sedate him with a little midozolam. Then insert a small vaginal speculum in his anus. As soon as you open it, you should be able to visualize the foreign body. Pull it out slowly with a Magill forceps and stand back because there's often a lot of fecal material behind it and the colon may go into spasm."

"Got it, thanks, Dr. Forester."

Jack turned to Kellogg. "John, I'm going to go find a nurse to help us, and I need to locate the toxicologist. We need drug levels. Eleanor, do you want to stay here with Dr. Gavin?"

"I'll volunteer for that job any day."

"You've done beautifully."

Jack checked his watch. Almost twenty minutes had elapsed since they'd left Gavin's room. Things would have to explode soon.

Striding back to the nursing station, he nearly bowled over Randy Delancy.

"Dr. Forester, what are you doing? This is way out of line. Even I know that."

"Out of my way, you little ass-kisser. And, by the way, you can clear out of my office. Your boss is through."

He saw Darcy McFeely and called to her.

"What's going on?"

"Darcy, if you aren't involved in something life-or-death right now, please help take care of the new patient I just put in Suite X. John Kellogg will explain. It's Dr. Gavin."

"Come again?"

"No time to talk."

He marched to the secretary's station.

"Kathy, any luck reaching Dr. Wick yet?"

"He hasn't returned the page."

"Page him again."

"You will do nothing of the kind," said Bryson Witner. "Put down that phone, or you're fired."

Jack swung around. The interim dean strode toward him, Nelson Debussy at his side.

"What in the name of God is going on here, Forester?" sputtered Debussy, his face purple, jabbing his finger at Jack. "I run into Dr. Witner in the hallway and he tells me you've kidnapped Jim Gavin. You are going down, sir. All the way down!"

Everyone within earshot turned to gape.

Witner cleared his throat.

"What you did was very unwise, Dr. Forester," he said. "Unwise."

"I'll say it was unwise," Debussy thundered. "If anything untoward happens to Gavin, I will personally rip your license to shreds."

"Dr. Gavin is doing fine," said Jack. "Not only is he doing fine, but there's a good chance he might be awake by tomorrow."

"What kind of garbage are you blithering!"

"Do you want to keep screaming at me, or would you like an explanation?"

"I want him back where he belongs. Now!"

"I'm afraid that can't happen yet," said Jack.

"What!"

"We're going to run some tests first."

Debussy turned to Witner. "Did he just say no to me?"

"Easy, Nelson," said Witner. "We'll get this straightened out. First of all, Forester, where, exactly, is Dr. Gavin?"

"Suite X," volunteered Delancy, who had come up next to Witner. "He's in Suite X, sir. I just saw him myself."

"Which is where he's going to stay," Jack said, "until we run some tests."

"Oh, I think you're wrong about that," Witner replied.

"You want to bet?" Jack took his cell phone off his belt. "I'm going to call the police. They can help us settle this."

Witner raised his hand. "You'll do nothing of the kind. We'll deal with this internally. I'm sure Mr. Debussy will agree we've had more than enough adverse publicity. Do not make that call."

"That's right," Debussy chimed in. "Put down the phone, and get that man back upstairs."

Ignoring him, Jack punched in three numbers—911. Witner reached for Jack's hand, but Debussy stopped him.

"Let him, Bryson. Let him cook his own goose."

"What's happening?" said Gail Scippino, striding into the station, crowded now as more staff stopped working and gathered around. "I was at a meeting. Why didn't someone page me?"

"Dispatcher?" said Jack into the phone. "This is Dr. Forester at the New Canterbury ED. There's an attempted murder going on here. That's right. Please send the closest unit immediately. Straight to the ED. No delay, please. That's right, it's Dr. Forester, medical director of the ED."

He stared over at Witner, whose face had darkened.

"Attempted murder?" said Gail Scippino. "Jack, what are you talking about? Why is everybody here?"

Debussy threw up his hands.

"For God's sake, would somebody go see how Dr. Gavin's doing?"

Darcy had just appeared from the corridor toward Suite X.

"He's doing fine," she called over. "Everything's stable. The respiratory tech's with him."

"Excellent," said Witner. "If he's stable, then there's no reason why we can't take him back upstairs. Let's go, Randy. You and I will personally wheel him up."

"Over my dead body," said Jack, stepping to block the corridor.

The ambulance port slid open, and in ran two gray-uniformed state troopers, handcuffs clanking on their belts.

"Where's the problem?" one of them demanded.

"There's the problem," said Debussy, pointing at Jack. "That man right there. He kidnapped a patient from upstairs and is now refusing to let him be moved. Arrest him."

The troopers stopped, confused expressions on their faces.

"Arrest Jack Forester?" one of them said.

"Yes. Immediately. He's endangering the life of a patient."

"And who are you?"

"I'm Nelson Debussy, president of the university."

"Sir, that doesn't sound like the Dr. Forester we know" said the other trooper.

"Enough talk," said Debussy. "Just take him away."

"Hold on just a minute," the trooper ordered. "What's your side of this, Jack?"

"Thank you," Jack said. "The patient in question is Dr. James Gavin, the former dean, who is supposed to be in a coma. But I believe he's being criminally overmedicated by Dr. Witner. That's Dr. Witner, right there."

A murmur went around the central station.

"Which proves he's off his rocker," said Debussy. "You can arrest him my authority. Just do it."

Tim Bonadonna pushed through the crowd.

"Jack Forester is telling the truth, officers. We believe Dr. Witner is trying to kill Dr. Gavin. He may have killed others."

"And who the hell are you?" Debussy demanded.

"That's the security guard I found in Dr. Gavin's bed," said Witner, whose face was composed but abnormally rigid and pale. "He's an accomplice."

"Well, *I'm* no accomplice," Eleanor Lane announced. Hearing the commotion, she had left Suite X and had been listening from the sidelines. "Dr. Forester is just trying to do what's best, and I'm helping him. You can arrest me, too."

"What?" Debussy said.

"I'm a thirty-five-year veteran of this hospital's volunteer service, young man, and you need to listen."

"Oh, my God, what's next?" said Debussy.

Jack held up his hands and raised his voice.

"Everybody—all I ask is to keep Dr. Gavin here in the emergency department until we can run some blood levels and get a toxicology consultation. He's perfectly stable, and he will get exactly the same care here he would upstairs. I promise we can have this sorted out in less than two hours."

"By which time," said Debussy, "you'll be behind bars."

"Sir," said the trooper, "we don't arrest people just because you'd like it to happen."

"What the devil *do* you do then?"

Witner cleared his throat.

"All right," he declared, pointing toward the troopers, "seeing as I'm being accused of something here, I deserve a word."

"Go right ahead," said the trooper.

"I agree with Dr. Forester."

"What are you talking about, Bryson?"

"That's right, Nelson. I see no harm in keeping Dr. Gavin here for a short while, if that's what it takes to clear the water. Any deleterious effects from dragging him here will already have occurred, I'm afraid. So, he can stay here, and let the chips fall where they may."

Debussy gazed around, speechless.

"It's all right, Nelson," Witner reassured him.

"Well, Bryson, if that's what you'd like. Ms. Scippino, as the nursing director, do you agree to keeping Dr. Gavin here for a while?"

"My head's still spinning. Certainly. I believe we can spare the room. We're not too busy."

"It's settled, then," Witner said. "Now, if no one objects I would like at least to check on my patient."

"Certainly," Debussy told him.

"But not alone," Jack added.

"I'd be happy to have an escort, if you think that's necessary," Witner agreed.

Jack stared at him. He had to be bluffing. There could be no doubt he wanted to be alone with Gavin. It was obvious from the smug look on his face Witner didn't think the game was over.

Something occurred to him. There might be a way to flush him into the open.

"Listen, I realize I could be wrong about all of this, Dr. Witner. You've been kind enough to let us keep him here, and I appreciate this. If you want to examine Dr. Gavin, that's your prerogative. I won't try to stop you."

"Jack?" Tim protested. "Are you sure?"

"Well, finally, we are hearing some common sense and consideration," Witner said. "Thank you, Dr. Forester. This may speak in your favor."

Jack nodded. "Listen, the respiratory tech is in there now. When you go in, would you tell him I need to speak with him?"

"Yes, I can do that, no problem." Witner held Jack's gaze for a moment, then turned and strode toward Suite X.

The window was closing fast, but a razor-thin chance still existed, glimmered on the horizon like the sun about to set. And the opportunity was courtesy of Dr. Forester himself.

Witner eased aside the curtain. The respiratory tech was adjusting ventilator settings. He looked up with a startled expression.

"Dr. Witner?"

"Where's the nurse?" Witner said, entering the cubicle.

"She had to check on another patient. She'll be back in a minute."

"How's our patient doing?"

"Fine."

Witner bent to read the man's name tag.

"Mr. Kellogg, Dr. Forester wants to see you. He's out by the nursing station."

Kellogg looked skeptical. He went to the wall, where a small intercom device connected to the central station.

"Dr. Forester, this is John," he said, pressing the button. "Did you want to see me?"

Jack's voice crackled back after a moment.

"It's okay, John. I need to speak with you for a minute."

"Dr. Witner's here."

"I know."

"I'll be right back," Kellogg told Witner, and stepped out.

He had to get the potassium in fast. The moment the tech disappeared, he took the syringe from his pocket. The potassium would work almost instantly, but it would not do for him to be in the room when Gavin's heart fibrillated.

A small bag of saline hung from an IV pole, slowly dripping into Gavin's arm. Perfect. He gave a quick look back at the curtain then reached up, slid the needle into the port and injected the entire contents of the syringe into it. He then turned the plastic flow regulator to wide open. The fluid began running in a steady stream. In fifteen minutes, there would be no more James Gavin.

The syringe back in his pocket, he stepped away from the bedside—and just in time, for he heard footfalls approaching. Someone was running. His muscles tensed.

Jack burst through the curtains and lunged for the IV bag, clamping off the tubing with his fingers and turning the bag upside down. The curtains parted wider and wider, and there appeared a number of faces, all staring at him—Debussy, the two troopers, Gail Scippino and Randy Delancy.

"Is something amiss?" Witner said, clasping his hands behind his back.

Jack didn't reply. He was busy disconnecting the IV tube from the catheter in Gavin's arm.

"Nelson." Witner turned toward Debussy. "What's going on?"

Debussy released a sigh that seemed to deflate his entire body, and he shook his head, his eyes glistening. There was an expression on his face Witner had never seen there before. Intense shame.

He heard the sound of handcuffs being opened. His eyes went from the trooper back to Debussy.

"Bryson," Debussy said, pointing to where the wall met the ceiling. "That's a video monitor. Dr. Forester turned it on a moment ago."

Witner saw the purplish eye of a camera lens, and the blood drained from his face.

Jack was staring at him, the IV bag in his hand, his hand trembling slightly.

"I'm not sure what you put in there, Witner, but it won't take long to find out. Or would you like to tell us?"

"For God's sake, all you'll find is an antibiotic."

A cacophony of whispers filled his ears. So, the window had shut. Or had it? Perhaps not completely.

Behind him lay the door from Suite X into the morgue. It was less than three feet away. Was it locked? Everyone—even the troopers—stood immobile, like somebody had poleaxed them. Good, let them all be dumbstruck.

He inched backward toward the door and began talking.

"I can't believe, Nelson, that you'd believe me capable of what Forester is suggesting."

These fools weren't going to stop him. Strange, but it seemed as if someone had turned up the volume on everything around him. He could hear the murmuring of all their viruses communicating.

"I think what you'll find is that Dr. Forester planted a pre-taped video you mistook for live action. That's the only explanation I can think of."

He was close now. The voices in his head were celebrating.

One of the troopers began approaching, the handcuffs ready.

"Dr. Witner, you have the right to remain silent," he began. "Anything you say—"

"Nelson," he said, nearly at the door now. "I doubt you'll survive the backlash from this. I doubt this measly place will survive. Believe it or not, the time will come when all of you will wish I had succeeded. In the meantime, I've got some loose ends to take care off."

"Good God," Gail Scippino said.

He reached behind him and felt the knob, turning it carefully. It wasn't locked.

The other trooper was the first to realize what was happening, but he wasn't fast enough by half.

"Look out!" he yelled. "There's a door."

But Witner was through. He slammed it shut, and luck was with him. There was a deadbolt on the morgue side.

Chapter 40

Within fifteen minutes of Witner's escape, every security guard in New Canterbury Hospital was combing the medical center, assisted by the state troopers and a dozen city police officers, led by Chief Bedford. They stationed an officer in Witner's office and another near his car.

By mid-afternoon, they still had not found the fugitive.

Time flew by for Jack. It seemed like every consultant in the medical center, from neurology to orthopedics, filed into Suite X to examine Dr. Gavin and discuss the bizarre turn of events. Dr. Wick arrived not long after Witner disappeared, and the toxicologic blood studies confirmed pancuronium and chlordiazepoxide. There was no doubt now that Gavin's coma was medication-induced.

It was three p.m. before Jack remembered the letter. As he was rushing out of the building, he ran into Chief Bedford standing by a coffee machine in the ED lobby, speaking into a walkie-talkie. Bedford lowered it from his ear and shook Jack's hand.

"Good work, young man."

"Any luck finding him yet, Chief?"

"Jack, that man must be a magician. It's like he's disappeared off the face of the earth. But there are only so many places he can hide, and we'll get him. But, I still can't believe I had him pegged so wrong."

"You and a lot of good people. Have you checked his house yet?"

"I detailed a couple of men to go out there in case he shows up, but he'd have to be walking. His car isn't an option, and we've gotten no reports of any stolen vehicles. I think he's probably still here somewhere. It's just a very big place, a lot of beds to hide under and closets to hole up in. This could take days. How's Jim doing? I heard he's starting to wake up."

"He is," Jack said smiling. "Just a little, but he's coming around."

"Thank God." Bedford blew on his coffee and took a sip. "I still can't figure out Witner's motives. Talk about somebody with a lot to lose. Goes to show how you can't judge a book by its cover."

Book cover. He had to get Zellie's letter.

"Chief, I've got to run

Bedford again reached out and shook his hand.

"I am going to need a formal statement from you."

"Later, please."

"Your mom and dad would have been awfully proud. If you ever want to change careers, you give me a call."

"With a little luck, I just might get my old job back. Chief, would you call me with any news?"

"Done," Bedford agreed.

"Just ask the hospital to page me."

A leaden overcast hung above the buildings, and the wind was picking up as he trotted to his truck, still parked in the handicapped spot, with an orange parking violation under the wiper blade. A few snowflakes fluttered onto the glass.

Tim Bonadonna ran up beside him.

"I'm coming with you, mate," he said.

Tim barely had time to shut the door before Jack jerked the truck into gear and pulled out. Jack's jaw was set, his lips clenched together. He accelerated through a light turning red.

"Where are we going?"

"Remember that letter from Zellie I told you about, the one I was going to pick up at the hotel until all this blew up?"

He zoomed through another changing light.

"Easy, partner."

"I got a bad feeling."

"Don't automatically jump to the worst-case scenario."

"Then why hasn't she called?"

"Any of a million reasons, Jack. She might have gone shopping or—"

"Would you shut up for once in your life?"

Jack left the truck idling by the front door and tore open the small white envelope. He read it then looked at the clerk.

"I'm sorry I grabbed your tie this morning."

"No problem."

"Listen, did Ms. Andersen call this in herself?"

"That's what I was told."

"Has anyone seen her today?"

"Not that I know of."

"How about Mrs. Gavin?"

"The redheaded lady from California?"

"Right."

The clerk shook his head and shrugged.

"Would you call Ms. Andersen's room for me?"

The clerk did as he was asked. Jack reread the letter.

"I'm sorry. No answer."

Back in the truck, Jack shut the door and sat for a moment, looking at the snow, which had now begun falling steadily.

"Boy," Tim said causually, "if the rest of the winter stays like this, we're in trouble. Aren't you going to tell me anything?"

"It was called in last evening. Nobody's apparently seen her or Daphne Gavin today."

"Not what I asked. What was the message?"

Jack handed it to him, and Tim read it out loud.

"I'm fine, not to worry. Daphne and I gone to stay with her friends for night. Have discovered absolutely vital information, you'll be pleased as punch, miss you." He hesitated for a moment, and then continued. "Please meet us tonight at five-thirty tonight on the dot, near the little bitty bridge by Deepwater Marina. Can't wait to see you, handsome. Love, Zellie."

Jack started the truck but made no motion to set it in gear.

"Sounds like good news," Tim said.

Jack looked at him, and slipped the truck into drive.

Tim raised his eyebrows. "It doesn't sound like good news?"

"Zellie's an artist with words, Tim. She'd never write something that stupid."

He stood with his friend on the little bridge near the marina. Beneath them in the darkness, Miller Creek gurgled. It was a little reed-bordered stream, flowing as it had for ten thousand years.

The floodlight in Hinkle's parking lot glowed. The snow had turned to freezing rain shortly after dusk, coating the bridge's metal grating. Jack checked his watch and stomped his feet.

"Quarter to six," he said. "We've been here half an hour."

"Without an umbrella."

Only two cars had passed since they'd arrived, both of them police cruisers heading toward the west shore in the direction of Witner's house. The second one had suddenly braked, backed up and stopped next to them. The window rolled down, and a high-intensity flashlight jabbed into their eyes.

"It's Dr. Forester," the cop said to his partner. "How you doing, doc?"

"Fine. We're waiting for someone."

"Okay. Stay warm."

That was twenty minutes ago, and nothing had come by since.

Then Jack saw lights coming down the western shore. They disappeared several times behind cottages then reappeared, much closer.

"Another car," Tim said. "Maybe it's them."

It passed by Hinkle's parking lot—it was another police cruiser. Jack's throat contracted. The car pulled off the road just before the bridge, braking hard. The doors opened, and two men strode over. One was Armand Bedford.

"Hell of a night," he said, moisture dripping from the brim of his cap. "One of the officers said he saw you two here. What the hell are you doing?"

Jack explained the message allegedly from Zellie about a meeting.

"Jesus, you should have called me. You don't have to shoulder these things alone, Jack. But listen, we've been investigating a crime scene at Witner's place, and I'd like you to come up there for a minute."

"What do you mean?" Jack's pulse quickened.

"We found two bodies. One is Fred Hinkle, but Jack, we might need your help..." His voice trailed off.

Jack felt like a hand had his vocal cords in a vise grip.

"No sign of Witner?"

"Still at large. Do you want to follow us, or would you rather ride with me?"

"We'll drive," Tim said, stepping closer to Jack.

There were two city patrol cars and one belonging to the state police parked in Witner's driveway, and light flooded from every window, including the attic. Jack stepped over a yellow tape, and a few minutes later found himself standing by the body of Fred Hinkle. Hinkle was stretched out face downwards, a small pistol still gripped in his right hand, and the back of his head caked with blood. Spread around his head lay a huge pool of it, congealed and thick.

"Did he shoot himself?" asked Tim.

"No. It's blunt trauma, Bedford said, pointing to a bloody hammer lying several feet away. "There's the murder weapon."

"Jeeze," Tim blurted, "I thought that was a couple of old guys sitting there."

"Yeah, it seems that Dr. Witner liked to play with life-sized dolls," Bedford replied. "There's more of them over on the other side of the furnace. They talk to you when you make a loud noise. Crazy."

"Crazy—not a bad description," Tim said. "But who killed Hinkle?"

"That's the million-dollar question. By the way, aren't you the one who's been calling us about some drug company monkey business?"

Tim shrugged. "Once or twice, maybe. Guess I was off-base."

Jack had been steeling himself. He didn't want to ask the question, but he had to.

"Chief, you said there were two bodies."

"This way."

Bedford led them to the freezer. He lifted the lid and switched on his flashlight. Daphne stared up, her eyes milky.

A mixture of revulsion and relief flooded though Jack.

"Good God."

"You know her?" Bedford said.

"Yes, and I think you do too. It's Dr. Gavin's daughter-in-law."

"Daphne Gavin? The one who was married to Jim's son?"

Jack nodded.

"Jesus." Bedford swiped his chin. "Yeah, I only met her once, maybe ten years ago at some party. She was quite a looker. What in the hell was she doing here?"

"She and Zellie were together," Jack answered. "Witner must have found out they knew. Unless…"

"Unless what?"

"Unless she and Witner were working together."

"Holy smokes," Tim said.

Jack swung toward Bedford.

"Is all you've found?"

"That's it so far, son. Our men are still working through the rest of the house. But, listen, come here and take a look at something."

Back next to Hinkle's corpse, Bedford played his flashlight over the floor.

"See that? And that?"

Jack dropped to a crouch and stared.

"Don't touch," Bedford said.

"They're footprints," Jack said, and the thought came to him that he had never seen Zellie's feet without shoes.

"Got to be," said Bedford. "Footprints in blood. They head for the back door over there."

Chapter 41

Zellie swung the hammer and felt the blow radiate up the handle all the way to her neck. Blood began pouring from his scalp, but Hinkle just stood there, straightening a little. One of the puppets was singing.

She lifted the hammer again, but he swayed, blood now oozing down his neck. Suddenly, his body arched, and he fell backward toward her. With a cry, she lunged and pushed him. His legs jerked, and he toppled forward in slow motion, making no effort to protect himself, his face slamming the concrete so hard she felt it on the soles of her bare feet.

The puppets stopped babbling, and she heard the ragged, gasping sound of her own breathing. She looked at the hammer. It was spattered with blood, as were her hands and forearms. Her fingers grasped the handle as if the hammer might strike her if she let it go.

What if he were still alive? What if he could still get up and grab her? But the longer she gazed at him, the more convinced she became that Fred Hinkle would never rise again. Nonetheless, should she bash his head a few more times to make doubly sure? Her stomach turned. She didn't think she could force herself to do it—not unless the killer began moving.

The blood from his scalp and the massive gash on his face wasn't flowing anymore, and she saw no sign he was breathing. She nudged his leg with her foot; it moved without resistance.

It was then she noticed he had a pistol in his right hand, the same one Daphne had pointed at her the night before. She crouched and tried to take it, but his fingers were locked around it. She recoiled at the thought of touching him. Was there any need for it?

She shuffled around the body and made for the basement door. Halfway there, she looked at the hammer, still gripped in both hands, and gave in to an impulse. Returning to the freezer, she lifted the lid and, with one blow, smashed the lock.

When she got to Hinkle's truck, the keys were not in the ignition. They must be in his pocket. The thought of rifling though those was too revolting to contemplate. Now that she was outside, breathing the fresh air, even though the gray sky was sputtering snow, even going back in the house to look for Daphne's purse and the keys to the rental was too awful to think about.

There was still the boat. She could see the other side of the lake. It wouldn't take her long to get there. She returned to the basement door, opened it just enough unhook the keys from the nail, then shuffled to the dock. Thanks to a friend who lived on Long Island Sound, she knew how to start an outboard. The engine kicked over on the second try.

It wasn't until she was far out on the water that she realized she'd forgotten to call Jack.

The cold rain had washed away any footprints that might have remained outside the back door. While Tim, Chief Bedford and two other officers methodically searched the lawn, moving toward the lakeshore, panning flashlights in front of them, Jack borrowed a light from one of the troopers and searched the woods, calling Zellie's name.

Bedford came up, collar pulled around his neck, water dripping from the brim of his hat.

"To judge by the state of Hinkle's body, she could have left here six or eight hours ago, Jack," he said. "Or maybe more. Damn this weather. Two more years, and I'm heading for Florida."

"This is not good."

"Listen, we're not going to give up until we find her. If I were the young lady, I'd have tried to get as far the hell away from here as possible and into some shelter. But I don't think I'd have trusted the neighbors. I'd have tried to find a phone."

An officer came bounding down the yard from around the front of the house.

"Chief! We just got a call from dispatch. They've found something."

"So, don't keep me in suspense."

"Jones and Simpson discovered a pair of shoes and a white coat with Witner's name on it."

"Where?"

"Out on the pedestrian walk of the Seneca River Bridge. About halfway across."

"Jesus Christ. All right, tell them to call out a crew to start dragging. And have them send any available people out here to help search for a missing person."

"Yes, sir."

"Jack, do you think Witner could have survived a plunge like that—ninety feet into swift current at forty degrees?"

"Not likely."

"It would save a bundle of taxpayer money. We should be so lucky."

They were walking along the lakeshore now. Jack studied the boathouse. It was the size of a one-car garage, and it hung out over the water next to a short dock. He knew Witner owned an old mahogany runabout; he had seen him on the water a few times, most recently late in the summer. Witner had zoomed past close enough to send spray into Jack's sailboat.

The boat wasn't tied up at the dock.

"Where are you going?" Bedford called after him.

"I'm going to see if Witner's boat is inside."

The dock was slick with ice. Skidding on the planks, Jack grabbed the side of the boathouse for balance.

"Don't come out here!" he warned Bedford. "It's treacherous."

He opened the door and shone the light inside. Waves splashed in the rocky shallows. The beam reflected off the surface and shimmered on the walls where a few dusty life jackets and a coil of rope hung. No boat.

Tim had joined Bedford, and they were waiting at the dock's edge.

"It's empty," he told them as he stepped onto solid ground. "Witner's boat is gone."

"Maybe he took it somewhere for repairs," suggested Bedford.

"Wait a minute—look at this," Tim said. He was shining his light on something dangling off the side of the dock. It was a rope. "Somebody left here in a hurry," he said. "They untied the rope from the boat but left it tied to the dock."

Bedford turned to Jack.

"What do you think?" he asked.

"I think it's possible, Chief."

"Highly unlikely, I'd say."

"I don't think so. Any woman resourceful enough to have gotten the drop on Hinkle," Jack said, pointing toward the house, "would consider using the boat."

"Then why haven't we heard anything from her? She's had plenty of time to get to a phone."

"Unless she had engine trouble," Jack said.

"It's pretty farfetched, Jack."

"Chief, the wind's out of the southwest. If she lost the engine, she'd drift toward the north end of the lake, and she wouldn't be dressed for this kind of weather."

"Do you realize what it will take to search that lake tonight?"

"All I know is that she might not survive a night out there."

"Jack's right," Tim blurted. "I know you guys have a search-and-rescue boat. What are we waiting for?"

Bedford glared at him.

"What are we waiting for, he asks. All we've got to go on is an empty boathouse and a frigging piece of rope." He hesitated and looked at Jack. "But what the hell—we'll make it a combined land and sea effort."

The rain had turned to snow. Wearing a yellow slicker given him by one of the officers, a ski hat pulled down over his ears, Jack took up station at the prow, and for the past several hours, he'd been swinging the searchlight in wide arcs as they surged through the rough water. His back and legs ached from bracing himself.

The plan had been simple. They would make one swing north up the center of the lake using GPS to guide them, then travel south down along the eastern shore, then back up the western side. Thanks to the chief's entreaties—and once Bedford made a decision, he didn't stint—three other boats would join in the search at some point, but that might not be for some hours.

It was now eleven-thirty. They'd already reached the northern end, where the lights of a hamlet called Amaretto flickered through the snow, and were on the way back south, following the shoreline about two hundred yards out. Though the wind seemed to be dying, the surface swell remained rough, and the snow fell thicker as the temperature dropped. The light made a swirling cone of flakes that at times made Jack feel as if they were moving sideways, or tilting, or even revolving.

Tim sat close, holding onto the gunnel and, at least for a while, had kept up a stream of small talk. However, he'd been quiet for some time. Jack looked over and saw that his friend's eyes were closed.

"Hey, Tim. Wake up. You don't want to fall overboard."

Turning back to the mesmerizing light, he thought he saw he saw something, a shape that shouldn't have been there. The next instant, it was gone. He played the light and caught another glimpse.

"Slow down!" he yelled to the officer piloting the search boat, aiming the light.

Tim fell forward into Jack as the engine cut back. Whatever was there seemed to have disappeared. Jack swung the beam farther, roaming it back and forth.

Something *was* out there.

A moment later, he clearly saw the outlines of a small open craft. They were heading straight toward it.

"There it is," he yelled to the pilot.

Gears clunking, the search boat went into reverse, and the sudden deceleration nearly tumbled him into the water. He lost control of the light for a moment, the beam careening up into the falling flakes. He fumbled it back, his fingers almost useless from the cold.

They glided slowly toward it, and the light glinted off a wooden hull, then a windshield, then the outboard motor. There was no cover over the craft—no shelter of any kind.

"I'll take the light," Tim yelled, clapping him on the back. "You go aboard."

The officer stepped forward carrying a rope.

"Good eye," he said. "I'll tie it up."

Jack yelled her name. No answer. Leaning far over the gunnel, he grabbed the smaller boat's side rail. There was no sign of her, just a snow-covered mound between the seats. Leaping in, he brushed the snow away. It was a plastic tarp. He lifted it.

She was curled on her side underneath, her face pale and her eyes closed. He couldn't see if she were still breathing. The light glinted off handcuffs.

"Zellie, wake up. Wake up."

No response. Yanking off his gloves, he felt for a pulse at her neck. As cold as his own fingers were, he was frightened by how frigid her skin felt.

Her eyes opened. He leaned close. Her lips moved, but he couldn't hear the words. He nodded anyway, and smiled.

"I wanted to show you the lake on a nicer day."

She said something else, and he put his face closer.

"I ran out of gas."

He kissed her and carefully picked her up. With the help of Tim and the officer, he lifted her over to safety.

Chapter 42

Two weeks later

The wintry days of late October gave way to a more seasonal November of clearer weather, and the snow soon melted. The trustees of New Canterbury University, led by Abe Delancy, gave Nelson Debussy a vote of confidence, since Bryson Witner had deceived every last one of them.

One of Debussy's first actions afterward was to reinstall Jack as the ED director. Jack accepted on the condition that his plan to modernize the department and start a training program be accepted, which the board agreed to. He also requested two weeks vacation to spend time with Zellie as she recuperated.

The days grew shorter as the winter solstice approached, and the nights colder. Thanksgiving was around the corner.

Zellie and Jack were taking a walk, as they had nearly every morning, hiking a trail that wove through the forest below his house to a hemlock grove at the edge of a little bluff where a brook made a waterfall. This morning, Jack had brewed a thermos of her favorite tea, and they planned to enjoy it in the grove.

Zellie had spent three days in the hospital recuperating from hypothermia and was still not back to full strength. She also suffered from nightmares but was sleeping a little better every night. Jack set her up an office in his study, and she wrote early in the morning and in the afternoons, sketching out scenes for the novel she had been working on the morning Jack drove to Boston. It would be autobiographical, about her childhood, and so far it felt good and real.

She also knew that someday she'd write about what she'd just been through, but not for a while. She told Jack the only thing that would ultimately bring her peace would be the finding of Witner's body.

Meanwhile, she treasured her time with Jack. Even Muriel, who had been up to visit twice, gave him a stamp of approval, not that Zellie needed anyone else's opinion. At Christmastime, if Jack could get a few days away, they were thinking about flying to Florida to see her sister Amy. They visited the Bonadonnas and had dinner twice with Dr. Gavin, whose recovery was complete and who had agreed to serve as the interim dean.

But these walks were the best, and this morning they had stopped to kiss more often than yesterday. Finally, though, they were inside the hemlock grove, and Zellie sat on a log where she could look over the little bluff onto the trees below.

"I wonder where Arbus is," she said. "It doesn't feel right not to have him tagging along."

"Maybe he's found a girlfriend," Jack suggested.

He poured her a cup of tea from the thermos then one for himself and sat next to her. She wrapped her hands around the cup and brought it to her lips. After being in the freezer, then all those hours on the boat, she did not take warmth for granted.

She looked up at Jack and noticed he was staring in the direction they had just hiked. There was a look of concern on his face. He must have heard something she couldn't.

"What is it?"

"Someone's coming down the trail."

"Arbus?"

"I think it's a person. Could be Tony, but he's usually quieter."

A chill climbed her spine as she saw a flash of orange though the hemlocks.

"It's only old Will Carter," Jack said. "Probably out for a little turkey hunting."

Zellie saw him then. He was carrying a shotgun and was dressed in Carhartt coveralls and an orange vest, and he had an old-fashioned red-and-black checkered hunting cap on his head, the brim pulled low.

But something didn't feel right. She looked at Jack and noticed his brow was furrowed.

Suddenly, he grabbed her hand and pulled her up, but the man had already raised the shotgun and leveled it at them.

"Don't move."

Jack stepped in front of her.

"Ah, yes, the urge to protect the beloved," Witner sneered. "I expected to see something like that. Predictable. So, how do you like my transformation to farmer? You've passed me on the road several times.

It's a shame for you, Ms. Andersen, that your friend Forester isn't more observant.

"I, on the other hand, have been very observant. I've been studying you from next door for three days. And here you are—right on schedule."

He was fifteen feet away from them. Taking off his hat, he tossed it onto the deep carpet of hemlock needles.

"So, you made it out of the river," Jack said.

"Stalling, are you, Forester? No, I was never in the river."

"Where are the Carters?"

"The same place your dog is." Witner clicked off the safety. "Here's a true-or-false question for you. If you place a body inside a manure pile, within a few months there's nothing left, not even the bones. Give up? True. A fact of nature."

His mind recoiling in horror, Jack realized there was only one thing to do. He could give Zellie a backwards shove toward the bluff and rush Witner at the same time. This might give her a fighting chance to tumble down there and run away. It was only twenty feet. There were no other options.

"I know it sounds trite, Witner, but you need some help."

Witner laughed. "Very good. But better sick than dead. You're a doctor, you should know that. The fact is, I have too much work left to do. I just wanted you both to know you didn't stop me."

He lowered his eye to sight down the barrel. Jack tensed to lunge and push Zellie away.

It was as if someone drew a line that penetrated Witner's neck and came out the back. The shotgun wobbled and began to droop, and Witner lifted his head, looking puzzled. Jack felt Zellie shudder behind him but was too startled to move.

Witner coughed, and blood trickled from the corner of his mouth. The second arrow hit him in the upper left chest, just in front of his arm. Unlike the first shaft, this one did not pass through. Eight inches of it with a fletching of dark brown feathers protruded from his chest.

Staggering, he looked down, and more blood drizzled from his mouth. Then he seemed to gather strength. From the arrow's angle, he now knew the direction of his attacker. He swiveled to his left and raised the gun.

A third arrow bored deep into his right eye socket.

As he toppled back, the shotgun discharged with an earsplitting roar, sending buckshot up into the hemlock boughs. For half a minute or more, fine needles rained down on his body, almost hiding him from view.

EPILOGUE

Two years later

The tiny island lay nearly a mile off the coast of Georgia, a windswept strip of white sand with a ridge running down the middle containing a forest of hardy scrub oaks and the ruins of a colonial fort. There wasn't much else to it except several weatherbeaten guesthouses and a boat landing on the landward side.

On the deeply shaded porch of one of the houses, Jack Forester sat reading the chapter Zellie had been working on that morning. He'd just returned from a swim, and his muscles felt pleasantly tired. It was going to be a wonderful book. Better than *Boardwalk*, in his opinion.

Next to him, Zellie lay on a lounge chair, sound asleep. She'd been sleeping a lot in the afternoons lately.

He gazed around. The barrier island had a Caribbean feel with its green water and white sand. Back home in New Canterbury, there was snow on the ground, and lots of it. They'd be back there soon enough, but in the meantime, he was happy to be away. He had plenty of help at the medical center now, and the first class of emergency medicine residents was more than halfway through their beginning year.

Far down the beach, a man and a dog approached. The dog darted into the surf, chasing breakers. By the looks of what Tony had slung over his shoulder, they'd be eating fresh fish for dinner again.

When they had gone to the Carter farm after Tony saved them from Witner, they'd found, to their great relief, Arbus and the Carters locked in the basement of the goat barn, left there to die of cold and starvation. Without Fred Hinkle to do the dirty work, Witner, it appeared, preferred to kill from a distance—except for his plan to dispatch Zellie and Jack that day in the hemlocks. He had come after them with the shotgun driven by rage and revenge for the way they'd spoiled his plans.

He hadn't counted on Tony Forester's hunting skills.

All that was past now. Zellie's nightmares had stopped. Jack reached out and rested his hand on the swell of her belly, and felt the life within as the wind stirred the palm fronds and a smile came unbidden to his face.

END

ABOUT THE AUTHOR

Born in Rochester NY, FRANK J. EDWARDS entered the Army in 1968 and served a tour in Vietnam as a helicopter pilot. He received a BA with honors in English from the University of North Carolina at Chapel Hill then attended medical school at the University of Rochester, graduating with an MD in 1979. In 1989 he received an MFA in writing from Warren Wilson College in Swannanoa, NC. After practicing for a decade in North Carolina, he returned to the Rochester area in 1990, where he remains in active practice.

Final Mercy draws from his personal experiences in the ED, but none of the people he's worked with at various hospitals, to his knowledge, has ever tried to murder him. He is married to an emergency nurse and lives on the shore of Lake Ontario.

ABOUT THE ARTIST

KAOLIN FIRE is a conglomeration of ideas, side projects, and experiments. Web development is his primary occupation, but he also develops computer games, edits *Greatest Uncommon Denominator Magazine*, and occasionally teaches computer science. He has had short fiction published in *Strange Horizons, Tuesday Shorts, Escape Velocity,* and *Alienskin Magazine,* among others. See more at http://www.erif.org/.

Made in the USA
Lexington, KY
17 March 2012